KIDNAPPING JESUS

KIDNAPPING JESUS

David Barnard
&
Samuel L. Brodie

KIDNAPPING JESUS
Second Edition
Copyright © 2024 David Barnard and Samuel L. Brodie

All rights reserved. No part of this publication may be reproduced, distributed, or transmitted in any form or by any means, including photocopying, recording, or other electronic or mechanical methods,
without the prior written permission of the publisher, except in the case of brief quotations embodied in critical reviews and certain other noncommercial uses permitted by copyright law. For permission requests, write to the publisher, addressed "Attention: Book Rights and Permission,"

Published in the United States of America

ISBN 979-8-9902809-0-8 Paperback
ISBN 979-8-9902809-1-5 Hardcover
ISBN 979-8-9902809-2-2 eBook
Library of Congress Control Number: 2024904816

Casca Publishing
Palm Bay, Florida

*DEDICATED TO THE MEMORIES OF OUR
FELLOW COMRADES
IN ARMS*

*THOSE WHO HAVE SERVED, ARE SERVING
AND WILL SERVE*

SPECIAL DEDICATION TO

SERGEANT JUSTIN CARTER,

STAFF SERGEANT CHARLES SKELTON,

&

CORPORAL R. HANKINS.

THEIR LIVES MADE A DIFFERENCE!

CONTENTS

	Prologue ix
I	Jesus, Last Testament to Man? 1
II	The Calm before the Storm 17
III	Time Well Spent after a Hard Tour Of Duty! 31
IV	Back at Camp 45
V	Another Beginning 59
VI	A New Stage 85
VII	Airpower 107
VIII	Wheels Up, 11/11/2001 115
IX	The Ground Campaign 155
X	Homecoming 195
XI	The Meeting 209
XII	The Cruise 233
XIII	Plan "S", a Good Place for a New Beginning .. 255
XIV	Mission to Turin 273
XV	Reality, or Is It? 309
XVI	The Rebirth 321

Acknowledgements 333
About the Authors 339

PROLOGUE

Kidnapping Jesus has been discussed and parts of it written over a ten- year period. Bringing to life an action-adventure story of this magnitude was a challenge, but well worth the emotional roller coaster for the authors and those who helped with their ideas. Those who listened provided much needed encouragement and direction along the way.

There are many characters in the book, but the major characters are based on the real-life adventures of six former Marines that wanted to make a difference. While this is a fictional story, it is based on fact and the possibility that man could bring Jesus back to life when man becomes worthy and the technology to do so is available.

There is the question then that if man is smarter, is man wiser? Has man learned? Has man earned the privilege of being able to talk to Jesus in a modern world? These Marines, and others, will take the reader on an emotional tour around the world, allowing the reader to experience their adventures and discoveries along the way. This book may question your belief in God and your belief in man. You may ask yourself, "Why has it taken thousands of years for us to come face to face with Jesus?"

If Jesus could speak to man, would he tell mankind why we exist on Earth? Would Jesus tell mankind how we came to exist? Would Jesus be able to answer the questions we have had for thousands of years? What have we done? Jesus, what have we done?

CHAPTER I

JESUS, LAST TESTAMENT TO MAN?

The air was still and so thick that a man, any man, could hardly breathe. It was an overcast day with the clouds dark and menacing, yet there were pockets of light shining through the clouds with a spectacular array of brilliance dancing on those majestic beams, As the frail, severely beaten man was led to His final judgment, those who were near Him stared at the blood streaming from the open wounds inflicted upon His body from the brutal punishment meted out by the Roman soldiers.

The man, beaten and bloody, dragged His Cross through the dirty, cobbled streets to Golgotha, the Place of the Skull, where He would be crucified for His beliefs. A crown of thorns cut deeply into His flesh as onlookers ridiculed Him, calling Him "King of the Jews." He suffered the indignities in silence, for He knew His destiny was even greater than this grueling march. His followers sighed as they watched Him stumble, but not all had abandoned Him.

The Sanhedrin, the Jewish lawgivers, was unwilling to share their power with this carpenter who could interpret the law better than they and spoke of their God as His Father. Many of the Jews believed in the prophecy that a baby would be born who would free them from Roman oppression. They believed this man would raise and lead an army to defeat the enemies of the Jews, but He did not follow their interpretations of those prophecies. He had come to create a pathway where any man could enter the Kingdom of God and forever enjoy the riches of life ever after. His true followers, those who had an amazing and unshakable faith, believed that He was truly the Son of God sent to Earth to save mankind and forgive their sins. After what seemed like an eternity, the man known as Jesus, and His tormentors arrived at Golgotha. The Roman soldiers had kicked, beaten, whipped, and spat on this good man.

The Cross, spattered with Jesus' blood and sweat, was thrown to the ground, and Jesus was grabbed and pinned to the Cross by three Roman soldiers. He was past resisting. His destiny was pre-ordained.

Two of the soldiers held His ankles while the remaining soldier held His feet. One of the soldiers positioned a steel pin against Jesus' right wrist and raised an old and weathered wooden hammer high above his head. He swung the large hammer downward with such force he drove the steel pin through Jesus' wrist. As His skin was penetrated, Jesus could feel the steel pin splitting the tendons and blood vessels. The pin ripped through His skin and was driven deep into the Cross made of olive wood.

After securing the right arm at the top of the Cross, the other soldier holding His left arm pulled with such rage that Jesus' arm was dislocated with a wrenching sound. Jesus' brow was etched with deep lines of human pain along with His suffering. He tried to focus his eyes on those around Him.

No man had ever endured so much and remained conscious. Mary, His mother, His mother's sister, Mary of Clopas, and Mary Magdalene were near His Cross. They were powerless to interfere as they watched, and their grief was so intense as they watched Jesus' suffering they were sobbing as if they could not catch their breath. It was a miracle Jesus was still alive, but the affliction He would suffer was not over.

The soldier driving the first steel pin came around and drove a second pin in the dislocated arm and again the pin was driven deep into the wood of the Cross. The pain was excruciating, so agonizing that a normal man would have passed out from the beating and the nails hammered through his badly beaten and bruised body. But not Jesus! He would remain awake even as the final pin was driven through His crossed legs. Although badly bruised and with three steel pins hammered through His body, not one of His bones had been broken. He took short breaths as His body struggled for life, but even then, He was in prayer with the Father. The Roman soldier placed a block of wood at the base of His feet. Under the block of wood was a plaque that Pontius Pilate, the Roman Prefect of Judea, decreed to be placed on the Cross with Jesus. The inscription read:

JESUS OF NAZARETH
THE KING OF THE JEWS

It was possible for Jesus to have a small ledge in which to support His weight, but the damage had been done. He would die an earthly death. Jesus, was He a man? Or, was He the Son of God? This was the question! Or, should the question be, Jesus, a man, and the Son of God?

The Roman Centurion, in his rich uniform with highly polished breastplate, could not believe his duty called upon him to be at this place at this moment. Where was the Glory? In battle, he fought soldiers and it was the best of the best who would survive the day. How could he be here after all the countless battles he had survived? Yes, he had scars and broken bones, but he had lived to tell the stories. He was well respected in battle, but the shame he felt for taking an unarmed man, a peacemaker, and nailing him to the Cross was unsettling. Thieves were different, but his duty to Rome was unwavering. He could not falter. To waiver would mean risking his Roman Citizenship and his loyalty to Rome and to Caesar would be questioned. If he were stripped of his Citizenship, what would he have? Nothing! He must finish this mission. It was his duty. It was his mission. There would be no charity given to Jesus just as he had never given quarter on the many battlefields that flashed through his memories.

The three soldiers hoisted the Cross and positioned it just on the edge of a prepared hole. When the Cross was almost upright, it slid as it slammed into its final resting place with such force that His Bones separated, and His flesh was ripped apart internally. One of the Sanhedrin mocked Jesus. "Show me your God now Jesus. Where is He? Call to Him! Ask Him to save you!"

Jesus' head was hanging downwards as He looked the Sanhedrin in the eyes and told the Priest, "You know not what you have done."

The moan that came from Jesus' lips was barely audible. His strength was ebbing. The Jewish Priest spat at Jesus calling His life a farce and condemning any who believed in this false prophet.

The Priest would go on to pronounce, in a booming voice, to those gathered at the Cross with his arms raised above his head, pointing one moment at Jesus and the next pointing towards the sky, "Jesus is no God! He is a liar and a thief! The words He spoke were words of blasphemy! For if this was the Son of God, why did not His Father save His Son? Why did He not free Himself?"

Another moan escaped from Jesus' lips as he hung limp and lifeless from the Cross. Someone entered the circle of those who gathered around the Cross with a stick and cloth wrapped around the end. It was wet and smelled like stale wine. The stick was lifted to Jesus' lips while people surrounded him. He took what moisture and momentary relief, he could from the wet rag as it was brushed across His lips. The Roman soldiers were now becoming afraid as the mood of the crowd seemed to change. People were streaming from the town to see what was happening to this man of God. Women were yelling for mercy and children were crying. The Jewish priest continued to yell insults at him, although the yells were dying down as the crowd's intensity grew. Jesus looked over at His people looking up at Him. Tears were running down the creviced lines upon His face.

Jesus looked up into the dark overcast sky. The light radiated from His face as beams from the sky penetrated through the clouds as they sped from Heaven towards Earth. The radiance made both He and His Cross stand out as though the crowd was in darkness. It was as if just He and His Father were alone in reverent silence. The radiance was so brilliant that many in the crowd could not distinguish Jesus from the Cross. In the distance, booming thunder grew louder as a storm neared Golgotha. The storm was growing in intensity and would soon be upon them. Quiet prayers were spoken in the surrounding silence among the faithful. It grew calm. It was sudden. There was darkness and intense light. There was a raging storm and then nothing. No one spoke. There was no sound. It was as if the moment was frozen in time.

JESUS, LAST TESTAMENT TO MAN?

Those who had no faith cast their gazes downward in shame for how they had treated this Godly man. They had judged Him.

Even the Centurion and the two Roman soldiers were shaken, for they had never encountered this eerie sense of foreboding, not even during their travels into the many conquered lands where they had fought mighty battles and won bloody wars in the name of Rome. They had never encountered a man who had withstood so much agony yet was still alive. They had faith in only their swords and their comrades in arms to gain what comfort that could be found. It did them no good to retrieve these past memories in order to muster courage. This crucifixion was no longer in their hands. Jesus and His Father were together in Prayer.

Jesus opened His eyes and spoke these words among the thunder and surrounding lightening. The light on the Cross was brilliant in the darkness when these words were received by every man, woman, and child in the gathered crowd. "Forgive them, Lord, for they know not what they have done!"

Even as the non-believers heard these words, they wondered how this man could forgive them. Did He have the power of forgiveness if He was only a man and not a, or, God? They did not understand, for their faith was in what they could see and not in what they felt in their hearts to be true.

On Jesus' left and on His right were two men who were also crucified. Jesus turned His attention to these men who were being killed for their deeds on Earth. He looked at them and spoke. "I forgive you of your sins and you will enter into Paradise with Me this very day and meet My Father if you repent your sins!"

One of the criminals asked Jesus to remember him when He entered the Kingdom of His Father, but the other hurled insults. Jesus assured the thief- turned-believer he would enter into His Father's House with Him. The clouds were now pitch black and the winds began to blow with such force that it was difficult to stand, and the words now spoken to be understood. The Jewish Priest stood before Jesus hurling the final insults at Him.

Jesus opens his eyes and said, "After I'm dead your church will be destroyed and all in it will die, this I promise you."

The Priest smiled at Jesus and yelled, "Where is your God?"

KIDNAPPING JESUS

Nine agonizing hours had passed. since Jesus was crucified by the Roman soldiers. Casca Rufio Longinus, the Roman Centurion, was ordered by the Priest to see if Jesus was dead. The winds were blowing harder and the crowd was becoming angry and afraid at the same time. They wanted this over. Though it was not night, there was no sunlight and darkness surrounded the crowd. The Centurion walked up to the Cross and stood in front of Jesus. He shook the Cross and looked at the limp body hanging there with the inscription and His head adorned with a crown of thorns buried deep into the flesh. His blood was drying on His face and on His body. His time on Earth was about to end. To complete the final struggle of earthly life for this man, Casca grabbed his spear and stabbed Jesus in His left side. Blood and water gushed from His body as Jesus' lung was pierced.

As the dark liquid ran down Casca's right arm, Casca looked into the open eyes of Jesus. Jesus looked directly at Casca. Jesus knew this man as He knew Himself. In the blink of an eye, Casca reflected inwardly and recalled the many battles he had fought in the name of Rome. He had killed more men, women, and children than he could count. He had fought in so many brutal wars he had no fear of man or beast. Yet, Casca could not lower his gaze from Jesus' penetrating eyes. This frail man who hung before him, the man whom people called Jesus, The Son of God, opened His eyes. In that instant, it was revealed to him by God that this beaten and bloody man before Casca was the Son of God and the Savior of the World.

Jesus spoke directly to Casca, His eyes clearly focused as He quietly whispered to Casca saying, "When man becomes worthy, I shall return to Earth!" Casca heard something else, or did he? Then, it was over. Jesus breathed His last. His body quivered and the breath from His mouth was raspy as the air in His lungs was exhaled.

The battle-hardened Roman Centurion cast aside his spear and ran away from The Place of the Skull. He was terrified and could not believe he was running. What had happened to him to make him afraid? Was it God who struck fear into his heart or the words Jesus spoke? He did not know, did not want to know. For this act of cowardice, he would be punished by his Battle Captain. Just how much and the type of punishment was never a doubt in his mind. He knew he would be publicly stripped of his rank, beaten, and whipped and would suffer many of

JESUS, LAST TESTAMENT TO MAN?

the indignities that were inflicted, that he had inflicted, upon Jesus. He did not care. He just wanted to get away, far away. The sand tore at his eyes as the wind howled about him, fighting him for his robes as he twisted and turned.

He fought to maintain his footing as he sought out the post where the soldiers' horses had been tied.

Stripped of his richly appointed robes as they sailed through the air out into the desert in the blinding sandstorm, Casca wore only his soldier's uniform. Casca grabbed his horse and rode off not knowing where he was going. He just wanted to get away from this place and the man known as Jesus. Casca rode for what seemed like weeks through the storm and into a changed landscape. The horse was tired and sweat dripped from its mane. Casca had never asked his horse for so much and the runaway soldier had pressed him to the edge of his endurance. Casca occasionally stopped to rest, ate next to nothing, and drank water from small wells that had been carefully dug by the Romans at critical crossings along the well-worn roads traveled by merchants, civilians, and the Roman Legions. Rome was able to maintain peace and march to war using the very roads that provided his escape route. The deep ruts in the roads were etched into stone from many years of use from both chariots and wagons. These roads were the arteries of war, in the past, present, and would be in the future. Time would tell!

He would often walk his horse and encountered other travelers journeying to where he had left as he headed towards a small village known as Turin. He was now in Italy and had traveled many miles through dusty villages, over rivers by boat and had even crossed the Aegean Sea in route to Italy. It was a long trip and he stayed to himself. He had traded his Roman uniform, breastplate, and shield along the way for comfortable clothes, so that he would look like a common traveler, not as a soldier. He kept his sword and short knife with him, but only kept the knife on his person. His sword was wrapped in a cloth tied to his saddle along with a pack he had acquired along the way in which he placed the food he purchased as he passed through small villages. No one ever caught him from behind. Casca stayed just out of reach of those he knew must be following. Yet, he could not outrun the events of that ill-fated day.

KIDNAPPING JESUS

Although it had been months since Jesus had spoken to him, he could not mask the memories of that day. It was forever branded in his mind! He had traveled far from the Place of the Skull in Judea, yet the pain Jesus felt penetrated him. He knew this man must be the Son of God and was inwardly disturbed by the thought, but he did not want to believe. He had run away and knew he would be hunted by the Roman soldiers, many of them his fellow comrades, until he was brought to Roman justice. For that, he was embarrassed. He was ashamed of murdering Jesus, an innocent man, and of running away as if he were a frightened child.

He did not stand his ground at the Place of the Skull— it was not a battlefield, but a battle, all the same, being waged in the very fiber of his being. All he wanted to do was to numb his mind with a drink. But he had to keep moving. He wanted release from that day. He wanted to forget about this man of God!

Casca was physically and mentally exhausted but could find no comfort when sleep finally overtook him each night. And, even though sleep provided a welcome shelter, he could not escape the words. The eyes of Jesus penetrated Casca's thoughts.

He replayed the words spoken to him when he thrust the dull spear into Jesus' side. He kept hearing, "When man becomes worthy, I shall return to Earth!" Yet, there was more! What was it? It haunted his very fiber!

Casca entered the town of Turin as darkness was falling. He had his coin purse with him just under his clothes. It was substantial in that he not only had gold and silver, but precious stones he had taken as loot during his victories over other men. He was a hardened soldier, and one not to be trifled with by anyone. He was also road weary and hungry. He tied his horse to a post in front of a hospitable looking tavern. He sought out the inn keeper as he entered the dimly lit tavern known simply as the Nights Rest. The shield that hung from the second floor was a light blue with crossed swords emblazoned with gold and silver and a small roof below the signpost. It was symbolic. The inn had seen travelers and soldiers for many years. The innkeeper's family members were no strangers to the mysterious and secretive comings and goings that brought an aura of surreal life to them from the adventures of the many travelers who visited from faraway lands. They had a good life compared to most. They were not wealthy by any stretch of the imagination, but they were not poor, and the family had connections in Turin, political as well as with highly placed merchants.

The inn keeper sent a small boy to take care of Casca's horse. He needed attention— to be fed, watered, and combed. They both needed rest. The inn keeper took Casca's silver coin and directed him to a room at the top of the stairs. A tub was sent to his room and filled with water by the inn keeper's wife and two young daughters. Casca was brought a clean robe, bread, and wine while he soaked in the tub. He was ravenous as he ate and drank. The young ladies giggled as they fetched more wine, bread, and water. They could see the scars Casca had received in his battles. He may have appeared as a lowly merchant, but he carried himself like a soldier, his muscles were taunting, his stomach hardened, and his scars vivid. He must have been a soldier.

One of the young girls asked him if he was a soldier. Casca replied, "I once was a soldier in another lifetime, but I am now just a man who has seen too much...too much bloodshed for any one man. I just want to rest and seek a peaceful life near here." He sent the girls away to fetch the innkeeper. Casca needed to be entertained and wanted women— women who knew how to please a man.

He finished his bath and as he stood up, he stretched his six-foot frame. He was tall for any man of his time and stood out in a crowd. He was strong and could easily best any man in any fight if there was some early warning. He dried himself off and threw the light robe around his body. His knife and sword were close by but out of sight. He needed to be always prepared and his instincts never failed him. He would have to worry about his hair and beard in the morning. He was tired. But he was not too tired for the two women that were now at his door. Each of them carried a pitcher of wine supplied by the owner. The clothes came off quickly and there were no preliminary courtesies extended. The women were here to pleasure Casca and provide him an escape from his reality.

They would more than earn their money that night. It was a long night of drinking, and the sex was hard and fast. Casca used the women

KIDNAPPING JESUS

to erase the memories in his mind and the final words spoken by Jesus as He died on the Cross. "When man becomes worthy, I shall return to Earth!" The buzz in his mind became louder. There was more.

As Casca rolled over from a long night of drinking with the two prostitutes in his bed, he shook himself awake. He took water from the bowl in the room and splashed his face. What a night! He was not yet satisfied, and his head was killing him. Finally, a pain he could understand and knew well.

He woke up in a killing mood and threw the two whores out of his room. He tossed their clothes out behind them as they scrambled to get out of his way. No matter how many times they had been treated in a similar fashion, they hated when they were accorded such disrespect, even if they were whores. This was the only way in which they could earn enough to eat. It was not much, but it allowed them, and their families, to live.

He went back to the bowl of water and splashed his face. He dressed in clean clothes placed near his door by the innkeeper's wife during the night. He tucked his short knife in his waistband, secured his coin purse, and left the room. He exited the inn and not a word was spoken by anyone in the dimly lit downstairs where the kitchen, eating area, and the inn keeper's rooms were located. He was hungry and wanted to get away to see what was in this town.

Casca found refreshment several streets away from the inn at another tavern. It was a dingy affair, but Casca wanted to go unnoticed if possible. Even in civilian clothing, this former Roman Centurion carried himself with self-assuredness. There were a couple of hard-looking men at another table. Casca was not looking for a fight, but if one came his way, he would not shrink from any confrontation.

Casca sat down near the entrance with his back to the wall. He ordered bread and wine and asked if there was meat. He was served a leg of mutton with a half loaf of bread. He drank his wine sparingly while overhearing the whispered conversation from the table nearby. His ears were attuned to hearing many things others could not. But one sensation never failed him and that was his instinct.

He looked into their eyes although he appeared not to notice his surroundings. The hair on the back of his neck was standing on end. His right hand slipped under the table and gripped his knife while his

JESUS, LAST TESTAMENT TO MAN?

left hand rested on the edge of the heavy table. Even out of uniform, the two thugs should have been more wary of this large man. Casca was a menacing- looking foe at six feet, 220 pounds. He was heavily muscled, his upper body rippled under his clothes with arms like tree trunks. These two should be careful of this man. He was a killer and spared no one. He was ready if they gave him reason, but he preferred not to fight this day and bring attention to himself.

His expertise with the broadsword and mace was renowned. In fact, Casca was an expert with every weapon in the Roman arsenal. He trained other soldiers to fight in battle and was keen in close-quarter combat where a sword could not be wielded with effect. His strength helped him in these combat situations as he slammed his shield with such force, he literally thrust people away from him. It was as if a scythe was being swung during the harvesting of grain. The short knife was a great tool for slashing and short thrusts into the gut of an opponent when fighting in close quarters. He had fought in forty different battles in his lifetime. His decorations were earned through his skill and bravery.

Casca was in one of the poorest parts of town, and seasoned thieves were bound to seek him out as a good target. They too knew how to wield a knife. They too had blood on their hands. They were no cowards, but they slashed throats often to steal. As Casca rose from his stool, the men flinched. It was the moment to fight. Casca lifted the heavy table by the edge with his left hand, and one of the two thieves caught the top corner of the table coming at him like a sledgehammer. The other thief came towards him with a menacing curved knife. Casca quickly thrust his short knife and hit the thief's hand with such force that blood spurted everywhere. The thief nearly tripped over himself as he headed for the door stumbling and yelling into the dusty streets. The other man had been knocked unconscious. He would bother no one for the moment. Casca looked at the tavern owner and tossed him a bronze coin for his meal and the damage. His menacing look along with his knife just resting on his lips ensured the owner would not speak of this fight or Casca would return to settle yet another debt.

Casca headed back to his room through the streets staying in the shadows as much as possible. He crossed several streets wanting to stay out of sight and created no pattern that could be picked up by eyes he

KIDNAPPING JESUS

knew must be watching from the safety of shadows and narrow alleys. There were thieves everywhere who would prey on the weak or those who let their guard down. Casca was always prepared.

Yet, though he had tried to escape them, the words spoken to him by Jesus haunted his waking moments: "When man becomes worthy, I shall return to Earth!" It was eerie! He needed to concentrate on this moment and his surroundings.

As Casca crossed a small alley, he was jumped by three robbers. "Where did these guys come from?" he asked himself. No pattern, or so he had thought. One of the robbers had his hand wrapped in cloth that was somewhat bloody. Casca knew immediately he had been trailed by the first thief from the tavern, and his friends were out for revenge and for his purse.

The fight was over in moments. The first robber had the advantage of surprise and was able to stab Casca in the back. There was pain. The pain was not new to him, and he knew he had to rise above the shock and kill these men or they would kill him. The knife was buried in his back. Casca spun around and ran his knife into the first thief's gut so quickly the thief just sneered at Casca not knowing for a moment he was already dead. Casca pushed this man off his knife grabbed the second thief and punched him in the face with his other hand. As the thief's head popped backward, the knife in Casca's right hand crossed his jugular vein. Blood spurted out as the thief hit the ground choking on his own blood. The last thief standing, whom Casca had previously encountered at the tavern, was trying to seek an advantage while his two brethren had attempted to distract Casca.

He only had one good hand remaining which clutched a heavy staff made of oak. He had it raised high, ready to smash Casca over the head, and would have been able to crush Casca's skull had not Casca reacted quickly. The wound in his back was painful, the knife still in place, but Casca's strength and agility overwhelmed the thug. Casca's knife swept upwards and split the robber in two halves beginning at his navel. The sharp instrument of death had done its job once more as the staff fell from the thief's hand as he hit the ground. There was a crowd, but this scene had been repeated many times in these streets. Some recognized the assassins, but no one recognized Casca. There had been rumors about a Roman Centurion that had been at the Cross of Jesus

12

JESUS, LAST TESTAMENT TO MAN?

of Nazareth, but this could not be the man, or could he? Blood was everywhere, and Casca backed through the crowd as they drew close to the three dead men. He turned and walked back to the Nights Rest. He was not followed.

He entered the inn and slowly ascended the steps to his room. He was unnoticed by the busy innkeeper and his wife as they were serving tables and keeping the guests occupied with food and drink. His room had been cleaned and the bowl of water refilled. He reached behind him and pulled the knife out of his back. Before he passed out from the pain, the voice in his head whispered to him, "When man becomes worthy, I shall return to Earth!" Was there more?

He awoke in the middle of the night, surprisingly refreshed from his sleep. How could this be? Were the day's events yet another dream? He knew he had killed three people that day. One thief had been left alive, yet unconscious, at the tavern where he had first been attacked. He knew he had been stabbed during the ambush. In the dimly lit room, a single oil lamp provided a yellowish flickering glow that reflected off the pale walls of his room. He could see the blood in the wash basin, on the floor and on the bed, but he could not feel the pain. Was he dead and now a spirit? He felt for the wound on his left side and found the hole in his robe. It was crusted with blood, his blood, but he could feel something else, a closed place that should be a hole in his back where the knife had been plunged during the second fight. It was sore, but the wound was closed. It was scabbed over. He was in discomfort, but he was alive and fresh. How could it be? This had never happened to him before, or to anyone he had known.

He sat down on the side of his bed. This was a miracle. His thoughts took him back to the Cross and the words Jesus spoke to him that day. He knew this man was Jesus, the Son of God. He took a piece of parchment and in Latin wrote those words that had troubled his thoughts for months. "When man becomes worthy, I shall return to Earth!" Casca would now remember the rest of what Jesus spoke to him that day. These words were, "You are content with what you are, you shall remain! Until we meet again." He did not want to write these last words but felt somehow compelled to complete His last testament to man. He did not understand what those words meant in the darkness of the room but would soon come to understand his destiny. Casca placed

KIDNAPPING JESUS

the leather parchment in a small chest and gathered his belongings to leave this town in the distance. He did not want to attract the attention of the Roman garrison nearby.

The word was out that a Roman Centurion had abandoned his post after the crucifixion of the King of the Jews and if they scrutinized him, they would know him to be that soldier. He had also heard that a temple had been destroyed near the time of the crucifixion, but he did not ever engage anyone in conversation, gathering what information he could in bits and pieces of information spoken by those people who milled around the shops and carts on the streets. There were rumors of the ascent of the man he stuck with his spear and who spoke to him at the Place of the Skull, but he was the only one who really knew that story, for he relived it moment by moment. He hoped the crowd spoke of the knife in his back and that the soldiers would believe him dead somewhere in an alley and not be searching for him.

He walked down the stairs and woke the inn keeper and his family. Although he had already paid them, he wanted to have his horse ready and something to eat so he could be on his way. As the horse was saddled and fed by the weary-eyed, the inn keeper's wife prepared the morning meal of mutton, bread, wine, and fruit. Casca went outside of the inn to a small church. He left the small wooden chest on the floor near the front of the church. Although there was no organized worship of Jesus at this time, the Church was growing in popularity and early Christians believed in a single God rather than the traditional pagan belief of a pantheon of gods. Inside the chest was the parchment along with three coins; one piece of gold and two of bronze representing the three men he had helped to crucify. It was a sign to anyone who sought interpretation of the message he had left.

Casca returned to the inn and ate his breakfast. He thanked the inn keeper and his family, left a silver coin, and went outside into the early dawn. The sun was beginning to rise, and the beams of light were radiant as they stole the darkness from the sky. It would be a better day for Casca. He mounted his horse, looked down at the ground, and could see his shadow and that of his horse. For a brief moment in time, he thought of this as a memory, yet he was very much alive. Bells were ringing as the town came to life. He reached behind him and felt where there should be pain in his back and found there was none. He could

JESUS, LAST TESTAMENT TO MAN?

not believe it, but he accepted this was a fact and it was his fate that he was healed. Casca pointed his horse towards Rome with thoughts of Jesus in his mind. He had been touched by His blood and by His words. And, those were the words he left behind.

WHEN MAN BECOMES WORTHY, I SHALL
RETURN TO EARTH.
WE SHALL MEET AGAIN.

CASCA RUFIO LONGINUS

CHAPTER II

THE CALM BEFORE THE STORM

Somewhere in the Indian Ocean, Gunnery Sergeant John Elder, the oldest of three brothers currently serving in the Marine Corps, received instructions from his Battalion Commander, Lieutenant Colonel (Lt. Col.) Harley J. Race. It was early and the unit had not yet assembled on the ship's deck for the morning formation. Along with the Battalion Staff, Company Commanders, Platoon Leaders and Platoon Sergeants, Gunny Elder was notified that the Infantry Battalion and his 1st Marine Platoon Tank Attachment would be going into Beirut, Lebanon.

It was October 23, 1983, and the Marine Corps Barracks had been attacked and decimated by a suicide truck bombing masterminded by Hezbollah with the funding and approval of Iran's senior governmental officials. The Marines were stunned as they received the heartbreaking news that their fellow Marines, many of them friends, had been murdered. It was later determined Osama Bin-Laden directed the extremist terrorist cell to attack the Marine Barracks.

With 12,000 pounds of plastic explosives packed into a yellow Mercedes-Benz truck, the determined bomber breached the outer defenses of the Marine Barracks in the early dawn and the resulting catastrophic explosion ended the lives of 241 Servicemen while they slept. The death toll included 220 Marines, 18 Navy personnel, and 3

Army soldiers. Many of the living would never fully recover, physically or mentally, from the devastation. This single murderous blow was demoralizing to the Marine Corps, their families, and friends, and to our Nation. They are among the unsung heroes of a grateful Nation and were serving our Nation's political will: American forces securing a tenuous peace in a war-ravaged country.

This hammer, wielded with such force, made the provision of future meaningful aid even more difficult in healing the political and ideological divisions of a country struggling for its very survival.

Once the Crown Jewel of the Middle East, Lebanon was about to enter another period of endless darkness. The peaceful future of all faiths, including Muslim and Christian, would soon be challenged once again in another historic life and death struggle. This terrorist attack by Bin-Laden was the initial new wave of terrorist attacks on governmental institutions throughout the world and was to set the pace of attacks that would affect all Nations in the years to come.

The 1st Marine Division was permanently stationed at Camp Pendleton, California. The Infantry unit was from Hawaii. All but a few of the Marines had seen combat but many of them had served in the same unit for the last several years, including the unit leaders. They were well trained and pre- deployment exercises had honed their peacemaking skills to a fine edge. They were ready for whatever challenges they were about to face. The operational name for the mission was Beirut VI, as it was the sixth rotation of Marines sent to Beirut with orders to maintain a troubled peace. For many, it was their third rotation. The business at hand was now anything but routine.

The early morning briefing from Lt. Col. Race to the Battalion leadership was disseminated to all subordinate commands. You could feel the tension on the ship. First, there was stunned silence, but that was just the beginning. These Marines were military professionals, but they were human beings, and were deeply affected by the announcement. Gunnery Sergeant John Elder from the 1st Marine Tank Platoon was a highly decorated Vietnam Veteran. He had received the Navy Cross for conspicuous gallantry during the Vietnamese TET Offensive in 1968 for personally risking his life while saving three of his fellow Marines.

His platoon had been ambushed by a Viet Cong Battalion while on routine patrol in the Trang Province, near the Mekong River. Then,

THE CALM BEFORE THE STORM

Private First Class (PFC) Elder, with complete and utter disregard for his life, shot one of the Cong at point blank range as he popped out of a spider hole. The battle was on. It was January 31st.

PFC Elder was one of ten who survived that day. Men all around him were chopped to pieces. The platoon formed a small perimeter that continually shrank in size.

Down to the dead, walking wounded, and a few who had not yet been hit, PFC Elder faced a bayonet charge from the Cong. He received a bloody wound to his left shoulder and while locked in combat, pulled his K-Bar knife, and stabbed the determined enemy soldier in his stomach. His buddy was wounded, and on his left all he could see was an intense fire fight with dead Marines and Cong everywhere.

It was getting dark, and he could just barely make out the glint of bloody steel heading his way. PFC Casey Long was unloading another magazine through the red-hot barrel of his M16 and was keeping the enemy's heads down. In fact, the firing was dying down. The Viet Cong Private was bloody and had been hit several times in the chest but was still coming forward yelling his battle cry at the top of his lungs. Elder could clearly see the eyes of his enemy coming nearer in the haze. Casey never saw him. PFC Elder jumped out of his position, bleeding badly, and took him down with a choke hold and snapped his neck. He did not die immediately.

PFC Elder woke up in a Military Army Surgical Hospital (M.A.S.H.) unit. He faintly remembered being carried to the designated Rally Point (RP), now a Pick-Up Zone (PZ) just large enough to handle two UH-1D Huey Air Ambulances. He could hear the slicing of the thick air by the huge rotor blades making that distinct "Womp Womp" sound and felt the vibration of this welcome machine. He felt warm and for a moment he was safe.

Looking up, a medical Corpsman was holding a syringe in his right hand; his left was hanging a bag of saline solution to the ceiling in the Helicopter. There were wounded in the Chopper, friends and buddies, all Marines. He remembered that Casey was next to him, he was wounded, wearing bandages on his head, arm, and leg. It looked like he had been torn up like the rest of them. The Morphine had done its job. Elder lost all recollection of the Huey Cobra AH-1G gunships flying overhead and the thunderous sounds of the 20mm guns firing into the darkness and the 2.75- inch rockets slamming into their targets while the Huey Ambulance Pilots continuously flew into harm's way to save his comrades-in-arms. The heroics of many that auspicious afternoon would linger in their memories throughout their military careers as well as follow them into their civilian pursuits.

Elder's Lieutenant was undergoing surgery but had been one of the few who were conscious as they were airlifted out of the combat area. An Air Force C-130, code named Alpha Charlie, was on station flying somewhat of a racetrack pattern over 300 miles away. The C-130 was waiting for the possibility of this type of immediate request. The pilot quickly responded to the radio call from the Battalion Operations Officer, Major Owen M. Johns, when the Platoon's Radio Telephone

THE CALM BEFORE THE STORM

Operator (RTO) provided the unit's updated situation report (SITREP) on the platoon radio, PRC 77. It was URGENT!

With the deafening sounds of conflict came the SITREP, "...Ready 3, this is Ready 8. Request urgent air support at my Grid Coordinates... break...enemy danger close...break...will pop smoke on our position on your command...over."

It was exactly two, very long, minutes when the reply came from Major Johns. "Ready 8, this is Ready 3."

The RTO clicked his Mike, "3, this is 8."

"8 this is 3...break...keep your heads down...break. pop smoke in five mikes, repeat...smoke in five mikes. Alpha Charlie, over."

"3, this is 8, Wilco...smoke in five mikes...Alpha Charlie. Tango Yankee, out." The order was silently passed to the men. In hand signals only, the men were ordered to get down as deep as they could, get into the dirt, cover-up, and ready the smoke.

Just as the sun went down and the purple smoke from three smoke canisters and lingering daylight played through the thick canopy, the C-130 gunship, known to the troops as, Puff, The Magic Dragon, opened up computer aimed Quad 50 caliber machine guns and carved the final epitaphs on the Viet Cong Battalion in a matter of seconds. The bullets ripped through the trees tearing through the canopy as the deadly missiles shredded the bodies of the enemy soldiers. It was close, danger close, but it was the only way in which these survivors could be helped by any type of effective friendly fire.

The Air Force Captain radioed the Battalion S-3, Operations Officer, after the brief engagement was over, "Ready 3 this is Alpha Charlie One...mission complete...standing by...over."

Very few of the Viet Cong that had ambushed the Marine Platoon were left alive, yet there were remaining pockets of fire coming from the woods and an occasional whistle of bullets coming close to the remaining perimeter of the Platoon. The Cong had set up a deliberate ambush that failed due to the heroic efforts of the Marine Platoon and the initial discovery of the attack when PFC Elder and the Viet Cong soldier all but collided at the spider hole. It was a discovery that helped determine the end to this isolated battle. It was a costly victory. It was

KIDNAPPING JESUS

all over. There were those that would live and those that were dead or dying. It was a bloody battle. Over 250 of the enemy were later confirmed dead. Thirty-one of the platoon's numbers perished that day. Of the ten survivors, not one was unscathed.

First Lieutenant Marvin Colby recommended PFC Elder for the Medal of Honor for his valor. In fact, the Platoon had three such recommendations. They each would receive the Navy Cross, including First Lieutenant Colby and Corporal Elder (now an acting Squad Leader in Charlie Company). The remaining seven surviving Marines received the Meritorious Service Medal with V (Valor) Device, and all ten Marines received the Purple Heart. The unit received a Presidential Unit Citation and a Combat Streamer from a grateful Nation that would be proudly displayed on the Battalion and Company Colors and remain part of the distinguished lineage of the 1st Battalion Marines that would be proudly etched in the annals of Marine Corps History. The Vietnamese Command recognized the unit and awarded them with the Vietnamese Cross of Gallantry. It was a proud day for these men, but a day they would always remember, and sometimes relive, throughout their lives, oftentimes when those repressed memories were not summoned. The survivors were reconstituted with another platoon except for PFC Long. Elder wondered what happened to Casey. It was a confusing time, and no one could seem to remember what unit he had been assigned to by Higher Headquarters.

Gunnery Sergeant Elder snapped back to his current reality as the unit prepared to debark from the ship. He knew his thoughts were unique in his personal daily struggle, yet there were others around him in that place and time facing their own demons and trying to conquer their individual internal battles to move forward into another situation that required their full attention and unwavering dedication to their fellow comrades, the Corps and to their Nation.

You could cut the air with a knife. It wasn't hot, but the air was still, and tension was high. The Marines were Combat Ready, and each had donned their web-gear, packs, and Load Carrying Equipment (LCE). It was a heavy load, about 75 pounds of gear, designed to protect each Marine and provide the basic comforts for this mission. Depending on their rank and requirements, the men were armed with M1911, 45 (Colt) Caliber Pistol, generally, for the Officers and Tank Crews, or

22

THE CALM BEFORE THE STORM

M16A1 rifles or M60 Machine Guns for the Machine Gun Teams for the Infantry Teams. Included in this arsenal were Grenade Launchers (known as M203s, which were attached to many of the M16A1s). The Grenade Launcher could provide indirect firepower at a moment's notice. There were several Dragon Antitank weapons for Infantry heavy duty work on armored vehicles. Rounding out the major weapons were a couple of M-2, heavy- duty, 50 Caliber Machine Guns that would slice through lightly armored vehicles like a hot knife through butter. Gunnery Sergeant John E. Elder, now a Tank commander on Tank 35 in Bravo Company, received word that B Company Tanks were going ashore, combat loaded with live rounds chambered ready for combat.

After the Paris Peace Agreement, the Vietnam Conflict was officially over. The Draft was abolished in 1973 and President Richard M. Nixon issued orders for the Department of Defense to reduce forces from wartime to a peacetime footing.

The withdrawal of the forces was now underway while in Vietnam the struggle for independence would continue into 1975. President Nixon's direct involvement in the Watergate break-in led to his resignation on August 8, 1974. It was a very difficult time for our Nation and for our Military men and women. The Reduction in Force, known as a RIF, was designed to keep the very best in uniform, while outstanding men and women were forced to leave all services and branches for assimilation back into a civilian peacetime environment. The United States of America was again leaving a war-time footing, as it has after World Wars I and II, the Korean Conflict, and now Vietnam. Millions had been trained prior to and during the Vietnam Era, 1962-1975. The loss of skills forged by intense training would be noticed by the military and the Nation, not immediately, but it would be noticed.

Elder continued to reminisce. Marines were anxious to get ashore to begin their mission, and to be able to react at a moment's notice to a myriad of possibilities. Knowing they were well-trained made them confident of success if the situation changed and new orders were received. They were disciplined and they were the best of the best.

As they were dismissed from the Company formation, a loud, and in unison, "Semper Fi" resounded in the silence. This scene was to be repeated as all the units prepared to debark into their landing craft as they were discharged from the USS Denver (LST) assigned to

Task Force Deep Green of the Nimitz Carrier Battle Group (CVG). Attached to the CVG was the Battleship New Jersey. Fresh from rearmament, the New Jersey was a welcome sight to many Marine and Navy veterans alike and an old friend to Gunnery Sergeant Elder from his days in Vietnam where the Battleship New Jersey performed support missions along the Vietnamese Coastline firing into or near the Demilitarized Zone (DMZ).

They were ready to begin their mission: to aid in reestablishing the security of the Marine Barracks with other Multi-National Force units, assist in recovery operations of the Marine remains of those who perished in the attack, and provide security at the Beirut International Airport in order to establish a secure resupply point for the exchange of Combat Troops and wounded men, and to help maintain the critical logistics resupply efforts needed to sustain the operations at the Operations Tempo (OPTEMPO) dictated by the combined security forces. Accompanying Elder would be the standard Tank crew of three Marines - the Loader, the Gunner and Driver.

There are five tanks to a Marine Corps Tank Platoon and five Tank Platoons in each Tank Company. There was only one Tank Platoon that was Task Organized and attached to the WESPAC, so there were only five Tanks that were assigned to this Battalion Task Force. Although they were professionals, highly trained, with many having previous combat experience, the atmosphere was thick with tension, not with fear of the unknown, but with wanting justice for their murdered Marine brothers in arms. WESPAC is a mission given to the Marine Corps to be combat ready in case United States interests are attacked anywhere in the Middle East. Elder's brothers John and Charles, also Marines, remained at Camp Pendleton with their units conducting rear detachment operations. They were not yet scheduled for rotation into the current theater of operations.

The first Marines went ashore at 1500 hours military time. They quickly moved across shore in combat formations and took up defensive positions around the rubble that was once a Barracks. Once the perimeter was secured, fields of fire for their deadly arsenal of weapons were sighted in on likely avenues of approach or zones where the enemy could assemble for a future attack.

THE CALM BEFORE THE STORM

The Infantry units began one of their assigned duties - to recover the dead and mangled bodies. Marines sifted through the rubble with their tools and machinery, moving heavy pieces of concrete and twisted steel beams while retrieving bloody bodies or body parts of the fallen Marines. The Mass Causality was overwhelming to many of the Marines. They were unprepared for the large scale of bloody carnage they had to face. It was a grim reminder of what a determined enemy could do with unsophisticated technology and the warped sense of direction these terrorists use for justification of death under the guise of religious beliefs.

Gunnery Sergeant Elder, and others, believed the terrorists used a sick interpretation of the Koran for justification. Mohammed's simple rules known as the Five Pillars of Islam were being interpreted and used to achieve the insane desires of a few. Their efforts were successfully aimed at taking the malleable minds of the Muslim downtrodden, without any future or hope, and molding them into sick and demented terrorists. The focus of their evil efforts was aimed at the peaceful and loving people of he world, including their Muslim brothers and sisters. Make no mistake, these extremists were in the initial stages of their ultimate mission: to wipe out every single Christian man, woman, or child in the world. This juggernaut will not stop until they are hunted down and brought to justice.

Secular positions of their belief would not provide any immunity whatsoever to their fellow Muslim brethren. It was with these thoughts that Gunny Elder focused. He was responsible for the detail of getting the mangled bodies into the body bags. He witnessed firsthand what twisted men under the guise of Allah could and would do to their fellow man by vilifying what had been established as a peaceful religion by the Prophet Mohammed.

The cleanup went on for weeks and the stench penetrated the nostrils and the clothes of each man in the vicinity of the Barracks. It was not just the smell that affected them, but as each body was removed, or a body part was located, each was treated with all the respect that could be accorded to these heroes. Physically exhausting, this duty was affecting these hardened Marines mentally as well.

Many of these men had been to see the Unit Chaplain and some had even been broken by the disturbed challenges presented by the

KIDNAPPING JESUS

detail and had to be hospitalized until they could get back to this perplexing task. None wanted to quit, but there are times when people cannot control what their environment does to them— no matter what they desire. There were a few who needed to be airlifted back to the States where they could receive more thorough medical attention at Military Hospitals, at Camp Pendleton and in extreme cases at Walter Reed. Bodies and body parts that were located were transported and placed in coolers onboard ships, later to be to be identified by a Graves Registration Team dedicated for this type of mission.

Gunny Elder had finally completed his mission. The tension he felt every moment during this delicate operation slowly drained from his tired body as the last of the body bags were picked up and placed on the hospital ship for transportation back to the United States. The silence was deafening as the Marine detail secured the final remains and the sharp salutes they rendered to their brave comrades in arms. The slow and downward movement of the salute ended at the seams of each Marine's dress uniform.

It was a moment that had been repeated on so many occasions, but it was never routine.

Gunnery Sergeant Elder was sent back to be with his Tank Platoon. His Tank Crew welcomed him with open arms, and he received multiple pats on the back for a job well done and punches in his shoulder. He was relieved and would not speak of this action for many years to come.

His fellow Marines respected his silence on this matter and his impact award of the Navy Commendation Medal for his outstanding duty in an adverse situation, although accepted, would never be worn, not even for his Official Military Photo that was placed in his Military Record Jacket.

When looking at his photo, one could tell Gunny Elder was every bit a hero and had served in many theaters of war. His uniform had seven rows of ribbons and combat awards that would make General Officers look twice. The highest decoration was the Navy Cross he had earned years ago while on a routine patrol in Vietnam. He was often reminded of that fateful day when his left arm would suddenly stiffen

THE CALM BEFORE THE STORM

just like it did when the bayonet was driven deeply into his flesh by the Viet Cong Private during the ambush. The lack of wearing an award is frowned upon by Promotion Boards. They are convened annually to select the very best Marines for promotion based upon their future potential service to the Corps. Though he chose not to wear the Navy Commendation Medal, his decision would not hinder Elder's promotion to First Sergeant for Bravo Company in the next several weeks.

The Tank Platoon had established a defensive perimeter around Beirut International Airport. Gunnery Sergeant Elder was personally walked around the perimeter by the Platoon Leader, First Lieutenant (P) Matthew R. Cavil. This Lieutenant was on the promotion list to Captain and would soon have a Company Command of his own. Cavil insisted that every man in his Command know where the unit defenses were located. A Private might have to assume a leadership position, should the current leadership be rendered combat ineffective. It might be as Commander of a Tank, Platoon Sergeant or acting Platoon Leader. The Chain of Command was firmly embedded in every Marine's mind. Cavil indicated the placement of Claymore Mines, including where the Platoon had established interlocking fields of fire with the two adjacent Platoons.

It was formidable defensive perimeter, and the Gunny had a wry grin on his face indicating he was well pleased with his Lieutenant. They worked well as a team and the Non-Commissioned Officer (NCO) ensured he took every opportunity to help train this leader as he prepared for subsequent positions of increased responsibility within the Corps.

It was 0300 hours on December 14, 1983, when the first wave of Shiite Muslims attacked the established defenses. They had done their homework well and were accurately firing their weapons in a well-coordinated attack on the Company's defensive perimeter. Rounds from the Russian-made AK47s, intermixed with green tracer rounds, sliced through the darkness of the night. If it had not been a combat situation, it would have been a beautiful sight to onlookers. There was a glow of light provided as the starlight tried to penetrate the low cloud ceiling, but the moon had already set around midnight. Rounds bounced off

KIDNAPPING JESUS

the tanks like hail on a tin roof Corporal David Reed, the Gunner on Elder's Tank 35, was from Rochester, New York, and was the second-in-command on the tank. Reed was also Elder's best friend. They had met while in boot camp years ago, but Corporal Reed had several incidents in which he had been reduced in rank and the highest rank he would ever achieve in the Corps was Staff Sergeant, the rank which he would later retire. He was an African American, a hardened Marine with almost as many decorations as Elder and, above all, a loyal friend.

As the Crew heard the incoming rounds pinging on the tank's outer hull, Gunny Elder radioed for permission to engage the enemy and repel the attack. A few of the emplaced Claymore mines were beginning to explode, but this was a defensive perimeter in depth. Many of the terrorists were already on their way to meet Allah and ready to count their anxiously awaiting Vestal Virgins. First Lieutenant (P) Matthew R. Cavil received permission and quickly gave orders to engage the enemy.

The entire Company perimeter was under attack and all Platoons were ordered to engage the enemy. The Company Commander, Captain Joseph R. Owens, radioed the Battalion Commander from his Command Post (CP). Lieutenant Colonel Race was located in the Battalion CP when the request on the Operations/Command Net requesting Naval gunnery support was received from Captain Owens. The request was quickly granted, and the pre-plotted coordinates established by the Battalion Fire Control Officer with the U.S.S. Battleship New Jersey were immediately brought up on the ship's fire-direction computers. The New Jersey, BB-62, was of the Iowa Class of Battleships built between 1940 and 1941 as part of the ship building program for this Class of Battleships. U.S.S. New Jersey was commissioned in May of 1943. It was recommissioned in 1982 and was a welcome sight to the Marines when it took up station off the coast of Beirut in 1983.

The massive guns dipped as the triple turrets swung into action. As they entered the fire solution, nine sixteen-inch guns lit up the night as the massive 2,700-pound shells sped their way toward the intended destination. The New Jersey rocked from the recoil of the shells being fired. The shells were deadly accurate as they slammed like boxcars on a train hitting the ground. The New Jersey fired 11 projectiles from her sixteen-inch guns at enemy positions. This was the first time that these huge shells were fired for effect anywhere in the world since the New Jersey ended her days of support in Vietnam in 1969.

The New Jersey - BB-62 (Iowa Class of Battleships)

The impact of the shells left huge craters as the sand was ripped from the earth. Terrorists disintegrated as their bodies were turned to liquid and scattered in a thousand different directions.

The tanks rocked from the impact. Elder ordered Corporal Reed to coax the enemy troops into the open, then do a "Z" pattern and put the enemy on the ground. Sergeant Marion R. Campbell, the Gunner, was on the internal tank communications when the order was given to load a beehive round in the Platoon's five tanks and to set the rounds to burst as they left the tank's main 105mm gun. This would create a burst much like a sawed-off shotgun would make at close range. The round spreads out ninety-five yards wide and reached the same height, providing an excellent killing field for an enemy penetrating or attempting to penetrate established defenses. Elder issued the command. The tank jumped with the recoil of the round being fired.

There were approximately five-thousand Muslims when the attack started and, although it seemed like a lifetime, by 0322 hours the attack was over and only twelve-hundred Muslims were limping, crawling, or running for their lives. The duration of the attack lasted for only 22 minutes. The combined arms of the Platoons Tanks, emplaced weapons, and 16-inch shells from the Battleship New Jersey had more than made their mark. The Marines were ready, and the Navy provided the firepower needed to disrupt the enemy deep into the rear of their attacking echelons, cutting their approach to the Airport. The prepared defenses disrupted and destroyed the paths of their retreat. It was a victory for the defenders and a devastating setback for a determined enemy. General George S. Patton could not have said it any better than the thoughts going through Gunny Elder's mind, "No bastard ever won a war dying for his country. He won it by making the other poor dumb bastard die for his country."

At first daylight, and as Navy helicopters circled overhead providing air cover, the Marines sent forth an Infantry Company to secure the battlefield. The Tank Platoon provided over-watch in case there was enemy resistance. Many of the enemy, who were dead, or dying, were stapled to their weapons or their bodies ripped apart. It was a kill zone of huge proportions. Each Beehive round was loaded with 5,000 flechettes that closely resembled sixteen-penny nails with their heads removed. The tank mounted M-60 caliber machine guns had done their job and had contributed to the battlefield success. The extremist bastards had paid the ultimate price in their pursuit of a demented side of a peaceful religion. These few extremists, pursuing their unrelenting quest for the lives of both Christian and Muslim fundamentalists, were driving a stake into the heart of the world.

In the Bible, it is the Book of Revelation that predicts the path to Armageddon according to the Word of God as written by the Apostle John.

"We all may well be on a collision course to meet our respective Maker no matter the name chosen by any given religion. A pale horse with a rider named Death appeared in Elder's mind, or was it just a mirage over the shimmering sands of time?"

Samuel L. (Lyons) Brodie

CHAPTER III

TIME WELL SPENT AFTER A HARD TOUR OF DUTY!

After the Marines completed their tour of duty in Beirut and transferred their responsibilities to the units replacing them, they embarked on the awaiting ships for the long journey back to Camp Pendleton, California. The trip was uneventful with the days filled with all Marines checking and rechecking their gear, going to classes to continue their training, doing PT (physical training) and taking a well needed break by catching up on some Rest and Relaxation (R&R). Although it seemed the perfect trip home, there were many who agonized in their personal struggle to make sense of the Barracks bombing. It just did not make sense to any rational human being that the carnage inflicted upon any person, regardless of religion, could ever be justified. Life was precious, wasn't it?

It was these thoughts that plagued the nightmares of Gunnery Sergeant (P) Elder. During the time Bravo Company had been in Beirut, the Master Sergeant (E-8) Promotion Board had convened and Elder had been selected for the next rank. This was a rank for which he was fully qualified, but he would have to assume new responsibilities in the coming months leaving some of his oldest and best friends behind. At least that was what he thought at the time. Little did he know how the future would shape many of his decisions.

KIDNAPPING JESUS

Upon arrival at Camp Pendleton, Gunny Elder was entitled to a month of R&R. He, and the rest of the Task Force, needed it after a normal workday of 12-14 hours, and some days, there had not been a moment where anyone could rest due to the intensity of the situation and the attacks the terrorists threw at Multi-National Forces. When rest did overtake Elder, his dreams were haunted by the recovery operations of his dead comrades. He also had been informed he had been selected to be the Bravo Company First Sergeant. Although he had to wait months to receive his promotion to E-8 because of the Promotion List and his selection number, he would be frocked in rank; he just would not receive the pay until he was officially promoted. The Marines in B Company were ecstatic with the announcement and the change of the Company Colors would take place upon their return from the long-anticipated trip to Mexico with Sergeant (P) David Reed and another Marine, Sergeant Justin Carter.

The three friends arrived in Mexico after a short flight from Los Angeles International Airport (LAX). They were in a great mood when they landed in Cozumel and grabbed a Taxi to take them to the Grand Hotel Coronado. It was party night and the three hoisted a few beers at the bar and toasted the Corps with a resounding "Semper Fi". In fact, there were many Veterans present and the three were treated to free drinks, especially when it slipped, they had just returned from Beirut. The details were spared in public, so a good time was had by all. It was late by Marine Corps standards when they all went down to breakfast in the morning at 0800 hours. Their boat was waiting for them nearby at the pier. Each of them anticipated the leisurely R&R, but it had been some time since they all had been SCUBA diving.

All their gear was on-board as previously arranged with one of the local Dive Centers. They cruised to their dive location not far from the coast. They could still see their hotel in the distance. The waters were warm and calm, and the boat was anchored in about 65 feet of clear blue water. The conditions were great. Each donned their weight belts and BCD (Buoyancy Control Device), slipped on their dive boots and fins and conducted one last safety check. Their air was on, and each tank was full - 3,000 PSI. They took their regulators, quickly pressing the purge button, and put them in their mouth. They were ready to dive, and all gave a thumbs up (OK). They took turns exiting the makeshift dive

TIME WELL SPENT AFTER A HARD TOUR OF DUTY!

platform on the back of the boat by doing a giant stride entry. Once in the clear water, they gave the OK sign and were ready to begin their descent to the ocean floor. The seas were relatively calm at the surface, but there was a slight current as they neared the sandy bottom.

At 40 feet, amid the reflected light playing off schools of fish of many different varieties too numerous to mention, they saw what they thought was a wrecked ship. Heartbeats seem to double in a split second, yet they maintained their composure as they continued a slow descent.

It had been a long time, and they were closely monitoring their Bottom Time and their descent. At a planned depth of about 65 feet, they could stay submerged for about 40 minutes, providing none of them used up the air in their tanks. It was also the limit of what is considered to be a safe dive, so in reality, 35 minutes of Actual Bottom Time (ABT) would keep them safe from Nitrogen Narcosis or from Decompression Sickness. The regulators only had a single second stage, so a shared air ascent was out of the question and none of the three friends wanted to do a buddy-breathing ascent. It was too deep of a dive to conduct a Controlled Emergency Safety Ascent (CESA). If they ascended too fast, faster than their exhaled bubbles, they risked one of many types of embolisms caused by an air bubble in their cardiovascular system which did not have time to be absorbed by the various tissues of the body.

They arrived at the wreck and were surprised at how well each of them had controlled their buoyancy as they used their legs and fins to power them through the water. It looked like this wreck was about 40-plus feet in length and that it was built for speed. Like Miami Vice, except this was not television. Each of them wanted to explore the interior of the boat. It was an easy entry after the door was opened. Elder, a certified Dive Master, had made many dives and had the most experience. One of his specialty courses included Wreck Diving. Although this was not the typical wreck they trained for, he was still cautious as he entered the wreck first. Reed followed. The quarters were fairly cramped, as you might imagine with their dive gear and fins, but the real issue was the disturbed silt and bubbles that were floating in the once luxuriously appointed cabin.

A myriad of thoughts ran through each of their minds while Elder and Reed were in the cabin. Carter remained just outside the entrance.

KIDNAPPING JESUS

He had the least diving experience, but was relaxed, although he had just completed his Advanced Diving Certification the previous year. In the small galley, there were several cabinets still intact and undisturbed. Those that were open had their contents scattered across the floor and those that were closed still contained dishes and cups, but Elder's attention was drawn to a locked cabinet. He checked his dive watch and the three of them had been down for about 25 minutes. They had about five minutes left before they needed to head back to the surface with a few minutes built in for safety.

Elder took his dive knife that was strapped to his right leg and dug at the door around the lock. The cabinet door gave way and through the bubbles they were exhaling through their regulators, both Elder and Reed could just make out three sealed metal boxes. They had no time to think, it was now 33 minutes into the dive, and they needed to head back to the boat before the air in their tanks was completely exhausted. Elder checked his pressure gauge on his console, and it read he had 1000 PSI remaining. He knew he was excited, and his two friends would probably have used more air than usual based on their level of experience and lack of recent dives. As Reed, and then Elder, exited the galley onto the wrecked ship's deck they were greeted by an enthusiastic Carter when he saw the metal containers Elder and Reed had with them.

As they kicked their fins back towards the distant, but visible, anchor line, Elder looked back at the wreck. He could just make out the ship's name on the back of the boat. It was named the Sandpiper XP. He could not make out the homeport as he turned his head back towards the anchor line. They reached the welcome anchor line when they were in 30 feet of water as they had begun their ascent while heading back to both the line and the boat. As they ascended and adjusted their buoyancy, Carter was running low on air and having difficulty getting a full breath. With his free hand, Reed reached over and helped Carter pull the J-Valve downward giving Carter more time to safely ascend.

They reached their safety stop at 15 feet, and Elder checked his watch. They had been down for 40 minutes and had pushed their dive time to the maximum. He hoped they would have enough time to complete their safety stop of three minutes, when Reed signaled to him that he was now low on air. Reed, again with his free right hand,

TIME WELL SPENT AFTER A HARD TOUR OF DUTY!

reached back and located the J- Valve. An OK sign flashed between Reed and Elder.

They completed their ascent and climbed on-board using the cruiser's ladder. Carter went first, helping Reed and then Elder with their fins and with the three boxes. It was somewhat of a surprise to Elder that they were able to safely complete this dive with the boxes in tow. Then again, they were trained and had been under worse conditions, including diving, than this. The gear came off quickly. The boxes were more challenging than they appeared and would have to wait until later for their inspection. Each looked the other in the eyes knowing this could be some sort of contraband being illegally shipped into or out of Mexico. It could even be gold, silver, or precious gems...they had no idea, but their imaginations did run the gamut.

They decided to take a break while the residual nitrogen slowly dissipated through their tissues, blood and finally exhaled through their lungs while they considered making another dive on the wreck to see what else they could locate. Maybe there were more treasures to be found.

About an hour passed and they returned to make a second dive. They looked around but could not see the wreck. The anchor had dragged in the sand as both wind and tide had pushed the boat around. The boat was only equipped with a depth finder and compass with no modern navigational equipment, so they doubted they would ever be able to locate the wreck again. After about 20 minutes of circling the anchor, they surfaced and readied the cruiser for the return trip.

After their leisurely trip back and drinking a few cold beers while looking at the beautiful sailing ships and yachts and their beautiful people topside, the boat was secured to the dock at the boat rental shop. They returned the dive gear and settled the bill. It was a great day's adventure, and the diving was fantastic. In each of their bags was a metal box, yet what was inside the boxes was yet a mystery and would have to wait until they got back to their rooms. Nothing was mentioned about the wreck to the boat rental manager when he asked about the dives. He wondered why only six of the nine tanks had been used and asked why the other three tanks were still full. Elder responded authoritatively. "After the second dive we were tired and, after all, we are here to relax and enjoy ourselves. If we are completely worn out from diving all day,

KIDNAPPING JESUS

then, the beautiful girls will be disappointed when we party tonight." The manager provided a knowing smile and Elder turned and winked at both Carter and Reed as they left.

It was a short distance back to the Hotel and there was always a party atmosphere in this city. Cozumel is a paradise where the colorful local merchants and tourists from all walks of life and from all corners of the world seemed to blend together for good times. Elder, Reed and Carter were having fun letting it all out. It was a good feeling to be in this type of sand, thousands of miles away from Beirut, and not in the Battle Dress Uniform (BDUs) with 75 pounds of gear on, weapons loaded and looking for someone, or someone looking for them and ready to shoot them for just being an American, much less a United States Marine doing his duty. They entered the front of the 5 Star Hotel and once in the ornate lobby, the Bell Boy hurried to them to help them with their bags. It was somewhat of an irritant, but that is how many of the young men get tips to help feed their families.

There was light conversation as the four of them rode up in the mirrored elevator. The mirror was highly polished, and the ornate gold glittered with the reflections of the Hotel patrons. Once they had been escorted to their suite by the young Mexican boy, Elder gave him a $5 dollar bill for his efforts. Although this tip, by all standards, was a small amount of money for Elder, this amount of money could feed a family of five for several days if they watched how they spent their pesos. Juan Estrada beamed from ear to ear at his newfound wealth. He vowed to help these Americans while they were guests of the Grand Hotel Coronado and would be ever-vigilant at any time, he saw them inside the hotel.

Once inside the room, they all let out a deep breath, almost in unison. It had been a great adventure, and they knew they had lived not far from the edge during the dive. With both Carter and Reed running low on air, carrying extra baggage back in the form of unopened metal cases, it was a dive that could have gone from recreational diving to an emergency that could have engulfed all three of them. Fortunately, cool heads prevailed, and once again, they had received excellent training from their Master Instructor at one of the local Dive shops near Camp Pendleton.

36

TIME WELL SPENT AFTER A HARD TOUR OF DUTY!

The name of the Dive Shop was West Coast Adventure SCUBA Divers. They were a fully certified dive facility and ran many levels of certification through their courses of instruction. John Richards became fast friends with the owner as he trained many of the classes during the weekends, if he did not have Marine duties at the Camp. Their SCUBA instructor had made thousands of dives, most of them training dives, was also a Marine.

Major John L. Richards had learned to dive while stationed in Izmir, Turkey when he was stationed there as an advisor to Land Southeast, a Component of NATO forces. He was a logistician assigned to the multi- National forces commanded by a Turkish Four-Star General with a U.S. Army Major General as the Deputy Commander.

One of the subordinate Commanders was a Brigadier Marine General. Within a year of arriving in country, he became an Open Water Instructor and had learned his skills from a Turkish dive instructor by the name of Friksos. Friksos was half-man and half-fish and was the best technical instructor Major Richards had ever had in his life. Friksos would have been a great Marine Drill Sergeant. However, he was quite spoken, but when he spoke, you would listen. What a great friend he became as Richards advanced through his levels of certification. In fact, Friksos gave Richards his dive knife and a gold SCUBA diver charm to go on a gold chain that Richards would always treasure as a deep, binding, level of friendship and mutual respect. Richards quickly became a Staff Instructor, one of the first two Americans in Turkey to be certified as an PADI Instructor in Turkey, as well and would later become a Master Instructor when he was stateside and stationed at Camp Pendleton.

Major Richards had taught all three how to dive, beginning with Elder. During the intervening months between deployments, there were many occasions to dive off the coast of California. It was challenging due to the icy water, currents and kelp beds, but that had made the dives they had just completed relatively relaxing except for the circumstances resulting in the low-air situation. They had been trained well and had reacted with textbook precision when they encountered the situations presented and ensured the dive was a successful dive. Major Richards always stated during his classes, "Remain alert during every dive. Continuously check out your buddy so you always enjoy your dives. This is recreational diving! Everybody wants to have fun and celebrate every dive by reliving their shared underwater experience." This advice holds true in many activities and was passed down from Friksos to all divers whom Richards trained.

The boxes had been removed from the carelessly tossed bags and placed on the coffee table between the two leather sofas. After a few moments of searching through the kitchen, Carter returned to Elder and Reed with a knife and ice pick. Elder took the pick to the lock and twisted. After a few moments of effort, the lock snapped. The knife was then inserted and turned to open the lock. The first box was now opened. Inside was a brick. At least it looked like a brick, but the contents were hidden and wrapped with silver duct tape. They removed the block from the box and began to unwrap the bundle they found. They wondered if they had retrieved illegal drugs or something else, they would later have to get rid of. They could always go diving again and throw away any drugs they may have found as none of them wanted any part of this type of deal.

The duct tape proved to be difficult as it was wrapped in three layers to prevent any type of damage to the contents. Carter again disappeared to the kitchen where he found a pair of cheap scissors. This helped to break the sealed bundle and their challenging work produced ten stacks of U.S. currency. As they thumbed through them, they quickly noticed they were all one hundred-dollar bills. The hundreds dated back to 1965 through 1973 and none were sequentially numbered. This was great news as they were not counterfeit. The same process was repeated on the remaining boxes, and they contained the same amount of cold hard U.S. cash as the first box. The money was dry and in excellent condition. Elder, Reed and Carter sat in the room for what seemed like hours without anyone saying anything.

Elder spoke first, "I think we should put the money in some type of investment, so when we get out of the Corps, we will be rich!" It was a somber statement coming from John when everyone was thinking about throwing the cash into the air like a New Year's Eve celebration in Times Square. They all laughed. It was the first real laugh anyone of them had had for months and they savored the moment.

Elder went on to say, "First, I think we should have a wonderful time while we are down here in Mexico." Reed and Carter unanimously

TIME WELL SPENT AFTER A HARD TOUR OF DUTY!

agreed with their friend. In fact, it was clear the wink that passed between them in the Boat Rental Store was real, the $300,000 they had was real, and the time they were about to have, would be very real.

They took $500 out of each of the boxes, and they agreed they would equally split the money three ways. The boxes were placed into a safe located in the closet. None were to ever speak of the money when they returned to Camp Pendleton, and they swore an oath of secrecy not to divulge where they found the loot, or that any of the others had the same amount of cash. They showered, had a couple of ice-cold beers, and headed down the escalator to the lobby. Juan Estrada, the Bell Boy who had helped them with their bags earlier when they returned from their dive trip, ran up to Elder and thanked him for the tip, and then ran to the Hotel door and held it wide open for the three friends. He made a sweeping bow that would make a Matador smile.

The three friends were on their way down the streets looking for an enjoyable time, and there would be blushing women in the morning after the pumped-up men swept them off their feet this evening. The sky was the limit and the Marines pocket full of cash represented a month's base pay for Sergeant Carter. This was a night to celebrate.

The friends partied for days, ate well, and had an exciting time with the senoritas. They were beautiful women, and none were bashful. It was, after all, a time when there should not be a care in the world, except to get home without being detected with the money.

The day finally arrived to leave. They had said goodbye to the beautiful ladies the night before. They had been paid well by the newly found riches, but not overly much so as not to raise any suspicions. The ladies had an enjoyable time too by being with only one guy for days as opposed to hustling for wages earned by high-class prostitutes. These ladies were independent as they were on their own, and not part of any of the institutions that give women of the evening a negative connotation. They were selective with their clientele and did not just jump into bed with anyone they met. They could only make money with the world's oldest profession as they really had no other opportunity and had hungry mouths to feed their extended families. Many of them were the sole source of income. They kept the frolics at a very low key. It was not time to attract too much attention from the locals, fellow tourists,

KIDNAPPING JESUS

or from some prying eyes in the crowd that would, or could, reveal themselves at an inopportune moment.

Carter called down to the Bell Captain requesting a Bell Boy. He recalled Juan's name and asked for him. Almost as quickly as the phone was cradled, the buzzer at the door sounded. Juan was there with a beaming smile and with a cart for the luggage. Juan said to Carter, "Senor Carter, if was a pleasure to have you and your friends stay with us in the Hotel Grand Coronado. You are honored guests and I hope to see you on your next visit. Please don't forget me as I will always remember you." Carter was somewhat amazed as Juan had been very reserved during their entire visit and had treated them with every courtesy. Yet, this small Mexican boy, although diminutive in stature, was fluent in the English language and was very well mannered. Carter would not be surprised if this little entrepreneur did not own the Hotel someday. This guy was going to be a survivor.

From the outside, the luggage was no different in appearance than it had been when they arrived in Cozumel from Los Angeles. Yet, inside, the luggage held nearly $300,000. The bags should not raise any eyebrows at the airport, but it was clear that this was the crucial part of this adventure. Juan gathered the luggage and took it to the elevator designated for the Hotel staff while the three friends jumped on the Hotel guest elevator on its downward trip to the lobby. They all looked at each other, silently worried, while it took just a few minutes to reach their destination. Not wanting to cause any undue suspicions, and just like they would normally do if they had no money, out came the plastic cards to pay for the rooms and beverages they had at the mini bar in the room and at the fully appointed bar on the top floor. They had also had a few meals indoors and one delivery charge from a lady's boutique for some fancy negligees the ladies modeled while running around the rooms. Clothes were optional, but at night, the suite quaked while the pent-up Marines were entertained.

The Bell Captain had called for a taxi, and it was waiting at the curb outside the Hotel entrance. He held the doors for the three men and had treated them with much respect during their visit. Carter was designated as the tip guy and laid a $10 bill in the Bell Captain's hand. Juan loaded the luggage in the trunk of the taxi slamming the lid down to ensure it was closed tightly. Carter waited until Elder and Reed were

40

TIME WELL SPENT AFTER A HARD TOUR OF DUTY!

in the back seat and then handed Juan a $5 bill wrapped around two $20 dollar bills. He did not want the Bell Captain to take Juan's tip. In this manner, Juan could pocket

$40, a wage that would feed his poor family for a month if the Bell Captain decided to take his tip. Juan could hide the real money with no problem as it appeared to be a small tip with the Bell Captain getting twice as much. Juan leaned in the back window at Elder's request.

Elder whispered to him, "Juan, thank you for your help. You are a special young man. Do not lead a routine life, seek adventure...dare to dream heroic dreams. Be careful, as there is ignorance that will prey upon you. Rise above it." Juan was not sure he understood the meaning, but in the years to come, he would heed these words and become greater than he could ever imagine. As a leader from the people and of the people, he would understand! Elder looked out the window of the taxi at the Grand Hotel Coronado. Memories were made there that would last a lifetime. These were good ones— memories that helped ease the painful flashbacks of the Barracks vividly painted in his mind, never to be forgotten, but living must go on. If not, they too are dead.

It was an uneventful trip back to the airport by Mexican taxi standards. The road was crowded and the lines on the highway were only a suggestion. Traffic was heavy, and it was a race to see who had the fastest Detroit denizen. This taxi was a 1957 Chevy with a 327 cubic inch engine. The outside was two-toned, red and white, while the inside was red leather. Nice tuck and roll job. The dual tailpipes had a nice throaty sound as they sped on their way. It was nice not having to drive, but the cab driver wanted to find out from the friends about their trip. They kept if low key. Just did some diving, drinking and dancing with the beautiful ladies. They spoke of nothing that would give the driver any inkling as to the treasure sitting in the trunk of this reconditioned classic.

They arrived at the airport in one piece. The silent prayers paid off. Checking their baggage at the ticket counter, they showed their passports and their military identification cards to the airline's agent. She was a pretty lady around 30 years old. She was very attractive to John Elder. She had a light complexion, olive skin, and nice, luscious lips. Her smile was radiant, and she seemed to be attracted to this man. If only there could be more time. But Elder and his friends were on their way out

KIDNAPPING JESUS

of Mexico, not coming in, so it was perhaps another match that could have been had the cards be dealt differently. But it was a good feeling to have a man look at her with both respect and admiration. It brought heat to her cheeks. The blush did not go unnoticed.

Rosita finished checking their passports and their ID cards. She had asked the routine questions about gifts and fruits while they were in Mexico. The Marines had nothing to declare except that they had a wonderful time, and it was a beautiful vacation paradise where they could unwind. She handed them each their passports with a small piece of tape on each indicating they had been properly scrutinized upon check in. Handing Elder back his passport, her hand lingered on the small book as Elder reached for his identification. The touch of his hand on hers made her gasp. Elder also was affected. It was only for a moment, but both knew this was something more than might have been.

There are endless matches in the world that would work if they were only acted upon. Why did many make the wrong choices, he would ask himself on countless occasions. Elder thanked Rosita, but their flight was being called and they still had to get through security.

They made their flight with 15 minutes to spare. Their carry- on luggage was stowed overhead where the three friends could keep their eyes on their valuables. They sat together on the DC- 737 and quietly discussed where, or better yet, how to invest the money. They choose not to have these discussions while in Mexico as you could never be sure when someone might be listening. They also had the prostitutes they hired with them most of the time and loose lips might have caused some questions among the ladies. One thing they each agreed upon was to divide the money into three equal amounts and place the money in three separate accounts in different banks in Los Angeles. They did not want to attract attention, so they would do this over a period of three weeks during their time away from Camp.

In each bank, approximately $98,000 would be deposited with Elder, Reed or Carter being the designated principal account holder. Just in case, Reed was designated as back-up for Elder, Carter for Reed and Elder for Carter with the accounts set up so that two of the three friend's signatures would be required. Although they were friends and fellow Marines, money often did evil things to people or split families apart. This agreement allowed all of them to feel good about each other.

TIME WELL SPENT AFTER A HARD TOUR OF DUTY!

Elder and Reed had gone through their Basic Training at Paris Island together and Carter became good friends with Elder and Reed when he joined Bravo Company and later would become a crewmember on Tank 35. They were like brothers although Elder and Reed were older than Carter by ten years. They were family!

They had a great flight and had a couple of free drinks during the uneventful trip. The flights attendants were friendly and very nice looking. It was a pleasant trip with beautiful skies. This was going to be the best trip any of them would ever have and they were relaxed as they neared the end of their vacation. Elder was thinking about the waiting First Sergeant position and the ceremony the Company Commander would hold as the Company Colors were passed from Company Commander to the previous First Sergeant to Brigadier General (BG) Marvin Colby then to Elder and the Company Commander. BG Colby was his Platoon Leader when the Platoon was ambushed in Vietnam in 1968 by a Viet Cong Battalion. They were brothers in arms and were always in close touch with one another during the intervening years. Each had kept up the correspondence and the Navy/Marine Times covered stories where one, or the other, had served. Beirut was still getting a lot of publicity in the news.

The jet touched down and they were back in the U.S. It would feel good to get back to their Billets at Camp. Yet, they still had to go through Customs. They each had their Passport, ID Card, and completed Declarations Form when they got to Security. Each was asked if they had anything they had not declared and each responded with, "No Sir...nothing to declare with the exception that we had a fantastic time in Mexico." Each was allowed to cross back in the States and breathe just a little bit easier.

CHAPTER IV

BACK AT CAMP

Once they arrived back at Camp Pendleton, they knew they would have to get ready for the Change of Command and then there was the Division Boxing Championship coming up in one month. Gunnery Sergeant (P) Elder had not put on a pair of gloves in over a year. While he worked out every day, even during his vacation in Cozumel, he was not in tip-top fighting condition, and he was almost 35 years old. His birthday was coming up on July 30th. It would take training every day if he were going to get into shape in order to have a chance of winning the heavy weight division. During his assignment in Lebanon, there had been no time for physical training or boxing. There was only time for gathering the dead, defending his Nation, and fighting the enemy.

Elder had grown up in a family of fighters. His Uncle Charles was a light heavyweight contender in 1941. Uncle Charles entered World War II when he joined the Marines on December 10th, 1941. Enlisting in the Marines would end his boxing career, but he wanted to fight for his Country like many of his friends after the cowardly attack by the Japanese at Pearl Harbor on December 7, 1941. He sped through Basic Training as his unit was rushed to the Pacific Theater of War.

He shipped out to Hawaii where he trained with his unit while preparations were made to begin the fight across the expanse of the

Pacific Ocean on many islands no one had ever heard of until the newsreels were shown at the movie theaters and newspapers covered the advances made during four years of fighting on the beaches and in the jungles. There were names like Bataan, Corregidor, Midway and Guadalcanal. These were names that would invoke emotions from the American public as the U.S. Military met setbacks or achieved costly victories throughout the Pacific Campaign. The devastation of the Pacific Fleet at Pearl Harbor was in the news and on the radio at home. It was like a rally cry for the military and for all Americans.

History is filled with battle cries like "Remember the Alamo" and "Remember the Maine" and now it was "Remember Pearl Harbor", a new battle cry to arms.

A sleeping giant was awakened. But, up close and personal, the devastation was real. There were the dead that would never be buried in a National Cemetery and heroics that would never be documented. The cleanup at Pearl continued while the United States prepared for battle and the industrial base of America focused on one goal, to aid the military might of the Allied Forces to win on the two distinct and separate Fronts, the war in Germany and the Atlantic Ocean, and the war against Japan in the Pacific Theatre of Operations. This was now a World War. The Campaign was bloody and took years to complete and achieve victory.

It was in one of the final historic battles where Uncle Charles would get his ticket home. It was during the bloody battle in 1945, at Iwo Jima, as the U.S. Marines stormed ashore where Staff Sergeant Charles L. Elder was severely wounded in his right shoulder. Elder was part of the legendary 5th Marine Division. He was evacuated with the dead, dying, and the wounded to a Navy Hospital Ship offshore. An angel must have been watching over him that day as his fellow Marines met the Japanese in their

BACK AT CAMP

defensive positions. It was a killing field. The shells from the mighty Battleships fired that day along with the bombs dropped should have riddled the emplaced Japanese Army, but they were prepared and were tenacious as American military fought the bloodybattles in order to gain the ground needed to take the war to Japanese soil. Many of Charles' friends died that day. Death had been a constant reminder as he moved through the Pacific Theater of Operations, island to island, as the stranglehold on Japan tightened. Yes, the bullet was his ticket home, but the ticket came with a price.

Coincidentally, the Battleship New Jersey was also involved with this invasion. The Elder's never served on the New Jersey, but it was a common thread through the colorful and distinguished military careers of the Elders that the New Jersey was nearby, providing much needed support for the battles they were fighting and later would fight. He recovered with others yet would be unable to box after the war ended. It took the explosions of two Atomic Bombs to bring the Japanese to surrender. "Little Boy" was dropped on Hiroshima by Colonel Paul Tibbets and the B-29 bomber known as the "Enola Gay" on August 6, 1945, and Major Charles Sweeney dropped "Fat Man" on Nagasaki on August 9, 1945 from his B-29 known as "Bockscar".

The devastation was unimaginable, and many Japanese civilians lost their lives or were severely scarred with radioactive poisoning that would make their lives a living hell. Yet, the Japanese now would surrender and both Japanese and American lives would be spared from a battle for the Japanese main islands. General Douglas MacArthur, Supreme Allied Commander, presided over the Japanese surrender in Tokyo Bay on the U.S.S. Battleship Missouri (BB-63), also of the Iowa Class of Battleships, sister ship to the U.S.S. New Jersey, on September 2, 1945. Two of the Japanese representatives were Foreign Minister Mamoru Shigemitsu and General Yoshijiro Umezu, Chief of the Army General Staff. Representatives from the Allied Powers were also on board the Missouri.

Mighty Mo" or "Big Mo" USS Missouri

So, what Uncle Charles did was coach John, Jack, and Charles Elder on how to fight. Their mother always was uncomfortable and thought the boys would get hurt, but aside from a few jabs and punches any boxer would have to absorb during matches and constant training, they never were seriously injured. There were no glass jaws in this family, and the solidly built young men would continue their boxing in the Marines. Uncle Charles was able to take John and Charles to the Golden Glove Nationals where they both won their respective weight divisions. John fought in the 147- pound division and Charles fought in the 135- pound division.

It was May 11, 1967, when John entered the Marine Corps. He joined several years ahead of his younger brothers. Charles and Jack enlisted under the buddy program. Charles was engaged when he joined the Corps while Jack, like many young men his age, liked to date

BACK AT CAMP

all the women. There were some uncomfortable moments when some of the girls he dated came in close contact with each other. Jack had many girlfriends when he joined the Corps, all believing this was their man and one day Jack would pick them to be his wife. He was going to be a Marine. Vietnam was still going strong in early 1970 when they signed up at the Recruiter's Office.

Both John and Charles compiled good boxing records and earned the respect of fellow boxers when they were matched. John was in 110 fights. He lost only 12. He knocked out his opponents 76 times and he was never knocked out or put down on the floor. His brother Charles had 80 fights, lost eight of them and had 65 knockouts. He too was never knocked off his feet or badly beaten. He had fast hands and was often jokingly referred to as a white Sugar Ray Leonard. Charles was married after Basic Training. It was a wonderful marriage to begin with, but with Vietnam and the deployments, the young couple could not make it work. Life was tough, and still is, for the family life of a service man or woman. Both John and Jack would remain single, at least for the time being. There would be a day each of them would be able to settle down; however, it would be many, many years before that day would come.

The Corps started every day before anyone in their right mind would be awake. The morning formation at 0500 hours would call for a morning report from the Platoon Sergeant or Lieutenant to the First Sergeant or Company Commander. Following the morning report, it was time for Physical Training (PT). In unison, the Company would expand the formation to do the stretching, jumping Jacks, bend and reach, and many more exercises including sit-ups and push-ups. This was the way to get everyone's blood pumping. Once the exercises were completed, the open formations would close and the First Sergeant (Top) took the formation from the Company Commander (the CO). Marching to Jodie calls, Top would get the formation lined up, the road guards out front, to block traffic, and the Company guidon, just left and behind the CO. Getting the unit started, Top would begin the colorful calls. Four or five of the enlisted would also rotate into the calls as units all through the Camp were exercising. It was a great sound, to hear Marines in the morning.

KIDNAPPING JESUS

The road work, in formations, helped the Marines stay in shape. It depended on the day of the week how far the unit would run, but you could always count on at least a three-mile run in formation. On Fridays, the unit would get a five-mile run and once a month, the Battalion would form a Battalion Run with all the Companies lined up behind the Battalion Commander, the Battalion Staff, and the Battalion Colors with the Unit's Battle Streamers. The Battalion Sergeant Major would police the rear of the formation for any stragglers and the First Sergeant having the most fallouts from their Company would get his call to Battalion Headquarters. In fact, all the Company First Sergeants would get a piece of their rear end handed to them for this major malfunction. The Battalion Sergeant Major kept great notes and there was not one Non-Commissioned Officer (NCO) that wanted to be on this list for long. The young officers looked to this NCO for mentoring as they learned about the Marines and how to be good officers. They too, did not want to be on his Shit List.

Gunnery Sergeant (P) Elder was lean and mean and always stayed in tip top shape. In addition to the morning runs, he would make time to run an additional two to three miles a day. On weekends, he always took one day to hit the trails running off the beaten path, so it was more than just running in a straight line on pavement. This paid off in later years. Charles always found a way to get out of road work with the training over and fight night only two days away, John was getting his game face on and was honed to a sharp fighting edge. Staying in good physical condition and his mental preparation paid off. Staff Sergeant Jack Elder covered all the bets. The betting went down racial lines with the Blacks betting on the Division cook.

Staff Sergeant Jerry Willis was the Division Champ for the previous two years. He weighed 186 pounds. He was a powerful man and his muscles rippled as he brought his gloves together. His record was 53 wins. He has lost eight fights, but he had an impressive record of 28 knockouts. Willis was 32 years old and like John, he had been fighting most of his life. They knew each other from previous assignments and often spoke of famous fights throughout history. Both liked to think back to the years of Jack Dempsey and Gentleman Jim Corbett. Jerry was from Detroit, Michigan and wanted to join the Marines and make a life for himself. The auto industry was where his family had worked

BACK AT CAMP

for years. He did not want to follow in the footsteps of his father, older brother, and several of his uncles. He witnessed firsthand what happened to his family over the years when there were strikes and when there were layoffs. Those were tough times when he was growing up. He too had joined the Corps in 1970 and went through Basic Training with John's younger brothers, Jack, and Charles.

John Elder was to enter the ring first. He grabbed the top rope and slipped through the middle and top ropes. He did not want a fancy entrance and wanted to conserve his strength. John weighed in at 188 pounds. Just a three-pound difference! Was it an advantage for Elder? Both fighters were even in reach, and both were six feet tall. John received shouts of support and also heard boos from the opposition. His brother Charles and his friends Reed and Carter were working in the corner.

The music was cranked up when Willis started his walk to the ring. Jerry was wearing a long white robe with a large black locomotive on the back with smoke billowing from the engine's smokestack. It looked like something from the 1800s and was very impressive. The caption over the heart on the left of the robe read, "The Willis Express." He took the top rope as he climbed into the ring and jumped over it easily with an effortless move. He was being cheered on by his fans and jeered by those who favored Elder. The announcer was on the microphone as the yelling died down. Willis was quite intimidating as he stripped out of his robe. Elder was pumped...there were no smiles exchanged between the two Marines.

This was a fight both wanted to win. It was pride, but it was for the right to be the First Marine Division Champ. This would be Elder's last match and he wanted a victory. Willis had a flat, washboard, stomach, and big arms. He was all muscle. He stared at Elder and said with a loud voice.

"You're going down." All of the Blacks started a chant, "Knock him out Willis...Knock him out! ...Knock him out Willis...Knock him out!" The crowd intensified when Elder turned to Willis and stared him in the eye. The noise seemed to disappear. It was quiet. You could hear a pin drop. Elder could hear Willis breathing and see the sweat popping out of his pores. He could see deep into the pupils of Willis' eyes. Did

KIDNAPPING JESUS

Willis have what it takes, or was the spark flickering deep within? A winner seizes the right opportunity.

When John said to Willis, "Bring it on!" The crowd erupted. It was pandemonium. The Marines cheered on the two in the ring and all eyes were focused on this center stage. The announcer brought them both together announcing the rules and cautioning them to fight fairly. They turned their respective corners. John looked at Charles. This was a look that Charles had seen many times before. John felt genuine support from his corner. He knew his team and they knew him. They were close. Charles spoke quietly to John while Reed and Carter readied John for the fight. "Feel him out with the jab and then set him up with a hard right." With their mouthpieces in place, the two fighters came to the center of the ring. The referee issued the final instructions, looked over at the bell. Willis pushed Elder's face with his glove rather than bringing the gloves together and the crowd went wild. The referee cautioned him for this insult, but this was unexpected. Then, as if in slow motion, the referee nodded, the bell rang, and the fight was on.

Elder and Willis were toe to toe dancing while each sized up their opponent. Willis stepped to his right after Elder jabbed him with a right hand to the head. Elder never took a step back. He continued to press Willis keeping him close and doubled up on the jabs moving Willis back towards his corner. Elder dropped a right hand down the pike and put Willis on his butt. The referee stepped in... The crowd was quiet... Elder was pushed back while the slow count started. Willis was stunned and he was in disbelief Elder had knocked him off his feet. He was no longer confident he could take this match.

He could hear the count hit three and then he heard the chant from his corner begin... "Choo...Choo." The rhythm came faster, and it sounded like a train was coming through the wall of the Marine Gymnasium.

Willis took his time to get up as the referee's arms came down at the sound of "eight." Willis took the eight count and was on his feet dancing to get his circulation going. He shook his head and the beaded sweat on his body shook off. Willis was trying to clear his head as the referee asked him if he was ok to continue. Willis nodded and Elder had to run him down.

BACK AT CAMP

He squared him up. Willis' hands blocked a left and then a right, but he did not see the second right come under his block. Willis doubled over and he took another left just glancing off his right jaw, but he was off balance and was on the mat again. It was a five count this time and again Willis got up slowly. This time, Willis was moving slower and was looking at his corner for encouragement. He could see it on their faces. Disbelief was evident even though words of encouragement were being given. Before Elder could close in another exchange, the bell rang ending the first round.

Without a doubt, the Marines knew what the score was. Somebody was going to lose, and it was probably going to be Staff Sergeant Willis. It was incredible. Two years of winning the Division Championship had put the odds-on Willis and it looked like the monthly paychecks that were bet would be lost. For those who were single and living in the Barracks, that would not be a problem as they would still get three hots and a cot, so to speak. They had their bunks and the mess hall served great food. For those that were married, kids or no kids, times would be tough, and the Pawn Shops would see increased traffic of items that could be pawned and sometimes later reclaimed.

Round Two was moments away. The corners were cleaning up their fighters and giving them last-minute advice. Elder was all business. He knew he had his man but did not want to be overly confident. If Willis connected, he would lose the advantage he had earned in the first round. The betting was over, but the fight was still on. There was a chance for Willis to pull this out. He was good, really good, and he knew it. But, his confidence in himself was being challenged by his opponent.

The bell sounded bringing the crowd to their feet. With the adrenaline pumping through his veins, his heart pounding, Elder came out of his corner like a man on fire. He met Willis in the middle of the boxing ring and the two titans began their personal battle. John was determined to end this match as soon as possible not wanting Willis to catch his breath.

Elder shot two left jabs at Willis' head. Not connecting, Elder sent him backwards. Elder closed in on Willis not allowing him to set his stance. They exchanged punches with each being deflected by the other's gloves. Elder came in with another right hand down to the middle just enough of a hit to get Willis to follow with his eyes. This was the

KIDNAPPING JESUS

mistake Elder was looking for. Elder followed the right hand with a left hook. The party was over. Willis hit the canvas like a sack of potatoes and the ring shook. The referee closed in and sent Elder to his corner while he administered the count. After the initial dead silence of a shocked crowd, they jumped in and counted out loud with the referee.

"One...Two...Three...Four...Five...
Six...Seven...Eight...Nine...Ten!"

Willis was out. His corner came in and the referee held up Elder's right hand signaling the fight over and declaring the new 1st Marine Division Champ. Elder checked out Willis and saw he was coming to and would be alright. The smelling salts were working. Most fighters would want to make fun of the fighter that was knocked out but not this Marine. He saluted Willis with his right glove. This was not a snappy salute, but a friendly salute to a brother at arms.

The bets were collected, and the crowds left the gym. The fighters went to their respective dressing rooms to get cleaned up and dressed into their civilian clothes. Elder entered the room where Willis and his friends were by him. Arms went out to hold Elder back, but Willis would have none of this. He motioned Elder forward with a big grin. It was a good fight, Elder had won fairly and earned his respect, not only as a fellow Marine, but as a great fighter.

The room was crowded, but Elder and Willis spoke to each other with respect. Elder let him know what he had done wrong during the fight. Weaknesses, once discovered, could be made into a new strength. Elder told Willis this was his last fight in the ring. He was getting too old, and the First Sergeant's job was going to take up any free time he would have in the future. He told Willis he would be in his corner next year when the next Championship was held if Willis would have him. The friendship between the two was sealed for a lifetime at that moment. They would remain friends until Elder left the Corps, but Elder would continue to keep in touch with his friend through the years.

BACK AT CAMP

It was June 1, 1984. Bravo Company, 1st Tank Battalion was in formation. The Company Commander, Captain Matthew R. Cavil, was facing his Command as the outgoing First Sergeant and First Sergeant Elder formed two steps in front of him facing each other. This was not a normal ceremony, and this was not going to be a normal day for Elder. Cavil was his Platoon Leader in Beirut. Earlier in the day at a promotion ceremony, Gunnery Sergeant (P) John Elder was frocked in rank to First Sergeant by General Colby. The diamond in the middle of the stripes indicated he was a First Sergeant. He would not get the pay for several months, but he would get the respect. The Company Colors were passed from Captain Cavil to the previous First Sergeant. They were then passed to Brigadier General (BG) Marvin Colby then to Elder and back to Captain Cavil.

BG Colby was his Platoon Leader when his Platoon was ambushed in Vietnam in 1968 by a Viet Cong Battalion during the TET Offensive (Lunar New Year) on January 30th. Both wore the Navy Cross on the top of their ribbons. Elder had seven rows of ribbons on his uniform and Colby had six rows. They were highly decorated, and both had two Purple Hearts. They were impressive and both deserved the respect they earned in the Corps. Once the Colors were passed, the General and First Sergeant saluted, the General embracing his friend, whispering good luck to each other. The General took his right hand and slapped Elder on the right shoulder and congratulated him on attaining this next level of responsibility. It was a day all would remember. History was being made, and the common thread was Elder and his two Lieutenants, one from 1967 and 1968 in Vietnam, and one from Lebanon in 1983 and 1984. He was proud of his promotion and this position, but he was proud Marine Non-Commissioned Officers made a difference when they trained the future leaders of the Corps. His duty was not yet over. He had more training to do before he left the Marines.

Two years quickly passed. 1st Sergeant John Elder and Staff Sergeant David Reed were finally at the long-awaited day when their careers in the Marines were finally at an end. They were at their appointed place of duty, at the Division Retirement Ceremony. This was a standard

KIDNAPPING JESUS

ceremony held on a monthly basis with the responsibilities for the Ceremony passed from unit to unit. They were among 15 fellow retirees. Friends, family, and fellow Marines were present. Major General (MG) Marvin Colby presided over the Ceremonies that day. He flew in from the Pentagon where he was serving with the Joint Chiefs of Staff. He was in daily meetings with the Commandant of the Marine Corps while the Nation's National Defense Strategy was being formulated to meet emerging threats throughout the world. He would not miss this moment.

For the service each of these retiring Marines had given their country, they would receive a Peacetime Award representing their entire careers along with their last assignment. They ranged from Meritorious Service Medals to the highest military peacetime award that could be given. There were two Colonels, four Lieutenant Colonels, one Major, one Sergeant Major, two Master Sergeants (including First Sergeant Elder), three Gunnery Sergeants and two Staff Sergeants (including Staff Sergeant Reed). First Sergeant Elder received the Legion of Merit for meritorious service to his country. It was another medal in the lengthy list of medals he had received during his 20 years of service to his Nation. MG Colby pinned on all the awards during the ceremony thanking each man and woman for their selfless service. When he reached First Sergeant Elder, he paused, spoke only to him for a few moments, looked him in the eye and thanked him for his mentorship when he was a green lieutenant in Vietnam.

The Navy Cross was well earned that fateful day when many of their comrades met their untimely deaths and had received their final awards posthumously. Colby and Elder would always have a special relationship, one that was earned by them both.

Just a few days after the Ceremony, newly retired Marines John Elder and David Reed went with Staff Sergeant Justin Carter to Los Angeles to the three banks where they had deposited nearly $300,000. They had found the treasure just over two years ago when they were on vacation in Cozumel. Systematically, they went into two of the banks and withdrew the money on deposit for John and David, leaving in place the money for Justin. The signatures for Justin were changed to either John or David in case Justin died. If Justin married, then the new wife would be on the signature line for the money. He still had 10 years to

56

BACK AT CAMP

go until he could retire unless he wanted to leave the service early. He could afford to do so if the money on deposit continued to grow.

He expected he would leave it on deposit until he felt it was needed. Independently, he could draw out the money at any time, just as Elder and Reed had taken out their money.

The money they had found had grown to about four hundred thousand dollars. Each of them had $133,000 at their disposal. Elder and Reed would begin to draw a nice retirement check in 30 days and Elder was now a disabled veteran. He was awarded 50% disability prior to his retirement and would begin to draw some of his retirement pay as non-taxable income. This was the last time they would see each other for a number of years.

It was June 1, 1986. John Elder would join the U.S. Marshal's Office on August 1, 1986. His friend David Reed would join the New York Police Department after his training on August 15, 1986. And Staff Sergeant Justin Carter would continue to serve his Nation as a Marine Corps NCO. They all would stay in touch with one another.

CHAPTER V

ANOTHER BEGINNING

It was August 1, 1986 when John Elder reported to the U.S. Marshals Academy at Glasgow, Georgia. The Marshals was the oldest law enforcement agency in the country. The Academy was not as hard as Marine Corps Boot Camp and the rigors of Academy training paled in comparison to Paris Island and the Drill Instructors that made the personal lives of each Marine recruit a living hell. Training was tough, but the Nation needed the men and women of the Corps tough, both mentally and physically. Many of the Marshals were former military veterans themselves.

The Federal Law was the hardest thing for Elder to learn. However, as the First Sergeant for Bravo Company, he knew the Uniform Code of Military Justice (UCMJ) like the back of his hand. The UCMJ was the bedrock of Military Law. John had not been in school for several years but had been put through the paces when he attended the. Marine Senior Non- Commissioned Officer Course at Quantico, Virginia. It was a struggle at first, but he was able to master his Law courses with a lot of studying late into the night and by joining a study group that met three times a week. Again, a former Marine, and seasoned U.S. Marshal, volunteered his free time to help the new recruits that wanted to learn the Law and become full- fledged Marshals.

KIDNAPPING JESUS

The physical aspect of the school was the easiest for Elder. The rigorous training Elder experienced on a daily basis in the Marines prepared him both mentally and physically. He was a leader, but real leaders must know how to follow and gain knowledge as they continue on life's road.

In one of the first self-defense classes Elder attended, he was selected to role play the crook. The instructor told John not to let his fellow classmates arrest him. Cadet Kathy Byrd was first to approach Elder. As she approached from Elder's front, her partner Robert (Bob) Clary moved to his left side. John was asked by Byrd what he was doing in the area. Elder shrugged his shoulders, judged the distances between himself. Bob and Kathy responded that it was a free country, and he could go anywhere he pleased. He turned to his right and started to walk away from Cadet Byrd. He was aware of Cadet Byrd's position when she grabbed Elder's arm and turned him around to face her. Elder was not the type of man that believed women should be out in the field playing cop. He believed a woman could provide support in many of administrative roles within these organizations, but due to many factors, a woman in this type of situation was not only in danger but placed their partners and civilians in danger as well.

Kathy was an attractive woman with blond hair and blue eyes, but she weighed only 105 pounds, and that was most likely dripping wet. As she spun elder around to face him, she told him "Sir, you are under arrest for suspicion of burglary! You must submit to my authority!" Elder took it easy on her when he gave her a short punching jab to her stomach just under the rib cage. She went down hard and rolled into a tight fetal position. She was on the ground sobbing and heaving unable to catch her breath.

Bob, her partner in the role play, was behind Elder as he looked down at Kathy shaking his head. He knew right where Clary was but was setting him up for his next move. Clary grabbed Elder in a choke hold around the neck. Elder had already flexed his neck muscles in preparation for the grab, and Elder grabbed Clary's little finger on his right hand with both of his hands and while breaking the failed hold, broke Bob's finger as he twisted away from the ill-advised, poorly attempted, choke hold on a hardened Marine role-playing a criminal subjected to a botched apprehension.

ANOTHER BEGINNING

Clary almost blacked out as he was falling backwards. Elder did not let go as he was attempting to keep Clary upright. Clary was no longer a danger to Elder, but he was to Byrd. As they were locked together, Clary fell over backwards dragging Elder with him causing Elder to fall forward. Although Elder did not believe women should be out in the public as law enforcement officers where they could be a danger to themselves, their partner or to the general public, he was not trying to hurt Byrd or Clary. As he was trying to prevent an injury, he was actually falling into Byrd lying on the floor. Elder fell on her ankle and severely sprained it. Kathy now started to cry out aloud like a little baby as she continued lying on the ground. Elder rolled and took Byrd's pistol from her. He shot Clary in the heart and Byrd in the head. Both were dead and the roll playing was over.

Soon after both Clary and Byrd were taken to the hospital, the Academy determined they would have to be recycled into the next class as they would be unable to complete the physical part of the course. Clary would attend the course and would go on to be successful as a U.S. Marshal. He had learned a valuable lesson from Elder and Byrd. Assumptions kill! Elder was not surprised when he found out that after Kathy's rehabilitation, she had submitted her resignation. Law enforcement was not for her, but maybe for other females. She knew she did not have the fortitude to be in this profession. Elder was a male chauvinist in many respects. Women have their place, but he believed police work was not one of them.

Elder would graduate from his class towards the bottom in academics but number one in pistol, rifle, and had a perfect score on the physical fitness test. During the remaining role-play-type classes involving possible physical confrontation, the instructor cautioned Elder not to injure any more students. Even with caution, it was difficult when the instructor nodded at the students for them to enter the ring with Elder. Elder was a third-degree Black Belt in Tai Kwon Do and no one could match him in boxing skills. He was still fast with his hands and had sharp mental discipline when someone approached him. He was always on guard. His tour in Vietnam taught him to respect his surroundings just as he respected his opponents. Assumptions kill!

The assignments were posted. Although his first assignment with the U.S. Marshals seemed to be punishment for his lack of academic

KIDNAPPING JESUS

achievement, it would serve him well in the future. He was assigned to Prisoner Transport for one year.

Within the Department, Captain Ronald M. Sullivan (nicknamed Lucky) was the Division Deputy Chief. He had visited the Academy on several occasions to check out the possible new Departmental recruits. It took a special Marshal to transport the worst of the worst criminals to their place of judgment or incarceration once they were tracked down and captured by the Marshals. It was during one of these routine trips Captain Sullivan saw Elder in action. He took a liking to Elder when he saw him during one of the many role-playings exercises the students encountered during their classes. The Captain spoke to the Instructor regarding Elder's abilities during situational encounters.

The instructor was a former U.S. Army Special Forces Master Sergeant with 23 years of seasoned experience. His career included two tours in Vietnam, and he was involved in the low altitude parachuting of the Rangers into Grenada during Operation Urgent Fury in the early morning hours of October 25, 1983. This was the first major operation conducted by the U.S. Military since the end of the Vietnam War. The Marxist-Leninist led regime was successfully toppled. The victory was decisive. The U.S. suffered casualties and 19 fellow comrades in arms lost their lives during this mission of restoring a legitimate government to power.

Marshal Elder was taking a prisoner down to Captain Sullivan for a disciplinary hearing. As Elder entered the well-appointed office, the Captain instructed Elder to remain in the room during the hearing. Elder didn't know what happened, but suddenly, the Captain and prisoner started yelling. The prisoner, Rick (nicknamed IcePick) Shelton shouted at the Captain, "You're a piece of dog shit and I'll kick your ass. If I were not here in this rotten prison with your trained apes, I'd rip your head off and piss down your throat." The Captain was not about to lose his cool now with this low-life, scum bag of the Earth, mass-murdering lunatic. He regained his composure and ordered Elder to remove the prisoner from his office.

62

ANOTHER BEGINNING

Elder told Icepick, "Let's go!" Shelton stood completely still and did not move as Elder had instructed. Marshal Elder grabbed IcePick by the arm and locked his right hand midway behind his back. He had his little finger in a hold ready to be snapped if IcePick made the wrong move. IcePick was being forced towards the door by Elder. The Captain was relieved. He was under a lot of stress from both the demands of the Marshal's Office, his position in his community, and from his wife and teenaged children. His son, Nicolas, was just out of High School and was trying to determine what he was going to do for the rest of his life and his daughter, Elaine, was 16 years old going on 23. She was named after his wife's sister.

Captain Sullivan snapped back to reality. The prisoner had pulled away from Elder's tightly held grip and was swinging a huge right hand directly at his face. Elder had seen the right hand coming a mile away.

IcePick was not a small man, but it would not make a difference even if he weighed 250 pounds. Elder was still relatively new to the Marshal's Office and had not yet gained a reputation. IcePick would end up sharing the news with the rest of the criminal community in short order. Elder's left hand blocked the blow short of contact with his face. He nearly broke IcePick's right arm when he made contact just above and behind IcePick's wrist. Before Captain Sullivan could blink, Elder followed with an overhand right to the loser's nose followed by a quick left hook knocking IcePick out as he hit the hard floor. There was no Ten Count. The prisoner hit the ground like a tub of lard splitting his head open.

The Captain yelled at Elder..."What are you doing?"

Elder wasn't doing anything. It was over in seconds. It was his training and his instincts that kept Elder safe from possible harm, yet when the Captain yelled, the Marshal stopped cold in his tracks. Just after all Hell broke loose, Elder thought he was going to get an ass chewing for taking this thug down even though it was self-protection and verbal threats were made at the Captain.

Thinking he was in deep shit, Elder looked up at the Captain and saw a huge grin on his face. The Captain told him to call down to the aide station and get this scum out of his office. There will be another disciplinary hearing, but not now. The punch Elder landed on IcePick's face was going to get a lot of attention in the weeks to come. It was

KIDNAPPING JESUS

broken in two places and blood was everywhere. His eyes were already turning black and blue. This was a no-gloves affair and Elder's knuckles were bleeding as well. IcePick would never hear the end of this to be sure. In fact, Elder was already thinking of a new nickname for this asshole, and it was not IcePick. IcePick looked more like a NosePick lying on the Captain's stained Oriental rug than anything else he could think of at the moment.

The gurney came. IcePick was lifted by a team of four, and his hands were strapped to the rails. He was on his way to getting some serious medical attention. Most of the Marshals that passed by the scene took one look at the former IcePick and at Elder. They shook their heads, smiled at Elder, and were off to tell the story. The Captain said to Elder, "Come back to see me after the nurse takes care of that hand. I need you at full strength. There's a mission coming up that is made to order for you and your special talents." Elder was intrigued. Elder trailed the team to the elevator and went to the aide station for some gauze to wrap around his fist. It was swollen and needed some tender loving care.

Elder dropped off the prisoner and went back to see the Captain. Captain Sullivan was indeed feeling "Lucky" to have Elder as a new recruit. This was a pleasant relief to this battered defender of the law. Elder knocked on the door and was instructed to enter. Elder entered the Captain's Office and stepped around the freshly cleaned carpet. "I'm reporting as ordered, sir," stated Elder. You can take the man out of the Marines, but you cannot take the Marine out of the man.

The Captain motioned to Elder to take a seat. A relaxed Elder was asked, "Where did you learn to fight like that Marshal? I know you know how to fight and defend yourself, but that was quick, really quick, and you put IcePick down before he could become a threat to others."

Marshal John Elder responded. "I was trained by my Uncle Charles from the time I was 12 years old in how to box. Uncle Charles was a light heavyweight contender in 1941 but he joined the Marines following the Japanese attack at Pearl Harbor. He continued my training after the war, but he could no longer fight due to the wounds he received during the battle at Iwo Jima. I also fought on the Marine Corps boxing team. I have had over 100 amateur fights."

The Captain replied. "John, I liked what I saw when I visited the Academy. Although I did not see you every visit, someone would update

ANOTHER BEGINNING

me on the latest events and your name usually came up during the discussions. Jack Rogers, one of your fitness instructors, suggested I check into bringing you into my department. He was a former Army Ranger and is a well-respected Marshal and that was good enough for me."

The Captain took a deep breath and looked Elder straight in the eyes. "John, I have a dangerous assignment for you, one for which only a few Marshals are selected. It is dangerous, requires independent field work, calls for you to work with local authorities, and has no pretense of being a choice assignment. I can only tell you this much. You could easily get yourself killed doing this job, but your background and unique talents make you eminently qualified. This is a one-year assignment and if you choose to accept it, you will be promoted to the rank of Sergeant effective immediately."

Elder asked the Captain about the position. "Sir, what exactly is the job?"

Captain Sullivan responded. "You would be tracking down the most dangerous felons in the country and serving them arrest warrants and bringing them back into the justice system. These are the worst of the worst and have eluded our abilities at the State and Local levels to bring them to justice in order to receive their just punishment. There is a team of ten Marshals assigned to this mission. It's a tough job, hard on the men and their families, and has the highest mortality rate in the Marshals. Are you in?"

Marshal John Elder looked at the Captain and with little hesitation, responded to the point, "Yes Sir, you can count on me!"

It was a break for Elder and he jumped at the chance to get out of the daily grind of transporting prisoners. It was boring, and he yearned to be on his own without all the bullshit. There was nothing like the Corps. You knew exactly where you stood with your superiors and subordinates. There may have been some instances when someone took a cheap shot at you because they wanted to make an impression with someone, but it did not happen often. The Officers and the NCOs knew the score and those that took cheap shots were passed over for promotion. Well, they were usually passed over. Yet, there were some that could cover their tracks. It was the same in every profession; some bad with the good. But, when you took a look at the U.S. Marshals, there were some real losers who just didn't belong. They were the lifers.

KIDNAPPING JESUS

And there were genuine heroes as well. Some of the Marshals were like school children telling their supervisors stories that did not need to be told, repeated or anything else in between. Gossip was not what Elder, and others needed as distractions to their duty. Remembering the good order and discipline they had been brought up on in the different branches of the military were who the true professionals were, and this was not even close. There was no loyalty among the identified backstabbers. They were easy enough to spot and were shunned by many. But some unsuspecting individual might be caught in the freshly spun spider web if the story was good enough to be believed. So, John Elder accepted the job in serving arrest warrants.

It was 1989...Marshal Elder had served in the department for nearly three years. He had arrested some serious felons and had a reputation for tracking down and bringing to justice anyone that the Department identified. He had been dragged through the dirtiest and most dangerous streets and alleys in America. The thugs he had captured were numerous. His days and nights were a blur, and he was getting tired. His year in taking felons out of circulation was nearing an end. In the beginning it was a welcome change to transporting criminals, but down the home stretch, it did work on him more than just physically. It was a mental struggle to be one step ahead of these rats that lived in the sewers and fed like vermin on the carcasses of the weak and powerless. Humanity has its levels, but there are those unsuspecting people who are trapped and dragged into the bottomless depths never to be able to reach upwards from the abyss they had landed in to live a normal life.

Elder was taking a much-needed break after he had just brought in a felon with a rap sheet two pages in length. This one took Elder all over the United States and at one time, into Canada where the trail grew cold. He was tired. When he caught up with him, it had been a real fight and it was not just a single rat John smoked out, but a whole pack of rats. He had help from the locals, but the San Francisco Police Department was the real muscle Marshal Elder needed to be successful. It was teamwork that brought these criminals to justice. Walter "The Cat" Johnson was a hit man for anyone who could pay his price. His

ANOTHER BEGINNING

team of assassins successfully accounted for over 20 known assassinations. They went down hard. Two of the four criminals were killed when the SWAT Team entered the flea infested building by the waterfront. Two were quickly captured and "The Cat" thought he would get another life as he was going out through a trap door under the building. The escape was over as out of the dark came a fast- right hand followed by a left uppercut. "The Cat" was on the ground trussed up like a pig when the building was finally declared cleared. Not one of the SWAT Team was injured. The mission was a complete success. Marshal Elder had another one to cross off his short list.

The call came in at 1400 hours in the afternoon. Elder was relaxing in his modest one-bedroom apartment. It had been four days since he and the San Francisco Police Department had brought "The Cat" and his thugs to justice. At least two of them would not cost the taxpayers the time and money it takes to bring the guilty bastards to justice while innocent lives are still in jeopardy. It was unbelievable to Elder that the Judicial System would even consider setting bail on this scum. Because "The Cat" was a felon, he did not get bail along with one of his cronies. But, due to insufficient evidence on the other asshole, he was released on $2 Million Dollars of bail money posted by a lawyer. The lawyer was well known to the Department, but the strings attached to this puppet could never be found. It would be figured out sooner or later. It always is. Elder would have liked to know who provided the bail money and why this guy was on a get out of jail card. There was something that did not smell right. As one of his former Battalion Commanders used to say, "There must be a turd in the punchbowl!"

It was just a few moments later that John had an idea as to why this shit- head had been released. A local newspaperman for the Los Angeles Times had been murdered. He and his wife were found dead in their home. Tom Livingston had been doing an exposé on the San Francisco crime wave and the similarities to crimes in the Los Angeles area. It was coincidental, or was it? The Marshal on the other end of the phone told Elder he had a bench warrant for the guy released on bail in San Francisco. His name was Don Walter Smith. He had a rap

KIDNAPPING JESUS

sheet that was only one page long, but included armed robbery with a firearm, rape, attempted murder, and aggravated battery on a law enforcement officer. Not to mention his association with "The Cat." It seemed ludicrous to Elder that this guy was walking the streets with unsuspecting citizens.

Although Smith had served three sentences, he had always remolded his life, found religion and was released once again into an unsuspecting society. It is amazing just how porous the cracks in the judicial system are that allow someone of this ilk to be recycled over and over. How could a man like this be changed? The answer was an unequivocal never! Until justice was final for these hardened souls, a restful night of sleep for many would be hard to come by. He never served a complete term and some of the charges were dropped prior to other trials and justice could not be served due to witnesses refusing to testify or because they had simply disappeared. This guy was a real bad ass. It was too bad that one of the two bullets fired by the SWAT Team did not kill this scum bag. Now, others had died and more could be in the Villain's crosshairs.

Armed with the information from the phone call, Marshal Elder was enroute to the last known location of Don Walter Smith, again suspected of yet another felony. He was at his girlfriend's apartment in a high-rise apartment building near the center of downtown Los Angeles. As Elder entered the downstairs of the building, he and another Marshal, who had picked up the Bench Warrant for Smith's arrest, moved quickly past the sleeping derelicts among the makeshift cardboard beds with what appeared to be donated blankets and pillows from well-meaning citizens and charitable organizations. There were a few empty whiskey bottles scattered around. It was not a large lobby and was not overly cluttered, but the homeless set up shop wherever they could and for as long as they were able to do so before they were kicked out to find another place to invade as if it were their own and they were entitled. Even with shelters nearby, the homeless seem to only go to a shelter in extreme situations, as if it were a place to go as a last resort.

John looked at Marshal Tom Roy. Roy had been a Marshal for eight years and was a prior policeman. He held a bachelor's degree in criminology he had earned by going to classes at night over a ten-year period while he was serving in the LAPD. It took time, but he was

ANOTHER BEGINNING

determined to better himself and wanted someday to be a Lieutenant within the Police Department. He was offered a position with the Marshal's Office. He accepted the rank of Sergeant and knew his goal was now within reach, although not with the branch of service he thought it would be with.

Marshals Elder and Roy moved up the staircase to the fourth floor. It was Apartment 313 and was located down the dimly lit hallway. Elder and Roy approached the apartment, and the door was slightly open. The Marshals covered each other as John stepped past the door. Roy signaled Elder and used his left hand to ease the door open. Each looked through the open space provided. They didn't see anything. Elder slowly entered the room and proceeded with caution, weapon drawn, and entered into the apartment. Roy was right behind him.

Around them, both Marshals could hear the sounds that come from apartment dwellings— kids yelling, Mom and Dad pleading and noises from the apartments above as people were walking or moving things across the floors. Instincts were sharp. Although there were many sounds and smells invading Elder's senses, he was clearly focused on his surroundings. In moments, Elder and Roy determined there was no one in the room. It looked like Smith had advance notice that a warrant was being served. Or maybe it was just a sixth sense Smith had that something, or someone, was coming for him.

Elder and Roy looked at each other as both heard shouting from outside. They looked out the window to see Smith being chased by three men who appeared to be undercover LAPD detectives.

Although it was not a coordinated operation between the two law enforcement departments, the Marshal's Department worked closely with LAPD and they had been notified of the Bench Warrant for Smith's arrest, so they must have been nearby in a support role when Elder and Roy entered the building.

Elder and Roy exited the apartment and ran down the hallway to the stairs. Skipping the steps as they ran downstairs, they exited the apartment building through the somewhat crowded and dimly lit lobby kicking bottles and trash as they hurried through the double doors. They looked to the left and could just make out the fleeing felon and his pursuers rounding the city block. Elder and Roy now joined in the pursuit of Smith but were clearly half a block behind. It would take

KIDNAPPING JESUS

time to catch up, but they were quickly on their way. It was a run that seemed like five miles, but the distance was only three short city blocks. The chase ended in a dead-end alley. Elder and Roy slowed their run to a walk as they approached the group with their guns aimed and badges upheld. They were both sweating and breathing hard. Elder stated, "I'm Deputy Marshal Elder. This is…this is Marshal Roy. We have a warrant for Smith's arrest."

The yet to be identified man turned his attention away from his captured prisoner lying on the ground. Smith was face down on the dirty asphalt with his arms handcuffed with plastic ties behind his back. He was heaving and you could hear small curses coming from his lips aimed at the five men standing around him. "I'm Chuck Taylor, Bounty Hunter. You boys are just a little too late. I found this guy hiding just outside his apartment building. Looks like you flushed him out in the open for my team. We were about to go into the apartment when you two showed up, so we decided to wait to see what was going to happen. Look, we didn't want any confusion. Smith had a $1 Million Dollar reward posted on his head. It seems like the newspapers made a big deal over the death of that newspaper man and his wife. Just want you to know we appreciate your help. This was a good night for us as the reward offer was just posted. We just made $200,000 by capturing him."

Elder and Roy holstered their pistols. Roy asked Mister Taylor, "How did you earn $200,000 for Smith's capture?"

Taylor replied, "We get ten percent of the reward posted, or of the bail that was set, for every capture. This makes our fifth bounty this week. It's been a great week; for me and my team!"

Marshal Elder was taken aback at Chuck Taylor's reply to Marshal Roy. He had heard about bounty hunters but thought they were only in the Wild West and not in the concrete and steel jungles of the modern world. Undercover teams were one thing, bounty hunters were something else altogether. And this man Chuck Taylor was real. Taylor was a Bounty Hunter and just made more money in one evening than Elder did in two years doing the same thing Elder did as a U.S. Marshal. He wanted to find out more information about becoming a Bounty Hunter. Elder looked at Taylor and asked, "May I have one of your business cards?"

ANOTHER BEGINNING

Chuck quickly responded. "No problem, be happy to." Handing it to him, Taylor spoke to Elder telling him, "If you want to make some real money give me a call. In the meantime, I need you to sign this paperwork for me so you can take custody of Smith. This gives me the clearance to pick up the bounty for capturing this piece of work." Elder signed the paperwork and took control of Smith. Marshal Roy had gone back to his car minutes ago to transport the prisoner. He knew of Bounty Hunters and about the money they made but was more interested in serving a traditional public service role in the Marshal's Department. This was what he wanted. Somehow, he knew he would be a public servant, but at a level far above his current station.

Roy put Smith into his unit and ensured the prisoner was safely secured. Marshals Elder and Roy said their goodbyes to Chuck Taylor and his team and got into the unit for a short trip down a couple of blocks to where Elder had parked his unit. Elder followed closely behind Roy and Smith as he was transported to the nearest LAPD jail.

It was not a long drive, but rush hour traffic was picking up on the crowded downtown streets. The red lights seemed to be lined up against them, but they did not need to put on their lights. No emergencies now to respond to at the moment. Although there was chatter on the police scanner, Elder was thinking and not paying any real attention to what was going on in the city. He was thinking of the job.

He was thinking back to the Marine Corps and the long days and nights for the last 24 years of service to his Nation both as a Marine and as a U.S. Marshal. The trip to get Smith locked up was uneventful. All the paperwork was completed in short order, personal effects taken and secured, new photos and prints made. Marshals Roy and Elder shook hands as they left the police station.

The next day Elder sat down at his desk and asked himself the same questions he had asked himself while getting Smith to jail. Did he really want to do this job? Was this what he really wanted to do? When he joined the Marshals office, he thought it was going to be like the Corps serving our Country out of pride and dedication. There were professionals like Marshals Tom Roy and Jack Rogers as well as Captain Sullivan, but it was not the same. Elder felt surrounded by both men and women that were complete idiots that would get someone killed. In the military, you knew who was on your right and left and

KIDNAPPING JESUS

who had your back. You ate with your fellow Marines and slept with them when duty to foreign countries called or the Operations Tempo (OPTEMPO) of training, or battle, demanded. You shared your foxhole with a stranger who became your best friend and you lived and died together protecting each other's asses.

It wasn't the same in the police department or in the Marshal's department. It was different and it was hard to adjust to the red tape and to people you couldn't trust to be there for you when the moment came. Those moments were rare, but a split-second decision cost people their lives. Elder had been to way too many memorial services where friends were gunned down in the streets and had left their families behind. He witnessed the tears from the men and women that loved them and the brave children that would never see or hold their father or mother again. Brothers and sisters and parents would suffer their loss the rest of their lives mourning a child that should have outlived them as they grew older. Yes, there are some good Marshals, many of them decorated veterans, but others wore a badge of honor they really would never understand.

Unfortunately for Elder, his trip down memory lane recalled an incident involving Marshal Lynn Connelly. She was severely overweight but had a medical condition that excused her from the physical fitness regime. It never looked like she had any conditioning, but she did have to pass the physical fitness gauntlet of the Academy. Lynn was John's backup, and he knew he had to be careful not to be accidentally shot by her as she entered the building with him. Elder moved; Lynn froze. Fear gripped her. She was shaking and John was now responsible for making the arrest. After the situation was over, Lynn asked John an amazing question. "John, are you going to write about what happened to me?" John remembered looking at her and responding with... "What happened, Lynn?"

She replied. "You know what happened. I froze!"

John spoke to her as if she were only a child. "You need to face it, Lynn. You are a coward. I'm not telling my fellow officers but do yourself a favor and quit the Marshals. You are going to get someone killed, and it might be you."

The last John had checked she was still on the job. John wondered if she had attended any of her partner's funerals and had to look into the

ANOTHER BEGINNING

eyes of their families. Marshal Elder had made his decision. No more thinking would be necessary. It was time for a change. Could this be a change for the better? Looking back, everything that had gone before in his life would prepare him for the next challenge.

With the decision to leave the U.S. Marshals, relief came to this Veteran Marine and Marshal. It had been almost four years since Master-Sergeant Elder retired from the Marine Corps. With absolutely no regrets, he tendered his resignation to Captain Sullivan. He accepted the resignation with regret but offered John his best and said that he would help him in any way that he could. The resignation was to take effect in 30 days. Elder was assigned limited office duty and had accumulated 20 days of vacation time. It was another milestone in his life and with a handshake with the Captain, Elder sharply saluted him, did a snappy about face and exited his office. This was the only senior U.S. Marshal Elder had respect for and the only one he would salute as he began his short timers' calendar with his first bold red X crossing out Thursday, May 30, 1990 and leaving his small office for his earned vacation.

He would call Chuck Taylor the following day and see what he had to offer. Elder wasn't worried about what was around the corner in his road of life as his bank account had increased substantially since the dive off the coast of Mexico. Elder was so busy with his life lately and wondered what his friends had been doing during the last few months. He would catch up with them in the next few days so they could get caught up with each other and what was happening in their lives. Each led a busy life but staying in touch with good friends should have been a priority. How many of his friends had said, "If I only had known they were going to die, I would have given them a call?" Way too many! Maybe they could get together for old times if their schedules allowed.

Elder contacted Chuck Taylor the next day. After a brief conversation, a short drive to Taylor's office and a knock on the office door, John Elder was instructed to enter when he heard the lock turn on the door once the remote control was activated. When he entered, he spoke to Taylor's beautiful assistant. As he glanced at her nameplate, he said, "I'm John Elder and I have an appointment with Chuck Taylor."

KIDNAPPING JESUS

The dark haired, blue eyed, tanned women, probably in her mid-30's rose from her desk and replied, "I know. He's expecting you. My name is Pearle. Please follow me."

Once inside Chuck's office, John was instructed to have a seat on the plush black sofa that faced Chuck's desk. He carried his concealed weapons, never leaving them behind. Just under his left shoulder was his 45-caliber pistol. It was not a standard 45, but was modified with a short barrel, night sights, and was special in that the barrel was tightly rifled to ensure accurate shooting beyond standard gun ranges. It was customized for the shooter and was deadly accurate at 50 feet. He also had a knife on his belt on his right side and another small pistol strapped to his right leg. He began to wonder if he was doing the right thing.

At that moment, the door opened and in walked Chuck Taylor. He was as massive as John recalled in the dark alley where Don Walter Smith was captured. Chuck was a large man. He looked like a professional football player on the offensive line. No one wanted to line up against a guy like this. He would crush you. And, despite his looks, he was in pretty good shape. John remembered the night when Taylor and his team captured Smith in the dead-end alley. It had been a run for all of them, but Chuck didn't seem to show any fatigue when John and Marshal Roy caught up to them. Taylor was 6'8" tall and weighed 350 pounds. His chest was huge. Elder was thinking that it would take one really large cannon to bring him down. His 45 might get Taylor's attention, but it would probably just piss a guy like this off.

Taylor sat down at his desk, leaned over, and said, "What is it that I can do for you Marshal Elder."

Elder replied, "I will no longer be a Marshal in 30 days, and I would like to work for you if the money is right. I would rather work for a professional than continue to work with someone who might get me killed."

Taylor replied, "This is the deal. I checked into your background the day after we met in the alley and was considering bringing you on my team. It seems like you made the choice for me. If you are as good as everybody I've talked to says you are, I will start you at a $75,000-a-year salary. There will be bonuses paid as well. If you do well, you can make $120,000 a year. What do you have to say about my offer?" Elder made no reply, and just looked silently at Taylor as he thought about a

ANOTHER BEGINNING

salary that was three times what he was making! "Well, can I welcome you aboard?" Taylor asked.

Without another thought, Elder reached out and shook his hand and replied, "You can count on me Mr. Taylor!"

"Call me Chuck. We're on a first name basis here. We count on each other and friends work harder to keep each other alive than do associates. You are one of the family beginning now," Taylor replied. Chuck quickly followed with, "When can you start?"

John replied, "I need to clean my desk out and finish some paperwork. I need to hand off a couple of cases I've been working on for a few months and I have some leave. My last day officially is June 29th."

Chuck reached out his hand and patted John on his back saying, "Welcome again to my team, I'll see you when you get your loose ends taken care of. Be ready to come to work. Let me know a date as soon as you have one. Let's catch some of America's scum and make some money."

It was June 20th. Elder had wrapped up loose ends at the office, taken a couple of days of vacation and to his disbelief, was ready to go to work and make some money with Chuck. He called Chuck on the phone. Pearle answered, "Taylor's Headhunters (TRH), may I help you?" Sounded like a place that found you a job.

John asked Pearle, "Can I make an appointment with Chuck?"

Pearle sweetly responded to John, "Why of course Mr. Elder, Chuck gave me instructions to clear his calendar for you at your convenience. When can you come by?" A time for that afternoon was agreed upon. Elder would meet Chuck for lunch at a high-class restaurant known for its great steaks.

John was early as was Chuck. It was 1245 hours, and their appointment was for 1300 hours. Years of training taught Elder to always be early, if possible, for an appointment. This is good advice when you are meeting with your future boss. It also allowed Elder to get his bearings, check entrances and exits and study the patrons of this fine establishment. When Chuck walked from where he parked his car, he could see he was being watched through the front door glass by the head waiter.

The waiter opened the door for Chuck and exchanged pleasantries with him. Elder knew immediately Chuck was a regular and as he came in the door, Chuck looked at Elder and extended his right hand. As they greeted each other, they were seated in an out of the

KIDNAPPING JESUS

way booth, with Chuck's back to the wall. Elder would have liked to have his back to the wall as well, but there were several mirrors and pictures that offered selective views towards his back. The waiter was at the table before they could speak. Chuck asked John, "What would you like to drink?"

Elder replied, "Whatever you are having Chuck."The waiter nodded at Chuck and left the table. Chuck asked Elder how everything was going and if he was finished with the Marshal's. Elder was still on vacation and would be paid his final check at the end of June. They had some minor discussions about the night they met, and they both were looking forward to working together. The waiter brought their drinks to the table. Chuck was served first and then John. They were having a Martini. It was very dry, and the smell of the Vermouth was pleasant.

Chuck picked up his glass, looked at John, and said, "Here's to us! May we always get our man before he gets us!"

John replied with, "Here, here!"

During the two Martini lunch, an excellent Caesar salad and a very large T-bone steak with a large, stuffed baked potato, was served. The waiter offered the pepper grinder and lunch was served. Chuck and John discussed the first mission. It was to get a criminal that had jumped bail on a $250,000 bond. Sounded simple enough but this scum bag was rumored to be connected to the mob. His name was Rick "The Weasel" Villisca. Chuck provided the background and said there was a folder at the office waiting for John's review.

Lunch was over. It was one of the best meals John had ever had. The reputation of this restaurant was never in question and the cuisine, and the service was excellent. Chuck and John had polite conversation and were like old friends catching up on old times. Chuck picked up the tab. After all, it was a business expense. They parted at the door, each checking out the way they would be going to get to their cars. Both were well trained, but their guards were never let down. There were no guarantees someone had not followed them, someone let the word out, or someone knew Chuck ate at this restaurant on a weekly basis. Times and days were always different, but it was hard not to have some routine.

There were only so many restaurants in town and eating at a different one on a daily basis had its challenges as well. Working or not, John always kept one lesson he learned well during his tours of duty

ANOTHER BEGINNING

in the Marines and with the Marshals as the foremost thought in his mind—assumptions could and do kill.

John met Chuck back at the office. Pearle West was as pretty as a Lilly in spring. She smelled nice, too. After taking John to a small office, Pearle said, "Welcome aboard, Mr. Elder. Glad to have you with us. I've heard a lot about you from Chuck. He speaks highly of you. If there's anything I can do for you, please don't hesitate to ask."

Elder replied politely. "Pearle thanks again. I appreciate your assistance and look forward to getting to know you."

Pearle smiled as she turned and walked out of the office. Elder took a deep breath as he looked around his tiny office and noticed he had a name plate on his desk. It simply read "John Elder — THH". It didn't take a rocket scientist, or was that rocket engineer, an imagination to figure out what THH stood for.

The folder was lying in front of him. It was tabbed with Rick "The Weasel" Villisca. Pictures were included along with the guy's rap sheet. It looked like an exact duplicate of a Police Department file. It was as if the Standard Operating Procedures (SOP) from the Military to the U.S. Marshals and to the Private Sector were closely followed. It avoided confusion and required less time to come up to speed when a recognizable routine was established. However, there was information that would, or might not, be known to the local cops. Friends, family, and things "The Weasel" did to get his kicks. Elder would start with the mother first thing in the morning before breakfast. One thing Elder had learned in the Corps and as a U.S. Marshal is that Italians love their families and especially their mothers and sisters and always stayed in close contact with them, even if they were on the run from the cops.

Elder met up with Ms. Villisca at her address on Sea Gull Drive. The small subdivision was right out of New Port Beach off the Ocean Highway. Ms. Villisca explained to Elder she had not heard from her son in more than three years. Elder gave her his new business card.

It was non-descriptive in that it had Elder's name, cell phone number from the phone given to him by Chuck, and that he was an Investment Broker. Bounty hunters tended to get people excited, so the

KIDNAPPING JESUS

only thing that might give Elder away was if someone caught a glimpse of his 45 pistol under his left arm, or the knife and the hideaway gun. As Elder left her the business card, he asked her, "Ms. Villisca, please have Rick call me as soon as you hear from him. His business accounts in the Cayman Islands need to be reviewed at the earliest possible time."

She knew that John was probably a cop although he didn't smell or look like a cop. Cops didn't drive in small truck like vehicles, but she was not about to let on that she knew where Rick was at that moment. Elder did have identification that he was a Bounty Hunter and had concealed weapons permits for the guns he carried and those in his new Ford Bronco. The Ford had also been provided by Chuck and was lightly armored plated with bullet-proof glass. Chuck believed in protection and in protecting his investments. John was an investment. Ms. Villisca replied, "I'll be sure to let Rick know you stopped by Mr. Elder if I should hear from him."

Elder knew she was lying. Elder thanked her and started to walk down the steps when he turned and looked at her asking if he could use her phone. "Why of course," she replied. Elder dialed his cell phone. He did not like to carry a phone with him. It was just another protrusion in his pocket or on his belt. The phone rang in his Bronco. Elder left a brief message that he would be home in time for supper and to let the kids know that daddy was bringing them home a surprise. Elder thanked Ms. Villisca once more. She smiled thinking that Mr. John Elder was a good family man and a loving son.

Back at the office, Elder contacted Lynda Saracen at the phone company. As a U.S. Marshal, Elder needed contacts to help get useful information. He had used her many times in the past to look up phone records.

It cost $100 each time, but it was always well worth it. Elder had an expense account now, and for information that could lead to a capture of any felon, it was a small price to pay. Lynda was always about the money. Elder didn't want to let her know he was now a Bounty Hunter, or her fee would triple. As long as she thought Elder was a U.S. Marshal, it would be

$100 dollars. Others on the force used her to get information as well. The speculation was that she would sell herself for the right amount of money. A couple of the Marshals had dated her from time to time,

ANOTHER BEGINNING

so everyone knew she was good-looking, but she was easy. Lynda gave John the information he was looking for.

The phone number that was listed once a week had an Area Code of 321. The number that came was listed to Nancy Luigi on Whitecap Way in Melbourne, Florida. Pearle booked the flight out of LAX and Elder arrived on Wednesday at the Melbourne International Airport. It was a long flight having to go through Atlanta. This was the first time that John had ever been to Melbourne. It really looked like a nice town compared to Los Angeles. There were no tall buildings and there did not seem to be much traffic on the roads as he looked out of the aircraft window prior to landing.

It was easy to get around this small city. Although spread out, you could easily see down the streets for some distance. Buildings were located off the main roads and parking areas were in front. No need for parking garages and meters everywhere. The Melbourne Police Department was easy to find. Bounty Hunter John Elder entered the Police Department and asked for a Police Lieutenant by the name of Harold K. Layman. After John Elder identified himself, he was advised by the Lieutenant to ensure he stayed within the legal limits of the law and if he could be of any further assistance to let him know. John was also asked to let the Lieutenant know the results so he could officially log the report. Since the local authorities did not know of Rick "The Weasel" Villisca, the Lieutenant hoped this Bounty Hunter would be successful. John shook his hand and assured him he would do so.

John drove by the house on Whitecap Way. He parked a couple of houses down from the suspect's house. It was 1700 hours, and the sun was still hanging midway in the west. It was hot, but the air conditioner in the rented Ford LTD was doing its job and keeping John comfortable. John had memorized the details surrounding Rick Villisca and it did not take long for him to get a good look at the man going into the house he was watching. It was a positive ID. He was "The Weasel." This was Elder's objective.

Elder drove off and went past the house noting where the doors were located, fences, and other streets. He mentally went through the possibilities as he went to find a hotel for the night.

Elder found a nice Hotel located just off New Haven with quick access to Interstate 95 and was close to his suspect. Just like back in his

KIDNAPPING JESUS

Marine days, he was up at 0500 hours for his daily run. He drove down to the beach, stretched the kinks out of his body from the long flight the previous day and ran three short miles. He did not want to overdo it but wanted a fresh mind for the task at hand.

He got back to the Hotel at 0630 hours for a shower and went for some breakfast. His bags were packed, but he went back to his room to ensure all was ready. He checked his pistols, his warrant for the arrest, and made a quick call to the Melbourne Police Department checking in with Lieutenant Layman. Layman informed Elder to give him a call just as soon as he made the collar.

Elder checked out of the Hotel and headed to his suspect's home around 0815 hours. Elder parked down the street and waited for him to show himself. He went over the plan in his head. Elder planned on following "The Weasel" to wherever he was going. He planned to take him down, handcuff him and place him in his car and drive him to New York. He would let the Lieutenant know the results. The scumbag came out of the house after about a three hour wait. Elder followed him to a full-service gas station with food store on New Haven Avenue. "The Weasel" pulled his unassuming car into a parking space in front of the store and went inside to do some shopping. Elder was ready. He would make his catch on his return to the car.

Villisca came out of the store not suspecting anything. Elder approached him like he was heading into the store to get some groceries as well. Villisca had a small bag of groceries in his left hand and was about to light up a cigarette with the lighter in his right hand. Elder had a stun gun in his left hand slightly behind him. Villisca was wearing a tank top, so a lot of flesh was exposed. Elder zapped him just under his left arm. Groceries went everywhere as Villisca hit the pavement hard flat on his face. Rubber handcuffs went on quickly with his hands behind him. Elder grabbed him and tossed him in the back of the LTD and was on 1-95 in five minutes with his suspect. It was unbelievable. In just moments, Elder had his prisoner. Not one person said anything. He could have been a kidnapper. Now, Elder thought to himself, "Why do so many people disappear, without a trace?"

John Elder and Villisca were on their way to New York. John picked up his cell phone and called Lieutenant Laymen. John simply said, "Lieutenant, I have Villisca in my custody, and we are on our way

80

ANOTHER BEGINNING

to New York." John let the Lieutenant know where he apprehended Villisca, and that the guy's car was there. It needed to be impounded by the Police Department. Villisca could always make a claim for it later.

Lieutenant Layman replied to John, "Have a safe trip! Appreciate the call. Let me know when you're back in town and we'll meet for a drink. I'm buying!" John was in Jacksonville before Villisca woke up. Villisca was advised that he was a Bounty Hunter, Villisca was in his legal custody, the Melbourne Police Department knew of his whereabouts, and he was being taken to New York to be surrendered to the proper authorities.

Villisca cleared his voice and it cracked with dryness when he asked John, "How did you find me? No one else came close."

Not wanting to give this scum bag too much information, John just smiled when he simply said, "You love your mother, right?"

Villisca replied, "I sure do!"

John smiled again with, "Me too!"

Villisca gave John a blank stare he could see in the adjusted rear-view mirror. Villisca would wonder what John meant for a long time. He would not put two and two together until Ms. Villisca visited her son in the Federal Penitentiary on a designated visitor's day in the months to come.

"I don't want any problems on this trip to New York. Or, your mother is going to be placing flowers on your grave. I will kill you. It makes no difference to me whether you are dead or alive. In twelve hours, I turn you over to the proper authorities and you get what you deserve. Are you clear with these simple instructions?"

He said, "I understand. I won't give you any problems. What's your name?"

"You can call me Elder." The Bounty Hunter relaxed somewhat with a grin on his face as he sat behind the wheel of the LTD. He was going 85 miles an hour and keeping up with traffic on the Interstate. His 45 was lying on the seat next to him just under a newspaper. The other was still strapped to his right leg. They would make a couple of quick rest stops on the way. Elder allowed Villisca to have one free hand while his left hand remained cuffed to his belt behind his back. With a light Jacket on, no one would notice. Elder always had his pistol at the ready and Villisca was a coward when he was not surrounded by a bunch of

KIDNAPPING JESUS

thugs against weak and law- abiding citizens. This was scum. Filth cultivated in the back alleys of America. The trip was uneventful. It was just under twelve hours from the time of the take down to when Elder turned over his suspect.

In New York, Villisca was handed over to Marshal's Department. It was late Thursday night when John turned in his paperwork. He called Chuck in Los Angeles and let him know the mission was completed and he would receive the check the following day. Later on, Friday, John turned in his rental car at John F. Kennedy International Airport and was on a flight back to Los Angeles that had been booked by Pearle.

He was in First Class. During the direct flight, John had a few martinis and quietly read an article that intrigued him about the life and death of Jesus. The Holy Land was in turmoil these days and almost daily there were front page articles. He dozed off, but he would deliver the check to Chuck on Monday and be paid his percentage for the capture. It was $10,500 for a week's work and all expenses were paid by Chuck's agency. This was a job he was going to like. Taking Weasels, IcePicks and Cats out of circulation was going to be his kind of fun.

John worked with Chuck for just over ten years. He went on with the job of catching the scumbags of society and removing men and women from the streets where a democratic society oftentimes turned a deaf ear to the pleas of the innocent of this land. Laws, it seemed, were not made equal for all people. John made a lot of money over the time he worked with Chuck. He had saved almost $550,000 dollars from hunting down criminals and the $100,000 dollars found on the dive trip to Cozumel had grown exponentially to somewhere around $450,000 dollars. Not bad having a cool Million. And, although not a significant monetary impact, he was still getting his Marine retirement pay and it continued to grow with the annual cost of living (COLA) increases. It all helped to make the decision he was about to share with his good friend and boss just a little easier. John felt it was time to make his move.

It was August 3, 2001. He was sitting at his desk near Chuck's office. Over the past few years, his office had changed and been richly furnished. It was mahogany and the rugs on the wooden floor were

ANOTHER BEGINNING

from the Orient and from Turkey. It was a nice office; the best John had ever had. Chuck was like an older brother and he and Chuck had become close friends over the years they had been associated. Chuck was not surprised. He had felt this moment would come someday soon, it always did, either through someone leaving out the front door, or the silent prayers said at a funeral.

It was with regret John told Chuck he would be leaving his employment. John informed Chuck, "I'm moving to a place that I liked when I went on my first case with you. You remember "The Weasel?" Well, I like the atmosphere of this small city and I have never been able to get the fresh, clean, smell of the saltwater out of my mind from the peaceful run I had on the quiet beach the morning before I picked Villisca up. It really refreshed me and cleared my mind for the task at hand. I'm looking for a change. My feet are itching for something new and if I was still in the Marines, I would have probably had at least five permanent changes (PCS's) of station. I'm going to Melbourne, Florida. Not sure what I am going to do, but it will come to me."

You could tell Chuck was hurt because he had deep feelings for John. They were more than just associates. More than just a few times, they had saved each other's life. Counting on someone like a brother went deeper than just a job; it was an extended part of each other's family.

A couple of weeks later, the furniture was packed and on its way across country from California to Florida. This was going to be a change— a big change. The same moving company would also transport John's 1966 Cheverly Corvette Coupe. It was canary yellow with a 427 cubic inch engine under the hood. This man-made beauty had a roaring 425 horsepower engine under the hood. It had been a few years since John had driven this Detroit Lion of the Road, but he would soon be back behind the wheel once more. While the movers were getting the precious cargo enroute to sunny Florida, John would drive his Ford F-150 Super Cab 2000 4x4 to Florida. It was a purchase he made after he turned in his 1999 Explorer back to Chuck. He remembered the look in Pearle's eyes. She was a handsome woman. They had had a love affair over the years.

It was not a daily, or even weekly, courtship, but each had needs and desires that needed to be fulfilled. Chuck knew of the liaison, but

KIDNAPPING JESUS

also knew John and Pearle kept it secret and it never interfered with the office. Pearle was like James Bond's Money Penny to some degree.

John wanted a real truck for the open roads of Florida. He wanted the security a big truck could provide and one that could help him as he set his sights on the next chapter in his life. Interstate 10 was a long road, but a road he wanted to take his time traveling. He spent one of the ten nights in the place where he grew up. It was Baton Rouge, Louisiana. John looked up his old high school friends. He, Ed Arider and John Spangle went out to a restaurant, had a few drinks, talked about the times when the rains were so heavy, they would take out the huge tire inner tubes they had and ride the small streams that had swollen into rivers. It was a wonder they were still alive with some of the pranks they used to pull on others and have pulled on them. The meal was fantastic. Cajun seafood was at its very best. Good food, good drinks and good times remembered by good friends...friends for life.

84

CHAPTER VI

A NEW STAGE

John Elder could not wait to arrive at his new house. He drove to Fairhope, Alabama, near Mobile and rented a small bungalow near the water. He would relax for a couple of days even though he was anxious to get to his new home. He had purchased the house using a well-known agency. Pictures were provided and a web-based tour was available. He had made one trip to scout out the possibilities, but this is the one he selected. It was located in central Melbourne right off Magnolia Avenue. Just less than 2,000 square feet, the three bedroom and two bath home sat on a one- acre lot. John paid cash and was able to purchase the house for $49,900. It was a steal. Better yet, it met his requirements.

John set out to make the place extremely nice with the amenities he had been somewhat deprived of for most of his life. It was a fixer upper, but John liked the possibilities the house had to offer a man of his background. He would give the house a makeover any former Marine and Bounty Hunter would be proud of. The carpet was ripped out and a new roof was installed by a privately owned roofing company owned by two brothers, Pete and Charles. These guys were the best. No job too small or too big. The name of the family-owned company was catchy but appropriate. CPR Carpentry — Cardiopulmonary Resuscitation (CPR). That's just what the doctor ordered for this sun and wind

KIDNAPPING JESUS

weathered roof, some good old CPR. John spoke to Charles and found out he too had been in Vietnam during the 1968 TET Offensive. It was a small world, after all, except John had been a Marine and Charles was in the Army. They could relate. Under the carpet were hardwood floors. John rented an industrial sander and took the floors down to bare wood. The floor was then varnished, and two weapons lockers were installed where they could be hidden with an area rug. The finished house looked great. Marble and plumbing additions made the two bathrooms elegant. The accessories added would make any woman comfortable while visiting his small chalet.

Elder notified the movers to deliver his car and furniture to his house. They had been placed in storage not far away, but John wanted the delivery to take place once the house was completely finished and the renovations were done. Everything looked great, but there were a few vacant areas in the new house that he would have to go shopping for.

There were four locked foot lockers that were on the truck. There were no questions asked by the moving company and none by the movers when they were delivered. In addition to the two weapons lockers John installed in the floor, there were compartments and small built-in areas located throughout the house in which to secure the small arsenal John had accumulated while serving as a U.S. Marshal and as a Bounty Hunter. It was impressive! How some of the weapons reached the hands of the lawless was not the mystery, and it was troublesome to him and others of his caliber. John managed to acquire three M-203 grenade launchers, two boxes of M-67 grenades, four AR-16s (7.62mm) with night vision, thermal, devices. He also had four 45-caliber Colt pistols, four M-16 Squad Automatic Weapons (SAWs) with 10,000 rounds of .223 caliber ammunition. Like many Americans blessed with the right to bear arms, he was ready with enough weapons and ammunition to rise to any occasion. With his money, he could start a small war almost anywhere in the world.

Time really went by quickly as John completed the repairs, moving and shopping for new furniture and appliances for his new house. He had not taken time to catch up with his friends lately and was anxious to do so. He turned on his computer and went to his news and weather page. What he saw was a familiar sight, the Twin Towers in New York. He turned up the volume just as a reporter screamed that a second jet

A NEW STAGE

was about to slam into the other tower. John knew immediately that this was no accident. War had been declared in America! And now it was on our shores. It was September 11, 2001. Over the next few days, the magnitude and horror Americans and citizens of other Nations would experience was surreal. There were so many tears shed in the days and months to come...so many that died horrible deaths...so many mothers, fathers, sons and daughters who would never come home. There were those who were lucky to be alive but would be forever scared. And the heroes! Thanks to the heroes, many of whom would scratch at anything in the rubble to see if they could save just one life. Life was precious, wasn't it?

It seemed as if those who painted the indescribable scenes at the Pentagon in Washington, D.C., over the fields of Pennsylvania and at the Twin Towers, that life was not precious to them. The death of the innocents of war were not an accidental tragedy, but a calculated means to an end to wipe out non-Muslim believers. There was the convenient mask of religion to form a coalition of fanatics under a disguise of lies.

Almost 18 years had passed since Beirut. This was yet another scene in the same struggle using religion as a cover for a manuscript of death. Using commercial airliners and innocent civilians as missiles to bomb designated targets was a similar theme of using truck, car, or personnel armed with explosives. It was deadly to anyone nearby, regardless of whom or how, death was delivered. This attack aimed at the will of the people, amid the daily struggle for survival, brings to question any government's ability to protect its citizens from a virtually unseen enemy. The impact of 9/11 reverberated throughout the world and the hunt was on for the terrorists, their leadership and financial underpinning. John Elder wanted to reach out and get those responsible for the carnage of 9/11. He wanted revenge like many others. Justice would have to wait. It was a matter of time.

Elder, along with the rest of the world, was stunned. It was amazing how polite people were to each other. Civilian planes were grounded, and nothing was in the air except military aircraft on alert. It was quiet. The world had stopped spinning. There may have been more planned attacks whose missions may well have been compromised due to the grounding of the aircraft at the closest airports wherever they were in the world and in their flight. Confusion would be plentiful in the days

KIDNAPPING JESUS

to come. The world was standing still. Strangers went out of their way to be courteous whether in a store or behind the wheel of their car. It was as if we were trying to communicate with each other and share in the personal tragedy that had befallen us all. This was sick. It made Elder mad at the extremists who planned and executed this attack on America.

Not far away, Ellis Island and the Statue of Liberty stood on the shores of this great Nation. America welcomed the immigration of all into this melting pot of humanity and now we are attacked. Not all Muslims were responsible, but now all were under a microscope. It was too bad, but it was like World War II and the Japanese Americans, and the internment camps put together after the attack on America at Pearl Harbor in 1941.

Not always right, but a course of action taken by a leadership desperately trying to protect the public from demonic fanatics trying to undermine determined people. Although this single attack was directed at America, Elder believed there were many other countries around the world that were, or soon would be, in the cross hairs of radical Jihads. Nineteen terrorists murdered 2,973 people of all nationalities and races on 9/11. The religion you believed in did not matter. Color did not matter. Age did not matter. Life did not matter for many as it ended for those who were dead and for those who lost their loved ones. The world was in mourning. No one was convinced this was a last attack. The question was when and where. Not if.

This was not the first attack on the World Trade Center. On February 26, 1993, a bomb packed into a rented moving truck exploded in the underground parking garage killing six and injuring over a thousand people. The planned attack on the North Tower was designed in order to collapse the foundation of the 110-story building. This in turn would cause it to collapse into the South Tower. Six Islamic extremists were convicted of the plot in during their trials in 1997 and 1998. Over 50,000 people work at the World Trade Center not to mention the thousands of visitors that come through the downtown area on a daily basis.

Within three days, the link to Al Queda and Osama Bin-Laden was firmly established by the United States government. Confirmation on who planned the attack was now a public fact. Bin-Laden was public

88

A NEW STAGE

enemy number one. The United States Government placed a $25 million dollar bounty on him, Dead or Alive. Elder, among many others, wanted Bin- Laden to suffer the maximum penalty for taking another life. Death was too good for this terrorist, but even if a single life if taken by another, it should be death. If only Bin-Laden had been taken out earlier, maybe this scene would not have taken place. It was wishful thinking, but probably this act was already chiseled in stone.

John never forgot Beirut and that Bin-Laden had been involved in the murder of his fellow Marines. Pictures of 9/11 continuously played in John's mind. Thinking back to the chronology of the events, the North Tower was first to be hit at 8:46. At 9:02, the South Tower would be slammed. Then the Pentagon at 9:37 and in Pennsylvania, near a small borough in Somerset County, by the name of Shanksville, another dramatic scene was unfolding. International attention would be drawn to this small town of 245 residents. Did the passengers of United Airlines Flight 93 save yet another attack on Washington, D.C.? Was the Capitol an intended target of Flight 93? Or did American Airlines Flight 77 miss its intended target and then hit the Pentagon as a secondary target? These were important questions, but never-the-less, there was no mistake we were at war with terrorists and whoever were their associates. Our Allies were united. Our people united. If the terrorists could fracture our resolve, then we could never win. We must win. John Elder wanted his revenge. He wanted to kill Osama Bin-Laden.

A plan began to take shape in Elder's mind. This plan would require a team of six men. He knew who he needed for the mission of a lifetime. This was going to be no cake walk and he and the team would be risking everything including their lives. But…one could sit back and let life pass them by, or, you could take a shot at the moment and get in the game.

Elder checked his bank statements to see how much money he had accumulated. Elder had paid cash for the truck, the house and the repairs. This still left him with just under $900,000 dollars in several established bank accounts and his monthly retirement pay was still being deposited every month just like clockwork. It would have to be enough. Elder looked into his rolodex card file and began making life changing calls to his friends.

KIDNAPPING JESUS

Retired Marine, Staff Sergeant David Reed was one of Elder's best friends in the Marines. At Beirut, he and Elder had solidified their friendship under fire. David Reed now owned a night club with a famous restaurant in New Orleans and he was an established man in the community. Married with four children, Reed was now a family man. Elder knew him as a Marine that could be counted on in any situation. They always kept up with one another through the years, so Elder knew he was still in good condition, could react under pressure and knew how to handle himself. The only question left was would Reed leave his family for another mission? Elder left a message on Reed's phone for him to return his call and that it was important.

Next on the short list was Justin Carter. Carter retired from the Marines as well. His rank at retirement was Gunnery Sergeant (E-7). He had matured quite a bit from his early Marine years. Carter moved to Mobil, Alabama.

He and John had dinner in Fairhope while John was traveling to Melbourne. He had continued his SCUBA training wherever he was stationed. His diving experience included diving in the pristine waters of Cozumel in 1984 when he, Elder and Reed had discovered the money on the small boat named the Sandpiper XP. Since then, he had been diving in the Great Lakes and in the Atlantic Ocean. Essentially, he had been diving just about everywhere in the world.

He downplayed the hours underwater, but he was a Master Instructor. The title meant nothing. The time underwater meant he was an expert diver that was also an expert in another field. In the Marines, he became an explosives expert. He was like Red Adair was to oil wells above ground, but what he did underwater included more than just oil pipelines, drilling rigs, and ships that were grounded in shallow waters or were floating hulks at sea. He was a good man in a fight. He knew what to do to take a man down fast and his expertise with explosives was unquestionable. Carter never married, but he was always in demand. He always carried a black book with him, and like a sailor, had several women listed for every port of call. Carter picked up the phone on the first ring. After a few moments of explanation, and after completion of the conversation, Carter was making his own reservations for a flight to Melbourne where the final details of Elder's plan would be explained.

A NEW STAGE

The last Marine on the list was Phillip Tucker. He was an excellent hunter. In the Marines, he was with Force Recon. He was good with all weapons, from knives to guns, and he was excellent with a crossbow. During his time in the Marines, Phil's vacations were always to exotic places to hunt: Alaska, South America, and even a trip to Africa on Safari. Big game hunting was his specialty. In fact, after the Marines, Phil opened up a premier hunting and fishing camp in Montana. He was able to purchase the property within ten years after he bought it. Due to his reputation for guiding and providing first-class accommodations, the wealthy hunters from California and New York would pay a small ransom to hunt with Phil and bring home trophy Elk, Mule Deer and Mountain Rams. He also had Quail and Pheasant on the property. And, if Phil didn't have what you wanted to hunt, a trip to someplace special could always be arranged. Phil was well connected within the hunting circles.

Elder tried to call Phil, but it seemed he must be out of country. After a call to Phil's mother, John was able to get an international number. Mrs. Tucker was a special lady. She had entertained John when Phil visited home during the Marines and while John was hunting criminals with Chuck Taylor. She was happy to provide the information wondering about the urgency of the call. John simply stated he was hosting a reunion in Florida for his best friends. He called Phil and found out he was in Argentina fishing for Marlin. After a short explanation, Phil agreed to meet with John in Florida to go over the details. They had to be circumspect with regards to their conversation, but they shared a rich past experience in the Marines and there were certain code words used that an uninformed eavesdropper would never be able to pick up on. The adrenaline was pumping through John's veins. One could never be too careful. Assumptions kill!

Reed returned the call later that evening. He would not be able to join John at this time. His nightclub and family were his responsibility and there was another Reed on his way into the world. Although Reed was intrigued, he knew his family responsibilities came first. How could he keep his head in the game if he was worried about the love of his life and the new baby?

Without Reed joining the team, the three brothers, Justin and Phil would make the team a team of five Marines not the six John had

KIDNAPPING JESUS

originally selected as he developed the plan. John silently thought to himself, "Semper Fi!" Five Marines were all that was needed for this next mission. Maybe Reed could be counted upon at a later date using the city of New Orleans as a vantage point for the team.

Only two more calls to make. Jack and Charles, John's brothers, would also be on their way to Florida the following day and would join Carter and John. Their tickets would be at the ticket counter in Las Vegas International Airport. Charles was a Private Investigator in Vegas and Jack worked for Caterpillar Tractors. Both had retired from the Corps as well and had distinguished careers while serving their Nation.

Elder waited for their arrival at the International Airport in Melbourne, Florida for his brothers and brothers in arms from the Corps. It was a convenient alternative to the International Airport in Orlando. Jack, Charles and Justin all arrived within an hour of each other. The four left the small airport around 1700 hours.

It was a short ride back to Elder's house off Magnolia Avenue. They all had a lot of catching up to do and did most of it on the way back to the house. John had everything the plan called for laid out at the house. He had taken one of the bedrooms and turned it into a command center. John had everything he knew about Bin-Laden posted on one wall. On another wall were maps of Pakistan and Afghanistan. In a corner or the room was a 42- inch flat screen TV tuned to FOX News. The TV set was never turned off. Any scrap of information was useful or could be useful. Even the disinformation often accompanying the factual stories could lead to a break in the whereabouts of this Terrorist.

The group drank a few beers, smoked cigars, and agreed to wait until Phil arrived on the following day to get into the details of the mission. The team assembled had to think as one man, even down to the smallest detail. If details were ignored, the mission was likely to fail. This was a mission for humanity; a mission to bring to justice a man that lived his creed, no matter how demonic. This was going to be a grueling mission, unlike any these Marines had previously encountered, including the shared experiences in Vietnam and in Beirut, and those that Justin, Charles and Jack had during the first Gulf War in Iraq and off the coast of Kuwait. It was likely someone on the team may not come back.

When Phil arrived the following day, the group met again as a team of five. In the discussions, a name was penned for the team. They were

92

A NEW STAGE

truly a hunting club when it was agreed the code name for the team would be "COBALT." The letters had meaning, but COBALT would serve as a medical recipe for taking on the Al Queda terrorists at the heart of their operation. The "Company for Elimination of Osama Bin-Laden and Al Queda Leadership" was now a formality. Reality would come if the team trained hard and was diligent in their mental preparation. COBALT would be a force to be reckoned with.

Each of the members was wealthy in their own right. All received retirement pay from serving in the Marines. Most had invested well after their service was complete, but John ensured they would be paid for their labors with the paycheck at the end of the operation being the big score they all anticipated. $10,000 dollars were given to each of the team members. This was upfront money to pay their immediate bills. Each would get this every month until John ran out of money or COBALT was declared a mission success. If this was to be a precise operation with any chance of success, the milestones of the plan would take shape over a three-month period. The date was selected, and the calendar of events established. Changes would be made along the way, but the plan was the plan. But first, they had to get into shape, fighting shape.

The training was to take place right off Florida Highway 192 nearby in the small town of Holopaw. John had scouted out this place when he was a U.S. Marshal and was arresting Rick "The Weasel" Villisca. The place was like a hunting camp. Stacey Greer owned and operated the camp year-round. It was ideal and would more than meet the needs of the team. John rented the land and the building for three months for $3,500 dollars with Stacey providing around the clock security. Stacey was never informed of the details of the mission, but in his own way, wanted to help the mission succeed. As a law-abiding member of society, he knew that this might help bring security, to a struggling country at war with terrorists who were plotting to undermine the rights of humanity around the world.

John and Stacey established a perimeter within the boundaries of the property line. Camera surveillance, along with fencing and a secured entrance with code access were already in place but needed to be tweaked. The cost to rent the property was a great deal for John. A shooting range, five cabins, an owner's residence, and a large cabin for

KIDNAPPING JESUS

three families with a shared kitchen were on the two-hundred-acre property. All reservations had been cancelled. The cover story provided by Stacey was very simple. A death in the family placed the property into litigation and until the legal heir of the estate was determined, the property could not be used for commercial purposes. It was simple but needed to keep the customers who had been coming to the restful campgrounds happy. Stacey promised the issue would be resolved shortly and all former customers would receive a fifteen percent discount on their next visit to the camp.

It was September 15, 2001, and the COBALT team of five was now completely assembled at what the team referred to as Camp Stacey. The team moved into the large cabin. John was in one room, Charles and Jack in another of the rooms and Phil and Justin shared the third room. The cabin would be referred to as the Barracks, a term the former Marines were all familiar with. Another cabin was made into a briefing/training room where the team would meet daily to review the current events in the daily news reports, review the plan in detail and take in a daily class from the individual best suited to discuss, teach and or train a particular topic or discipline. It was like Non-Commissioned Officer Professional Development (NCOPD) in the Corps. Although they were all former Marines, each had a specialty that made them uniquely suited for the team. John was an expert with handguns and an expert in both martial arts and boxing. He was once a Marine Division Boxing Champion when he was stationed at Camp Pendleton. He would never forget the last semiprofessional fight he had when he beat Staff Sergeant Jerry "Choo Choo" Willis. Of course, that was almost 15 years ago. He kept up with the medicine bag when he worked out at the gym.

Charles was an expert in heavy weapons when he was in the Marines. His skill with 4.2 (Four Deuce) and with the 81MM (Millimeter) Mortar was exceptional. Additionally, as a Private Investigator in Las Vegas, he was able to keep up his training with local law officials. His marksmanship skills were impressive and he was often called upon to teach heavy weapons training. He was even called in on some of the cases when it seemed important informational leads crossed official and unofficial paths. Charles worked with local law enforcement and was never at odds with them on any of the cases he undertook. Charles also had access to departmental officials for information that might be useful to COBALT.

Jack was an expert with pistols and heavy equipment operations. Not only could Jack operate a Tank like his two brothers, he knew all the heavy-duty machines Caterpillar produced and how they operated like the back of his hand. He had only been with the corporation about ten years following his and Charles' retirement in July 1991, but his experience as the Motor Pool Sergeant in the Company Motor Pool made him an expert with the machinery aspects as well as with recovery operations when the vehicles would break down during exercises or during operations like the one he was involved with during Operation Desert Shield and Desert Storm in 1990 and 1991. The heat and the sand would take a toll on both men and equipment during the build-up and during the fight. He was in the Marine Central Command (CENTCOM) in the Theater of Operations. Charles was in the 1st Marine Division near the Al Wafrah Oil Fields.

Jack was involved with the feints and raids along the coastline of Iraq and Kuwait with the 5th Marine Expeditionary Brigade. Jack was a highly successful Platoon Sergeant. Although he had planned on retiring in 1990, he voluntarily stayed in the unit with his fellow Marines. Retirements in the Armed Forces were on hold during the buildup and during the operations. The Department of Defense could ill afford to let go of manpower and expertise in a time where the military was needed as an extension of political will. The Nation had rallied once again to support the troops. Jack was well trained with all manner of watercraft and was SCUBA certified. The 5th MEB was also stationed at Camp Pendleton along with the 1st Marine Division. The 5th MEB landed at Al Mish'ab, Saudi Arabia, about 28 miles south of the Kuwait border on February 24, 1991. The threat of a Marine Amphibious Assault in the Persian Gulf forced the Iraqi Command to hold at least four Iraqi Divisions out of the war in anticipation of an amphibious assault. Just the threat of an amphibious assault was a force multiplier to the operations of CENTCOM.

Phillip Tucker was a hunter. He could track any man or animal over any terrain and knew instinctively where an animal might be located based on the track, time of day and the weather. Once the animal of choice was found, Phil was a dead shot. Rarely did he have to track an

KIDNAPPING JESUS

animal once the bullet hit the intended target, but there were circumstances that often called for him to use his skills in finding a wounded animal. The crossbow was his favorite weapon. Using a compound bow was a close second choice. Using either weapon required stealth, something he both liked and was good at. He never failed to find those animals his clients wounded wherever in the world he was hunting.

Phil was also a former Marine that had the same infantry training as did his brethren. As a member of Force Recon, Phil would often find himself behind enemy lines in Iraq. His was a special mission. Iraqi unit positions were located, and the target coordinates passed through channels. This was a coordinated operation. Night was an ally to his team.

Once the air campaign and the air and sea launched cruise missiles eliminated the Iraq Command structure, further confusion on the battlefield came from his team and many more just like his team, both Army and Marines. Phil was personally involved with the capture of over 500 Iraqi soldiers. These men were not willing to die for Allah or for President Saddam Hussein. Most were in poor shape. They were leaderless, ill-fed and poorly equipped. Phil and his team would round up the soldiers and turn them into the first units headed in their direction. The Enemy Prisoners of War (EPWs) were soon overwhelming. After a while, it seemed the Iraqi soldiers were looking for any Coalition soldier they could find to give themselves up. There were some that resisted, but in the days following the decisive victory, the resistance ebbed. After being bombed, used for target practice and underfed, they were a beaten force.

Justin Carter was a Master SCUBA Instructor. His ability to use explosives both above and under water was phenomenal. During the last ten years, he had formed his own underwater demolition business in Mobile, Alabama. His duties as a team member would be to take care of the explosives work above or below the water. Like the rest of the team, Justin knew the infantry weapons of the Marines like the back of his hand. However, he was exceptional at taking care of large targets requiring finesse.

Justin retired from the Corps in 1991 as well. It was a coincidence Charles, Jack, Phil and Justin all retired the same year following the successful campaign of defeating Iraq. They all felt the mission was never complete even with the decisive victory of the coalition forces. The

96

A NEW STAGE

push to Baghdad was halted and Saddam Hussein and his henchmen were allowed to stay in power. Now ten years later, America was under attack. Like many others, Justin thought there might be a link to the terrorists and Saddam. Afghanistan and Iraq might be safe harbors for terrorist's cells and training. Shortly, the Taliban and Al Queda terrorists would meet up with Operation Enduring Freedom with forces from the North Atlantic Treaty Organization (NATO). Osama Bin-Laden, the leader of Al Queda, was literally in cross hairs. Everyone wanted to pull the trigger on this sick bastard. His responsibility for the deaths of innocent men, women and children was no myth. It was reality. He was only a man. Every man leaves a trail. A trail can be followed. A man can be killed. Assumptions kill!

After everyone settled into their quarters, John had the team assembled for their first day of exercise. It would be a light workout. Just like the military training they were all accustomed to on a daily basis; they stretched, did their calisthenics, and went for a short run in the Florida afternoon heat. Although it was September, it was still hot in Florida. Three miles later, John brought the team from the pace he had established to a walk. John was 52 years old and although he was the old man of the bunch, was still in pretty good shape. Phil was in good shape but was not running very often. Justin did not run very much as well due to his time spent in the water. He would have to retrain the muscles in his legs. Jack and Charles still kept up with their running, so their breathing was a little more relaxed. But the heat of central Florida would make or break even the best.

By the seventh day, the running increased by a mile. Training continued to take place on weapons every morning until the team was familiar with each one of them, even when blindfolded. Each COBALT team member took their turns leading the training. There was an old adage that held true: you learn more by teaching than by reading or listening. Each member of the team would learn each other's job almost as well as their own. It was all about assuming responsibility. One of John's former mentors had taught him well. You could choose three courses of action in life. The first and foremost was being responsible. The second and third choice were definitely out of the question. They were being irresponsible or unresponsive. Again, they were choices, but not the choices of these hardened men on a mission of extreme importance.

KIDNAPPING JESUS

In three weeks, the team was beginning to become physically fit. It was Saturday, October 6, 2001, and the team was now running eight miles a day. Although, as a team, the physical abilities were above average, John wanted to ensure the men would be at peak performance. In order for this to be accomplished, John sought out a friend of his that was a doctor. While working as a bounty hunter with Chuck, John and his associates had injuries that needed an expert surgeon who was also an orthopedic specialist. Although not an official member of COBALT, Doctor Frank A. Leone would be on the extended team should an incident occur requiring his medical expertise. John had a list of former associates he knew he could depend upon. During the training sessions each of the team members would share their list of contacts and the resources that could be brought to bear if necessary. Some were now in contact with John.

None knew the mission, but all knew what was required of them should they receive a call from COBALT with the code word "**BLUE**". The response of the contact if all was ok on their end would be "**FIRE.**" If it came down to the one of the other of the contacts being in a questionable situation, one letter of the code word could be used, followed by a response that was either the next letter or letters. For example, if John contacted Doctor Leone, John would say, "Frank, this is John. The weather in Florida is fantastic and the skies are extremely *"blue"* today. How's everything going with you and your family?" If everything was fine with Frank, he could simply respond with, "John, everything is great in Tampa. It looks as if the *"fire"* is out in the swamp. It's good to hear from you!" Or, Frank could have stated, "John good to hear from you. You still owe me *"five"* dollars from the game last week." John would respond to *"five"* with the following. "Frank, I'll send the *"five"* I owe you tomorrow. I need to renew a prescription."

Frank faxed prescriptions for mild steroids for each of the team members. None of the five would go to the same pharmacy but each team member, when they left Camp Stacey would go with at least one more team member.

Each Saturday afternoon at 1300 hours, the group would go into either Melbourne or Orlando. They would take John's Ford Truck, the F-150 he had purchased in Los Angeles when he left Chuck's employment. It was a chance to get a meal out and to see some of the local

98

A NEW STAGE

area. They would always leave the Camp with Stacey on guard. Stacey had borrowed two of the nastiest pit bulls one could ever imagine from a friend of his that lived out in the swamp. These boys were really nasty, and they smelled. The only bath they would ever get is when they jumped in one of the many creeks on Stacey's property. They had the run of the property and were used to everyone on the team. They would wag the nubby tails at each of them while slobbering out of their mouths. They were disgusting but would certainly be effective if needed.

The men were going to Orlando to get their prescriptions filled, get some groceries, and eat a steak dinner at one of the local steakhouses. The were trying to build muscle and the carbohydrates they were eating combined with the daily-dozen exercises and running were beginning to take effect. The steroids would be the extra kick they needed. This would allow muscle growth and shorter recovery time after the workouts. Classes in the afternoon were extremely interesting to all of them, but even John caught himself yawning at inappropriate times. They were each disciplined men with a goal in mind, but they were not young men any longer.

It was a great meal. The team indulged themselves with a real cattleman's plate of T-bone steak or a Porterhouse Cut, with Texas toast and a baked potato. The appetizers were small lobster tails roasted over an open fire on a stick. It was a fantastic meal. The red Pinot Noir was an excellent complement to the meal. Before the meal was served, a before dinner drink of martinis was served. A silent toast to COBALT was made. John was feeling great about the progress of the team. They were all friends, and they had to become a team of five that worked together as one.

It was around 2000 hours when the team left the fancy restaurant and headed back to Holopaw and Camp Stacey. They were tired, but in good spirits. John asked Justin to drive as the team reviewed the day's events.

They would need to hit the rack at 2200 hours. Tomorrow, John informed the team they would do a 25-mile road march. Stacey would follow at a distance. The Camp was now completely wired with cameras and security devices. Someone could get themselves killed if they got past the outer security and managed to hook up with the two devil dogs.

KIDNAPPING JESUS

On Sunday, October 7th, the team assembled at 0700 hours. They had a good breakfast at 0600 hours. It was Chuck's turn to cook, and the venison and wild boar served with hash brown potatoes and scrambled eggs was excellent. They all took their steroids and were soon on the march.

Each had a backpack, and each carried an array of weapons. None were visible. They had to be careful. If the hunters became the hunted, then their plan could be foiled, or their mission compromised. The United States government would not sanction this type of behavior from its citizens. The road march was a combination run and quick march. It was humid and Stacey went ahead to the first five-mile stop. When the team arrived at the first of three rest stops, the team was in good spirits. They had covered the distance in just under an hour. This was good time, but could they keep the pace?

After a five-minute break, stretching and getting the gator aid down, they then headed out on the next stretch. The packs only weighed 35 pounds but represented key equipment each would have to take on the mission. The next leg of the 25-mile course was at the halfway point. It took almost two hours to travel seven and a half miles. The team was a little haggard but still had plenty of pride and not one was a quitter. John thought each of them would rather die than quit.

After another short break, the team began the route back to Camp Stacey. It was getting hot as the Florida sun slowly rose in the east. It was around 1000 hours and if the team arrived on schedule at the Camp, it would be around 1300 hours. They caught up to Stacey at the first stop they had made that morning. It was only five more miles back to Camp. Just after noon, they were all getting a bit slower. John instructed the team to shed the packs and give them to Stacey to take back to the Camp. Each carried their pistols. Every one of the team had a concealed weapons permit from the state where they lived: but none wanted to be scrutinized if they could help it. Stacey headed off to the Camp; the team of five was on the road for the last stretch. When they were two miles away from the Camp, John began to jog. A Jodie call soon followed as they all began to hit their left foot on the pavement as if they were one man. Justin started the song they all knew so well. It was a favorite of all the armed forces.

A NEW STAGE

"C130 rolling down the strip, airborne daddy going to take a little trip. Stand up, hook up, shuffle to the door…we're going to jump on the count of four. Hup, two, three, four. If my chute don't open wide, I got another one by my side. If that one should fail me too, bury me in the lean and rest. Am I right or am I wrong? You're right! Bury me in the lean and rest. Bury me in my best dress. Am I right or am I wrong? You're right!"

And so it went. Many calls were made as the team headed to the finish line. Five miles were covered in just over one hour. The team had what it took. Now it was time to hone those skills and build up the muscles.

When the team returned, Stacey met them at the gate with water. A portable shower was just inside the gate so the team could cool down before they hit the chin up bars in front of the cabin that was designated as the training center. The dogs were happy to see the team and wanted to play. John, Jack, Charles, Justin and Phil were in good spirits and slapped and kicked at the dogs. Stacey threw what looked like a piece of firewood and both the dogs were on their way to play fetch. It was a riot when the dogs would return with the wood in both their mouths and each wagging their nubby tails in sheer excitement that they had done what their master wanted them to do.

Stacey took John aside after a few moments. The news was that Operation Enduring Freedom was underway in Afghanistan. This was good news. The official story was that the mission of the NATO forces was to destroy and to deny sanctuary to Al Queda provided by the Taliban. Osama Bin-Laden had established an alliance of sorts with the Taliban and had been living in Afghanistan since 1996. It was a safe haven for terrorists, or it had been a safe haven. Time would tell. The clock on this terrorist's life was ticking. Although Bin-Laden was implicated with gathered evidence, it could not be proved he was involved. It made not one bit of difference to John. There was a posted bounty for Bin-Laden of $25 million dollars, Dead or Alive, under the Rewards for Justice Program.

The team was officially notified of the events of the day once they cleaned up from the morning's road march. They assembled in the training cabin and were caught up with the news on FOX.

This was the channel that was fair and balanced. Some of the best reporters were on FOX. The fair and balanced news and the no spin

101

KIDNAPPING JESUS

zone were always of interest. International news was about the same providing pictures from different vantage points, but FOX could be watched almost at any time and there would be the same news, but updated as the events took place either for clarification or more news obtained from new sources.

The team was now briefed on their target. Their training calendar was now on the wall. They were on increased alert and the large red X on the calendar indicated the last day of training for the team. COBALT would complete training by October 31st. John informed the team of the travel plans. The team would be going to Afghanistan to meet with the Al Queda terrorists. Everyone was released for the remainder of the day. The next phase of training was heavy weapons and explosives.

Justin Carter was the explosives expert and would lead the training. Charles Elder would lead the heavy weapons training. On Monday morning, there was no running. Muscles from the 25-mile road march were still healing. The steroids had not kicked in yet but would soon begin to work their youthful magic on the men. Claymore mines and hand grenades were on the Monday morning schedule. In the afternoon, actual emplacement of Claymores was reviewed, and each of the team had to set and detonate a mine. The steel balls would rip the air towards the target range taking out all the silhouette targets in the deadly field of fire. Steel and wooden posts were ripped apart or shredded beyond recognition. These were great tools when you needed to cover an area too large for one man to defend. It was a force multiplier for the team.

Grenade training was on the calendar for the following day. The team used inert training rounds in the morning and in the afternoon, real grenades. It must have sounded like a small war was taking place in the neighborhood, but no one seemed to believe the noise was out of the ordinary. In any case, the heavy weapons training would begin on Wednesday.

John provided training on the M-16A4 and the M-249 SAW (Squad Automatic Weapon). Charles led the team in learning about the M-240G machine gun and M-203 grenade launcher.

Phil rounded out weapons training on Friday. His class included the sawed-off shotgun and the crossbow. The crossbow was simple to operate and was as deadly as it was silent. Using watermelons and

A NEW STAGE

cantaloupes as targets, the demonstration was graphic and effective. The crossbow was easy to learn, but Phil was three times faster than anyone in loading and shooting accurately than was the closest team member.

Justin took everyone to the Campground pool for SCUBA review on Saturday morning. It was refreshing to be in the water again. Charles, Jack and Phil needed some additional attention provided by both John and Justin. All the basic skills were covered, and each could set a charge to any surface at the conclusion of the training session. It was afternoon and it definitely was time to take a well-needed break in the activities they had been concentrating on for what seemed like endless days and nights.

The team headed to Orlando for another steak dinner. They went to the same restaurant and essentially ordered the same meal. Each member had a voracious appetite. It seemed as if the steroids were beginning to work their magic. Muscles were not as sore as they were in the past, and there was a radiant glow on the faces of the team. Martinis were served and again a silent toast was exchanged. COBALT was almost ready. The team was going to do a short five mile run the following morning and then hit the Ranger Tower in the afternoon.

Stacey had set up the training site with ropes and ladders. They needed to be able to conduct assaults like professionals using Air Assault techniques taught by the Marines and by the Army. Rappelling was fairly simple but needed to be combined with mountain climbing techniques. COBALT had to be deadly and regardless of the type of insertion taken to get to Bin-Laden, must be flawless.

During the training, two of the team seemed as if they were frozen to the tower. They had made the climb to the top and were about 100 feet above the ground. John had already completed his first trip up and was now executing the belay man on the ground ensuring the ropes would not be tangled as the men made their descent to the ground. There were two ropes for the team at the top of the tower. Justin was on belay on the other rope. Charles and Jack were at the top of the tower.

"Shit!" Exclaimed John. "What the hell are you two doing up there. Swapping spit?"

Charles and Jack did not like heights...anything but heights. Charles replied, "Hell, do you think we like it up here? I want to get my ass on the ground. Just leave us alone and well make it."

KIDNAPPING JESUS

After what seemed like hours, Charles and Jack nodded at each other and in unison yelled, "Geronimo!" The famous Apache leader seemed to be there in spirit and somehow provided the strength for these two brothers to begin their descent using their break hand as the rope passed through the snap link. They used their feet to bounce off the tower as they came closer to the ground. John was proud of the two and they overcame their basic fear of heights.

Justin and Phil scampered up the tower like two young Marines full of pride. They wanted to show Jack, Charles and John they could handle the tower. Both got to the top about the same time. Each winked at each other and rapidly headed to the ground. It was almost an Australian rappel in that it took just a few seconds for them to travel the 100 feet to the ground.

Now it was time to get up the rope one more time with a pack and weapons. Each donned their side arms, picked up their respective weapons, and moved to the ropes for their ascent. The first up the rope ladder was Phil. He was carrying a crossbow. A small grease gun was on his back, and he carried a large hunting knife on the left side of his belt. In the holster on his right side was an M1911, 45 caliber, pistol. It was modified and could accurately take out a target 50 feet away. It was no longer a basic weapon of issue once used by the military. Phil reached the top, rolled up his rope and tied the pack to it, and then threw it to the ground. No one would be on belay for Phil. He began his descent and about halfway down locked his break hand in place. He swung his crossbow with his left hand and aimed into the brush surrounding the tower.

The team was puzzled at the move but didn't utter a word. They trusted each other. As the bolt was released, a loud thump was heard by everyone. In fact, you could hear the ground shake. In a moment, each member had their weapons raised towards the noise and all were on alert as they hastily formed a perimeter. The grass was moving as the hidden target let out the gasp of air that spelled death. In moments, Phil was standing beside John with a big grin on his face. John asked him quietly, "What's so funny?"

Phil replied. "I just shot one of the biggest pigs I've ever seen in my life. There are a couple of big sows in that bunch, so everyone be careful. They just don't know the big guy is dead yet. They'll come out

A NEW STAGE

soon or run back into the woods." Just about then, you could hear the snorting begin. They were gone in seconds. The team moved to where the noise came from, and the wild boar was huge. Just like one of the early Volkswagen Beetles from the late 60s. It must have been 600 pounds. The tusks were razor sharp and about 8 inches long. They could cut man or dog to ribbons in minutes. The shaft of the bolt was right in the top of the wild boar's head and was buried deep. Phil had made a great kill. The team was nearly ready. That was no demonstration. It was the real deal.

Justin went next and was followed by Charles, Jack and John. They completed the tower with no more events. There was no longer need to invoke the name of Geronimo and bring the Apache War Chief back to life. In fact, Charles inwardly yelled out to himself as he began his descent, COBALT. That sounded good to him and at the same time was reassuring. The team quartered out the wild hog and loaded it into Stacey's F-150.

Both trucks headed back to camp. It was a good day. Dinner would consist of BBQ pork. It would be a late night and it was time to have a party. This was a great excuse. Cigars went around. Cold Budweiser Beer along with Jack Daniels and Jim Beam were available in the coolers around the fire pit. John had informed the team that Monday would be a holiday as a reward for the team. All work and no play do not always make a team better. Later, it would be time to be all business.

Today, it was time to party. It was a hell of a shot that brought down that wild boar. Phil recounted the story from his perspective above the team while he was rappelling from the tower, including the looks on the faces below first in puzzlement, then in disbelief when the bolt was fired from the powerful crossbow.

CHAPTER VII

AIRPOWER

The training was over. COBALT was now a hardened team to be reckoned with. It was October 31st. The war in Afghanistan was now in full swing. Operation Enduring Freedom began on October 7th and was having immediate success. Osama Bin-Laden was hunted in the mountains of Afghanistan and was likely in hiding somewhere along the shared border between Pakistan and Afghanistan. There were tunnels in the mountains and established defensive positions manned by hardened men who had fought in the mountains since they were children and knew them like the back of their hands. It was rugged territory and winter was fast approaching. If anything was going to be done by NATO forces before the next year arrived, it would have to be done soon.

The United States led a coalition of forces from many nations and had entered into an agreement with the Afghanistan Northern Alliance in order to remove the Taliban regime and their support and sanctuary provided by the Taliban to Al Queda. Al Qaeda training camps and strongholds were deep in the Hindu Kush Mountains east of Kabul near the Khyber Pass. He may have been located in the vicinity of Tora Bora or somewhere in the Waziristan region of Pakistan. Reports were somewhat sketchy. The posted bounty for Bin-Laden of $25 million dollars, Dead or Alive, under the Rewards for Justice Program,

KIDNAPPING JESUS

was on the line for those who could deliver Bin-Laden to justice. It was going to be a difficult operation and for those who were about to risk their lives, it could be rewarding to bring this evil man to justice. Someone was going to cash in on this terrorist before he could continue to lead his twisted network of militant Islamic assassins under a religious banner.

John Elder had purchased a McDonnell Douglas DC-6C from an auction nearly ten-years ago. The plane had been confiscated in a failed drug running attempt and auctioned to the public. This was just one of many law enforcement seizures over the years that included a wide range of cars, boats, and planes. John's bid of $35,000 was accepted and he was the proud owner of this vintage, four-engine, aircraft. The plane's cargo capacity was over 12,000 pounds with a cruising range of over 3,000 miles at a speed of 309 miles per hour. While working with Chuck Taylor, John wanted to learn to fly and it became one of his passions. He had some experience while growing up, as well as in the Marines, where he was able to gain an understanding of aerodynamics and how to fly planes but had never pursued formal flight training. The time had come to learn when he purchased the DC-6C at auction. He would now have to earn his wings.

It took several years to get his multi-engine rating, but John was a natural pilot and his ability to fly a plane was never questioned by his instructor, Bradley (Brad) Joseph Lyons. Brad was a seasoned instructor pilot as well as a Major in the Air Force Reserve at the time and he currently was flying the new C-17, transport aircraft. In fact, the DC-6C was ferried to Melbourne International Airport from John Wayne International Airport with John sitting in the right seat and Brad in the left seat when he transported the plane late in September of 2001.

This was the second trip that John had made from Los Angeles in the last two months and would probably not be his last. John had nicknamed the plane "LAPEARLE" after Pearle, his girlfriend, for almost ten years while he worked with "Chuck's Headhunters." Just like Pearle, the plane was 42 years old.

The DC-6C was built in 1959, the last year of production of this plane. This plane was one of fifty still in operation in 2001 and was well appointed. John and Pearle had had many midnight flights in the DC-6C and John had even used the plane on a couple of missions when

108

he was working with Chuck. It was expensive to maintain and operate, but she had been kept in good shape. Some of the costs incurred on these missions were able to be written

off as a business expense due to the affiliation with Chuck. On occasion, the U.S. Marshals would team up with the Headhunters due to the increased success rate of clandestine operations and the cover that could be used with the DC-6C.

With the 3,000-mile range, LAPEARLE could transport COBALT virtually anywhere in the world. The illegal drug running operations out of Columbia had netted the FBI one of the largest marijuana seizures in history. There were other drugs on-board including cocaine hydrochloride (cocaine HCI) and illegal automatic weapons, cargo destined for the local markets in the United States. There was no way to be sure of how this drug deal gone bad could have impacted the young men and women of America, but the seizure of handguns, a variety of machine guns, and sniper rifles could have started a small war with local police along the southern borders of the United States. Additionally, there were three Light Antitank Weapons (LAWS) on board the aircraft. It took some time for the authorities to go through the aircraft due to the nature of the many hidden compartments. It was also discovered by the Federal Aviation Administration (FAA) that this DC-6C had been owned by a leader in the Columbian Drug Cartel for at least fifteen years and had been in and out of United States airspace on twenty known occasions. This was before the discovery that a distinguished businessman, Jose Santacruz Londono, from Bogota, Columbia was the drug kingpin of the Cali Drug Mafia. The seizure was aimed directly at him. It was not until March 5, 1996, that Londono was gunned down near Medellin, Columbia where Pablo Escobar had

KIDNAPPING JESUS

established another drug kingdom, but had been killed in 1993. With the seizure of the DC-6C, it was the beginning of closing the drug air bridge from South America to the United States. John had run across a quotation that seemed to sum up a significant event that surrounded the seizure of LAPEARLE:

"They say that one should not celebrate the death of a person. However, there exist people in this world who are not honorable and bring no good at all to humanity. I have to admit that I feel good. I finally feel as if justice has been done. All those involved in the crime are in jail save the author of the crime José Santacruz Londono. And now he has paid with his life."

Vicky de Dios Unanue

Widow of murdered journalist Manuel de Dios Unanue, commenting on the shooting of Londono by Colombian police.

The gear was hidden in secret compartments to prevent detection by both the authorities and the terrorists. It was a dangerous game COBALT was playing. John had been in touch with friends in the FBI and Captain Sullivan was now the Deputy Director of the FBI. "Lucky" was doing well at his chosen profession. It was chance that put Sullivan and Elder together years ago when Elder became a U.S. Marshal. John needed to have a friend in high places that was informed of the team's mission. It was risky, but the U.S. Government had sanctioned the mission with Deputy Director Sullivan's recommendation. This was a very important step that would lead to several changes in the composition of the team and the direction the team would take. They were no longer an independent operation. They had support. Support from the United States Government.

John had been contacted by Sullivan. The FBI had assembled a small cadre of members that would support the team administratively and would be assigned under the operational control of John. The three-man team was fluent in Arabic. Two of the three members were devout Muslims and all three were highly educated in American Universities. The remaining member of the team was an Afghanistan political

AIRPOWER

refugee that escaped to the United States with his family seeking political asylum in 1985. He had joined the Central Intelligence Agency (CIA) at the age of 25. He was on- loan to the FBI for this mission at the direction of the Secretary of State. His wife and two children thanked Allah each day that they were U.S. citizens and would repay both Afghanistan and the United States for their struggle to gain and maintain a democratic government free from tyranny in both countries. COBALT was now a team of eight, the three Elder Brothers, John, Charles and Jack, Phil Tucker and Justin Carter and now the three men that joined the team from both the FBI and CIA. The two men from the FBI were Sergeant Aasim Rasheed and Sergeant Abdul-Hafiz Sahar. Joining the team from the CIA was Mustafa Basher.

The eight-man team assembled at Camp Stacey to review COBALT's mission. It was quite simple. The team had one target. And the abbreviation of COBALT stated the mission best — "Company for Elimination of Osama Bin-Laden and Al Queda Leadership." The team needed to make a few adjustments to the plan due to the increase in personnel. It would take about a week to iron out responsibilities. The mission date was set for November 11th (Veterans Day). The 11/11 date coincided with the moon phase of the calendar. Using the 22nd as Target OBL, this gave the team time to travel to Pakistan, cross the border and enter into Afghanistan. Hopefully, the weather will cooperate along with the new moon going into the first quarter phase. Light was the enemy when surprise was needed. The long dark nights were the ally of this team.

Deputy Director Sullivan was focused on the support for the team. This mission needed to be successful for any hope of world peace. One man can make a difference in either a positive or negative way in world events. Do the actions of one-man matter in the overarching grand scheme of things? World events throughout history gave the easy answer. Monday morning quarterbacks were plentiful. Sidelines participation never made a difference. Heroes versus dictators!

The National Intelligence Agency (NIA) was directed to share Photographic Intelligence (PHOTOINT), also known as Imagery Intelligence (IMINT), with the team through one of the FBI agents. It would be Abdul's responsibility to provide daily Situation Reports (SITREPS) to the team. Photographic intelligence can be interpreted

KIDNAPPING JESUS

in many different fashions. The NIA reviews for the region would be provided and reviewed along with the unaltered Top Secret NOFORN (No Foreign Dissemination) satellite photographs. It was hard to believe that with an array of intelligence gathering techniques, ground and air combined, from many different nations, one terrorist could not be located even with the concerted efforts put forth for his capture or termination. It would seem the posted bounty for Bin-Laden would bring this one man down. COBALT was undertaking a Herculean task. Only eight men on the team, was it enough? Something of a story from Greek Mythology regarding a Trojan Horse and the fall of Troy allayed many doubts. John was thinking to himself, "Assumptions Kill!"

In just eleven days, the team would depart. If the mission was successful, COBALT would be on their way out of Afghanistan into Pakistan with OBL, dead or alive. The key question regarding the mission to John was in order for COBALT to be completely successful; OBL must be killed or captured. If killed, then proof would be needed of his death. For that to happen, COBALT needed to return to the United States. Hopefully, everyone will make it back. That was the question he often asked. Who would make it home?

It was November 8th. COBALT was working out the final details in a hangar at the airport. The DC-6C was ready for the mission. The weapons had been carefully stored in the hidden compartments. It was quite an arsenal of lethality that had been assembled in one place. Not all would be used as it was a question of how much one man could carry in addition to the cold weather gear, food and mountain climbing equipment.

In addition to the three M-16s with M-203 grenade launchers, two boxes of M-67 grenades, four AR- 10s (7.62mm) with night vision, thermal, devices, four 45 caliber Colt pistols, four M-16 Squad Automatic Weapons with 10,000 rounds of .223 caliber ammunition, there were the weapons the new members of the team brought to the upcoming battle. The CIA Agent, Mustafa, brought his personal 45 caliber pistol and a M-50 Sniper Rifle. Both FBI agents wanted to carry their 9mm pistols but were issued 45 caliber pistols to help keep down having additional ammunition requirements. Phil Tucker carried his 45-caliber pistol, a compound bow and a crossbow along with his Bowie Knife. Justin carried his 45-caliber pistol, with an M-203

112

AIRPOWER

combined with an AR-16. Justin was designated as the indirect fire support element of the team and would be last in the column of six men. Phil was the point man. John was the leader and Charles and Jack protected the flanks. Abdul-Hafiz was originally slated to stay with the plane in Pakistan to ensure the plane would remain safe and provide interpretation, when necessary, with local officials; however, it was decided he would join John to provide direct communications with the other team and to ensure Arabic conversations did not go awry.

Mustafa, from the CIA and Aasim from the FBI would form a team of two and provide overwatch for the team with radio and the 50 caliber snipers' rifle. If some intelligence came by way of U.S. contacts, Abdul, Mustafa and Aasim could relay via the satellite phones he and each COBALT team member would have with them. It was the only way to provide communications in the mountainous regions where the team would be operating.

With high visibility of the operation at the National level, there was the possibility additional resources may be needed to carry out the clandestine operations. If the team failed in their mission, but discovered OBL, an array of weapons could be brought to bear on the coordinates provided by the two-man team designated as Team Cat. The core of COBALT, the six men in the lead to get OBL, was code named Team Mouse. The remaining team members that were yet to be assigned would continue to stay with the DC- 6C in Pakistan and receive real time intelligence from the NIA and relay information back to Deputy Director Sullivan. The FBI was the focal point for the team's progress and all information was funneled through what was now known as the COBALT Operations Center. The Vice-Chairman of Joint Chiefs of Staff in the Pentagon received updates directly from Deputy Director Sullivan. Those involved were on a need-to-know basis. Although the profile of the team was larger than John wanted, he knew the assistance of everyone involved was needed to make the mission a success.

On November 9th, COBALT moved into the hanger. Cots were set up as the team reviewed the flight plan and their team tactics. They ensured the DC-6C was set up like a Command Post (CP), complete with the latest computers, software, and radios. Uncle Sam had delivered the best equipment and set up the COBALT Command Communications Center (C3) on-board. Two mission specialists

KIDNAPPING JESUS

were added to the team to provide intelligence coverage around the clock. They would in effect be the team's base of operations located in Pakistan. Flying in with the mission specialists was an Air Force Lieutenant Colonel. It was Brad Lyons. He was an Air Force Reserve pilot and had been activated for active duty for this mission. He knew the DC-6C as well as did anyone and had logged quite a few hours when he was training John on the multi-engine aircraft. It was a welcome, yet unexpected, reunion. This would bring number of men on the team to eleven. Eleven seemed to be a repeating number for this mission.

The mission specialists would be in touch with the National Command Authority (NCA) directly. It was determined to move the operations from FBI authority to the NCA due to the sensitivity of the mission. It made no difference to John and the team. They had a limited window of opportunity for the mission and John knew the involvement of United States intelligence was crucial to success. He was surprised he, or his team, had not been replaced, but there was a prevalent belief this hardened war veteran and his determined team could pull off the mission and bring OBL to justice. Others had failed. This was another means to achieve an end— cut off the head of the terrorist led group who had gained influence in Arab nations and was an outlaw to international justice.

114

CHAPTER VIII

WHEELS UP, 11/11/2001

John was awakened by his alarm clock. It was 0500 hours. The team of eleven men were coming out of a deep, yet restless sleep. They had been tired when they hit their cots around 2200 hours. Reviewing the mission requirements was the single most important topic discussed among the team. Stacey was also involved. It was up to Stacey to secure the Camp and the hanger. Everything must be ready in case the team arrives back into the States with wounded or with OBL. While the team was away, it would be up to Stacey to ensure medical supplies were in the hanger and at the Camp. Doctor Frank Leone was their primary physician and would be on standby for the team's return. Both men were part of the rear detachment operations for Team COBALT.

At 0530 hours, the team was in the briefing area of the hanger. The hanger was affectionately referred to as Hanger 51. It was a Top-Secret operation being initiated in a small city with an international airport. Had this been at a military installation or at one of the large airfields, someone most likely would have stumbled into the team and blew their cover. John looked at the team. Team Cat was Mustafa, and Aasim. Team Mouse was made up of Justin Carter, Phil Tucker, Jack, Charles and John Elder. Abdul would now go with the team and would communicate in Arabic with Team Cat as they drew near their objective. If their conversation was picked up by OBL and his security, it would

KIDNAPPING JESUS

seem as if a couple of goat herders were operating in the mountains. It was a common practice, and the area was rural. Brad and the two mission specialists would remain with the C3 and remain in touch with the NCA around the clock providing real time intelligence to COBALT. John nodded at everyone and placed his hands behind his back. Looking at everyone directly in the eyes, he said, "Good morning, men, let's get this show on the road!"

Breakfast arrived from a local restaurant and was placed in the kitchen on the plane. The plane was outfitted with a superb kitchen, master bedroom, 20 seats, and ten bunk beds that allowed some degree of privacy. The master bedroom had a queen size bed and a separate bathroom. There were two other bathrooms on the plane. The Cali Drug Mafia had really spared no expense in outfitting the plane. The bunk beds had been added to the plane before the final number of men had been selected either by John or directed by the Vice-Chairman of the Joint Chiefs of Staff. In the center of the seating area was a large screen split into four separate areas. The two mission specialists, Air Force Captain Ted K. Knight and Army Captain David R. Kimble were on-line with the NIA. On screen were weather updates for Florida and for Afghanistan and Pakistan. There was a smile on his face as the hanger doors were opened. Jack and Charles boarded last, and Stacey moved the ladder from the plane's door. The aircraft door was closed, and cross checked even though there were no flight attendants on board.

John and Brad entered the flight deck and were going through the final preflight check list. They had already walked around the plane many times making sure that nothing had happened to LAPEARLE. The 42-year-old plane was still in great shape. What a buy the plane had been. Although it had a sordid past, the future of the plane was for freedom of fear from Al Queda terrorists and retribution for 9/11. It had been two months since the cowardly attack on the twin towers. Operation Enduring Freedom was in full swing. COBALT was the team and OBL was the target. If the intelligence was correct, he should be easy to find. Bombs could not reach him in his mountain stronghold, but stealth and deception would be the team's strength.

The engines started with a roar as each one of the four engines came to life. It felt good. Stacey removed the chock blocks from the wheels. John, sitting in the left seat, was the Pilot in Command. He moved the

WHEELS UP, 11/11/2001

throttles forward and the plane began to roll out of Hanger 51. It was 0630 hours, and it was still dark outside although it was beginning to get light in the east.

All the men had their own way of dealing with the trip. Justin had taken out a life insurance policy of $250,000 dollars made out to his only living relative, his sister Mille. It was mailed on Friday evening. Phil just made out a will stating that if he was dead, he wanted to be buried with his fellow Marines in Arlington National Cemetery. His money in his accounts, as well as his land holdings, was to go to his mother. She could decide to distribute his wealth as she saw fit. As for Jack and Charles, their wills were already in place. Hopefully, they were still correct in that they were made just prior to them retiring from the Marines in 1991. Jack had never married but had several girlfriends over the years. The money they left behind would go to their families, apportioned equitably among the surviving relatives.

John's will was made out, and Pearle was designated as his benefi-ciary. She was the only woman he really ever knew. If he died, it was only fair she got the money. His brothers would not need the money. She deserved the very best. The FBI and CIA agents all had families and it was standard for them to have a will due to the dangers of ser-vice. Brad also had a family. He was married and had three boys and two girls. He also had a twin brother, in the U.S. Army The oldest children already had left home, but he still had a high school student in the house. She was 17 going on 30 and quite a beautiful young lady. She was a straight A student and the President of her High School Class. Odds were in her favor that when she graduated, she would be the Class Valedictorian and receive offers from all the best colleges. She was considering going to the United States Air Force Academy in Colorado Springs or to the United States Military Academy at West Point. Ted and Dave also had families and their wills left all they had to their wives. It was simple, yet effective. They also had Servicemen Group Life Insurance (SGLI) in the amount of

$100,000 dollars that would go to their families. Not much, when you consider the danger of the mission and how much they could earn if they remained alive to collect their monthly paychecks. It was at this moment John recalled the Jodie call from his past life in the Marine Corps:

KIDNAPPING JESUS

"C130 rolling down the strip... airborne daddy going to take a little trip. Stand up, hook up, shuffle to the door... we're going to Jump on the count of four. Hup, two, three, four. If my chute don't open wide, I got another one by my side. If that one should fail me too, bury me in the lean and rest Am I right or am I wrong? Your right! Bury me in the lean and rest. Bury me in my best dress. Am I right or am I wrong? Your right!"

Just bury me in the lean and rest and pin my medals on my chest. Just tell the world we did our best. Strike that last thought! The world would never know of the team's involvement no matter what. It made no difference as far as the headline whether or not the mission's outcome was a success or failure. The Pratt & Whitney Double Wasp engines sounded really good and would get COBALT to their final destination. It was a "Rendezvous with Destiny".

John ran all four engines up to 3,500 RPM to get a proficient reading on the gauges. Brad and John looked at each other and smiled. Thumbs up! The DC-6C began to taxi from just outside the hanger as Brad radioed the Melbourne Tower. "This is DC 01145...do you copy?"

The tower quickly answered. "DC 01145...this is Melbourne tower...we copy loud and clear."

"Tower, request permission to take off, over?"

"Permission granted DC 01145. Continue to runway Alpha 2 Tango, copy?'

"Tower, I Roger, proceeding to runway Alpha 2 Tango." Elder's heart started to race as he positioned LAPEARLE for takeoff. The brakes were on and the engines were taken to 6,500 RPM. You could feel the power in the Pratt and Whitney Double Wasp engines. Damn, that sounds really good!

The headsets came to life with the welcome sound from the tower, "DC 01145, you are cleared for takeoff...have a safe trip." With the go ahead from the tower, John Elder let loose of the brakes and the McDonnell Douglas aircraft slowly moved forward. As the plane rolled down the runway faster and faster, the wheels left the tarmac. It was exactly 0711 hours when John checked his ROLEX dive watch. The time...again...another coincidence?

WHEELS UP, 11 /11 /2001

The numbers continued to repeat themselves. Melbourne International Airport was soon distant from them in the west as LAPERLE headed east for a few minutes and then headed south for the first leg of the three-leg journey that would take them to Pakistan. It would be a long flight for the team.

John turned over the flight deck to Brad and headed back to the passenger compartment. The altitude of the DC-6C was 27,000 feet above sea level. The plane was humming along at 300 miles per hour and had an approximate range of 3,000 miles. COBALT was heading to Bogota, Columbia for the first leg of the journey. It was ironic the DC-6C was heading back to Columbia where it had been for so many years after it was purchased by the Cali Drug Mafia for the transportation of both illegal drugs as well as soldiers of the Mafia including their leadership.

Jack, Charles, Carter, and Tucker along with the FBI and CIA and mission specialists were assembled in the COBALT C3. After a short briefing by Captains Knight and Kimble on the weather along the flight plan and in both Pakistan and Afghanistan and a brief review of Operations Security (OPSEC) and the gathered Combat Intelligence Preparation of the Battlefield (Combat IPB), John addressed the assembled team. The instructions were short and definitely applied to the KISS principle followed by many wartime leaders. KISS stands for Keep it Simple Stupid. The more complex a battle plan, the easier it is to FUBAR (Fuck Up Beyond Any Recognition) any operation. John simply said, "Gentleman, some of you have chosen to be here at this time and at this moment. Some have not. We have the same goal for our country, to bring OBL to justice, Dead or Alive. Preferably Alive! None of the team can be sacrificed for the life of this terrorist. In the Corps, everyone comes home. I will bring you back. You have my promise. Give me you're all on this mission so we can all come home to those who love us. Now, check your gear. Check, recheck, and then check it one more time. We cannot tolerate a single mistake. There are no assumptions to be made. Assumptions kill! Any questions?"

There were no questions. John headed to his room and checked in with Brad on his intercom. All was fine on the flight deck. Jack took charge of the review of the weapons inventory. Each checked their assigned weapons. It was all the same way they had been stored a few

KIDNAPPING JESUS

days ago. Jack called out the inventory to Justin. Three AR-10s with M-203 grenade launchers attached. Charles would check off on the list: 50 M-67 hand grenades, 25 claymore mines with detonators, two automatic SAWS (.223cal) with 10,000 rounds of ammunition, eleven 45 caliber M1911 Colt pistols with 3,000 rounds, holsters and three 9 round magazines. There were two spools of detonation (DET) cord with 500 feet to each spool and three LAW, Light Anti-Tank Weapons, shoulder fired rockets. Each man had an individual set of web gear, but Team Cat and Team Mouse were probably the only members of COBALT that would be actually wearing the gear. Additionally, there were eleven cases of Meals Ready to Eat (MREs). It took an hour to check, recheck and check again. Although it seemed like the hundredth time, it was important not only for each member to check their equipment, but the checking-built rapport with the team and strengthened the team as a unit, rather than as individual members. Assumptions kill!

Although John was family to Jack and Charles, friends with Phil, Justin and Brad, John was the leader of these former Marines. He was in charge of this mission! He was responsible for mission success. It wasn't just about the money. It was about justice! It was about freedom! It was about America! He was proud of the team. He was proud of his lineage. He would do his best…he would do his absolute best! The alternative was failure. Second best was death, not only his; it would mean more than just one life…it would be many, many, and more than ever could be counted.

Jack eased out of the secret compartment in the belly of the airplane. It was a cramped area that allowed both Jack and Charles entry and allowed them to review the inventory and restore the weapons into their proper compartments underneath the aircraft floor. Smaller compartments were located throughout the plane where individual weapons were concealed. Or, the weapons could be concealed at opportune moments for a time when they may be needed. In the cockpit, there were two 45 caliber Colts, semiautomatic pistols. These were not part of the inventory. John and Brad, along with Jack and Charles knew of the two pistols, but the knowledge of these two pistols, along with several other weapons, were not to be released to the rest of the team. This was for their protection as well as the protection of the team and the mission.

120

WHEELS UP, 11/11/2001

Jack looked up at Charles as he was exiting the floor compartment and said, "I bet he has us check it again in a few hours." Charles just smiled as he gave his hand to Jack and helped him up the three steps that disappeared underneath the floor. They slid the steel plate back into place and used their battery powered screw drivers to tighten the screws. The carpet was rolled back down, and two seats slid back into place. No one would ever find the weapons catch on this plane, not unless they were looking at a schematic, and even then, the hole was an access point to the many cables used to control the aerodynamic wing surfaces of the aircraft.

Jack did give credit where credit was due when he looked at Charles and said, "That John is one smart man. He knows what he's doing."

As Jack and Charles eased back up the aisle to the C3 where Captain's Knight and Kimble were in contact with the NIA, and the on-screen display on their computer laptops were also projected onto the screens so all could easily see, they bumped into Justin just as he was finishing up inventory on the radios and the satellite cell phones. Jack was completing his report for John. Justin reported all was in order and the equipment checked and rechecked. The communications calls did not need to be made. Keeping their radio signature to a minimum was in the best interests of the team. The profile needed to be kept as low as possible to avoid detection by the prying eyes that were always watching and waiting.

Brad used the intercom from the flight deck to the passenger compartment. It wasn't really an announcement of where they were located as the team followed the route of the aircraft on the overhead projections on the screen. The Global Positioning System (GPS) was great. Pinpoint accuracy of their location along their flight path was real time. Brad's announcement to buckle up and prepare for landing in Bogota, Columbia was exciting. The first leg of the journey was nearly complete. John headed to the flight deck and took over the right seat. He was the Pilot in Command (PIC). Brad would be the PIC for the next leg of the journey.

Everyone was strapped in and all could follow the flight as LAPEARLE began the descent from an altitude of 23,000 feet into El Dorado International Airport (SKBO). The elevation was 8,361 feet. This was an international flight although not all major airlines

KIDNAPPING JESUS

and all legal international traffic comes through Bogota. The terminal they would go through was also known as El Dorado. However, they would park the aircraft at a rented hanger. The hanger was rented by an American Airline Carrier from a small airline that provides support to oil companies. This was routine procedure and the State Department often contacted major air carriers around the world with such requests. It did draw attention, but that could not be helped when security was the major goal of any operation. The hanger was guarded by both Columbian and private guards.

Diplomatic relations with Columbia and the United States were like a roller coaster due to the drug traffic coming from Columbia into the United States supported by illegal operations run by gang like organizations. These were the gangsters that make their money by using the weak, including those that can be brought under absolute control. Control comes in many forms. Drugs and prostitution are but a few of the means to gain and maintain control.

The plane was covered under Diplomatic Immunity obtained by the State Department through the U.S. Embassy in Bogota. Each member of COBALT had a red passport that gave them the same privileges as those assigned to any country's Embassy. It was powerful. They had a cover story that would not change as they made their way to Pakistan. They were after a trail of counterfeit money making its way into the United States. One of the shipping points was traced to Columbia.

Brad radioed the control tower. "El Dorado Tower, this is DC 01145. Request landing instructions?"

The reply came back from the tower. "DC 01145, this is El Dorado Tower. Begin your descent to runway Three One (31) Right. Wind from the west, gusting from five to fifteen miles per hour. Upon exiting the runway, please follow the truck to your hanger."

Brad responded, "Roger Tower…Runway 31 Right. Thanks much."

The Pratt and Whitney engines were throttled back, and the flaps were extended. Not all the way. They were at an altitude of 27,000 feet and the airport and the runway where they were landing was at 8,356 feet. The snowcapped Andes Mountains were breathtaking, and you could plainly see the Meta River flowing from the mountains. The country was beautiful. Plantations outside of the capitol city were laid out perfectly and you could see small farms.

WHEELS UP, 11/11/2001

There were cattle and horse ranches as well. John had descended to 10,000 feet and was still about a mile from the airport. He was lined up on runway 31R and was barely having to crab the aircraft into the wind from the west. The winds from the Andes Mountains could be treacherous and many airplanes have had bumpy rides on both takeoffs and landings and people have had their lives pass before their very eyes.

The wheels were lowered, and the flaps were almost completely down. The DC-6C was about to come home. It had been many years since the DC-6C flew into, or out of, this International Airport. Keeping the aircraft undercover was a precautionary measure. Yet, John knew there were eyes watching the plane wondering what kind of mission was taking place and speculation was surely questioning COBALT's cover story. The aircraft's wheels hit the runway and the engines were throttled back and brakes were applied as the aircraft sailed down the runway. The runway was over 12,000 feet long and the DC-6C only needed about 5,000 feet to land comfortably. LAPEARLE came off the main runway and was greeted by an orange vehicle with a sign that read "FOLLOW ME."

They taxied behind the truck to a small hanger on the northeast side of the airport, located between both of the active runways. A fuel truck was waiting along with two black Chevrolet Suburban SUVs. The DC-6C was waived to a stop just outside the hanger. It had been a seven-and-a-half-hour flight. Not bad. LAPEARLE still had it in her. They were greeted as the door was opened and a small set of stairs pushed forward to the door. Outside at the bottom of the stairway was the Consular General, Charles K. Mathews, second in rank to the U.S. Ambassador. Mister Mathews was accompanied by two drivers and four more men. Although they were all in civilian clothes, John knew these men were Marines stationed at the Embassy for security reasons. This was expected due to the sensitivity of the mission. However, they could rest assured the mission they knew had to do with tracing counterfeit money. The plane was being fueled. Mister Mathews had already signed the paperwork. The State Department would pick up the tab for both the hanger and the fuel. It was easier if the contacts the team of eleven had with the Columbian public were kept to an absolute minimum.

Once the plane was fueled, including the two additional 500-gallon gas tanks installed on the plane during a retrofit when John worked with

KIDNAPPING JESUS

Chuck and non-stop flights across the United States were required, a small tug hooked up to the front landing gear and began to move the aircraft into the hanger. They would need the extra gas for the next leg of their journey. John had already secured the door, and the team had their gear. Two of the men from the Embassy remained behind with the aircraft. They were armed.

John and his team loaded into the large Suburban trucks for their ride to the Embassy compound where they would spend the night. As they left through one of the gates near the El Dorado International Terminal, they showed their Red Passports to the Customs agent. Their gear would not be checked nor would the airplane. Like many airports in the world, you had the best and the worst. Conditions outside the International Airport were great even though there was a State Department Travel Warning in effect warning U.S. citizens of the dangers from narcoterrorism and other criminal groups in the country.

It was beautiful. This was a thriving city and the architecture was breathtaking. Taxis were everywhere and in the different neighborhoods there were upscale shops and great looking restaurants. However, the team would not get to experience the culinary delights of this beautiful Andean city of about seven-million people. The mission was the priority. No matter which mission one was thinking about, John and the team knew the truth.

They arrived at the compound. The vehicle was checked with mirrors. Since the vehicles had not been out of sight of the Embassy Staff, it was quick. Once inside, the team was escorted to the building that controlled the access to the remaining areas of the compound. The team was issued temporary badges but would have an escort during their short stay.

They secured their suitcases and headed to a set of quarters used to house dignitaries when they were in town. As they entered, they could not help noticing the richly appointed apartments to which they were assigned. It was stunning. The local art and furniture were rich. Congressmen and Congresswomen often visited Columbia along with State Department officials. In fact, President Ronald Reagan visited Bogota in 1982 and had stayed in these very quarters with his Staff. It was around 1800 hours when they had finally settled into their quarters. It was 1700 hours back in Melbourne. They had an in-flight lunch of

WHEELS UP, 11 /11 /2001

subway type sandwiches, and all were hungry. They were directed to the cafeteria where dinner was served from 1700 to 2000 hours.

Once they had finished dinner, the Ambassador wanted to meet with the team. He had a message for them received in the Embassy message center via secure communications. It was an "EYES ONLY" message and labeled "TOP SECRET" for the Ambassador alone. It was 1900 hours when the team entered the Ambassador's chambers, and the team was ushered in by an Army Colonel. The Colonel was the senior military officer and advisor to the Ambassador and in charge of the Security Assistance Office. The Ambassador had already opened the sealed folder and had been briefed. He asked the Colonel to step outside the office doors.

Before he asked the team to sit down, he stood up and greeted each of the team members. He already knew their names. This Ambassador had a gift for retaining many details. It had been his life's training, and when the President asked him to take on this assignment, it was a request that could not be refused. The Ambassador and the team took their seats.

As Ambassador Don F. Lynn spoke, the team listened quietly as if the President of the United States were in the Ambassador's chambers himself. "I wish the team much success in the common objective of every law- abiding citizen in the world as you pursue your objective for peace and harmony. It is a task that must be undertaken and won. We will take the fight to any corner in the world if it will but save one life. Your mission is worth the risk. I wish you God's speed and know you will be successful in bringing this operation to successful closure."

The Ambassador did not have to know what the President was inferring to in his message to this team. It was clear from his combined 32 years of service within the Foreign Service, the State Department and two tours in the Navy what this team's mission was. They were hunting public enemy number one, OBL. The Ambassador asked John if he could be of any more assistance.

John replied, "Ambassador, my team and I want to thank you and your Staff for their courtesies. We have been treated extremely well and did not want to draw any undue attention. We are focused on our goal, and in the morning will depart Bogotá enroute to Seville, Spain. It is a long journey, and we will be in the air upwards of 20 to 24 hours

KIDNAPPING JESUS

depending on the prevailing winds. If all goes well, we'll be landing in Seville on the 13th. So, what I would like to ask you is that we all share a shot of bourbon whiskey with you toasting our future success and thanking you for your hospitality. With that, the Ambassador asked the Colonel to step back into his quarters and pour a round of drinks for them all. John simply said, "Here, here!" The shot glasses filled with Wild Turkey 101 were quickly drained, handshakes were extended by all, and the Colonel escorted the team back to their apartments. Nothing else was needed. A lone Marine sentry was on duty and would be relieved at midnight. The team's day was done. Nothing needed to be said as they all retired to their respective rooms and prepared for the next day. It would be rise and shine at zero-dark-thirty.

The team was awakened at 0430 hours when their alarms went off. Although they were tired, they met in the lobby of the apartments and did their stretches. Some light exercises, pushups and sit-ups, then outside for a short run around the compound. A couple of the Marines joined them as they ran. They would need the exercise just to keep loose. At 0500 hours, they headed for their rooms, showered and packed, and then met again at 0600 hours. They went to the cafeteria where the Colonel and the Ambassador had a table ready for the team. The 13 of them had a great breakfast of sausage, eggs and pancakes with juice and coffee.

At 0645 hours, they were met by two black Chevrolet Suburban's and taken to the hanger the American carrier had rented on their behalf. It was an uneventful trip. It did not take long to get to the airport and traffic was light. The sun was already on the rise and it looked like it would be another great day. So far, they had done very well, but it only would take one slip of the tongue or something unforeseen to put COBALT in harm's way. The ground crew had already pulled the plane out of the hanger and the Marines left with the plane were present as well. They saluted the arriving entourage and then exchanged some small talk with a couple of the Team members while John and Brad performed the walk around of the aircraft while the team loaded up the plane with their luggage.

John and Brad entered the aircraft, and the ladder was removed and the door closed and cross checked. John fired up the Pratt and Whitney engines and checked his gauges. All was ready. Waves were exchanged

WHEELS UP, 11/11/2001

through the cockpit windows; the tower was called and the request for departure from El Dorado International Airport was granted. DC 01145 was cleared to Runway 31L and takeoff towards the northwest. The winds were about 20 miles per hour and were almost from due north. Once airborne, they would head to the east and to Seville, Spain. Brad radioed the tower for final clearance as LAPEARLE revved up the engines and checked the flaps of the DC-6C. LAPEARLE began the takeoff roll down the runway and soon they were airborne. It was 0811 hours in the morning when the wheels left the runway. The landing gear was retracted and LAPEARLE slowly banked to a heading of 90 degrees. It was bumpy and they experienced some Clear Air Turbulence (CAT) as they climbed to an altitude of 33,000 feet. This day would be a long one for the team. It was November 12th, another day, and another leg of the journey. Just one day at a time.

The Pratt and Whitney engines were running flawlessly. LAPEARLE was quite a lady. John thought back to his days with Pearle. Now there was a lady. She was the real "McCoy". It was too bad that both John and Pearle were so independent. They needed each other and were a comfort to each other, but each needed their space. It had been a hectic life being a bounty hunter and knowing someone depended on you could be dangerous should your attention be drawn away from the task at hand. Brad had the first shift. The plane was on automatic pilot. Jack was called to the cockpit on the intercom and would keep Brad company. John eased out of the right-hand seat and Jack took his place. Brad was the Pilot in Command for this leg of the journey. Brad knew the plane as well as John. John checked on Ted and David. They were at the Command Center. Both screens were on. FOX News was covering the cleanup efforts at the Twin Towers and recapping the events from both Pennsylvania and from the Pentagon.

President George W. Bush was holding a press conference. He addressed America's effort on the Global War against terrorism, the progress in Afghanistan against the Taliban and Americas hunt for the World's public enemy number one, Osama Bin-Laden. The reaction of the team could be felt. It was like there was static electricity in the air. There were no words spoken, but each could feel the tenseness. The hairs on the backs of their necks were standing on edge. The President knew of the covert mission and John knew the President of

KIDNAPPING JESUS

the United States was relying on the team to be successful. Again, due to the secrecy of the mission, only a handful of people in the Nation's Capital knew of the true intent of the team's mission. A leak to the press could destroy any chance of success.

On the other screen was a Global Positioning System and the airspace they were in was displayed. You could make out in any details if you chose to do so with the functions that were available. They were just beginning to reach the coast of Venezuela and the North Atlantic Ocean. They were north of the Equator and beginning to head to the northeast just north of Grenada. Many of the West Indie's islands would be below them for some time as they stretched LAPEARLE towards Gibraltar and Seville, Spain. The flight distance was almost 5,000 miles. In the approach to Seville, they would fly along the coast of Morocco and keep Africa on the starboard side of the DC-6C. It would be quite a ride.

John asked both Captains for an update, but there was nothing to report. No news on America's Number One enemy. Apparently, OBL was still somewhere in Afghanistan in his mountain headquarters safely tucked away from the prying eyes of Uncle Sam. The National Intelligence Agency (NIA) was gathering both Signals Intelligence (SIGINT) and Human Intelligence (HUMINT) from many different sectors and from many allies. OBL was not just America's number one enemy but an enemy to the entire population of a peace- loving world. OBL had many followers and supporters and there is never a shortage for sponsors to support terrorism. John thanked the team for their dedication and professionalism and suggested they get their rest. They would need it in the days and weeks to come. Ted and David, the mission specialists, maintained communications with the Pentagon and the NIA and anyone with a need to know that contacted the flight. David would get a break first as the two Captains worked their own schedule. One of the two would always be awake during the operation. Ted had already contacted the Embassy in Seville and notified them they were enroute and were advised that the Ambassador in Bogota was awaiting news of their arrival in Spain.

John headed for his cabin to catch up on some reading. Maps were on the wall of both Pakistan and Afghanistan with OBL's last known location plotted on the map. The terrain was absolutely horrible.

WHEELS UP, 11/11/2001

However, there were trails that had been used for years for goats and sheep that covered the mountainous region. One point was very clear. OBL needed logistics to survive. He had to have supplies. He also had to have power to run his equipment. Even in the most extreme conditions in the world, from the North Pole to the Antarctic, in the Deserts or in outer space, signals are generated. Cell phones can be traced, movement on ground can be tracked, and if generators are being used, then the output can be located. Heat is generated and can be seen through infrared sensors on satellites. Even submarines can be tracked by the disturbance they make on the surface of the oceans when they are completely submerged, or at least, they once could be during the old days before the Cold War was over and the Berlin Wall came down.

John had read the dispatches concerning the factions involved among the terrorist cells, including the Taliban tribes. For the differences, there was little to be done to recognize how the tribes were linked to the cells, except the tribes were concerned about their real estate and ruling all that ventured into their domain. The price Al Queda paid could not be measured in simple dollars, but in an unbinding loyalty to each other and a common enemy in non-Arab nations, or nations that embrace democracy, whether they be Arab or not. Sunnis versus Shiites versus the Kurds, it was a real mess. How could this even be about religion and how could the name of Allah be invoked in all the bloodshed that was daily life, the political turbulence in these countries contributes to the inability to hunt down the terrorist bastards.

Just like in Vietnam, the enemy had learned the importance of digging in and popping out to hit their enemy. In Nam, the enemy was literally able to hide whole Cong Battalions underground. John had seen the caves and had fought hand-to-hand for every inch of ground when they went underground to smoke out the determined enemy. In Pakistan, John must trust his CIA and FBI team members. They were great guys, and each had a story about their personal trials in Afghanistan and in the United States. Aasim, Abdul, and Mustafa were professionals, and both the CIA and FBI were absolutely sure these men were totally trustworthy, Regardless, John was absolutely sure about one thing, assumptions kill and these three were last minute additions to COBALT.

KIDNAPPING JESUS

John would have liked more time to check them out. Deputy Director Sullivan had not been able to dig up any dirt concerning any of these three men, but once in Pakistan or in Afghanistan, something could change and John wanted to ensure that if one of these three men were going to give the team's true mission away, John would have a permanent solution to their treacherous act, if, or when, it occurred. John checked out his watch. It was two hours into the flight, and he was going to get some rest as Brad and Jack had the flight deck under control. Ted had the COBALT Command Communications Center under control. It was time to get some rack time.

John was abruptly awakened by a loud noise. It sounded like a small explosion and the DC-6C was shaking violently. Everyone was awake and trying to get to their seats and get their seatbelts on. The plane pitched to the left. John reached the cockpit and both Brad and Jack had their hands on the wheel. Brad was feathering the number two engine and John was looking at the instrument panel in order to get a better idea what was taking place. The number two engine was dead and there was no oil pressure.

There was no point in jumping in to assist. Brad was the seasoned pilot and was making all the necessary decisions that must be made. John had confidence in his friend and to step in now would complicate matters even more. Once the number two engine was feathered, Brad throttled back the number three engine to keep the plane steady. The altitude would have to be dropped.

"Brad how far are we from Seville?" John asked.

"We are about 500 miles out, and our airspeed has dropped to 250mph. Ground speed is 260mph. We should be on the ground in less than two hours. I need to call Seville Air Traffic Control and declare an in-flight emergency as we drop out of our flight level. We could maintain 33,000 feet but I recommend we drop down to 12,000 feet in case we have problems with pressurization."

John changed seats with Jack. Jack lingered in the cockpit before he headed back to the cabin. Brad and John spoke about the engine and the situation.

130

WHEELS UP, 11/11/2001

Brad made the call. He had checked in when they reached the airspace controlled by Air Traffic Control in Seville. "Seville Tower (SVQ), this is DC 01145, over."

"DC 01145 this is SVQ, over."

"SVQ, this is DC 01145 declaring an in-flight emergency. We have a blown engine on the portside and have throttled back. Request permission to descend to 12,000 feet as we make our approach to land, over."

"DC 01145, is there any other trouble with the plane other than the engine and do you request rescue standing by over?"

"Negative for rescue standing by SVQ, the situation is under control, over."

"DC 01145, descend to a flight level of 12,000 feet and turn to a heading of 110 degrees. You are cleared to Runway 3C…The pattern has been cleared for your approach. Contact Seville Air Traffic Control if there is a requirement for ground support."

"SVQ, this is DC 01145, Roger, Out."

LAPEARLE would need a new engine. This was a major complication and the delay was not calculated into the timetable. John used the intercom and requested Captain Knight to come forward. "Ted, I need you to make a call before we touch down. Get the Pentagon on the phone and find out where the nearest operational spare Pratt and Whitney engine is located. It's time to get some support from Uncle Sam. We'll pay for it; just get one to Seville ASAP. We don't have a week or more to sit on the ground in Spain. We're not here for the scenery. Let me know what you find out. Thanks!"

Ted replied, "Not a problem, I'll make the call."

It was 1000 hours in the morning. It was almost a 21-hour flight through five time-zones as they crossed the Atlantic Ocean.

Time was also the enemy and the weather conditions in the mountainous passes could be as insurmountable as any wall ever built by man and it was now November 14th. A day was lost in time as the team continued to close the distance to their objective. Thirty-thousand dollars for a replacement engine was a drop in the bucket compared to the reward money offered for OBL, Dead or Alive. The cost was not the issue. However, the issue at hand was time that would be lost. Time and the weather this time of year in the mountains of Afghanistan was unpredictable. If the snow hit hard, it would be futile to try and traverse

131

KIDNAPPING JESUS

the mountains. They needed a quick exit. The more time spent trying to escape would lead to their detection and destruction.

The approach was beginning to take shape as LAPEARLE descended to flight level 50 (5,000 feet) Above Ground Level (AGL). The Seville Airport was only 20 feet above sea level and was located about six miles northwest of Seville. John and Brad could make out the Guadalquivir River running through Seville into the Gulf of Cadiz and into the Atlantic Ocean. This was quite a large seaport with oceangoing vessels. Spain's second longest river was beautiful and a significant landmark from the air as they followed the southwesterly flowing river to the Seville Airport. They began their approach as directed by SVQ onto Runway 09N.

Once they touched down, they were sent to a hanger rented by a British Air Carrier. Yes, the British government had been contacted and requested the airlines rent a hanger for the DC-6C. It was a great arrangement and John was thankful the British were among America's allies in the war against terrorism. The flaps were down, and the airspeed dropped as they neared the welcome runway. The wheels touched down. It was 1001 hours, local time in Seville. Just like in Bogota, they were met by military members of the American Consulate General from Seville. The American Embassy was located in Madrid. The Consulate General had sent two Suburban SUVs from the motor pool to meet the team. Knowing the team back in the United States was providing the much-needed ground support at each of the stops along the journey was a relief. They were greeted by first-class service. Here again, they wanted to keep a low profile. Terrorists were operating throughout the world under many guises, including charitable organizations that supplied a cover for money being laundered around the world supporting many illicit causes including terrorist acts directed at peace loving governments and their citizens. The threads were like a noose around every law-abiding citizen in the world.

Two U.S. Marines secured the aircraft as it was parked in the hanger. COBALT had their gear, and the plane was in safe hands. A Customs Agent was at the hanger along with the State and Foreign Service Departmental Officials. He quickly reviewed the diplomatic passports and spoke to the Consular General. Mr. Mark C. Clarke had been on station for two years in his current position and knew the ropes. He

WHEELS UP, 11/11/2001

also knew this senior Customs Agent and his background check was impeccable. Senor Ferdinand Torres was a trusted agent and could be counted upon not to speak of the people exiting the aircraft.

Senor Torres simply said to Mr. Clarke, "There will be no problems with the plane. We will ensure no one enters the surrounding area except as cleared through your orders. We expect your engine will arrive tomorrow. We were contacted by the British and informed that a British Air Carrier would be delivering the engine from London's Heathrow Airport. It will be treated as a diplomatic package and will be sent to the hanger for your inspection and installation. A team of mechanics have been notified. They are cleared to work on the engine, and you should have your men present during the installation." Senor Torres did not know any more of the details of how the engine was to be delivered to Heathrow. It did not matter to him. The British were delivering the engine so as not to arouse undue suspicion of a U.S. Air Carrier landing at the San Pablo Airport in Seville.

It was a fantastic ride to the Consulate. No incidents. There were so many historic sites along the way; it was very difficult to comprehend what they were seeing although they were getting the dime tour from Mark Clarke. They arrived shortly before noon. As soon as they were checked and rechecked at the gate to the Consulate, the vehicles were parked next to a small building that served as quarters for guests. It would be tight. Several of the team members would have to share rooms. It would not be like the accommodations in Bogota, but better than what they could expect once they hit the ground in Pakistan. It was a journey. Life was a journey, and they were on a mission as important as any mission undertaken throughout history. The consequences of their actions could immobilize terrorist activities for the foreseeable future. Cutting the head off a serpent was never easy, but hopefully the body would whither. It was almost as if this was a battle in yet another World War being waged throughout the world. The gear was quickly unloaded, and a Marine Captain introduced himself to the group.

Captain Mike Harbin was a decorated hero from the first Gulf War. He had risen in rank from Staff Sergeant to Captain by way of the Officer Candidate School he applied for after the war was over. He had earned a bachelor's degree during his ten years of enlisted service, and, while in Desert Storm, earned the Navy Cross for his heroism in

KIDNAPPING JESUS

saving many of the men in his squad from certain death while risking his own life many times over. Captain Harbin was awarded the second highest medal for valor allowed by the Marine Corps, Navy and the Coast Guard. He had joined the ranks of a group of heroes.

The details were spared, but John, Jack and Charles had heard of this Marine and knew of his heroism. It was an honor to meet this Marine type just like the Army Audie Murphy and Marine Gregory "Pappy" Boyington of World War II.

They got their chow at the small cafeteria. It was great. Spanish cuisine was always welcome. Mike was to be their escort. Captains Knight and Kimble left the cafeteria and were directed to the small communications center with their laptop computers. They would monitor the situation in Pakistan and in the mountainous regions of Afghanistan, updates from the U.S., and the progress of delivering the rebuilt Pratt and Whitney engine from Heathrow to Seville. They would be on shifts for the next 24 hours or more.

After their lunch, the teams, minus the two Captains, went to their small apartments and were able to unwind and get a change of clothes and clean up. They should have done the three S's (Shit, Shower and Shave) before lunch, but meals were always better fresh than warmed over. A nap was in order for most of the team. John wanted to check in with the Captains at the Consulate Command Center. The mobile COLBALT C3 was in high gear and John wanted an update.

Captain Knight greeted John when he came into the Command Center. There were several Marines present as well as a couple of civilians that were part of the State Department contingent stationed at the Consulate. Ted and John stepped over to one of the unoccupied cubicles in the Center. Nothing changed. The cover story remained one of fishing for the currency trail funding the terrorists. Although Mike was suspicious, as were many who were assigned Consular duty, none asked the nagging questions they might have thought about asking. It was always on a need-to-know basis. Keep your suspicions to yourself and don't start rumors. If a rumor led back to the originator, then someone could get in serious trouble even though there were no serious intentions. The consequences could be permanent. Nothing had changed except the timetable. Ted updated John with a weather report. The Pratt and Whitney engine was inbound to Heathrow from Ireland and should

134

WHEELS UP, 11 /11 /2001

arrive in about two hours. The engine should be on its way to Seville in about four hours and then on the ground and installed the next day. If everything went according to the new timetable, COBALT would be on their way to Afghanistan on the morning of the 16th". It would take the maintenance team an estimated 20 hours to install the new engine.

The equipment was being readied and the blown engine being removed. Captain Kimble was at the hanger with another Marine, Gunnery Sergeant Les Hanson. He had radioed back to Ted that all was going well. There was no cover issue with the maintenance crew and Senor Torres was at the hanger along with the two Marines on Security duty for the plane. The only one issue was that the new engine was $40,000 dollars. This was not a budget concern, but additional expenses were never a welcome sight. Uncle Sam had found the engine and arranged the transportation, but John owed the money to a major British airline and to the crew for replacing the engine. He and Brad would have to take it for a test flight with the head mechanic once the work was completed.

Rather than having a bank transfer the needed funds, John would pay using a special line of credit he had established through the Bank of the Greater Grand Cayman Islands. John had placed $1 Million dollars in the account. Another $500,000 dollars was deposited as an advance by the U.S. State Department. It was his money and he wanted it available if and when it was needed regardless of the situation. One of his mentors had taught him that "a scared dollar never made a dollar"! Those words of wisdom were from Chuck Taylor. When going for the bad guys, sometimes a couple of $20 dollar bills would go a long way in the apprehension and the bounty money was really good in sharp comparison if just a few dollars more would, or could, make a huge difference in success or failure. John easily adopted Chuck's philosophy and it became his own rule.

If all went well, the engine should arrive that evening and the crew of engineers could complete the installation the next day. When their work was finished, a test flight would be needed to ensure all systems were ago. The team then should be able to be on their way the following day for the third, and last, leg of their flight in their attempt to attain their objective. Target OBL was coming closer to Team COBALT's sights and the need for speed was paramount; however, the Team knew

KIDNAPPING JESUS

that rushing headlong into any situation, without the requisite planning and attention to detail, could be devastating.

John rounded up the team and brought them to his apartment. All were assembled. John briefed the team on the current situation. Captains Knight and Kimble presented the Combat Intelligence gathered from both SIGINT and HUMINT. The weather report for Pakistan and Afghanistan was reviewed. If predictions held true, winter was on its way for the mountain passes they would have to travel through to get to their final objective. The team believed that their target was already on the ground. In fact, the Pentagon believed many of the Al Queda leadership had made their pilgrimage to the mountains to meet personally with Osama Bin-Laden before winter set in so they could begin their winter offensive. Planning more major attacks throughout the world with the magnitude of a 9/11 was their goal. If the team could capture, or kill, many of the terrorist leadership, there was the distinct possibility plans could be disrupted and potential plots of death and destruction in the planning stages avoided. Targeted countries included Spain and Britain, as well as selected Embassies throughout the world. High value targets were always on the threat list.

John's inner thoughts moved right along with the briefing. His team was an instrument of politics. It was a balancing act of every government. The National Security Strategy of the United States is supported through the National Military Strategy with the ways, means and ends (just like a three- legged stool) used to achieve National Security. Team COBALT was the "means," a capability that could possibly achieve an objective with acceptable risk. The covert operation was the "ways", the concept to achieve the objective. And the elimination of Osama Bin-Laden was the "ends." The elimination of OBL was the objective for COBALT.

Although they were expendable, plausible deniability could be used to mask the intentions of the United States Government. Everyone knew that should the operation be compromised, they would be dead, the mission a failure, and the news media would print a story that would put all the cards on the table. The Press would be able to buy someone and the story for a traitorous amount of cash. Judas sold out our Savior and Benedict Arnold sold out our Nation. There was always someone

136

WHEELS UP, 11 /11 /2001

out there that could be bought for a few coins of the realm. Life was very cheap to many as were liquid loyalties. Whores know no country.

John jumped back to reality. The briefing was over. John looked at the team and thanked them for their commitment. John looked at Ted and Dave and asked for a volunteer to man the Operations Center for the evening. Ted was it. John asked Brad and Jack to go to the hanger to oversee the operations. The engine was out, the aircraft mechanics and engineers were on stand-by and Senor Torres would be on hand to ensure all was well with Customs. John looked at the rest of the team and stated that in 30 minutes, they would head into town and have a great meal and see if they could find some quiet trouble. He apologized to those stuck with the dirty duty, but if another opportunity came up, they would be taken care of. There was no problem. They knew their duty and they were all responsible. To be irresponsible or to be unresponsive was not an option. Captain Mike Harbin and Gunny Les Hanson would be joining the remaining eight members of the team. They were part of the escort and would ensure the team was taken care of in establishments visited by locals and many of the different nationalities of the various consulates located in Seville. It would be upscale and relatively safe.

As they loaded into the Suburban, John looked at the drivers just to verify he knew who they were. John was good with faces and names. He knew the two young drivers were both Marines and would stay with the vehicles or would pick them up. It was suggested they just get dropped off and walk to their destination. This would be safer and allow them to blend into the public. Aasim, Mustafa, Abdul, Charles, Dave, Justin, Phil, and John loaded up along with Les and Mike. Les went with Aasim, Abdul, Charles and Phil, and Mike went with the rest of the team in the other vehicle.

This is the way they would go into town. Two separate groups, but they would never be out of sight of one another. The best club in town with great food and dancing was the Black Diamond. Locals rubbed the shoulders of the elite consulate members that would gravitate to this nightspot. The best- looking women from all walks of life were also on the hunt for a good time. The conditions were perfect. John had set up a bet with his group just like it was old times at the Non-Commissioned Officers Club back at Camp Pendleton when he bet

KIDNAPPING JESUS

with other First Sergeants and Sergeants Majors on who would get lucky. The first to dance with a girl gets $20 dollars from each of the group. And the first to get laid, an added $20 dollars. It was chump change, but a bet just raised the heightened state of the hunt. Although some of the team members were married, they were all in. What happened in Seville, stayed in Seville! After all, sex was an aphrodisiac, and the hormones of these warriors were raging.

They were dropped off a couple of blocks away at different locations and about ten minutes apart. It was going to be a night out in the town. John was pleased with his team. The workouts continued even during the long flights. There were no weights on board, but there were compact isometric machines that worked out the muscles. There was even a treadmill. With their booster shot of steroids, the core of the team was rock hard. Those who had joined the team after the training regimen at Camp Stacey were fit, but not like John, Jack, Charles, Phil and Justin. It was the fountain of youth. If used properly, men could look like they came out of Soldier of Fortune magazine. John's group got to the Club before the other team. Dinner and drinks were soon ordered. They had a reserved table and just about 30 feet away another table had been reserved. It was for the other group.

Mike had shared it with them while they were walking to the famous nightclub that the Palace they could see was known as Casa Pilatos. It was ironic that this 16th century palace was a copy of the palace of Pontius Pilate in Jerusalem. Pilate was the Roman Governor that history remembers as the reluctant instrument to the crucifixion of Jesus Christ.

138

WHEELS UP, 11/11/2001

Casa Pilatos in Seville, Spain – Reproduction of Palace of Pontius Pilate

John wanted to have a prime rib. Spain was famous for their cuisine. Mike took the liberty of ordering the wine and sherry. Along with the order, gazpacho, a cold, tomato-based soup, was ordered as an appetizer.

They were just relaxing when the other group came into the club and were escorted to their table. There were no exchanges except a brief look by John. The team knew they needed to be on their guard, even if they were out to have a good time. The band was getting started. It was just after 1800 hours. Mixed drinks were brought out as were the wine and sherry. The gazpacho was great. The drinks were great, and the background music was excellent. The club was upstairs, and the party would really begin around 2000 hours.

The meal would be served at a leisurely pace. After the soup, there was a salad. A very nice salad with fresh vegetables and oil-based dressing. The bread was hot and freshly made. The steaks arrived around 1900

KIDNAPPING JESUS

hours. The Prime Rib was one of the many specialties of the Club. There was also the Rack of Lamb, Lobster and huge prawn shrimp, and other meals fit for a king and his queen. But John was a meat eater as were most of the team. Mustafa ordered the Lamb and Mike ordered the Lobster. Dave ordered a Filet Mignon and Justin ordered the Prime Rib as well. Served with their meals were baked potatoes, mixed vegetables, mashed potatoes. There were waiters walking around with skewers of meat, chicken, lamb, and shrimp. You could add it to your plate if you wanted something else to go with your main meal. There was also a choice of vegetables offered. It was a feast.

It was around 2030 hours when the group pushed away from their table. John picked up the tab and left a generous tip. They had been served well. No courtesy was spared. The other group would soon be finished. John and half the team went upstairs to join the festivities. There was a small group of guitarists on the stage playing Spanish ballads. It was nice, but it helped to relax, have an after-dinner drink, and scope out the early arrivals.

John did a double take as he looked towards the entrance to the upstairs dance floor. His heart skipped a beat. He was staring at a black-haired beauty. She was with a couple of girlfriends, but John seemed not to notice. She could have been Pearle's younger sister. She was five-foot six-inches tall. Her hair was so dark; it looked like it had blue highlights. Her eyes, well, her eyes were dark blue. And, when she looked at John, she stopped for a moment. Her friends on either side first looked at her, then at John. And, then their looks switched from John to the others seated around him.

John stood up and made a sweeping gesture as he invited the ladies to their table. The introductions began with John introducing the men at the table. Mustafa's name was altered to Markus. Markus was from the Philippines. Elaine, the dark-haired beauty introduced her to two friends. The blond was Stephanie and Mary was the redhead. All three were beauties. Elaine sat next to John and although they were in a fairly large group, quiet conversations were taking place with the music in the background. It sounded like Smooth Operator. Elaine was about 120 pounds, slender and sensuous in every respect. Smiles and whispers led to some closeness. The others had made their friends as well. Mike

140

WHEELS UP, 11 /11 /2001

and Mustafa, alias Markus, were the odd men out, for the time being. It would not be long until they were paired up as well.

When the other group of five walked in, they had moved to another table with two dark-haired beauties. Mike knew one of the ladies they were with, but the other he had never seen. Just as the band began to play dance music, John jumped up with Elaine and headed to the dance floor. That was an $80 dollar dance that the team would have to pay later. It was a slow dance and Elaine and John felt the heat of the night. Elaine was limber and her hands were like a torch when they touched John on the shoulder. It was like a storybook love story. As the night grew late, all the men started to pair off with their ladies of choice. Mike and Les informed the team the Chevrolet Suburban's would come back to their drop off points at 30- minute intervals beginning at midnight until the last man was picked up. This had been prearranged with the team. Each had their cell phones.

In fact, shortly after 2200 hours, John was called by Jack. The Pratt and Whitney engine, code named Painted Egg, was in the Basket. The Basket was the Hanger. LAPEARLE was the Goose. Jack only said, "John, hope you are having a great time! The Painted Egg is in the Basket and will be united with the Goose." That was it. John closed his phone. Dave was with Stephanie and Justin was dancing with Mary. John looked around at his men, and they were all having a great time. It was around 2300 hours when John informed Mike he was heading out. His men saw him leave the Club with Elaine. They too would soon leave. At least most of them would leave the Club with a lady.

Not all would be lucky tonight. However, they all checked their watches. It would be the honor system as to who was laid first. The odds were on John at this point in the ball game, but you never knew.

John went with Elaine to her small one-bedroom flat. It was just down the street. In fact, Elaine's other two girlfriends lived in the same small apartment complex over the stores that were on the streets. The buildings were hundreds of years old and the rooms, although air con-ditioned, were 14 feet high with large archways to keep the heat up towards the ceiling. John went inside and sat down for a glass of wine. There was some small talk about the city, but Elaine had other ideas. She was a wild one. She was 35 years old, liked rugged men, and when she

141

got what she wanted, she cut to the chase. No games and no gimmicks. She was all woman.

Elaine was all over John. She first removed his shirt and then her own. John was muscular and that was exciting to Elaine. Even though he was 52 years old, John looked like he could be 40 years old; he was in that good of shape. He also had a full head of hair, dark brown with a few gray hairs, but not a head full of gray hair. Elaine turned down the lights and removed her own shirt. Her bra was black lace. She was close. He was taken aback a little by her aggressiveness and yet she had seemed fairly calm in the Club even though the dancing was danger close as they gently touched each other. But Elaine was like an "un-caged" wild cat behind doors. John always liked taming wild cats...it was something he was adept at doing. After four hours of love making, John kissed Elaine tenderly as he left her apartment at 0330 hours in the morning. He promised he would return as soon as possible. It was not going to be a problem. It was all about the sex, nothing more.

He headed to the street corner where the Suburban should be, and he could just make it out. Although the lights were off, John was walking down the dimly lit street unaware of a man watching his every move. As he walked by a street crossing, the driver of the Suburban flashed his lights about the same time. John stopped in his tracks. Something was wrong. The hairs on the back of his neck were standing.

He was ready when the shadow of a large man came to life and jumped out at him with a knife in his hand trying to sink it into his heart. John could make out the sound of the Suburban door close and the footsteps of a Marine coming quickly in his direction. His senses were heightened. John saw the flash of the knife as the dim streetlight hit the shiny blade. He turned just in time as the robber's knife came across his chest missing flesh but catching his light Jacket. John's response was textbook perfect. The robber just didn't know he was already dead but continued with his initial thought of trying to kill John for his money. It was over in seconds as John grabbed the thief's wrist and turned it upward causing the tendons to stretch and the large knife to drop from his useless hand. It was a painful hold and the thief was already on his toes in excruciating pain. Holding the wrist with his left hand, Elder took his right hand and brought it up with such force he heard the bone snap like dried wood.

WHEELS UP, 11 /11 /2001

It was a bad night in Seville for this guy. The robber would have killed his prey by now, but this was different. This was a man who knew how to protect himself. That was the last thought that went through the robber's brain as Elder moved so quickly and placed the would-be thief in a Special Forces choke hold removing his wind pipe with one swift jerk.

The Marine Sergeant caught up with him searching to see if there were any more. He was on his portable phone to the Consulate. Along with a barking dog down the street, a small choking sound could be heard that came from the robber but there was no one around to hear death. John turned to the Marine as they both walked back to the Suburban. The other truck showed up and five Marines and a Spanish diplomat assigned to the Consulate got out. It was over. John left with the Marine. The cleanup detail would contact the local authorities with a cover story.

It was just after 0400 hours when John finally arrived back at his apartment. He needed a quick shower and shave. He read the notes left for him by Captain Knight. Brad was at the hanger monitoring the installation as the rebuilt Pratt and Whitney engine was being installed. The SITREPS were short and concise. No problems, weather perfect at destination for the next one to two weeks, but after that, it looked as if the snow would begin in earnest. At this point, weather predictions were educated guesses.

The engine should be installed by 1500 hours. If an engine test could be completed with an in-flight safety check performed by Brad, John and the Senior Flight Engineer, COBALT could be on its way in short order. It would come down to Brad and the Flight Engineer making the flight as John, being the leader of COBALT, could not be risked at this stage of the mission. That decision was already made by the Pentagon, John just was not yet aware it had been decided for him. There was one other note for him from Charles. It was basic. All team members accounted for and present for duty. You win if you were first to bed Elaine before 0025 hours. John smiled. He would wait until the group met and they would settle the wager like true gentlemen. The last thing from Charles was breakfast would be at 1000 hours following a short run at 0900 hours. John hit the rack hard.

KIDNAPPING JESUS

It was soon 0830 hours in the morning. John had visions of sweet sugar plums spinning in his head. Of course, the sugar plums reminded him of Elaine. He jumped into his running clothes and tennis shoes and met some of the team members outside. Phil, Justin, Charles and Mustafa were there. John was coming out of the apartments rubbing the sleep out of his eyes. Brad was still at the hanger and Dave was in the rack getting some sleep. Ted was on duty at the Command Center. Aasim and Abdul were already in the weight room. They were not much for running, but their upper and lower body strength was impressive. It looked like all were present for duty. Mike Harbin was jogging towards them. He would run the circuit with them. Mike was always ready for a run. In fact, the Marines were always ready for a run. It was an individual sport, but one where camaraderie could be shared at the same time.

It was a short run, being just over three miles. Many of them silently hummed the Jodie calls to themselves as they ran. It kept their minds off the run. It was a mental skill they had learned. The joke was that if they didn't mind, then it wouldn't matter. It was truly mind over matter. John laughed out loud. They did their daily dozen and knocked out push-ups and sit-ups. Then they hit the showers and dressed for breakfast.

Once breakfast had been served, they met at the Consulate Command Center. Mr. Clarke met the team there. Mike was asked to step out and ensure that while the team met with Mr. Clarke they would not be interrupted. Mark reviewed the incident from the night before. The rest of the team looked at John. Nothing was said, and there were no exchanges of questions. It was how they were all supposed to act if they were confronted. Make the kill, ask questions later. The Consulate would absorb the heat. It was a diplomatic affair. COBALT could not be delayed.

Mark said something interesting as well. It appeared there was some chatter on the channels and back channels as to the mission the team was undertaking. Some eyes were turning their direction. The search for the counterfeit money trail, although a cover for the intent of the team's focus, was still dangerous ground to be treaded upon. Money was the root of all evil, and man and woman lusted over it, dreamed of it, and killed and died for it.

WHEELS UP, 11 /11 /2001

Mr. Clarke believed this team was on a mission of the utmost secrecy and he felt after his years of service with both the Navy and later in the Foreign Service he could sniff out the real target. This one was difficult, but he felt with all the movement at the highest levels in support of this team, it was unlikely it was just counterfeit money they were after. It might be the carrot, but the team was the stick. Someone was going down. This team was good. Not a scratch on John, and a hardened thief dead on the streets of Seville? John, the oldest of the team, looked as if he were in his early 40's and in tip top shape. The others in the team were in great shape as well. Although he was an observer, Mark felt this small contingent could wage a small war anywhere and win. John thanked Mark for his support and asked if the team could borrow the Command Center for a few minutes.

John looked at the team and smiled. They all wanted to know who won the money. Charles asked the team if any of them could beat 0025. Looking around, none spoke. Charles looked at John at said, "John, I know you are quite a lover, and you're my brother, but if you beat my time, I'll double our personal wager. Did you take Elaine to bed before 0025 hours?"

John responded, "Charles, you're a good man, but yes I did. We were going at it by 2345 hours. She was a wild one, an untamed cat. And, yes, it was sex, sex and more sex. And she had a body men kill for. It is hard to believe I had any energy this morning. In fact, I am glad you doubled the wage. I'm not a hundred percent sure, but I think I may have beat your time twice."

They all laughed at that. Now, it was back to the business at hand. He needed the status of the engine replacement, so John called Brad. It was still on time for a 1500 hours completion. The weather was still holding in the mountains near the famous Khyber Pass. Conditions along the route looked good. John felt encouraged.

It was believed by the National Command Authority, from the intelligence gathered by the National Intelligence Agency, that the heads of Al Queda were meeting in one of the mountainous hideaways in Afghanistan. The speculation was that they were planning multiple attacks throughout the world. It appeared to be sort of a chain reaction that could cripple governments and attack the will of the people causing destabilization of entire economies. According to intelligence estimates, there was a lot of movement this time of year through the mountain passes. Equipment and people were moving. Moving exactly where was the question. Some of this movement had to be diversionary in nature.

OBL was a smart man and knew he was being watched. He knew when and where the satellites were and when they would cross his airspace. He also knew there were U.S. military led three-man or four-man Long Range Reconnaissance Patrol (LRRP) teams on the ground trying to pick up his trail. These teams were very skilled at killing from a distance while remaining hidden. He also knew there were plans to capture or kill him. He also knew he had a price on his head and one of his own trusted servants would turn on him if they could. He was a hunted man. He was both a man on the run and a man on the attack. He had been the mastermind of many such attacks, and his mission, he believed, was to continue to wage war until all Christians and non-believers were dead. His was a pathetic attempt to feed the fervor of terrorist ideals in a sandwich of religion. John knew from his years of experience with the U.S. Marshals, and as a Headhunter for Chuck Taylor, anyone could sell this crap on any side street of despair and poverty. Loyalty could be purchased. Fear of reprisal and throats slit would keep the sheep from straying out of the pens woven out of the threads of terror.

COBALT reviewed the assembled questions for the planned interview with Osama Bin-Laden and what John would be asking and the way he would ask. Mustafa, Aasim and Abdul also reiterated how the culture worked. Beginning tomorrow, there will be no more shaving among the group. The three Muslims already had been working on their cover, but now it would serve them all well if they became more homegrown. The non-Muslims could not change that fact, but a little facial hair went a long way with this society and their status including their manhood. The team was dismissed.

Mustafa, Aasim and Abdul were asked to remain behind with John. John wanted to know if any of the hairs on the back of his neck needed to be on edge with these three. They were important to the success of the mission. Team Cat and Team Mouse needed to be one-hundred and ten percent ready. This was a once in a lifetime operation; they must get it completely right. John was reassured each member of the team was completely loyal to him and this mission, regardless of their

WHEELS UP, 11/11/2001

background. This was not business as usual. This was for the security of their Nation.

John headed back to his room where he watched other interviews with OBL. He had his laptop and was wired into the computer network. Anyone can watch world events at any time. The world was connected thanks to former Vice-President Al Gore. That was another story that brought him some minor amusement.

He must confess OBL had a large pair of balls to piss off the great Satan as certain Muslims liked to refer to as the United States. John was watching the FOX News Channel. It was by far the best coverage of all the news channels. Of course, one needed to be fair and balanced, so John routinely checked out the other famous news channels to see what was going on in their news coverage. John's favorite was Bill O'Reilly. You could always count on Bill to persuasively lead a discussion of virtually any topic. He was like Jack Webb to Dragnet in that it was just the facts. It was always hard to dispute facts, but it seemed Bill could always ensure the facts were viewed objectively. Of course, bias crept into his commentary, but if Bill recognized he was bias, he would ensure his audience would know where his bias came from. He wanted the truth to be told. At this moment in time, Bill was interviewing Nancy Pelosi.

John's impression of her was she was a left-wing extremist who would like to have women in charge of everything. Just to listen to her views on politics and government indicated that if she was ever vested to a position of power in the Democratic Party, the United States would be in for a roller coaster ride. She might be a great Congresswoman, a good mother and grandmother, but there was lingering doubt in John's mind that she was good for anything else. They don't make Democrats like they use to when John Kennedy was President of the United States. John could still not figure out how JFK's brother Ted remained a Senator, much less as a candidate in the presidential election of 1980 when he ran against the incumbent democrat, President Jimmy Carter. What about Chappaquiddick in July of 1969? Maybe another "Bridge Over Troubled Water" would be written regarding the years while Congresswoman Pelosi from California's 8th District served in the House of Representatives. She represented most of the City of San Francisco. John hoped this woman would never be in charge of

KIDNAPPING JESUS

anything that really mattered. He rationalized that he was only one man and had only one vote. That's what a Democracy was all about. Rule of the people by the people.

John's cell phone rang. It was Brad. It was just after 1400 hours and the engine was installed. John was on his way out the door. He called for Mike as he knocked on Jack's door, then on Charles' door. He also knocked on Phil's door to let him know he was headed out and to keep a low profile. Only short conversations on the phone and none back to the States and to their families. It was a reminder. They had been on radio silence back home since the beginning of the mission. It was strict, but necessary. As far as all of them were concerned, this was a Black Operations mission. No one, but no one, outside of their small group, and the backup team at the Pentagon, CIA, FBI and the NIA, had a need to know. There were only selected officials within the State Department, to include the Secretary of State, the Secretary of Defense, the Vice-President and the President and only the closest of his inner staff knew what the team was doing and trying to accomplish. The reason this team was selected was in fact that the team was trying to succeed where the government had failed in four previous attempts in the capture or killing of OBL. None of those attempts ever reached the news. They were largely unsuccessful. Launched air strikes and ground operations failed. Many of the terrorist foot soldiers and some of their leadership had been killed, but the hydra's heads remained. This was another avenue of approach.

The small group headed to the San Pablo Airport. Shortly before 1500 hours, the team arrived at the "Basket".

A somewhat tired Senor Torres greeted John and the team as they all headed into the hanger. The Marine guards were present, and the team of engineers was replacing the cowling on the engine.

All systems had been checked and rechecked. The plane was about to be rolled out of the hanger and the engine run through its tests. Brad was smiling and he was anxious to go up in the aircraft. John had received his instructions from Ambassador Clarke not to test flight the aircraft himself. John was disappointed, but knew Brad was more qualified than he was. Jack would fly with him and the Chief Engineer, Gus Morgan.

148

WHEELS UP, 11/11/2001

Gus was short for Gustafson. Born in Spain, Gus was part Swedish and part English, but he was one-hundred percent Spanish. He was married to a Spanish lady and had five children. He actually had dual citizenship from two very distinct countries, Spain and Sweden. He had even been a member of the Olympic Basketball Team from Spain. He represented his adopted country as so many athletes have done throughout history. This was somewhat ironic as the Swedish teams had always performed well in the Winter Olympic sports. His personal favorite was Bobsledding.

Gus, John, Jack and Brad conducted a pre-flight check of the air-craft. They were cleared. John came off the flight deck while Gus took over the right seat and Brad was in the left seat. Jack was in the third seat in the aircraft in the cockpit. Gus radioed the Seville Tower and was cleared for takeoff and wished good luck.

John watched as LAPEARLE taxied down and prepared for takeoff. The flaps and tail rudder were checked as the engine revved up to the recommended RPMs. Everything looked and sounded good from his location. The plane began its roll down the runway and was near the middle of the runway when the plane gently lifted off into the sky. It was a beautiful sight. John wanted to be in the cockpit, but knew he would have to give up his leadership on occasion to let others lead when it was necessary for the success of the mission. A good leader could always lead but had to know how to follow.

A great leader knew when to listen and when to follow. An important quote from his days in the Marine Corps came back to him. "You don't get the opportunity to lead, unless you know how to follow." This was deep. And, this was one of those moments.

As the plane gained altitude, it slowly banked to the left and continued to gain altitude. Other engineers were near John and Senor Torres and the rest of the team. All had crossed their fingers. LAPEARLE continued to climb to a flight level of 5,000 feet, continued to make the 180 degrees turn and fly back across the runway. Everything looked and sounded good, once the plane went far enough, to warrant a small grin of success on John's face. He looked at the team of engineers and their look also spelled success. It seemed as if the larger team had been successful on this occasion. They headed back to the hanger where they could see the DC-6C make its final approach.

KIDNAPPING JESUS

As the wheels touched the tarmac, a collective sigh from all could be faintly heard by John. It may have been his imagination, but he thought he felt the sigh. Once the plane had taxied to the hanger and the engines shut down, John met Brad and Gus, along with Jack, at the foot of the steps as they exited the aircraft. Their thumbs were up. Brad looked at John. "There is nothing to report. The test flight was a complete success. The loss of the engine may have been a temporary setback, but had this happened in Pakistan, the gloves might have been off in trying to get a replacement engine or even a ticket out of the country."

There were, of course, contingency plans and a multitude of alternatives. John spoke with Gus for a few minutes and passed him $35,000 dollars in cash in a black leather briefcase. This was not unusual, but Gus was completely satisfied. He would pay British carrier directly for the engine and pay his crew. The British carrier would take care of the engine that came from Ireland through Heathrow Airport. It had already been arranged with Mr. Clarke, that the Consulate would pay the carrier the balance of $5,000 dollars for use of the hanger. It would not be cash, but a credit from one government to another. COBALT would be back in the air within the next 24 hours. It was about 1830 hours in the evening.

The group headed back to the Consulate. It would be a late meal, yet the group needed to prepare for the next leg of the journey. Although they had spoken of another night out, John needed the team fresh in the morning. It would be early. The team needed to get together for some basic calisthenics and then a quick breakfast. Dinner was very good; the team ate through the meal in record time. Not much was spoken except John reiterated the time. No one will be on shift tonight. Wake up was at 0430 hours. This was referred to as "zero, dark thirty". They all headed to their rooms. It would be a short night. John called Elaine to let her know he was unable to join her this evening. He said, "Elaine, you are a beautiful lady, a real woman, and it was great fun. I'll be back this way in a week or so and really would like to get together with you if you are available".

Elaine's reply did not come as a shock to John. "John, you are the best. I really enjoyed being with you. I'll always remember you. Stay safe. I am always available for only you."

150

WHEELS UP, 11/11/2001

John replied, "Keep me in your thoughts. I assure you that you will be in my dreams. Until next time!"

"Me too", she replied. And they hung up their phones at the same time. Elaine stared at her walls in her tiny apartment. A single tear ran down her face from her left eye. In the short time she had known John; she knew this man was all man. She had heard of the attempted robbery and that the robber had been killed about the same time John had left her apartment. She felt there was a connection. Her intuition was always right. She would miss John. She hoped he would be well, but was afraid too she would see him again and her heart would be broken beyond repair. This feeling had only happened to her on one previous occasion. The man she loved was killed tragically in a train accident when the bridge collapsed into a ravine in the Alps in Northern Italy. It was a tragedy as hundreds of people died that day.

Life was precious and Elaine did not allow love to come into her life. She would always mourn her lover and her best friend throughout eternity.

Morning came all too quickly. No one really slept the entire night. This was the final event, so to speak. The adrenaline was high. Their nerves were on edge. Their eyesight seemed to be keener. They were focused, and the objective was the only target in sight. Nothing else mattered. Once the exercises were done, showers were taken and a quick breakfast in the Consulate cafeteria was finished. A meal to go had been packed for the team courtesy of Mike Harbin. He knew the plane was totally equipped, but the team probably would not take the time to eat properly.

The two suburban vehicles left the gate at 0630 hours. The team would arrive at Seville Airport by 0705 hours with a takeoff time of 0730 hours. Everything was on time down to the last minute. John thanked Mike and Les, along with Senor Torres and Mr. Clarke. They had quite a sendoff when the two Marine drivers and the two Marine guards were included in the farewell party. Although they tried, it was too much for the team to expect success in keeping, and maintaining, a low profile.

They taxied the aircraft to the end of Runway 09 and requested permission for takeoff. It was as smooth as a takeoff John or Brad could remember, and it felt good, really good. They could just make out the

KIDNAPPING JESUS

Guadalquivir River running through Seville into the Gulf of Cadiz and into the Atlantic Ocean. It was a beautiful sight once again, but from a different viewpoint. It was morning and the sun was rising from the east. And, LAPEARLE had four engines all running smoothly. And, they were on the last leg of their air journey to Target OBL.

They were headed to the southeast and were on their way to Pakistan. Once they landed, COBALT would secure the plane and find their local contact to meet with Osama Bin-Laden. It was prearranged and their guide was a trusted agent of the Pakistani government. The government's involvement was extremely low key for this mission. John just hoped their guide was not a double agent. Abdul was the lead as he would be with Team Mouse. He had to be the contact from start to finish. The plans were made. John's palms started to sweat as he thought about interviewing the madman who had been responsible for so much death and carnage. Whether or not OBL was responsible for the bombing of the Marine Barracks in Beirut was of no consequence. It made no difference at all to John. OBL could be directly traced to the planning of the bombing of the Twin Towers during 9/11 but had also been directly linked to the truck bombing of the tower's years earlier when 1,500 pounds of explosives were detonated in the underground garage of the North Tower. It was February 26,1993 when six people died as a result of the Islamic extremist actions. It was a wakeup call to our Nation that was not heeded. Failure that day would lead later to success with devastation unparalleled in the history of this country. One could argue where to place the blame, but in 2001, it was President George W. Bush who would take up the crusade against terrorism worldwide. John's team was one instrument in the global war on tenor. COBALT was now one of the many arrows in the quiver aimed at the enemies of democratic nations of the world.

It was going to be at least an 18–20-hour flight to Pakistan but the reward would be well worth the long flight. Jack was in the left seat while Brad was taking a break in the back. The auto pilot was engaged and the conversations up front on the flight deck were centered on the infiltration of the inner circle of OBL.

Back in the C3 of COBALT, Captains Knight and Kimble were gathering the latest available intelligence. The NIA was continuously updating the weather reports as well as the latest information on the

WHEELS UP, 11 /11 /2001

last reported location of OBL. It was difficult information to acquire, but it was reliable although in most cases, it was information that was days old. John shared with Jack it was time to get mentally ready for what was coming their way. It was a plan that could be followed, but like any plan, it was a plan until the first encounter took place. That's where the training they had all been through together took over. John simply said, "Jack, let's get our game faces on."

CHAPTER IX

THE GROUND CAMPAIGN

They were almost in Western Pakistan when John radioed Peshawar tower. "This is DC 01145 over."

"DC 01145 this is Peshawar Tower, we have you on radar at heading of 045 degrees, over."

"Peshawar Tower, this is DC 01145, request permission to land, over."

"DC 01145, permission granted. Turn to 090 degrees for the next ten miles and begin your approach to runway 29. Your approach is from the west, and on your downwind leg you will see the runway on your left. You may begin your descent to 5,000 feet at this time. The wind is 270 degrees at 15 miles per hour. Do you copy?"

"Roger, we copy runway 29. Tango Yankee, and see you on the ground."

Once they landed, the team could really see this runway was very different from the runways they had landed on in Bogota and in Seville. There were no State Department Officials or Marines to greet them, nor were there any U.S. Air Carriers or affiliates to help them sort out any maintenance issues. John taxied the plane into a private hangar where it would be during their stay in Pakistan. This too was pre-arranged through a private security organization. The plane would be looked after by security guards hired through the same agency. Background investigations were all well and good, but John and his team could be

KIDNAPPING JESUS

identified if the price was right. Ted and David would remain with the plane alone in the COBALT C3. They were the only security John could trust.

John shut the plane down and went out to meet Rajeev on the ground. Rajeev was the COBALT point of contact in Pakistan. Rajeev knew nothing of the team's unofficial objective, but the cover story of meeting with OBL for a news story had been quietly arranged with a well-known news agency in the United States.

Very few western journalists had ever had the chance to meet directly with OBL, and it seemed as if an interview was going to be granted. It was time for Team Cat to leave the group. They would not be part of Team Mouse while they were with Rajeev. Mustafa and Aasim would be on their own as they set about their specific duties. Rajeev gave them the vehicle he had been driving. It was an old Russian style truck. Talk about inconspicuous.

Abdul was assigned to work closely with Rajeev. Abdul began to lay out the teams' requirements. In order to do a story on Osama Bin-Laden they would need to purchase transportation. They would need a jeep and a truck to carry their equipment and the rest of the news crew. Four of the team could ride in the jeep, and the remaining three could ride in the truck. Rajeev informed John he had arranged for what was needed the day before they landed. Rajeev just needed the money to pay for the transportation before it could be delivered. Additionally, John requested a two-man security team of locals with their own transportation, another jeep, so as not to slow the group down. Nearly $20,000 dollars in Pakistan Rupees would be needed to foot the bill. John had brought $50,000 dollars' worth of Pakistan currency and $40,000 dollars of Afghanistan money. $20,000 dollars equaled nearly 1,200,000 Pakistan Rupees, and $40,000 dollars was nearly 2,000,000 Afghanistan Afghanis.

The additional security would be needed to get through the local defenses and to help protect the team's equipment. It was really just for a show. They were just trying to stay under the radar of any inquisitive locals whose possible network with OBL should not be taken for granted. Rajeev told Elder he would need 24 hours to make everything happen. In the meantime, Rajeev would made arrangements for them to stay at a local hotel. Elder shook his head. "No, all of my crew

156

THE GROUND CAMPAIGN

will stay on the plane until we get ready to have our interview with Osama." Rajeev shook his head and he understood. He had a feeling this American was not to be trifled with as he went about the task he was given.

Rajeev showed up with the jeep and Abdul was driving the truck. Neither of the vehicles was new; however, both vehicles were in pretty good shape. The security team would meet them at the border between Afghanistan and Pakistan. The truck ride to the camp would be about eight hours but it seemed like days. The roads were fairly decent to begin with, but as the distance from the airport increased, and they neared the mountains, the roads became bumpy, had potholes, and curved from left to right, right to left, and were up and down. They turned into what John jokingly referred to as Improved Goat Trails (IGTs) once they passed through the security checkpoint on the Pakistan/Afghanistan border. Once they entered into the mountains, they would be met by men who would check out the vehicles and the equipment and would then place blind folds on each of them. The jeep was left behind and all the equipment and the entire team loaded up in the rear of the truck. The canvas was down on the truck and none of the team could see outside the truck much less what was, or who was, inside the back of the truck. John's thoughts went to Team Cat.

The truck came to a sudden stop, and they were instructed to get out of the truck. Once on the ground, the blind folds were taken off. They blinked as they looked around. The days were short this time of year, but, even inside the cave, they could sense the daylight was fading fast in the mountainous region where they were located. They were inside a large cave capable of holding many vehicles like their own. This is how the satellites missed locations where equipment could be hidden from the prying eyes in the sky.

One of the guards spoke to Rajeev, he quickly translated to John and the others. "Do not go outside of the cave or you will be shot." Abdul was listening as well to the conversation. They had very little of the equipment needed to take down any of the terrorists in this nest, so the team made themselves as comfortable as possible. John wondered where Team Cat was. He knew Team Mouse was surrounded but the GPS transponder in his button on his overcoat had to be transmitting. Not only would Team Cat be able to pick up their present position, but

KIDNAPPING JESUS

the NIA should also be able to zero in on their location. John began to sweat it out that he might be the cheese in a huge mousetrap, a thought that was disconcerting even to this hardened Marine.

It was about three more hours when another man came into the cave. It was already dark outside, and the lamps lit were burning low with the yellowish light dancing on the walls of the cave. You could hear and feel the rumble of generators coming from beneath their feet. There had to be a system of caves and tunnels running through the mountain. John could not make out the individual in the low light. He looked like any other man John had met since he and the team reached Pakistan.

Rajeev introduced Ayman Al-Zawahiri, Al Qaeda second-in-command next to Osama Bin-Laden. This was incredible. OBL's second in command this close to OBL. So close. Something big was going on in this mountain hideaway. This must mean that the Al Queda leadership must be near-by.

Dr. Ayman Muhammad Al-Zawahiri was a little man even if he had been soaking wet. John was sizing him up as were the others. He was approximately 150 pounds on a good day. John had studied about this man and knew he was from a prominent family. Al-Zawahiri was born in Cairo. Al-Zawahiri studied behavioral science at Cairo University and graduated in 1974. He also had a master's degree in surgery. He moved on in his religious pursuits to a more radical Islamic Jihad and was one of many arrested following the assassination of Anwar Sadat. He was released after serving jail time for illegal arms possession. This bothered John. Usually, where there is smoke, there's fire. He later journeyed to Afghanistan and participated in the resistance movement against the Soviet Union's occupation of that county. There he met Bin-Laden, who was running a base for the Mujahideen. It was hard to believe men like these were able to bring so much mass destruction to the United States and to other nations throughout the world. This truly boggled John Elder's mind. In fact, Bin- Laden and Al-Zawahiri were products of an extension of the political will of the United States. Both OBL and Zawahiri were mercenaries hired to repel the Soviets from Afghanistan.

Al-Zawahiri went over the rules for the interview. He went on to say, "Osama Bin-Laden will be doing the interview in the morning.

THE GROUND CAMPAIGN

There will be no touching of Bin-Laden unless he makes the gesture. There will be no shouting or disrespect towards him in any way, or you will be shot and a film of the execution will be released to the entire world." That was as plain language and direct as a man could possibly expect to ever receive.

"These were good rules to live by." John was thinking out loud when he stated for all the team to hear, "So gentlemen, don't piss off Mr. Bin-Laden, in general, or we will die!"

There was a nervous chuckle among the group. It had to seem like the team was cowered in order to make the illusion realistic. Zawahiri was dressed in the traditional clothing of the area, long beard and glasses with an AK- 47 on his shoulder.

As he was leaving the cave, he turned to look John directly in the eyes. His words were clear and a translation was not necessary as he spoke perfect English. "It is ok to move around the camp. Observe our people. Learn from us. Feel free to take pictures for all of America to see what a great force we are and how brave our fighters are. You can use this cave, but do not enter any other caves without permission. Stay together in your group. You may ask any questions, but you cannot use any communications devices if you still have them. Enjoy your brief stay with us Gentlemen, I will see you tomorrow before you leave us."

John thanked him. John told him, "America will be able to see why you believed you had to attack the United States." When Zawahiri used the word "brief," John felt the perspiration run down the back of his neck. This was an uncomfortable thought.

Food was brought into the cave in several baskets. Hospitality was well known in the mountains when food was available. The equipment was being reassembled by the team after it had been thoroughly and roughly inspected. As the meal was being consumed, John went over the plan one last time by the numbers with the Team. It seemed everyone knew his part. The meal was fairly basic, but the kabob was very good. The bread and the olive oil were refreshing. The goat cheese was strong, but delicious.

John looked at his watch. It was 2100 hours, and the camp was dark. There were a few outside fires. John did not prolong his look at his watch, but the dials pulsated. He hit one of the three buttons on the

KIDNAPPING JESUS

watch. He knew at that moment Team Cat had found them. They had their guardian angel!

In looking at the camp, it was backed up to the snowcapped mountains to the north and to the east there were more mountains also with snow. It was the same in the west. It seemed to John there was only one way in and one way out. This route was only open for as long as the inevitable deep winter was temporarily at bay.

As he walked around camp, he observed two 50 caliber machine gun positions and several mortar positions. They had interlocking fields of fire and could bring a great deal of firepower to bear at a moment's notice. Abdul was with John while Justin, Jack, Phil and Charles carried cameras and camera equipment. From what John could see, there were more soldiers in the camp than he first thought. And, he felt sure there were more underneath the ground that he could not see. The enemy profile on top of a warren of interlocking caves and escape routes, to include ambush points, was likely possible. No mission was ever easy against a determined enemy. There were about twelve in all from his count. All were armed to the teeth.

John was able to take pictures of everything he wanted. He even posed with the Al Qaeda soldiers and made jokes with them with as much as he could understand from what they were saying to him. They smiled at him, some with crooked or missing teeth. It seemed a visit to the local dentist was not the major priority of these people. The other team members were doing the same. COBALT would review the plans in detail and determine if the mission was a go. It could be scrubbed, but the team had come too far to even think of that option as a real possibility. John went over the plan with the team and now all of their equipment had been returned to them. The equipment was in perfect working order and the team was primed and ready for whatever came their way. They had no real weapons, those that are traditionally thought as weapons, like guns and knives, but they had weapons that could not be seen. They also had an arsenal they could tap into when the time was right.

The team hit the rack, if you could call it that. Their sleeping bags and cots were a welcome sight along with the rest of their equipment. They needed some rest for the upcoming events. Jack stood first watch. John, and the rest of the team, drifted off to sleep. The fires they had

THE GROUND CAMPAIGN

in the cave were a hot bed of embers and the firelight, mixed with the kerosene lamps, danced off the cave walls like ghosts from the past. John wondered how many men had slept in these caves in the tens of thousands of years of history of these mountainous people.

It wasn't very long until John was fast asleep. His dreams took him back to an all too familiar reality. It was one of the patrols in Vietnam when his platoon had been ambushed. He remembered vividly. The newly assigned Private First Class (PFC) had just come over from another platoon that had been all but decimated in an ambush. He, along with the survivors, was being used to reconstitute other platoons that had lost some of their personnel. It was a practice used when a platoon became combat ineffective due to significant losses of personnel. Those platoons were broken up to fill the ranks needing replacements throughout Vietnam.

Casey Long was an intimidating looking man. He appeared to be in his late twenties to early thirties. He had blue eyes, blond hair and was about six-feet tall. He was muscular and was assigned the M-60 machine gun. He also had an assistant gunner, the ammo bearer for the 7.62 rounds that would be fired through the machine gun. He came from the same platoon and spoke very highly of this Marine from the battles they had been in together. John and Casey had now been on several patrols and the one John was dreaming of tonight was one that reoccurred prior to any mission he had been on since that particular patrol. It was not their most important patrol together, but it was sur-realistic, almost like a modem day movie shot in slow motion.

The platoon had encountered a small Viet Cong patrol of fifteen men. The platoon leader wanted to let them go by, but they were already in a hasty ambush formation. The orders were quite clear. There was to be no engagement of the enemy. The platoon was searching out a much larger formation, battalion or brigade level, and this VC patrol could possibly lead them to that location. No Marine was moving. Bugs were crawling everywhere, and the sweat was dripping. One of the Viet Cong stopped to relieve himself and had stepped out of the patrol line for just a moment to unzip his fly. He was peeing when he noticed he was peeing on the leg of his enemy.

Before he could sound the alarm, Casey engaged him with his entrenching tool that had been sharpened to a razor's edge. The fight

KIDNAPPING JESUS

was on. It was hand-to-hand combat as the VC patrol had literally stepped on the Marine Platoon. Casey took out the Viet Cong soldier with one blow that removed his head. Blood was everywhere. The rest of the enemy platoon was hitting the ground just as fast. They never knew what hit them. Casey turned quickly to the next soldier. As he turned, Casey lopped off his arm and the soldier fell to the ground screaming. Three other soldiers turned around to help their friend, but it was too late to do any good but to die themselves. Casey impaled the shovel into the chest of the soldier, then threw his knife into the eye socket of another and split the skull of the last remaining Viet Cong with the butt of his pistol. He turned and shot the VC Private dead in the head that was still screaming with his M1911.

Blood was gushing like Old Faithful in Yellowstone Park. It was a mercy killing, except the soldier was trying to reach for a grenade. John had three kills himself, but it was like Casey was in a dance with the enemy hacking them up like he was doing the two-step dance back in a local bar in his hometown.

Elder had never seen anything like that before or after. He felt sure that Casey probably could have taken out the entire VC patrol had not the platoon been present to kill the remaining ten men. There had only been one shot fired during the ambush that should not have taken place. Not one Marine had a life-threatening injury. Yes, there were scratches and cuts, but nothing significant although a few of the platoon would receive Purple Hearts. It had been their moment, and the team seized it and used it to their advantage. It was not their mission, but the victory they earned could not be taken away from this hardened team. It was a morale booster that brought the team closer together and more than ready for the next challenge that lay ahead of them.

After the encounter with the Viet Cong, the Platoon Leader and Platoon Sergeant always picked Casey for any high-risk mission. PFC Casey would earn another medal that day to go with his many previous awards. John wondered why he was not promoted on the spot to Lance Corporal. Apparently, the orders for the promotion had been lost, but Casey did not seem to be worried about the recognition. Casey was a natural fighter. John often wondered what happened to him after the TET offensive. That was the last thought Elder had before he came to his feet like he had been shot from a rocket.

THE GROUND CAMPAIGN

Carter was telling him it was time for the interview. He had dreamed all night and it felt like he had slept for a week. Located next to the fire burning in the center of the cave, was a basket of simple flat bread and donar kebab. Along with hard boiled eggs and feta cheese, he also noticed bottles of milk and water. While he appreciated the hospitality of his host, he knew if his team was discovered, failed in their mission, or were caught trying to complete their mission; there would be baskets reserved for each of their heads. His team snacked on the morning meal.

It was simple but filling. He looked over at Carter and the rest of the men and said, "Let's get this show on the road."

It was well past the established time for the interview when the team was taken to another cave. The team was in the process of setting up their equipment when Zawahiri came into the cave with his AK-47 on his shoulder. Al-Zawahiri said to John, "I trust you slept well in the fresh mountain air and enjoyed our simple food."

John replied, "We appreciate your hospitality. You have been very kind in allowing us to interview your people."

The cave appeared to be a central location where many meetings often took place. There was electricity and heat. There were also rugs on the floor and kilims hanging on the walls where many Arab country flags were also displayed. In addition to the one camera, they were allowed to set up, another camera team was also set up. They were clearly of Arabic descent. There were pillows on the floor that appeared to be stuffed carpets but looked very comfortable.

This cave definitely was used for dignitaries or for interviewing supporters, but John did not believe this was where major meetings were held for extended periods of time. The rest of their gear was at the entrance of the cave just inside the makeshift door. It was now 1230 hours and the team continued to wait for OBL. John knew this was a sound military tactic, to keep your opposition off their game plan. Bin-Laden was no fool.

Had John and his team been on a timetable with OBL's adversaries, not knowing when and where a meeting took place, added in the security of both Bin-Laden and his leadership. A few moments after John once again thanked Al-Zawahiri, Bin-Laden walked into the cave.

In perfect English, OBL said, "Thank you for coming all this way, Mr.

KIDNAPPING JESUS

Elder to let me tell my side of the story."

Elder was taken aback on how good his English was. John had only heard the translated interviews with Osama speaking Arabic and someone providing a translation. However, he really wasn't surprised as many people in foreign countries were fluent in many different languages.

All John could manage to say was, "Thank you for meeting with us, Mr. Bin-Laden."

OBL sat down on a large pillow in front of the lights that had been set up and motioned to John to sit down across from him. Both camera crews were ready. Jack was behind the news team's camera. John looked at Jack and then at Abdul. Abdul was close by, but Bin-Laden motioned him back. Bin-Laden looked at John. "There will be two interviews: one in English and one in Arabic. The first interview will be in English. During the second interview, I will use my own interpreter to ensure the translation is correct. We will have no need of your interpreter."

John simply nodded. It had to appear changes like this were commonplace for him and he was flexible and thankful for the lifetime opportunity of any newsman's career to interview a man that was not only notorious in the hearts and minds of free loving people around the world, but was worshipped, in a fashion, by extremist factions everywhere.

John began the interview with a simple, but direct, question. "Sir, let me ask, why did you use civilian passenger aircraft to attack the Twin Towers in New York, and, then the Pentagon in Washington, D.C.? Was the jet that crashed in Pennsylvania headed to the United States Capital when the high Jacked aircraft crashed? Not only Americans perished that day, but men, women and children from many countries throughout the world. These citizens of the world were non-combatants, yet they died horrible deaths and left so many families without their loved ones. The world is in mourning over these events. Can their loss be justified?"

Bin-Laden stated, "I wanted to send a clear message not only to your country but to the world. We will no longer put up with your policy towards my Muslim brethren. I will no longer endure Washington politicians telling us what to do and how we should live. We defeated the Russians fighting along with the Mujahideen and we will defeat the

164

THE GROUND CAMPAIGN

U.S. by attacking your civilian populace indiscriminately with any means, we have at our disposal, we will impose our will upon your society until your people have no will to fight. The only regret I have is that New York City did not burn to the ground and the White House was spared."

John knew his history. This was not the first battle or war aimed at the will of the people. If you can't cut off the head of your enemy, hit the enemy hard enough and long enough, the will of the people will allow strong governments to crumble from within. It has worked where all the battles have been won, but the war lost. John replied, "Well, I understand completely the desires you have stated, but could you have sent Washington your message by another means, one that would use diplomatic channels? A peaceful way! Instead of killing innocent women and children, and allowing such an unconventional method of warfare, could a treaty have been formed to look at a peaceful means of coexistence?"

OBL was clearly irritated with the line of questioning John had chosen. It was clear to John that Bin-Laden was not used this method of questioning. John knew the interview was coming to an end with the next response. "This was the only way to get the attention our cause needs and to have the entire world know we are serious. This is a war of attrition. We are followers of Islam. We are the guardians of our, the one and only, true religion. We will kill more of your people in the future with a great weapon that will kill millions in the name of Allah. We will take over the world and Islam will be the only religion that will be worshipped. It will be as Mohamed ordained and it will be the will of Allah."

John wanted to reach over and snap the terrorist bastard's neck. It was all he could do to appear to be fully composed as he refrained from doing so at this time. He doubted if he would live had he made the attempt, but knew it would be one less head of a hydra that would continue to kill and consume the peace-loving people of the world, both Christians and Muslims, along with many other major religions too numerous to contemplate at this time.

"Sir, I can assure you that you have Washington's full attention as well and that of the American people. It is my hope as well as that of my countrymen that we can all live in peace someday soon. Our wish for future generations is a peace forged out of these dark days that will provide light, everlasting light, for our children and their children. Please allow me to ask just one more question. What would you like from Washington?"

It took a few moments, but one could clearly see Bin-Laden was contemplating his response. John's expectations were soon answered. Had he been a true newsman, he would have been disappointed with the response from Mr. Bin-Laden. The reply from OBL, "I want your President Bush to release all Muslim prisoners held captive by the Israelis and in your prison facilities throughout the world. We know where our brothers are located. Your prisons are only walls made to hold our innocent people. Allah will prevail. You cannot change the heart of a warrior for Allah. It makes no difference if they are part of the movement or not. I will provide you with a list. It only makes a difference to my Muslim brethren. In addition, I want your President to not attack my people and I want an apology made to the Muslim people from the Pope."

Elder knew this man was serious in his demands and also knew Bin-Laden clearly understood these impossible demands could and would never be satisfied. President George W. Bush would not give into any demands from him or anyone else. National policy would never allow any free nation to give into the demands of terrorists or criminals. Once demands were satisfied, they would never end. This was an attempt to kidnap societal values for a ransom of freedoms that could not be allowed. It may start out with small gains, but the end result would be tyranny. A world dominated by terrorists would be no better than a world dominated by a Lenin, Stalin, or Hitler. There are others within history that would have laid ruin to the world, but John had no time to recall those names that also echoed within his head.

John was exhausted. It was an interview lasting about 15 minutes. It was clear this deluded bastard had one thing coming. He may have known someday, he might die a martyr's death that would serve as a rally cry to the extremists who blindly followed his lead, but there were other alternatives to a death he preached to his followers. Bin-Laden looked at John. No words were exchanged. Bin-Laden stood up, nodded to John and the others, and looked directly at Al-Zawahiri. The interview was over in just 15 minutes.

THE GROUND CAMPAIGN

OBL started to leave before Elder was to give him a token of appreciation. John cleared his throat and said a courteous "thank you" for the interview. "Mr. Bin-Laden, I know the interview was as difficult for you as it was for me. I would consider it an honor from my network affiliate and myself, and my crew, to present you this small gift to you for granting this interview and for letting me tell your story to the American people. Your hospitality has been greatly appreciated." Elder asked Abdul to hand him the box. He then presented the watch to Zawahiri. Al-Zawahiri opened the box and removed the Rolex watch. After careful examination, he passed the watch to Bin-Laden.

OBL knew this was an expensive watch and said, "Thank you Mr. Elder for such a gift. I am sure it will come in very handy to me. Time in the mountains goes by slowly, but the world waits to hear from me. It is only a matter of time."

A wry grin could be seen on Bin-Laden's bearded face. His eyes were as tired as they were sharp. He was a terrorist. Unfortunately, he was an educated terrorist, and one of many. There were no handshakes. Elder was, and represented, the infidels he would kill...exterminate. It was just a matter of where and when. John thought about Bin-Laden's last statement. No, he thought. It would not be that way at all. We, free men and free women, would never give up. In the words of Patrick Henry, "Give me liberty, or give me death!" John thought to himself. The media was simply a tool to be used by the radical extremists in order to fervor their cause. With that said, Bin-Laden was escorted out of the cave and into a waiting jeep.

Zawahiri stayed behind. He explained to John and his crew they would be taken back to the place they had been met by his men before coming to the camp. As it was late in the day, they would remain honored guests of Bin-Laden. They had the free run of the camp to finish the story. John thanked him and told the crew to get the equipment loaded in the truck as they would begin their journey home in the morning. The men cheered. Appearances were everything. The deception must work. It must appear as if the team was leaving tomorrow.

The team loaded the equipment into the truck. So, all the team did for the next several hours was perform news reporter type missions like reviewing the tape of the interview and listening to Bin-Laden. They also conducted campfire interviews and continued to look at how the

KIDNAPPING JESUS

camp was laid out. As they spoke to the soldiers, it gave Elder's team the time to review their escape route.

Soon, the team was back inside the cave given to them when they arrived. Lunch was waiting for them. Although it was late in the afternoon, the meal was freshly cooked. John knew there were campfires, but the one thing he had not noticed was where the food was being prepared. This was not the simple fare of the normal soldier but had the look of food being prepared for everyone. The soldiers were not cooking or preparing their meals, and it was also noticeable they only saw a few women present around the camp, and only at mealtimes. There was a shift operation in place as the soldiers' rotated duties in the camp. This was an organized military structure, not just a gathering of a few mercenary soldiers. The jeep taking Bin-Laden away from the cave was not just going around the block to another cave, but was traveling some distance away.

It was part of the overall security in effect of this radical military organization. A delay of the team's departure might affect a timetable established previously by the team with the enemy of these terrorists. John was thinking of Team Cat. Were they successful in tracking Bin-Laden? If they were not able to track him to his lair, then the next question was what about the remotely controlled Predator aircraft that should be overhead, or one of the many satellites? Not one soldier was watching them. It felt like after the interview was over, the team was treated like they were just part of the family. This was probably not anywhere near the fact. It might just be a ploy to put the news team off their guard.

The sun was setting quickly, and oncoming darkness was beginning to surround the small camp. John was taking one final look around before he entered the cave. Except for a few small campfires, a man could hardly see his hand in front of his face. John entered the cave. There were no guards present. John thanked the crew for the conduct of the interview, and they spoke like professional newsmen in case they were being watched or monitored. There was some small talk and code words used to cover their short discussions. The plans were reviewed once again with teams with a few small changes. John checked his watch. It was 2000 hours. At 2001 hours, a glow pulsated through the watch dial. It stopped. Then at 2011, it pulsated again. John had held

THE GROUND CAMPAIGN

his breath for almost 10 minutes. Team Cat had tracked the specially modified Rolex watch. It was basically a homing device. Jack secured the other GPS device hidden into the camera equipment. Phil was standing outside the cave entrance smoking a cigarette. What a reputation the American cigarette had made throughout many different battles in countries throughout the world. It was better than gold in getting provisions, and even answers, from tightly guarded lips. It also put an enemy into a relaxed mode.

John turned the device on and immediately it was receiving a signal. It showed that OBL, or the watch, was only about a mile from them. That was the good news. The bad news was he probably was surrounded by an additional fifty soldiers. Team Cat had visual information vital to the success of the operation. This Human Intelligence (HUMINT) would be combined with information that would come from the Signals Intelligence (SIGINT) provided by the NIA coming directly from satellites and Predator aircraft loitering somewhere nearby. The COBALT C3 was doing what they did best— coordinating gathered intelligence information relevant to the mission and passing to Team Cat. Mustafa and Aasim should be at a Rally Point (RP) nearby while protecting their exit route from the camp. They were providing overwatch protection John hoped would not be needed at this time. Discovery was the enemy. John knew his team was on top of it while Team Mouse was out of touch via communications.

John told the team. "Get some rest. We begin the end at 0200 hours." The final phase of the plan was about to take place. The team would know in about four hours whether the breaking news team story would be a success or failure. It was their story, and they were writing it. It had a beginning, a story, and an ending. John knew where he was and where he was going, but the next few hours would tell if he had chosen the right path.

John drifted off to a shallow sleep. He awoke to the humming sound of his watch. The team was waking. Quickly, and quietly, they began pulling out the surgical steel sown into the seams on their khakis in the low light provided by the embers of the fire. It was an eerie glow.

Their eyes were used to the low light. They had worn their khakis throughout and had been checked on many occasions. They knew it was the only way to get any kind of weapon into camp. The belt buckles

KIDNAPPING JESUS

would be used as the handles on the garrotes. This was a nice tool for the silent work that would have to be done that night. The team must be victorious. Elder got out his garrote and quickly went over the plan once again.

Phil was the first one out of the cave. He ambled outside and pulled his Jacket up against the deep chill in the air. While his eyes adjusted to the moonlight, he checked out his surroundings, opened his fly and pissed. He could see a guard at a campfire and walked over to him. He kneeled down to warm his hands. The Taliban soldier spoke to him in broken English. "Do you have please, a cigarette?"

Phil smiled and pulled out his pack of Marlboro Regulars. He tapped out a cigarette for each of them. The soldier picked up a stick from the fire and offered Phil a light. Then, as he lit his cigarette, Phil made his move, With the garrote in position, looped to go around his neck, Tucker leaped upon his prey and pulled the garrote so quickly, and with so much force the head of the Taliban soldier came off hitting the ground with a thud. His dark blood flowed from his neck like an oil gusher from a Texas oil rig. Tucker had enemy blood on his hands. This was a man he had previously spoken with. The body hit the ground flopping like a fish out of water. Tucker armed himself with the dead man's knife, his AK-47, three grenades and a bandoleer of rounds.

Just then, Jack moved in. Hand signals exchanged, Jack policed up the small battle area and leaned the dead man against an outcropping. He put his head back on his torso. If one did not look too closely, the vigilant guard appeared to be asleep at his post. Phil handed a small 9mm pistol to Jack with the only spare clip provided. As he made his way to another Taliban soldier about 20 yards away, Tucker used the knife he had removed from the dead soldier. He inserted it at the base of the man's skull with a quick back and forth motion, scrambling his brains. It was an immediate death. There was no sound. John, Justin, Charles and Abdul followed. They had Rajeev in tow. His allegiance could have been questionable and there could have been no risk of an alarm sounding. It was the beginning of the hunt. There was no sound from the two Taliban soldiers. Their dreams of the vestal virgins were now a reality.

There were twelve Taliban soldiers left on guard. It was a beginning. Ten more to go before Phase One could be completed. Tucker held his

THE GROUND CAMPAIGN

position while Carter took out his targets. Carter stalked his prey the same way as Tucker did except, he broke the neck of the Taliban soldier. John, Charles and Abdul silently moved in behind Carter. Jack was securing his perimeter to ensure some walking guard did not accidentally discover the actions of the team. Carter armed himself with the dead man's knife and his 9mm pistol, holster and two magazines. John secured the AK-47 and two bandoleers. Charles secured the six hand grenades.

Carter's next target put up somewhat of a fight. Carter slipped up behind him just as the he turned around to look over at his fellow soldier. There was immediate disbelief on his face and then rage as he confronted Carter just before he was about to die. The two went hand to hand with knives cutting and slashing while trying to gain the advantage and deliver a deadly blow to each other. It seemed everyone was engaged about the same time. While Carter was up to his elbows in deep shit, John, Jack, Charles, Abdul and Phil were fighting or preparing to fight. Metal against metal from the knives was drawing attention, unwanted attention.

The Taliban soldier drew blood first by cutting Carter on his left forearm just above his wrist. A vein may have been cut, as there was a lot of blood, but just as Carter was about to finish, his quarry pitched sideways and flipped in midair. The bullet must have passed close to another soldier coming in to help Carter's quarry. The velocity of the bullet coming in close proximity to the soldier's face had ripped the skin off the left side of his face and blood was coming out of his mouth, nose and ears. Two of the enemy killed with one shot. One with a direct hit, and the other poor bastard was just plain unlucky. There was no sound. The 50 caliber snipers' rifles in the hands of Mustafa had done its work. Carter was disappointed his kill was taken from him, but relieved Team Cat was watching from a considerable distance.

Carter had to give the SOB credit. He gave respect one soldier gives another— he did not let out a sound. Another one, no, make that two, dispatched. Carter held up his hand with what appeared to be a peace sign. Mustafa could see Carter in his sights with a count of two. Mustafa had made a great shot! While Carter wrapped the injured forearm and put pressure on the wound, he secured his perimeter holding the ground he had just gained. Jack was about to take

171

KIDNAPPING JESUS

out a sentry covering the road. He had to low crawl fifty yards on his stomach through camel shit to get at this Taliban. Carter could clearly see through the firelight as Jack jumped to his feet to make the leap to use the garrote. The Taliban was bigger than Jack by at least fifty pounds. The soldier threw his arm up as Jack tried to slip the garrote around his neck. The thin piano wire of the garrote cut deep into his hand severing two of the guard's fingers, but the defensive move allowed him to throw Jack over his head. Jack was flying through the air just on the edge of one of the fires. He knew he needed to hit the ground rolling and to get to his feet quickly.

That was one thought that was interrupted when he hit a large rock on the way to the ground. He blacked out for just a split second. That's all the time the Taliban soldier needed. Just as he was about to deliver the killing blow, he arched up in momentary pain, grabbed at his back and fell over Jack. Another enemy soldier was on the pathway to Allah. Jack rolled him over and saw a knife sticking out of his back about halfway down his spine. This was teamwork. Jack had Justin Carter to thank. The men were on alert back-to-back. Justin had a smile on his face: Jack could be barely heard by Justin as he quietly said, "I owe you one!"

Justin wrenched the deeply embedded knife out of the dead Taliban's back, grabbed him by the back of his head and slit his throat ear to ear. This move, known as a Texas necktie, was sure to win friends and kill your enemies. You always wanted to make sure your quarry was dead. Any noise could give the team away, and that could spell disaster.

Jack and Justin moved in opposite directions to the next targets. Some of the soldiers were deep in sleep and slumped over. Knives did the work. They would wake up in the afterlife. Jack delivered a knife at the base of the skull scrambling brains resulting in instant death. Jack secured his section of the camp and was awaiting word from John and Charles. Charles was to take out the two soldiers that manned the machine gun nest. This would be a little delicate as both soldiers were in a prepared defensive position. Charles crouched behind a boulder watching the soldiers for what seemed like hours. It was only a few minutes. Charles was hoping everyone was successful and so far, he had only heard some scuffling and some metal clanging, but so far, he had not

172

THE GROUND CAMPAIGN

heard shots fired. That was a good sign. He just wished the men in the machine gun nest had not heard any of the noises from back in the camp.

Just as Charles was thinking about his companions, one of the soldiers left the gun emplacement and went behind a tree. Charles thanked his lucky stars when he heard urine hitting the ground. This was the opportunity he needed. Charles low crawled to the soldier, slowly rose behind him in the shadows, and as the soldier used both of his hands to organize himself and shake out the last drop, Charles slipped the garrote over the soldier's neck, pulled and went with him as he sank to his knees and then to the ground. There was no noise.

Charles armed himself with the dead man's knife and the soldier's clothes. He slipped on his shirt and the headdress and walked back to the machine gun nest with his head down so the other soldier could not see his face. It was quick and quiet work. Charles climbed into the nest and found the other soldier half asleep. Charles grabbed the soldier with his left arm around his head, inserted his knife at the base of the throat into the windpipe and made a short twist cutting both the windpipe and the carotid artery. He jammed a single round in the barrel of the machine gun. If the gun was turned on them, someone would likely die as a result. He went to the first soldier he had just killed and dragged him back to the nest.

He removed his newly found clothes and redressed the soldier. He secured the knives, two pistols, one AK-47 and two more bandoliers of rounds. He looked like Pancho Villa, the famous Mexican Revolutionary General, with the arsenal of weapons he was now carrying along with the crossed bandoliers.

John was taking care of the other three soldiers along with the help of Abdul. Carter was assisting and Jack was providing security. Charles was coming in. It was give and take for about thirty seconds. John was able to walk up behind one of the Taliban and decapitate him with one blow from the E-tool (entrenching tool) he had found. The body hit the ground flopping around like a fish out of water. Blood gushed everywhere. The other two remaining soldiers turned to run over to their fallen comrade to help him if they could.

Carter took the first soldier off his feet before he could jump on John's back. He grabbed him around the neck in a choke hold and snapped his neck. The soldier's legs quivered as death had taken him to

173

KIDNAPPING JESUS

the next level. Abdul rushed the other soldier just as Tucker seized the opportunity to take his knife and throw it through the air. It embedded in the last soldier's throat. Abdul heard the knife pass his left ear just before it slammed into the enemy's throat. The enemy was dropping to his knees while he grabbed his throat. Abdul put his hand over his mouth and finished the kill by pushing the hilt of the knife while the blade made its way through the back of his head. The soldier fell over dead.

The team came in just as John, Justin and Abdul cleaned up the area. It was 0300 hours. It took just five minutes to kill the enemy encamped with them. John was sure there were more, and they needed to get on the move to Target OBL before they were discovered. It was life or death.

John gathered the team and went over all the weapons they had acquired. Distribution was quick. All would be armed with two bandoleers for the AK-47s, at least three hand grenades, a pistol and fighting knives. There were a couple of extra weapons left behind minus firing pins. Extra pistols were secured by a couple of the team members. Phase One was complete. John had been informed one round was fired. It was Team Cat. John quietly spoke to the team. "This operation went very well. Good job! Don't get cocky and don't expect Phase Two to go as smooth when we grab OBL." Carter had the only real wound. Jack applied a new pressure bandage with gunpowder on the wound to help the cauterization and a light tourniquet to the left arm to help stem the bleeding.

They had all done very well in their mission when Tucker asked John, "Where did you learn to use an entrenching tool like that?"

John replied, "In Vietnam dumb ass. I'll tell you later. Let's go get our man."

John moved out towards the signal from the GPS. The next stop was Osama Bin-Laden himself. The team was moving over the mountains towards the signal about a mile from them, so John figured it would take the team about an hour or so to move the distance and get into position to make a strike on OBL himself. That would put the time around 0400 hours and would give the team two hours before the sun came up and what John had determined when the night changed today. Along the way, they would link up with Team Cat; discuss the

174

THE GROUND CAMPAIGN

intelligence they had obtained on the camp with OBL and other possible enemy targets. This could be dicey. They needed transportation and it would have to be obtained at the new camp.

They had assigned Carter to take care of Rajeev. Abdul had made it perfectly clear. This was for his protection along with the team. "Rajeev, you have a choice to live or die. Choose wisely. You will die either way, by our hand, or by the hand of the Taliban. You are a dead man either way unless you choose to make your fight with us." Rajeev quickly nodded his understanding. He had to make a choice. Or did he? For now, he chose to be on Team COBALT, although he had no knowledge of the team's name. He was pretty sure OBL was the target, although he was not too sure about that as well. He did not revere Osama Bin-Laden, but he was more, or less, a fellow countryman and had been paid well in the past for courtesies granted in moving terrorists across the borders of Pakistan and Afghanistan. He was a good double agent. Although he remained gagged, his left hand was tied behind him. He would need one hand to keep from making noise as they silently moved out of the camp. Justin was weak from the loss of blood, but he was in step with Rajeev and would kill him in an instant if he muttered anything other than a heavy breath. The team needed Rajeev for the escape route in order to have a better chance of the mission succeeding.

It was just after 0400 hours in the morning when the team reached the main camp. The GPS was on target as they traveled on the constantly changing road OBL must have used to get from the camp following the interview. John thought back to his days in the Marines. It was several clicks to the target although line of sight distance had been just about a mile.

The camp's position was very well hidden in the mountains of Tora Bora very near the Khyber Pass. No wonder the combined efforts of many nations had not been able to track down this killer. John had to admit to himself that this man was a tactical genius the way he had evaded the military might of the United States and her Allies in this epic battle. And, to think it was done with the experience OBL gained in the war against Russian troops in Afghanistan. With the help of the U.S., he had learned his lessons well.

The team sure could have used night vision goggles, but they would have to make do without them. Team Cat had the night vision devices brought with them and they had the piece-de-resistance as well. They had four claymore mines they could serve up as one of the ala-carte specials. Team Cat silently worked their way around the camp and again would be providing over-watch coverage from about a half a mile away. They were on the escape route chosen by the team and were in position just after 0430 hours.

Mustafa had signaled with his watch. The glow on the watch dial on John's left wrist pulsated. It was 0434 hours. OBL's main force was not as large as John had thought. He could make out only about twenty-five Taliban soldiers from his vantage point from just a slight distance up the mountain located off the path they followed from the upper camp. They were on the eastern side of the camp; Team Cat was in the west.

There was another road that passed through the camp, somewhat of a crossroads, but a route that could allow additional support to come to the aid of the Al Queda forces at this encampment. They probably had dispersed their forces in a hub and spoke wagon wheel type arrangement. The route would have to be guarded. John motioned for Charles to cover the northern approach and for Justin to cover the southern approach. Team COBALT fanned out in different directions. Phil and Jack followed Charles at a short distance while John, Abdul and Justin, with Rajeev headed to the southern approach.

John left Justin, Abdul and Rajeev and worked his way back to Rally Point One (RP1), where the team first arrived outside of OBL's camp. He met Phil while Jack remained with Charles. COBALT had all the needed information. Phil whispered, "John the main force seems to be around the northeast corner of the pass. They are just on the other side of the road that enters the canyon from the south. There are several vehicles in the camp and two we can easily use. There are no guards on the vehicles; it looks like a light perimeter with most of the men in small groups. The jeep and a two- and-a-half-ton truck should do the trick. Both are U.S., left over from the war with our friends against the Russians."

Phil took a deep breath and then went on with the SITREP (Situation Report). "John, on north side of the canyon, I saw a machine gun emplacement. It looks like a ring mounted 50-caliber machine gun. It has been modified as a ground, rather than vehicle, mounted crew served weapon. There are large rocks all around it, and I could just

THE GROUND CAMPAIGN

make out two soldiers with the weapon. I'll need to take that one out first. That's about all. My count is 14 enemy soldiers I need to take out. Charles and Jack are already in position and are close enough to hear the soldiers talking, so we are ready."

John stated, "Our approach on the southern side of the camp located another 50-caliber machine gun set up the same way and manned by two soldiers. Coming in from the south entrance, there were claymore mines every 30 feet. I have Justin, Abdul and a somewhat reluctant Rajeev reversing most of the mines, so hopefully, we are out of the camp when they start hitting the clickers. It should be nice fireworks show, at least for a moment. We will have to watch our step if we have to come back through that area. That would mean we were retreating instead of advancing, and that would mean we failed. There is also an ammunition bunker across the road with one guard on it."

Phil asked John, "So, how do you know it's an ammunition bunker?"

John replied, "I saw two soldiers carrying supplies. My count is 12 soldiers' total. That makes 26 on the outside we can clearly identify. We have to take out the machine gun nest too. Charles and Jack should have closed the gap and should be really close." John looked at his watch. It was 0515 hours. John asked Phil if he had anything else to add to his report.

Phil's reply was short, "No, we're ready when you are."

"Phil, you, and your team, take out the machine gun nest on the north side of the camp. Justin, Abdul and I will take out the other machine gun. Neutralize the guards and meet us at the vehicles. The motor pool is RP2. I don't intend on using this RP for action. Don't start the engines until you hear from us. We still have to get OBL, and I think I know where he is located. There are a couple of guards at an entrance to a cave, just on the other side of the road beyond the ammunition point. The GPS signal was strong from that location. The machine gun seems to be oriented with the cave in mind, a covering fire. If we time this right, we should be taking out the machine gun nests at 0535 hours. Jam the gun with a single round and take the two men you kill and hide them in the rocks. I don't want a sign there was a struggle. I intend to be in that cave by 0545 and out by 0600 hours. Be ready to get your vehicles started and pick us up on the way out of the camp. That will be RP3. Team Cat is at RP4 and they should

177

KIDNAPPING JESUS

be calling in for covering fire once they see us departing the camp or hear a fire fight in progress. But, get those trucks moving not later than 0605 hours regardless." Phil watched John disappear into the night. Phil quickly headed back to the north and then to the east.

Exactly at 0535 hours, the two teams went into action. The machine gun nests were taken without incident. Four enemy soldiers were down and there were about twenty more left to neutralize. The guns were jammed, and the bodies hidden in the rocks. Within minutes, Jack, Phil and Charles approached a group of four guards around one of the campfires. They were wearing the clothes they had secured from the soldiers they killed during the night. They reached for their cigarettes and just as they reached for a stick in the fire with their left hand, three guards were instantly dead when they were grabbed with the left hands and the blades on the razor-sharp knives held in the right hands silently slit their throats. The last remaining soldier was coming to his feet just as Charles karate chopped the soldier with his left hand across his windpipe. He hit the ground like a sack of potatoes. Charles slit his throat. All four soldiers were propped up against the rocks with their weapons laid across their laps. Each of the bodies was given a gift. One grenade each with pins pulled. If the bodies were moved, more of the enemy would join the already dead. Phil, Jack and Charles headed to the small motor pool to silence the contingent there and secure the escape vehicles.

John's team was also successful. They jammed the machine gun and added two grenades for an added punch. If the guns were turned on them, the barrel would explode as well as the gunners killed with grenades lodged into the bottom of the nest. Legs would disappear. With the guards dead and moved, John and Abdul headed to the cave entrance while Justin and Rajeev headed to the ammunition depot. Each had their mission. Rajeev could not believe his eyes. He was now part of the team out to kill or capture OBL. He had no choice. His knife was ready when he addressed the guard at the entrance to the sturdy cave built of rock and wood and covered with dirt and plants. This ammunition point could probably withstand a direct hit from a 500-pound bomb, but with precision guided munitions (PCMs), and penetrating ground busters, it would just disintegrate. The trick was that you had to have a location for PCMs to work.

THE GROUND CAMPAIGN

Rajeev and the guard spoke pleasantries and Justin lit a smoke and offered the guard a cigarette as well. Once his hand came away from his trigger finger, Rajeev leapt into action. His knife slit the guard's right wrist while Rajeev's left hand chopped the guard's neck dropping the soldier into a gasping heap. Justin finished him off with a knife twisted into the base of the skull. Blood was everywhere. They slipped into the ammunition depot dragging the dead soldier. They used the robes to wipe up the blood as they jammed the dead soldier into an empty box. Another grenade was placed underneath the dead body.

Justin rigged a cigarette detonator with a pack of matches near a keg of gun powder. Breaking open another keg, Justin poured powder trails into the bunker, covering weapons and other explosive devices. Coming back to the original keg, another hand grenade was placed under the keg in case someone got there before the explosion could take place or if the homemade fuse did not work. Always, always, always have a backup plan! The matches were lit. Justin and Rajeev were coming out of the ammunition depot as John and Abdul were entering the cave. This was going to be close.

John and Abdul had taken out the two guards. Justin and Rajeev were on their way to the cave entrance, when they heard some muffled noises. Al-Zawahiri was quickly killed and left in his bed with another grenade under his dead body. The bodies of the two guards were brought into the cave. One of the bodies was thrown into OBL's bed along with a grenade just under his head and another under his torso. It was a deception needed to create a moment in time for plausible deniability. OBL was in a camel position with his face on the ground. John was on his back and had jammed a rag into his mouth. He looped a garrote around his neck and twisted it into the rope that bound his arms behind his back. If Bin-Laden struggled too much, he would choke himself to death, a slow death as the razor-sharp wire would act as a saw slowly cutting through his rotten flesh.

Justin entered the cave with Rajeev. OBL's murderous eyes met Rajeev's and Rajeev felt he had met his death. John quickly placed a bag over OBL's head and the leader was in tow. Justin placed four additional grenades throughout the cave: one in each of the beds, one under a book lying on the table, and one at the entrance. No one else was in the richly appointed cave. It was warm inside as heat was being generated by a

179

KIDNAPPING JESUS

portable heater. There was propaganda everywhere. President Bush's and Prime Minister Blair's photos were on the wall. They each had a bull's eye on them and a single bullet hole right between the eyes. A note in Arabic read death to all infidels. John grabbed the photos. Justin and Rajeev took the point. John and Abdul were right behind with their captive. It was 0555 hours.

They headed to the vehicles about 50 yards away. The light from the moon was fading, and soon, the sun would be rising. Just as they were getting to the vehicles, a large explosion came from the ammunitions bunker. The fuse had worked. It was like the Fourth of July fireworks special near a major theme park just south of Orlando, Florida.

The team moved fast as they headed to the trucks. Charles was on watch and Jack and Phil were already in the driver's seats of both vehicles. The engines roared to life as everyone jumped aboard. With the tailgate down on the truck, OBL was tossed into the back and laid flat on the metal truck bed. John and Abdul leaped into the jeep with Charles. Charles had thrown an M60 with several bandoleers of ammunition into the back of the jeep. Justin and Rajeev were in the back of the truck with the prisoner.

Phil was driving. Bombs began to explode in the south of the base camp they had just left and in the east, probably at the first camp where Team Cobalt had interviewed OBL. It must be a diversion or reinforcements were being taken out by airborne assets John could not see or hear. In fact, the enemy seemed to be more worried about the explosions from both the ammunition point and those in the south and east than about looking for an enemy. This would soon change.

Team COBALT roared out of camp with the jeep in the lead. John had the M-60 ready for bear. In the rear of the truck, Justin and Rajeev had their AK-47s ready to rock and roll. Soldiers were pouring out the rocks like an ants' nest that had just been stepped on by an unsuspecting victim. They had just discovered they were under attack and their leader was gone or dead as those who entered the cave were being blown to bits by the grenades left behind. The sounds of machine guns and gunfire were all around them. A few of the claymores and grenades were going off in camp and screams could be heard in the distance. A roadblock was just ahead. Damn it all! There was no way around and

180

THE GROUND CAMPAIGN

there were five or six enemy soldiers raising their guns. John looked at Charles, "We might have run out of luck!"

Just then, the AK-47s in the back of the truck were firing. Charles looked at John, "You just might be right. We are in a squeeze play, no way back. We can only go forward."

The team was in pure fight mode. John looked back to the front and saw the enemy soldiers dropping to the ground, first one on the left, then one on the right. They were bewildered. Guns just were beginning to fire, a third and then a fourth soldier hit the ground, except one of the soldiers looked like he was tossed like a Raggedy Andy doll. It was the work of Team Cat. John opened up the M-60 and the other two enemy soldiers were dead.

The road was not clear. Charles hit the brakes and slid to a stop. John and Rajeev jumped out and opened the gate. They closed the gate once the truck cleared it and then put two more grenades on the gate to get maximum kill for their pursuers.

John ran up beside the truck and shouted at Phil, "Let's make it like the Lone Ranger and Tonto and get the hell out of Dodge!"

Tucker looked at John and smiled. "John, we are with you. Let's move!"

Hell had been uncorked. The sun was rising, yet the flashes and thunder of explosions echoed through the mountains. Moments later, the jeep came to a stop at RP4. Team Cat was waiting for their ride. John grabbed Aasim by the hand as he jumped into the jeep. Mustafa would get in the truck along with Phil. The plan had gone the way John had planned, not exactly to the point, but a plan was just a plan. The team was successful in the execution and in the reality, they would have to improvise. The American soldier always knew how to take a plan and make it work. Aasim was giving John the SITREP while Mustafa briefed Phil in the truck. They used their Satellite radio to notify COBALT'S C3 located in LAPEARLE just inside of Pakistan. Captains Ted Knight and Dave Kimble, along with Brad Lyons were notified their package would be delivered within several hours. The NIA was also notified that a certain watch was telling time accurately. It was the homing device needed to bomb the camp. It was now 0630 hours. Adrenaline was high.

There had been wounds, but they were superficial. Carter's wrist was throbbing, but he continued to drive the truck like a stunt driver.

181

KIDNAPPING JESUS

Mustafa would need to drive soon after they stopped moving. In fact, John, at that very moment, signaled a stop. Just overhead, he had seen a Cruise Missile flying up the valley heading towards the camp. Mustafa switched seats with Justin. All eyes turned towards the camp. There were at least 30 trails of missiles flying towards a single target. First the flashes, then the explosions; then the earth was shaking like it was coming apart. You could hear avalanches coming down. There would be collateral damage, but it would be months, even years, before the camp could be dug out.

The team was cheering. John yelled out, "Men, we are almost there. Keep your eyes open. We are too close to become part of history... ...Settle down, let's move out." Just like John Wayne, John waived his hand forward as Team COBALT moved forward. "Semper Fi!"

They hit the border of Pakistan. It was just after 1000 hours. Peshawar was not too far away. Aasim spoke to the guards. They were not the same guards they had met when they came through just a few days back. They looked at Charles and John, then at Abdul and Aasim. It was clear John and Charles were not Muslims. One of the guards spoke, in Arabic, to Aasim. "Where do you go and where do you come from?"

Rajeev jumped out of the truck and was coming forward with the papers. Rajeev spoke to the guard. "We just came from an interview with Osama Bin-Laden. These are Western journalists. We are returning to Peshawar to fly home with the films we took from the interviews. And my host has a gift for you. We need to be on our way quickly."

John was watching what the soldiers were doing. He reached into his pocket and pulled out the value of a hundred dollars in Pakistani Rupees. This was a fortune for these guards, but they were used to being bribed.

It was part of daily life. They looked at the money and reached out for more. John handed them another stack of Rupees. This was for the second vehicle. They had pointed at it the same time the hand was outstretched. The guards went to the gate and lifted it upwards. The jeep, closely followed by the truck, headed through the gate and was soon in Pakistan. It was lucky the guards did not check the truck. Had they stumbled onto the man bagged and gagged, there would have been questions. Of course, the guards would have met their deaths, but this

THE GROUND CAMPAIGN

would have raised the alert level and may have hindered their exit from utter chaos.

The team headed towards the airport and LAPEARLE as fast as they could drive. Aasim had radioed the COBALT C3 they had crossed the border. Brad had the aircraft out of the hanger, the security team was deployed. Dave Kimble was on secure communications with the Pentagon. Captain Knight was standing outside the aircraft with his M-16 and M1911, 45-caliber pistol, in the shoulder mounted holster that was concealed. Brad could see the dust from the small convoy enroute to the airport. But, there was a second cloud of dust!

They were passing through a small ghetto just outside the airport. Although it was sporadic, a couple of gunshots could be made out by Captain Knight as the vehicles cleared the town.

The drive back to the plane was quite an ordeal. Although it was only about 200 miles from the camp, the roads, the IGTs, made it seem like 1,000 miles. It had taken almost six hours to get back to the plane. The vehicles had been punished. Gas for the jeep and diesel for the old Army truck had been secured at one of the few filling stations along the way. They had endured herds of sheep and goats on the road being escorted by their herders. Dogs were always in the little towns they passed through and the children, the beautiful children, always waved. There were stop and go moments, but no incidents along the way, until now.

The chase was on. Speed was the only hope. John looked back. He could see his pursuit. It was growing closer. They were not yet near enough for them to engage. Grenades would be no good. The security team at the airport would probably run.

John hoped they would run and not turn on them. John grabbed the radio from Aasim. "Cool, this is Blue. We have company and need to get our friend home."

Brad radioed back, "Blue this is Cool, ready to help." Brad yelled back to Dave that this was going to be a hot load and to get to the door and provide cover with Ted if needed. First, though, they needed to get a message out that air cover might be needed and that if any of the Drones were available to put them to use. Of course, Dave already knew the eyes were in the sky and hovering nearby and ready to assist.

KIDNAPPING JESUS

The pilot of the Predator, although thousands of miles away, had cameras trained on the pursuers.

As the jeep and truck entered the airport, the security team motioned them to pass to the aircraft. One of the vehicles in pursuit crashed and exploded. The Predator had fired a single shot, and three of the five vehicles crashed. Two of the vehicles were following so close that it was like a slow- motion train wreck as the vehicles ran into the back of the vehicle in front of them. Back at the U.S./Turkish Air Base located in Incirlik, Turkey, the expert Air Force pilot and marksman, smiled to himself.

Another round chambered; another vehicle crashed. The last vehicle stopped, and everyone jumped out. There were about 10 men in the truck. Just as the last man jumped, it appeared to the men, as well as to Ted who was watching, that he was a superhero as he seemed to fly into the air. It was as if a large, invisible, hand reached down and picked him up and threw him. The rest of the group were digging into the sand and were shooting at LAPEARLE. The pursuit for the moment was over, but the battle continued with the dismounted terrorists. They needed to be killed to the last man. They may have knowledge of the OBL abduction, probably not, but assumptions kill.

Charles pulled the jeep to a stop just behind LAPEARLE. Rajeev, Aasim and John jumped out of the jeep. Aasim grabbed the M-60 and started to return fire. The truck pulled up alongside the jeep. Mustafa had the sniper's rifle and also had taken up position in the back of the truck while OBL was being dragged out of the truck bed and being manhandled on his way to the plane. John yelled out to Aasim and Mustafa. "Keep your heads down while we get the package on the plane." Just then, Carter took a hit in his left leg. Justin fell down the steps of LAPEARLE. Blood was flowing freely and he was clearly in pain.

He yelled to John. "John, I'm hit. hit bad. Shit! This really is fucked up. Almost there and the mother fucker gets me with a lucky shot."

John yelled at Ted. "Get Justin onto the plane and make him comfortable. I want Dave to radio the coordinates of those bastards to the Pentagon and get air support." The Predator could not bring effective fire to bear. "Do it now!" John looked over at his team. COBALT was reacting well. An occasional bullet would zing by their heads. The

184

THE GROUND CAMPAIGN

security team they had hired wanted no part of this skirmish. They had quietly slithered away.

John said to his team, "Rally on me when I give the signal. Mustafa and Aasim continue to provide cover. This is how this goes down. Phil, Charles and I will head towards the enemy using available cover. Rajeev, get into the aircraft and stay there. Jack, you and Abdul, slip back to the hanger to make sure it is clear and that I don't have someone run up our ass while we are out front. Mustafa and Aasim, make sure no one breaches the perimeter around the aircraft. The three of us will take the lead. Tell Brad to keep the plane running and heading in the right direction. If you see us not making it, shoot the bastard and save yourself. But, get the plane in the sky. If we don't get air support fast, get your ass out of here."

The three-man team spread out in a fire team line. Charles and Phil were fifty yards abreast of each other moving and providing cover. John brought up the rear. It only took a few minutes to close the distance to the enemy. They mostly had their heads down. The Predator had them nervous and Mustafa would hit a terrorist whenever he popped up like a whack-a-mole game. But that did not prevent an occasional bullet to be fired, although mostly inaccurately. It only would take one shot, and the mission would be over. Jack and Abdul encountered an enemy soldier one hundred yards behind the hangar. Jack spotted him first letting Abdul know. Jack raised the AK-47, sighted the iron lights on the unsuspecting soldier and squeezed the trigger.

The familiar sound of the AK-47 was a distinct sound to John. He had heard shots fired from this weapon in several battles. It was over for this terrorist. One round hit him right between the eyes. "This one is for Justin you dirty bastard."

Jack motioned to Abdul; he had just observed eight more soldiers. "Where did these guys come from, he whispered?"

John, Phil and Charles continued to move towards the remaining enemy soldiers. The hanger was only twenty yards behind them as they moved through a grove of trees that gave them some cover. John held the team up at the grove giving them new instructions. About the same time, John heard gunfire from behind the Hanger. He looked at his small team. "I hope that's Jack and Abdul making short work of those bastards. We have to get these guys, or we are history." Just then, John

185

KIDNAPPING JESUS

heard a whirring sound in the air. It was just a glance, upwards by most of the team but at the same time, Charles took a round in the chest. As John grabbed Charles, the Air Launched Cruise Missile (ALCM) slammed into the enemy position. They were gone, obliterated in a moment of time. But they had done their damage. Justin was shot in the leg, and now his brother was shot in the chest. He would have to get him back to the plane. Phil and John quickly placed a pressure dressing on Charles' chest and wrapped it tightly. Charles was unconscious but was still breathing. John and Phil picked up Charles, his arms across the back and neck of his friend and his brother and although his feet were dragging, he was heading home, one way or the other.

John yelled at Aasim and Mustafa to help Jack and Abdul. That was the last fire fight to finish, and then to get airborne. John and Phil helped Dave and Ted get Charles onto the plane. Then they headed off to provide additional cover to the rest of the team. There were now six versus the eight enemy soldiers. The odds were very much in COBALT's favor. It was just like a hasty ambush. Jack and Abdul were on the end, with Mustafa and Aasim in the middle and John and Phil on the other end with the six bastards dug in. Shots were popping everywhere. Just as the bastards thought they were safe, another shot, another one dead, they would try to gain more cover. It was to no avail. John lobbed a couple of grenades. Then Aasim threw a grenade and Jack followed suit. Their job was done. The team closed in on the dead to make sure they were dead. The 9mm pistols they had blazed. John yelled at Phil and Jack to ensure the other bastards were dead as they headed back to LAPEARLE. Phil and Jack took off at a trot. The small airport was closed. Everyone had left and it would be moments before Pakistani soldiers arrived. They were running out of time.

John jumped into the aircraft, did a quick check on Charles and Justin. He looked at Bin-Laden and smiled. The gag would remain unless he was being fed or given drink. John spoke to him, "Now, you are my guest. We will speak to you, but you will not speak back. You will remain bound. Do you understand?"

Bin-Laden nodded his understanding. However, he did it with utter contempt. John put a cloth bag over his head. Both Charles and Justin were out but hooked up to a drip line of morphine and plasma. Dave was working on Charles. All soldiers have basic medical skills, but Dave

THE GROUND CAMPAIGN

had been a medic before he became an officer. He had prior service and had served as a combat medic during the first Gulf War. John could hear a couple of shots in the distance. Jack and Phil were jumping up the short ladder and closing the doors. John headed up to the cockpit and Brad was already rolling LAPEARLE to the takeoff position. He was going faster than normal. There were no communications to the tower. Everyone had their heads down. It was just gun and go.

It was just 1415 hours when LAPEARLE lifted off the runway and slowly banked to the southwest. John looked out the window and saw what appeared to be a Pakistani military convoy.

What they needed was air cover for the flight back. John called back to the C3 of Team COBALT. "Ted, please tell me we have air support for the ride home!"

"Roger that, we have support. We just received a change of plans based on the package and the walking wounded. We are now cleared all the way to Turkey. Our air cover is at 33,000 feet and I have them on a closed channel. The State Department had already spoken to the Pakistani government. They will not pursue. The incident at Peshawar will be quietly dealt with. The Pentagon knows we have the package. We should be at Incirlik Air Base in Adana, Turkey by 1800 hours, local time. The flight plan now takes us south of Iran, and we have permission to fly a narrow corridor over Iraq in U.S. airspace and then into Turkey just north of Syria. It looks like the State Department worked overtime. I wonder how many favors have been called in and who is asking questions about an old DC- 6C vintage aircraft. Someone has to be talking somewhere?"

John replied, "I appreciate the hard work. Thanks for getting the route approved. Where's the air support?"

The reply came quickly. "They have us in sight. They are just above and to the starboard side of the LAPEARLE."

"Roger and thanks! One more question, did our request for Air Force transportation to the States get approved?"

"That's affirmative! Transportation is already on the ground in Turkey and standing by. We should make a quick transfer and be on our way back to the States courtesy of the United States Air Force."

John looked across at Brad and pointed up at the eleven o'clock position. Two Navy fighter aircraft were on station. They were F/A-18

187

KIDNAPPING JESUS

Fighter/Bombers. They were from the Navy Aircraft Carrier Carl Vinson, a Nimitz Class Carrier on station just off the coast of Iraq in the Persian Gulf. It was likely some of the Tomahawk Cruise Missiles were launched from the Carrier Battle Group (CVBG). They were supporting Operation Enduring Freedom, so these must be battle-hardened pilots. John called back to Ted. "Have our friends visually. Please get a closed channel to them so we can talk, if necessary."

Ted called back to John in a few minutes. "Their radio frequency is as follows…157.175." Next stop was going to be Turkey. John looked over at Brad and took a deep breath.

"Brad, I know you must have had your hands full while we were going to visit OBL. I'm sure Team Cat kept you informed of our every step. It was close. Real close! But the team is the real thing. Everyone did really well. I appreciate you taking the lead back at the hanger. It seemed like an eternity although we have only been gone for three days. Where has the time gone? This is November 18th. I feel like we have earned some rest and relaxation. We're not out of hot water yet, but keep your fingers crossed. I'm going back to the cabin. I'll send Jack forward. He'll need his rest. We're all exhausted, but still pumped up. I'll tell you about it over a couple of drinks when we can really recount the last couple of days, especially the last eight hours."

Brad replied, "I can't wait to hear the story. We've had some moments as well. We have to put them together. Who knows, maybe we'll write a book someday and it will be a best seller."

John laughed out loud and replied, "Who knows, maybe when we get a minute to catch our breath."

John felt a lot better now that COBALT was in the air headed towards friendly territory. The flight would take about eight hours traveling at 33,000 thousand feet. He would have to land the team there and transfer them to the C-141B Star lifter. Charles and Justin would receive the much- needed medical attention and receive it earlier. John was thankful there was a change in plans. COBALT was bone tired. The adrenaline rush for the last three days had taken its toll.

188

THE GROUND CAMPAIGN

John was dozing in his small cabin when Jack radioed that they were now flying over the Persian Gulf as two more F/A-18 Fighter/Bombers joined LAPEARLE. John made his way to the flight deck as the two Fighter/Bombers that had joined them over Pakistan did a wave of their wings and began their descent to the Carrier Battle Group below. The sky was crystal clear, and John, Brad and Jack looked out the window of LAPEARLE at the CVBG spread out across the Gulf below them.

It was an impressive sight. The new escort also did a wave of their wings acknowledging LAPEARLE and Team COBALT. Radio silence had not been broken. John placed his hand on Jack's left shoulder and squeezed. "Jack, take a moment and check on Charles and Justin. If they are conscious, let them know that medical support is just around the cornet. Let them know the military might of the United States is protecting them and our cargo."

John looked at Brad. "Brad, I'll need you and Phil Tucker to stay in Incirlik and get LAPEARLE checked out. Then, I will need you to make your way back to Melbourne once you get everything ready for the flight. COBALT has to get OBL back to the States and get the team back to a hundred percent. Remember, the reward money we are receiving for the success of this mission. I am going to ensure you get a fair share of the spoils. You've earned it. Once the dust settles, you'll receive a bank book with money held in a Cayman's Island bank account. I won't disclose the amount to you. You were on active duty for this mission, so I don't want any of this repeated so someone can state there is a conflict of interest." Brad nodded and thanked John for his generosity. They had been friends for a long time. This would help him out when he retired from the Air Force in a couple of years.

Brad's combined active and reserve duty of 26 years made him eligible for 65 percent of his base pay. That was, of course, if he retired in the next four years and was not selected for the next rank. Promotion to Colonel was not foremost on his mind at this time. Colonels, after all, were just lucky Lieutenant Colonels who were selected over their peers, who were also fully qualified to be Colonels. Not bad for someone who did not think a career in Air Force was part of his future when he was growing up in Huntsville, Alabama.

His dad retired from the Army. His twenty-two years of service took him on a wild roller coaster ride during World War II from North Africa into Italy. His travels took him to Oran and to other small towns in Algeria. He also traveled to Casablanca, Morocco and into Rabat. During the invasion of Italy, he hitched a ride from Oran on a B-25 to Tunisia and into Sicily, then into Italy where he located his unit and began flying reconnaissance. The reason he hitched a ride was due to some major forced landings that had caused him abdominal pain and an ulcer. On his last flight in Africa, and before being admitted to an Army General Hospital located at Sidi-Bou-Hanifia, about 50 miles south of Oran, he had passed out while flying on a mission. Another pilot saw him slumped over but kept him company in the air until he woke up. He was lucky. His Duodenal ulcer was cured, but his unit had already deployed and he had tracked them down.

Pilot Log Book from WW II - Lieutenant P.O. Lyons

As with many others who had gone to war, there were many amazing stories that could be recounted. One story Brad recalled almost immediately. His father struck up a conversation with him about the time he was completing his Air Force Flight Training. It bore a striking resemblance to what was happening this very day. Then, First Lieutenant Payne O. Lyons and another Lieutenant were doing absolutely nothing at the airport in Naples. They were approached by an Army Doctor that asked them if they could fly some blood up to Anzio. The blood was badly needed. The two Lieutenants placed two large cases of blood in the back seat of a Piper Cub. They flew by large emplaced German guns located at Gaeta Point and into strong headwinds but made their landing just before nightfall and were low on fuel. The shipment of blood was well received and his dad later received the Air Medal for this flight. His tour of duty during World War II was recorded on an American One Dollar Bill the American Soldiers named a "Short Snorter."

Short Snorter from Lieutenant Lyons – WW II

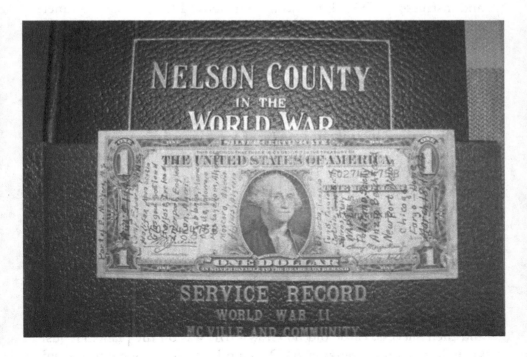

KIDNAPPING JESUS

He was a hero. He served in Korea during the Korean Conflict and later was stationed in Japan for three years. He had quite a military career and Brad was very proud of this man who had grown up on a large farm in a rural Nelson County in North Dakota (b. April 22, 1920). His paternal grandfather had come over to America from Bergen, Norway aboard the Cunard Steam Ship Company's ship, Lusitania, in 1914. His maternal grandfather had come to the States from Germany, lied about his age, and enlisted in the Army and fought in World War I. Both his father and his grandfather were from Nelson County. His dad retired from the Army at Camp Wolters, Texas in 1963 after serving in the Army for over 22 years. His dad flew NASA personnel as well as parts needed for the Space Program at Redstone. Brad wanted to fly like his dad who was both a fixed wing pilot as well as a helicopter pilot. Brad took Aerospace Administration in College. Brad converted from the Army Reserve Officer's Training Program (ROTC) program to the Air Force where he transferred his private pilots training and knowledge to become a full-fledged military pilot and instructor. When Brad was not on Active Duty, he flew commercially and became an instructor pilot. The recollections of his early years flashed back, and it seemed like it was only yesterday the two brothers were on the Tennessee River in their dad's boat with their childhood friends or at Guntersville Lake with their girlfriends. Oh well, back to reality.

John was snoozing, LAPEARLE was an auto pilot. Brad radioed Incirlik Tower. "Incirlik, this is DC 01145."

"DC 01145, this is Incirlik Tower. We have you on radar. You are northeast of Iskenderun. Turn to a heading of 285 degrees and begin your descent to 10,000 feet."

"Roger thanks."

It was a smooth landing. They were met by the Base Commander, an Air Force Major General (MG). John was the first out of the aircraft. Security was tight in the hanger and the Air Force C-141B was already standing by. It would be a quick exchange. No one was allowed inside the perimeter. The security team had strict orders to remain facing outward. Major General Smith thanked each of them for their dedication and their success. Little did he know OBL was on the plane. He just knew it was a high-ranking Al Queda official. An aero medical team

THE GROUND CAMPAIGN

from the Star lifter was taking Charles and Justin from LAPEARLE to the waiting plane. A surgeon from the Base Hospital joined the nurses and the medical technicians in evaluating and in transporting the wounded to their new quarters on board the plane. It was first class. The C-141B is the workhorse of the Air Mobility Command. This plane was from Andrews Air Force Base in Maryland.

Joining MG Smith was Lucky Sullivan who had just walked into the security perimeter. John did a double take. Without too many words and a pat on the back, Lucky told John, "Son, you and your team did great. The satellite photos are still coming in and ground intelligence indicates allot of damage in the two enclaves you visited while in Afghanistan. We also have confirmation your pursuers you had in Peshawar are all dead. We'll be flying to Patrick Air Force Base in Florida where there will be a special delegation on hand to meet you. That's enough said for now. Let's get your team aboard and out of here."

MG Smith thanked John personally. "John, I'm not sure what you and your team accomplished in Afghanistan, but I know each of you risked your lives and likely saved many lives that would have been lost had you not accomplished your mission. On behalf of my command and from a grateful nation, we wish you God's speed home and a safe trip." With a handshake, a Commander's Coin was given to John by the General.

John thanked the General, and he and Lucky followed the stretchers to the waiting C-141B. John turned and waved to Brad and Phil and said, "See you in the States in a couple of days. Be safe."

The doors of the Starlifter closed. The surgical team would begin their work once the plane reached cruising altitude. The remainder of the team would take turns guarding their prisoner in an isolated part of the plane while getting cleaned up, shaved, and putting on fresh clothes. What they were wearing would have to be burned. John was thinking ahead about the transfer of OBL into the waiting hands of the United States Government and wondering what the team's next adventure would be. You could be sure there were interesting times ahead. Only, in time, would they know just how interesting it would be.

CHAPTER X

HOMECOMING

Once airborne, John checked with the Air Force pilots of the C-141B to find out what information they had on the operation. Major Ward (Howdy) Clemons indicated the trip was anything but routine. "John, you stirred up a hornet's nest. Not sure what you boys were doing, but it's fairly safe to assume you have someone on board this aircraft we've been hunting for a long time. Everyone on board has a Top Secret, No Foreign Dissemination (TSNOFORN) Security Clearance, and each of us is forbidden from discussing this operation with each other or with anyone else. This operation is highly compartmentalized. I can only speak of this mission with my Commander. Everyone has to be debriefed when we arrive at Patrick Air Force Base on what we know. We'll probably be there for days."

John replied, "We appreciate the lift and sorry about the inconvenience. It's been interesting to say the least. I need to get back to my team and to our prisoner. He will also need some attention from your medical staff for a condition he has been suffering from for years. I don't want him to die now. We are so close to making this mission a total success."

When John returned back into the cabin from the flight deck, he checked to see how Charles and Justin were doing. The nurse stated, "They both are resting, and an injection of morphine was provided for

KIDNAPPING JESUS

the pain. Justin's wound was not life threatening, but Charles, on the other hand, is being monitored closely. His wounds are serious. Justin's hit in the leg, although bloody, just missed the bones, but did clip a vein. The surgery was successful, blood was lost, and some muscle tissue torn apart. He will recover, but will have a slight limp for the rest of his life. His arm really is ok. Here again, it could have been much worse. Your brother Charles has not regained consciousness. The surgery was successful, but the patient has to have the will and spirit to live. He is strong, so it is my belief he will choose to live, not to die. The body will work better while he sleeps. He is resting. The wound to his right lung did some major damage, but we have the bullet and the bone fragments out of the body. If you had bought him to us an hour later, he most likely would have had no chance at all." John thanked the Air Force Captain. She was great looking, but John was too tired to think of sugar plums.

After a brief moment, John continued…"One more thing, I need someone to check on our prisoner. He may need an injection of insulin. I would like to leave that in your hands. If you need the Doctor, then, that is a decision you will have to make. And, you cannot speak of this person's identity to anyone, ever. I know you will understand completely."

John went over to where Jack was sitting. "Hey brother, it could have been worse. Everyone is going to make it. I know you and Charles are close but hang in there. Get some sleep and think about our pay day." Jack walked back down to the rear of the plane where he saw OBL sitting upright and getting a shot from the Nurse that John had just spoken with. She gave a thumbs up to Jack, one of pride and one of success. You could tell she was happy that this terrorist was in the hands of Uncle Sam, and she was now contributing to bringing the bastard to justice, the American way.

In just a few minutes, Mustafa was back with Aasim as they took turns guarding the prisoner. John headed towards the center of the plane. As he approached the World's Number One Terrorist, he looked him straight in the eye. "I wanted to kill you when we had our interview and later when I had you in the cave. Yes, I wanted to kill you for all of the innocent people, men, women, and children, brothers, sisters, mothers and fathers, sons, and daughters you have slaughtered. They have died for a cause that is a sin in God's eyes, and yes, in the eyes of Mohammad as well. Your prophet never taught the insanity you

HOMECOMING

prophesize. Instead, I bring you back to America where the American Government will deal with you. You are the head of the world's most despicable organization, and with your capture, the demise of your demonic aspirations will be forthcoming."

John heard OBL's quiet whispers as he said, "I was always a fool for interviews. You made a fool of me, but you will never get me to America and let the news media feed off of me. I will never stand trial in American Courts. Your government will not allow me to say what I know."

John replied. "We will see Bin-Laden, we will see."

John looked at Mustafa and Aasim. "Do not speak to this man or let him speak. If he does, gag and bag him. Have the Nurse check on him every hour. Ensure he is fed. When he needs to go to the bathroom, he is to be restrained. Let him have use of his right hand only. Both of you ensure Jack is backing you up if you move him. No chances to be taken, none. Double check him again and then check him again. No ropes, nothing he can use. Take his shoes off and throw them away. There are no assumptions allowed. Also, I want your guns. Each of you will have no weapons, period."

Jack was watching and listening. John took off the restraints on OBL's feet and wrists allowing him to sit completely upright but his hands were handcuffed behind his back and attached to the airframe of the plane. His feet were still shackled together. Bin Laden was not going anywhere until the plane landed. John motioned Jack over. "Watch while Aasim gets some sleep. Rotate every two hours so each of you gets four hours of rest. I'll be in and out. Here are the keys. Stay away, at least ten feet away from him, no matter what. Pass the keys but get them back. You have the gun. Use it if necessary."

John headed back to the passenger seats that had been installed in the C-141B. The rest of the team was sleeping. They had done a great job. John sat down in the seat next to Lucky Sullivan. Lucky spoke to John. "I never imagined I would be looking in the eyes of Osama Bin-Laden. John, he will not stand trial. We have a very private CIA Prison for this man. He will be alone...very alone!"

He turned to John. "When we arrive at Patrick, President Bush will be on hand to meet you. He will be there to talk to the Air Force Airmen and Women who support military operations in Iraq and

197

KIDNAPPING JESUS

Afghanistan and also into Space, access to the high frontier including global operations. His primary objective, not to minimize the importance of the sacrifice of these American heroes, is to meet you and your team. In a way, your operation complements their mission. Success for you is not only success for them, our Nation, but the entire World. There is a special CIA team that will be on hand to move your prisoner to a secluded area. One of the team members is on board. He is a back-up to your security. He will come forth if needed, but like an Air Marshall, he will not be identified. Trust me; he is here to help only as a last resort if something goes wrong. President Bush does not want to see this man and he does not want OBL to see him. It would send a political statement to world terrorists if OBL saw President Bush in person. We will not grant these bastards any moment that they could claim as a victory regardless of who controls the situation."

John nodded his understanding. "Lucky, appreciate all the support we received during the mission. It was great! We had the most amazing support from all the government agencies as well as from the Air Force and the Navy. The State Department made a huge difference between success and failure. This was one wild ride. It was quite a step up from the U.S. Marshals office and from my days of bounty hunting. What a rush! The team was really good. The mission specialists, Captain's Knight and Kimble, along with our FBI and CIA agents, made it work. I cannot say enough about each of them including Brad Lyons and Phil Tucker. I know it's strange to feel this way but let me ask you if you remember the quotation from Colonel Jack Hayes during the Mexican War."

Lucky nodded his affirmation and acknowledgement of this legendary Texas Ranger. In fact, it is often used as a Maneuver Warrior's Prayer and any Army Division probably uses it during Terrain Walks or during Officer's and Non-Commissioned Officer's Professional Development Sessions or Trips.

John began the recitation....

"Oh Lord, we are about to join battle with vastly superior numbers of the enemy, and heavenly Father, we would like for you to be on our side and help us; but, if you can't do it, for Christ's sake, don't go over to the "enemy", but

HOMECOMING

just lie low and keep dark, and you'll see one of the damnest fights you ever saw in all your born days. Amen."

Lucky smiled. John went on to say, "It was really something...not sure how we got out of there alive...not sure why we are still alive except that the team...the team worked and lived not only because they were a team, but because they are a team. We are thankful for the assistance, but boots on the ground, in the long run made all the difference." The famous quote echoed in his mind as he drifted off to a restless sleep. Lucky let him go. John and his team were exhausted, but Lucky knew that the leader of any mission has a huge responsibility, a responsibility like a ton of rocks on their shoulders. One that rest would relieve over time, but not until the mission was completed.

The C-141B Starlifter was nearing American airspace and flying along the coast of Florida. Jacksonville was on the starboard side of the plane. One of the two surgeons came from the Operating Room and sat next to John. John slowly opened his eyes to see Major (Doctor) Don D. Sasser. John asked Doctor Sasser about the two team casualties. "Doctor, how's my team!"

"Both patients are doing well," the Major replied. "Justin will need to stay with us for several weeks so I can make sure his infection is under control."

"What about Charles?" John replied.

"Charles, well, Charles is going to make it. But it is my belief his running days are over. It will be months before he is back on his feet and on the road to recovery. Don't get me wrong. He is lucky to be alive. But he will recover in time. If it was not for Captain Kimble, Justin may have had serious problems and your brother would be dead. There is no doubt in my mind this Army Officer saved their lives. He would have made a great doctor. Your bother has a chance because of him."

The descent into Patrick Air Force Base was smooth and the landing was by the book. Not a real bump was felt. The plane taxied and was escorted into a hanger where several teams of both Air Force personnel and another group of camouflaged men were waiting. They were armed to the teeth and were wearing special Kevlar Jackets. John sized it up quickly. These men were taking OBL. There were three black Suburban SUVs. The C-141B shut down its engines and the flight crew departed

KIDNAPPING JESUS

the aircraft while the aero medical team unloaded their patients from the rear of the aircraft. The Air Force Load Master had lowered the ramp as the medical team was met by two ambulances and several staff cars for their ride to the hospital. Their debriefings would take place over the next several days.

All that remained on-board was Team COBALT, including Rajeev, Lucky Sullivan and one lone Air Force Load Master. So, he was the CIA agent on board! And, of course, there was the prisoner.

Jack followed Mustafa and Aasim as they escorted OBL. The terrorist was bagged and gagged and had his head lowered. He looked like a bag of rags, but everyone knew who it was. The CIA agent met the ground team and took physical control of the prisoner. It was a somber occasion. Not one word was spoken. COBALT was now alone with Deputy Director Sullivan. It was the team, minus Brad Lyons and Phil Tucker, as well as Charles and Justin. John looked around the small circle with pride including the agents that had been added to the team, Mustafa, Aasim and Abdul along with Rajeev. Rajeev had become a member of the team out of necessity, but Sullivan had plans for him in the CIA that would be part of his future Black Operations. Rajeev just did not know it, yet. Then there were Captains Kimble and Knight. They did good, real good! They both would receive Silver Stars with V Device from their respective services including a Presidential Citation for conspicuous gallantry. Lieutenant Colonel Lyons would also receive the same decorations for his contributions to the overall success of COBALT's mission. That left Jack and John. The team had grown to twelve with their adoption of Rajeev. There were eight standing in the small group with Lucky Sullivan.

Lucky turned to John. "We will keep OBL alive. We know we will get information from him. It is just a matter of time. We have plans to use Rajeev to help us achieve our goals. He will join Mustafa, Aasim and Abdul as an undercover team. They will return home to their families for only a short time and will reassemble and go dark for an extended period of time. They will be the core of many teams to follow. We will infiltrate the hydra and continue to cut off the heads as they grow. Our forces in Iraq and in Afghanistan will continue their pursuit as well, and our allies in the region, including Pakistan, will continue to pass

HOMECOMING

crucial information to our undercover assets. You are sure Al-Zawahiri is dead, John?"

"I am positive! His throat was slit from ear to ear when I left the cave. Plus, there was a grenade under his stomach, so if he was rolled over, then others would join him in his search for his prearranged treasures."

Lucky quickly followed. "The pictures you took with Al-Zawahiri in the cave will be used for the media. There will be no mention of OBL to the press. He was not there. His body is missing from the cave, which provides plausibility he is alive both to Al Queda and to the world."

"Why the switch, Lucky?"

Lucky thought to himself for just a moment before he answered this question, a question that had been asked many times in the hours since the capture of OBL had been confirmed. "There would be so much pressure for us to end the war if the American public knew we had captured Bin-Laden."

"Ok, you have my undivided attention. What about the $25 million dollars, Dead or Alive, under the Rewards for Justice program for the capture of OBL? Not that I was in this just for the money, but I have the team to think of as well, plus my out-of-pocket expenses."

"John, there is a check waiting for you, which was made out to you and will be presented by President Bush in front of the Press. In moments, a bus load of reporters, along with heavy duty security, and the President will be arriving. I just needed time to prepare you. We have already sent word that Al-Zawahiri has been killed and his body is on display at the morgue right here at Patrick. With your pictures and the dead body that was on board your aircraft, positive identification was made. Not to mention that the Press already has news of what is being referred to as "Retribution at Tora Bora."

The bus arrived and cameras set up. It was not a large crowd. John had seen Air Force One on the ground when they landed. This should have alerted the Press. It was seldom a plane could land or take off from any airport when the President or the Vice-President was on the ground. The limousines arrived. The cameras swung into motion. A small podium had been set up that bore the Presidential Seal. Security personnel established a perimeter around the Presidential Limo.

KIDNAPPING JESUS

White House Press Agent Scott McClellan greeted John and his team. "You must be John Elder?" John nodded as he met the firm hand shake offered to him. "Glad to meet you, John!"

"Scott, this is my brother Jack and the team minus my other brother Charles, Lieutenant Colonel Brad Lyons, Phil Tucker and Justin Carter. Scott shook Jack's hand, and in turn, Aasim, Mustafa, Abdul, Rajeev and Captains Kimble and Knight.

Scott took the podium and announced, "Ladies and gentlemen, the President of the United States of America." President and Mrs. Bush exited their limousine and made their way to the podium amid the applause of the audience to include COBALT.

Scott turned to the audience. "It is my pleasure to introduce the President and the First Lady to a dedicated team of professionals. Mr. President, it is a distinct honor to present Marine First Sergeant (Retired) John Elder, Gunnery Sergeant (Retired) Jack Elder, Agents Rasheed, Sahar and Basher. Also, please meet the newest member of the team, Mr. Rajeev. Sir, there are two active-duty Captains that were mission specialists during the operation; Army Captain Kimble and Air Force Captain Knight. Two of the team members are still in Turkey and two have been moved to the hospital."

President Bush motioned for John to stand next to him. A waiting Nation had not been informed as to the subject of this news conference. They were here to cover the President's visit to speak to the men and women of the United States Air Force stationed at Patrick Air Force Base. The Nation, and the World, was about to learn that John and his team killed Al- Zawahiri, Osama Bin-Laden's second in charge.

Ladies and gentlemen, fellow Americans, the men I have the pleasure to introduce to you have killed Doctor Ayman Al-Zawahiri, second in charge of the Al Queda network established by Osama Bin-Laden. As you, and the rest of the World are about to learn, this team of professionals took out many terrorists in the mountains of Tora Bora. Satellite photos will be released to the news agencies of the world showing the incredible damage at two terrorist camps established deep in the mountains of Afghanistan near the Khyber Pass. The team before you have four additional members that could not be with us at this moment, but I know they are watching. (President Bush looked directly at the cameras.) Gentlemen, you have my thanks and the deep appreciation of a

HOMECOMING

grateful Nation. Military support was brought to bear and State and Foreign Service Departments greatly assisted."

"This team, well, this team is a dream team. They did it all. I know there are many questions to ask, but there are only a few answers they can provide. I know you will respect their answers. They are also extremely tired. John, it is my pleasure to present to you a check in the amount of $25 million dollars, tax-free, as part of the Rewards for Justice Program for bringing these terrorists to justice and disrupting the Al Queda network." John stepped forward to accept the check and the President stepped back from the podium and stood between Jack Elder and Laura Bush.

John was not really new at the speech game because of his military service, but he was glad he had time to think of what he wanted to say. "First, I would like to thank my team for making our mission a success. We had the right plan, although it changed constantly. And our support was flawless. I also want to thank the President for his support, without which, we would not be here at this moment. This was a plan that was approved at the highest levels and was on a need-to-know basis. I am grateful for those who provided the closest support possible and kept their knowledge of the mission to themselves. It was a journey. It was our time. Failure was never an option, but I can assure you that death was a constant factor to be reckoned with. There were many close calls, too many! The right and might of the United States shone through the dust and the dirt. And I would like to thank my extended team. I would also like to thank people in the government whose names I cannot mention. There is one specialist somewhere in the world that provided us much needed cover at a critical juncture on our way out of Pakistan. His shot took out most of our pursuit. It was a team effort. Without all the assistance we received, this mission would have failed."

There was a shattering applause from everyone in the hanger. It seemed like a long time. John looked back at his team and then gestured to the cameras. He knew Charles and Justin were watching from the Base Hospital and Brad and Phil were watching from Incirlik Air Base in Turkey. His last communication with Brad indicated LAPEARLE would be flight worthy in a few more days. They would fly back to Seville, then into the United States. John told Brad and Phil to relax in Seville for a couple of days. He wanted Phil to see Elaine and explain,

KIDNAPPING JESUS

in person, to her that the team was on a mission...a secret mission...and that, well, that...he would be in touch when things quieted down. He didn't know if there was something there or not. Only time would tell. The applause died down. John snapped back to reality.

"I guess I will answer questions from all of you now. I know you have some." There was laughter from the group. "Let's begin with Katie Couric of CBS news."

"Mr. Elder, where do you come from?"

His reply was short and sweet. "Mrs. Couric, I was born in Baton Rouge, but I was raised on a small farm. I'm just a country boy. I served over twenty years in the Marine Corps. My team also has credentials. My brothers, Charles and Jack, served in the Marine Corps along with Justin Carter and Phil Tucker. Others assembled before you have their training as well. Captain Knight is active-duty Air Force and Captain Kimble is in the Army. My co-pilot, Brad Lyons, is active-duty Air Force Reserve. We all trained, lived and fought together. This team became a family. I served as a U.S. Marshal and later as a bounty hunter after my retirement from the Corps."

Mr. Sam Donaldson asked the next question. "John, why did you... why this mission? What was your incentive?"

John responded. "I planned this mission after Osama Bin-Laden was labeled as the mastermind behind the attacks of 9/11. I was in Beirut after the Barracks were blown up. It left a hollow feeling in me. I wanted payback. No, that's not quite accurate. I wanted revenge. The devastation! It was incomprehensible that such devastation was aimed at innocent people during their daily lives. The families bore unspeakable suffering. I looked into their eyes as our Nation reeled from the senseless actions of these terrorists. Our Nation had been attacked. No, we have been ambushed. The enemy was in our midst, taking advantage of the freedom our Nation takes for granted. They used our rights for their evil. But there was no way one man could make a difference. When it was revealed that Bin-Laden attacked our country, I began to come up with a plan."

John pointed at Wolf Blitzer from CNN. "John did you have many casualties?"

204

HOMECOMING

My brother Charles was severely wounded. Justin Carter sustained multiple wounds, although not as severe; this indicates how close the mission was to imminent danger and death. They will recover."

There was a follow-on question from Mr. Blitzer. "Where did you train and did the U.S. provide any money for this operation?"

"We trained at several different locations. That's all I can say. To give out an exact location would jeopardize the overall secrecy of the mission and may compromise any possibilities of future missions. Let it be said, without the logistical support provided by an extended network, one that involved other nations as well, the mission would have failed. As to the second part of your question, I financed the entire mission with my own money. There was support provided by the government that will not be released. Now, my team has been through quite an ordeal, and I think it is time to take one last question."

Brian Williams had his hand in the air and John pointed to him. "What do you plan do with the money?"

"I am going to take a long vacation and think about that very question?" John stepped away from the podium amid the laughter. It sounded like he was about to respond with what has become a famous response for the Most Valuable Player of the Super Bowls.

The President of the United States of America shook each hand and spoke to each of them individually. He spent some time whispering to John. No one could hear what was being said. John would think about that conversation for days. The first lady followed suit. They were quite an engaging couple. John thought to himself that this honest man would be remembered in years to come as a great President whose career of public service made a difference to both the United States and to the World. It was a different time, and the front lines had all but disappeared. This was World War III. The World needed a wakeup call. It was unlike any war that had been fought in the past. The enemy fought by none of the rules of engagement. There was no Geneva Convention. How do you fight an enemy with your hands all but tied behind you?

Reporters had their hands up. Scott McClellan took back the chores of finishing off this hastily assembled news conference. Many of the reporters now knew why they had been asked by Mr. McClellan to be present. They were highly respected newsmen and newswomen. They

KIDNAPPING JESUS

would take the lead in spreading the word about the work this team had accomplished.

John and his team were heroes. They would soon answer more questions. One was going to be a tough sell. Where was Osama Bin Laden? And who was the prisoner they brought back? And where was the body? Those questions would only come up if there was a leak to the Press. OBL had departed with the closest shroud of security that ever engulfed anyone. A secret would only remain a secret if they all continued to do their job. He was surprised the question had not come up regarding OBL's whereabouts. With doubt of his death in the future, John thought the American government might fill the information gap with news of sightings, that is, if Al Queda did not find it necessary to provide their own propaganda to keep their unjust cause alive.

Back in Melbourne, a Florida native was sitting in his den. He was not an ordinary man, and this was not an ordinary home. His mansion was located on eighteen acres on the Indian River. He was leaning forward in his overstuffed chair in his large and richly appointed office glued to his Television set with the volume turned up. His name was George E. Hastings, the Owner of BIOTECH150, the largest biotechnical company in the World. The company cloned plants and animals as well as human organs. He was a leader in the field of biotechnology. Yes, George W. Hastings III was to be directly connected in history to cloning like Bill Gates was to Microsoft.

While the interview was in progress he called his assistant, Ken Parker, on his intercom. Ken had been with Hastings for over twenty years and was a trusted friend and associate. Parker knew the good, the bad and the ugly about George Hastings.

Hastings spoke and Parker listened. "Parker, I want you to find out everything about John Elder. I mean everything." Parker knew to leave no stone unturned and not to make any assumptions. Just provide the facts. "He's the man I want for the mission you and I spoke about."

"Yes sir, Mr. Hastings. I'm on it." Parker left the room.

Hastings walked over to the wall and read the words in Latin from a framed piece of old leather parchment. It was a simple frame but was

HOMECOMING

sealed to protect the contents. It was kept in a dimly lit place in his office for two reasons.

The first was so it would not draw undue attention and the second was to keep the exposure to the light at an absolute minimum, even though it was sealed in protective UV glass. In fact, if the frame, or the contents, were ever disturbed, you would think that you were in lockdown at a maximum- security unit in the military. This was Hastings' treasure. It was in old Roman, but Hastings knew the translation like the back of his hand.

WHEN MAN BECOMES WORTHY, I SHALL
RETURN TO EARTH.
WE SHALL MEET AGAIN.

CASCA RUFIO LONGINUS

The parchment had a signature. It was from the Roman Centurion, Casca Rufio Longinus. These were the words spoken to him by Jesus. It was Longinus who was ordered by Pilate to crucify Jesus at Golgotha, the Place of the Skull. Hastings thought out loud, "What did Jesus mean? When man becomes worthy, I shall return to earth!" That day had come. Hastings knew the answer. Quietly, he spoke as if there were someone in the room with him. It was eerie. "I know what you meant, Jesus...I know what you meant!"

CHAPTER XI

THE MEETING

George Elmore Hastings III was born on July 4, 1958. He was the only son of George Elmore Hastings II who also was an only child. Their money was old money. The family fortune began back when the United States was just beginning to develop as a country. The Hastings were direct descents of John Hancock, one of the signers of the Declaration of Independence. He went to the best private school's money could buy. George Hastings III graduated from Harvard Medical School with a specialty in human reproduction and cloning. His mother and father passed away while he was attending graduate studies at Harvard. His father was flying a small aircraft on the way to a business meeting when the plane disappeared from radar. Flying with his father and mother was one of Hastings' employees…He was a young John Washington Jefferson, a family friend and trusted servant in many ways. His family had served the Hastings for six generations. He was survived by his wife, Martha and his son, James Winfield Jefferson. The plane was located several weeks later after an area search finally discovered the plane had crashed into a hillside in the Mohave Desert. Sometime, after the tragic accident, George sold the family construction business for a record $5.5 Billion dollars. The sale of his father's company made him one of the top-ten richest men in America.

KIDNAPPING JESUS

George started the parent company of BIOTECH150 in 1983. It was a small beginning. At the age of 25, he made a breakthrough in the field of reproduction that was a headline article in the Journal of Medicine. It drew National attention and was a topic of conversation in many households. It was a subject that drew heated discussions due to the nature of the controversy that stirred up old prophesies, stories that could well have been the past and could become the future. It depended on your beliefs. It depended on your reality. What was once science fiction was now the present and could become the future. He was up for a Nobel Peace Prize for his work in human reproduction and mapping the entire human genetic code. He had paved the way for human and animal cloning. His company quickly entered the realm of the very rich and famous. The company was quickly catapulted into the Fortune 500 area, and in 2001, was reported to be worth over $100 Billion dollars and climbing. Hastings had his hands on almost everything to do with reproduction and cloning. His company now owned the patents on over a thousand different types of drugs and enzymes.

George wanted to meet this man who had just killed Al-Zawahiri, Osama Bin-Laden's second in charge. He knew Ken Parker would be able to arrange a meeting and have all the intelligence on Elder and his men. Parker had been with him for twenty years. They first met while George was in Turin, Italy in 1981 when George was finishing his research paper, *"Humans! Cloning Would Alter the State of Mankind."* In fact, Hastings truly believed humans should not be cloned. This feeling was not based on morality reasons, but because evil men could use this technology, any technology created for both good and evil, to rid the world of every man, woman and child that did not meet the rules of reproduction brought to bear on this controversial topic. Powerful nations had attempted this very thing in the past. Nazi Germany led by Adolph Hitler, in the 1930s and 1940s and now a limit of how many and type of children a family could have in a large nation like China. It was merely a matter of time when George would have to embrace the eventuality of what he feared and hated.

While visiting Turin, Italy, he left his apartment as he had done so on many evenings. He was on his way to the Royal Library of Turin when he became the victim of a robbery. Two men jumped him and started to beat him up when Parker came out of nowhere and saved his

THE MEETING

life. George offered him a job on the spot with his father's company. George Hastings II was happy to bring his son's guardian angel on board and on the company payroll for as long as he lived.

Ken remained with George and was faithful to only this man that had provided a life after the French Foreign Legion. He had a destiny. More to the point, Ken Parker had a rendezvous with destiny with George Hastings III after that night. Events seemed to be falling into place where Ken Parker and George Hastings III would be inextricably linked for their entire lives.

Ken Parker came from a small family. His mother and father worked all of their lives and had nothing to show for their efforts. His parents died penniless and were buried in a small graveyard in the rural countryside just outside of Paris, France. Parker had a younger sister, but she passed away from an undiagnosed fever when she was just a child. With no other family around, Parker joined the French Foreign Legion. He served his required five-year tour of duty and was ready to reenlist when he ran into Hastings.

Parker's job description was written as the days, weeks and years passed. It was his job to ensure everyone who met his boss was checked out thoroughly. He was very good at it and learned his job quickly. There was no room for error, for Hastings or for Parker. Hasting depended on Parker. Parker did all of the preplanning and background checks on anyone Hastings hired. These were Top-Secret experiments that were being conducted by BIOTECH150 and the formulas of the drugs and enzymes were always trying to be reengineered by unscrupulous individuals and companies. His work ventured into gene therapy and cloning was closely scrutinized by both the public and the government.

This job turned into the best job a single man could ask for. Its sure beat getting his daily ass chewing from the Legion's Brass. Those military men and women in America can only think an ass-chewing was a hands-off experience. The Legion Non-Commissioned Officers, and the Officers, had all experienced the tough discipline that made the Legion the best fighting force in the world. Parker would always be a Legionnaire at heart. His daily training prepared him, and kept him razor-sharp, and mentally tough. He could kill you before you could blink an eye. He was good…very good! Now, he had to get back to reality. The accommodations were much better. He had the Legion to

KIDNAPPING JESUS

thank for his physical conditioning and his mental agility. Unlike the old days of the French Foreign Legion, they had been trained and honed into thinking, killing machines.

A Legionnaire could survive under many different weather conditions and corporate types of environments were not so different. It was truly survival of the fittest, no matter the conditions. In each situation, there were tributes the victor could associate with a type of character much like James Bond in a 007 novel or of an inventive secret agent character like Angus MacGyver from the television, MacGyver, series in the mid-1980s and early 1990s. They each could be, and usually were, very resourceful. And, Parker had one of James Bond-type characteristics that helped to make him irresistible. He was ruggedly handsome. There was a dirty side to his job, but it was not anything Parker had not enjoyed doing. Hastings did not want to be stuck with a single woman and was quite a playboy when work permitted. Along the way, Parker was involved with making enemies disappear. Some had accidents. Others just disappeared. These people all had something in common. Either they were trying to kill Hastings or were trying to steal from his corporation.

BIOTECH150 was born from those early days after the family business was sold. It took some time for it to finally sink in, but there was a reality that occurred to Hastings during the early years just after BIOTECH was founded. There was a definitive reason to change the name from BIOTECH. There was a tie to the past, a bridge to the future. It was in the last words of Jesus. It was possible! Parker's rescue of Hastings allowed Hastings to live.

Over the weeks it took him to recover, he completed his paper for submission to his college professor. He would have to wait sometime before he received his final score, so he decided to extend his time in Turin and make it into a fact-finding vacation. He toured several museums and libraries as well as many of the churches in the area. The Duomo di San Giovanni, built in 1498, is Turin's last vestige of Renaissance architecture and was home to the Shroud. Although the Shroud of Turin was not on display, when Hastings visited the museum, there was interest generated by the many news events regarding the Shroud. This was important in the grand scheme of things. It weighed on Hasting's mind for years.

THE MEETING

Hastings visited Turin during the ten-week public exhibition of the Shroud in 2000 that commemorated the Jubilee anniversary of the Birth of Christ. His visit occurred during the annual Columbus celebration held in Genoa. Christopher Columbus was one of the most famous people who had come from the small town. Still, one of the most amazing sights was the Tower of Pisa located in Pisa. He was on his journey to see the Shroud of Turin. The Shroud was now first and foremost in his mind. The bridge from the past to the present was the parchment from Longinus. The knowledge Hastings learned about Longinus caused him to change the name from BIOTECH to BIOTECH150 in the early 1990s. The pieces of the puzzle were coming together.

Hastings had purchased the parchment in 1981 for $5,000 dollars from a curator in the Royal Museum. It really was just another piece of parchment that had never been authenticated and probably would never be missed due to the catalog problems associated with the many artifacts uncovered throughout time. The practice of selling artifacts from museums was, and is, well known and widespread. The fact is that this practice occurred before the Pyramids were conceived and built and ancient burial sites in the Valley of the Kings had been pillaged throughout time is part of history's footnotes. Some of this history in Egypt occasionally would come to the surface in strange and mysterious ways. Just like the goat herder who discovered the Dead Sea Scrolls near the Dead Sea in 1947. It was a huge discovery that unleashed controversy during the late 1940s and early 1950s. Again, something had occurred in the sands of time from the past to meet the present and affect the future. Had anyone suspected the value of this cloth, then this future may have been in question.

Hastings had the parchment carbon dated. It was from the period of Christ. There was a margin of error, but if Casca Rufio Longinus was the author of this parchment, he was present at the death of Jesus. And, if he was present at the crucifixion, he likely heard the last words spoken by Jesus.

Where had Casca gone after the parchment was left at the church in Turin? This was the question Hastings wanted an answer to. His search had revealed nothing save a Roman Centurion had run from Golgotha, briefly appeared, possibly in Turin, and then a man fitting

KIDNAPPING JESUS

the description of this Centurion arriving in Rome many years later and participated in the gladiatorial games in the Coliseum of Rome. Two-thousand years of rumor...it was a cold trail.

How in the world could this have been the same man? The years between the crucifixion and the inaugural games in the Coliseum in 80AD were too much of a stretch in time. Where did this man disappear to following the crucifixion of Christ? He followed the orders of Pontius Pilate to crucify Jesus Christ. Then, he was gone! Time...time marched onward. The parchment caught the eye of Hastings. It was his link to the past, present and quite possibly the future.

In the next several days, Parker developed a detailed background package on John Elder and his entire team. Parker was determined Hastings would like the material he had assembled. Each person had an established file, with the exception of Mr. Rajeev. There was information on this man, but it was limited, and Parker could not figure out how the team had been augmented by this individual. It was a mystery that would be unraveled, but it would be some time before his actions were completely known by Parker.

John was one tough man and the people he surrounded himself with where only the best. He knew Hastings would like this fact of information due to Hastings' own stringent requirements for his employees, regardless of their long-standing relationship to the family. There had been the faithful, and then there had been the rebellious. Those who could meet the perfection demanded by the Hastings lifestyle were employed. Those who could not meet the high expectations were taken care of and worked outside the household on the grounds of the mansion. They were not allowed inside the household once they were excused from the duties they once performed. Their lives were closely monitored.

He put the information in his briefcase and headed to his truck. The brand new 2002 F-150 FX4 was purchased for him by Hastings. Parker received a new truck every year and could dispose of it any way he saw fit. It was a write off. On his drive to provide the information to Hastings, Parker was thinking of what else he needed from Elder. He was almost 100% sure he wanted to be involved in this mission. It would be intrigue at its finest. He had a smile on his face. The French Foreign Legion had trained him well. He had grown to respect this man of courage.

THE MEETING

George walked to the fireplace in his den, looked up, and read once more from the faded leather parchment on the wall.

WHEN MAN BECOMES WORTHY, I SHALL RETURN TO EARTH. WE SHALL MEET AGAIN.

CASCA RUFIO LONGINUS

"When man becomes worthy, I shall return to Earth!" Then, the final line..."We shall meet again." With a smile on his face, Hastings walked out of the office and up the several flights of stairs of his mansion.

It was 1500 hours in the afternoon. Hastings showered and waited for Ken Parker to return with the information gathered on John Elder and his team. Parker pulled his FX4 into the iron gates of 1140 North Riverside Drive in Melbourne, Florida. The golden "H" was prominent on both iron gates as they swung open to admit Parker's shiny F-150. The mansion had a guard shack on the entrance and sophisticated security hardware both inside and outside of the home his family had built in the late 1800's. Although not as large as the Vanderbilt's home in Ashville, North Carolina, it had the trappings associated with wealth, unimaginable wealth, amassed by America's aristocracy. Flanked by the Indian River on the east, it was situated on 25 acres of manicured real estate. There was a helicopter landing pad in the rear of the estate with a short road between the pad and the house and a small yacht, about 60 feet in length, complemented with an amazing guest house combined with a boathouse from right out of the early 1900s. Yes, Mr. Hastings lived a nice life. Parker was very proud to work for him and knew this man was part of history. In fact, Parker was part of history as it unfolded and added to books that would one day be read. His name would be linked to this man in those annals.

He pulled his truck up to the front of the house and was met by one of the many staff employed by Hastings. He knew James as he knew all the staff. James, a driver, butler, and bodyguard had been with the Hastings family for 55 years. He was a trusted agent of Mr. Hastings.

KIDNAPPING JESUS

It was common knowledge James Winfield Jefferson was a member of the same secretive societies George belonged to and was closely tied with George. As was his father and mother, including his sister and brother, this family served the Hastings for years. In fact, their ancestry could be traced back to Africa. When they were freed from slavery, they made a choice to continue in the service of the Hastings family. That service had turned into a deep friendship and the protective nature of their service to this family had cost them many family lives over the two centuries and seven generations from the time they had emigrated to America and made the beginnings of the family fortune in agriculture, then in cattle and later in the shipping industry. George Hastings III was born into unimaginable wealth.

Yet, he was interested in the new, undiscovered, territory of medicine and cloning. It had not happened overnight, but like his forefathers, he wanted to go where man was just on the verge of new discoveries. It was exciting to him. Managing the family fortune was never an option. He wanted to build upon what had already been established and become famous in his own right. He wanted to make a name for himself. It was about power. He knew power corrupted, and with the knowledge he had discovered, absolute power could corrupt absolutely. George was determined not to open Pandora's Box, but history was about discovery. It was about knowledge. And, it was about unleashing the ability to link the past with the present and being able to affect the future. He was on the very verge of greatness. A greatness not one person on earth could ever imagine. Or, was it possible someone could fathom the concept emerging within his mind?

James escorted Parker to the impressive den located downstairs just outside a formal dining room. Parker had been to this room many times. Dinners with the rich and famous always led to the men being invited to this very room. There were occasions when a select few ladies would be allowed entry. If they were not royalty, they were certainly undressed and undressed quickly. Cigars and Brandy were staples. It was only the very best. The leather chairs and immense bookcases along with the rich engravings on the wall made this study one of the largest rooms in the mansion. Just outside the study was Hastings' office. Parker activated the built in DVD player and the 54-inch Panasonic Plasma TV

THE MEETING

screen that dropped down from a panel located in the bookcase. He loaded the DVD as he waited for Mr. George Hastings III to join him.

Hastings had just finished his shower. He had worked out in the gymnasium located in the basement. This was a weights day for George, and he worked with the medicine ball to get his rhythm in order. George was well trained. After the incident in Turin, Parker became his coach and worked George extremely hard. He knew George would ask him for a rematch in the next several weeks. George never let him off the hook. Parker would have to give his best and not let George win, regardless of the blows exchanged.

George walked down the long stairs and entered the den and library primarily decorated with art by Michael Angelo and statues from Remington. He relished the idea regarding the Holy Trinity... The Father, The Son and the Holy Spirit. On the ceiling of the study was a mural of the Crucifixion of Jesus. Hastings entered the room and walked over to his desk without saying a word to Parker. It was plain he was excited to hear about Elder and his Team but was in deep thought. He sat down in a comfortable chair, reached for his humidor, and offered Parker a cigar. Ken declined but did accept a glass of iced sweet tea when James brought in a tray of assorted drinks and a pitcher of ice. When James left and closed the massive doors to the den, Hastings looked at Ken. "I hope your fact finding went well. I am looking forward to seeing what you have. What were you able to uncover on these men?"

"I know you will like what you are about to see. Let me take you through the slide show I prepared. Each man has his own history, but you will shortly see there is a common thread among them all, culminating with the killing of Ayman Al-Zawahiri, Al Qaeda second-in-command next to Osama Bin-Laden. However, there is one thing I would like you to consider when I finish the presentation. These are the satellite photos I obtained from our source in the Pentagon and clearly show the damage done to Bin- Laden's camps at Tora Bora. This is significant damage done to two separate camps held by Al Queda. The Press labeled the mission "Revenge at Tora Bora". However, as you know, when the C-141B landed with the team, a dead individual on board was transferred to the morgue at Patrick Air Force Base. Security was as tight as it could possibly be.

KIDNAPPING JESUS

There is something else that happened. This is still a mystery. I could only get a rumor there was not only a dead body, but someone else who left the plane under intense security. There is no trail. Officially, it was only a dead body. There was no one who was not accounted for. The crew of the C-141 was sequestered for two days. They were interrogated and the flight log is classified. In fact, the crew's name was struck by all flight records. It's as if the flight never took place. If I could be so bold as to offer up an idea with a possible explanation of what took place, I would suggest, based on the evidence, or the lack of evidence, and the fact there seems to be a struggle for power in the Al Queda leadership and a suspension of terrorist activities, I believe we have a new prisoner at Guantanamo Bay Naval Base. That prisoner would be Bin-Laden himself."

Hastings looked at Parker. He stared at the ceiling in his huge den. Parker knew this man was thinking. Hastings reached for the humidor and took out two cigars and clipped off the ends. Parker leaned over and Hasting lit his cigar and then his own. He reached over for his Brandy decanter and poured two drinks into the crystal shot glasses. George Hastings III lifted his glass and Parker followed suit. There was a slight ching as the glasses came together. Hastings smiled. "Ken, I would bet you are 100% correct. My instincts are in tune with yours. Now you've given me this fantastic news, let's hear the rest."

Parker pointed to the slide show and provided a detailed description of each member of the team. Parker spoke of Rajeev, Aasim Rasheed, Mustafa Basher and Abdul—Hafiz Sahar. "There is a relationship with the FBI and CIA. It's probable Rajeev was coerced into joining the team during the mission since nothing could be found on this man. In fact, all four men, to include those who had families, were no longer on any radar. They probably had gone underground with new identities and deeply imbedded into Black Operations. Their houses were sold, and the extended families had no real information to offer. The only people on the radar were the Elder brothers, Justin Carter, Phil Tucker and Air Force Lieutenant Colonel Brad Lyons who was now on the Colonel's Promotion List. He was now on active duty. There were two mission specialists on the team as well. From what I can tell, they were both selected to be promoted early to Major and will be promoted once the new promotion lists are released for the Army and the Air Force. They

218

THE MEETING

were both assigned to Special Operations at Fort Bragg. Their names are Captain Kimble and Captain Knight. Not sure we could locate them or if we should even try."

Ken continued to advance the slides. "I found their training camp located outside of Melbourne, Florida. It was referred to as Camp Stacey. It is in mothballs currently. No activity, but you can tell the camp was well laid out complete with shooting ranges and training towers. There were a lot of rumors from the locals, but nothing concrete. I believe we should talk directly to John Elder." His picture was on the TV. "This man is a leader. His team followed him to the letter. They managed to have support from the Pentagon, FBI, CIA and the NIA. They also had support from the Navy and the Air Force, not to mention the State and Foreign Service Departments. They put it together rapidly and this was the chief reason why they were successful. They had a purpose. They are hardened professionals. John Elder's service in the Marine Corps was exemplary. He retired as a First Sergeant, with two tours in Vietnam, a mission in Beirut with his Tank Company successfully defending their established security perimeter at the Beirut International Airport. His awards include the Navy Cross and Silver Star with cluster. He served in the U.S. Marshals office. He holds a commercial pilots license with 1800 hours of logged flight time. He was a bounty hunter. That shows me he is interested in money. He left the bounty-hunter business to begin his own business and work for himself. After September 11, he formed Team COBALT. Here's what I believe the letters stand for based on the information I can find. Team COBALT... Company for Elimination of Osama Bin-Laden and Al Queda Leadership. This briefing is concluded, subject, of course, to your questions."

"Parker, I believe Elder made a lot of contacts while he was in the Marine Corps and as a U.S. Marshal. I also think as a bounty-hunter he made a lot of connections with the right people to help him with this mission. The government backed this mission; and he ended up being the spearhead of a monumental mission kept Top-Secret. Currently, this in itself is a miracle. The flight from the United States to Columbia and then into Spain is nothing less than remarkable, considering the plane and the difficulties they encountered. And, then into Pakistan... you know...into nowhere and then coming out alive with a prisoner and

KIDNAPPING JESUS

a viable cover story. This is yet another remarkable feat. I would hate to have this man, and his team, aimed at me, no matter how good I think my security. I have to believe he can succeed. Ken, what can I offer this man to do a job he has not already earned or accomplished? He has $15 million dollars we know about and a couple of smaller accounts in the Cayman Islands. I assume many men from the team also have off-shore accounts. Is that correct?"

Ken nodded affirmatively. "Sir, what do you want him to do?" "Ok. Ken, it's time to put all the cards on the table. I want Elder to steal the Shroud of Turin."

Now it was Parker's turn to stare at the ceiling. It was all coming together. Parker let out a slow breath. "I see. And, with what I've learned about this man in the last several weeks, I think the only way you will get this man to retrieve the Shroud for you is to offer him a very large sum of money. And I believe it will not just be about the money, but the thrill. This is a great adventure. Part of the thrill is in the planning and executing a successful mission."

"Ken I am in complete agreement with you. I'm thinking of $100 Million dollars; $50 Million dollars up front and the balance on delivery. I think this offer will get his attention and should seal the deal. What do you think?"

Parker's mind was swirling as to why his boss wanted the Shroud. He has everything money can buy. Money and the thrill of discovery are the motivators for Hastings. Hastings looked at Ken. Ken was staring at the ceiling.

Upon hearing the question from Hastings, Ken snapped back to reality. "Arrange a meeting for Elder on my yacht. Ensure my security team is on board. I want you there leading my team and taking care of the details. I don't want any problems or distractions. We will cruise a few days out on the ocean and then return to the mansion. I want you to arrange for five or six beautiful women to be aboard. I will provide you with a list. These ladies are the best and very discreet. Their social skills are unquestionable, and they are not only beautiful, but they are smart. I keep them on a monthly retainer as you know. Elder may like to indulge himself or at least relax. I believe you informed me he was a SCUBA diver, so make sure we have all the gear in order. The ladies will also be SCUBA qualified. I have not been diving in some time and

THE MEETING

would not mind getting my feet wet in some warm water. No cameras on board, except for our security. Ensure you sweep the boat for listening devices. You know what to do. Set this up quickly. I want this to go down fast. Do you have any questions?"

Parker shook his head. He had no questions. He put out his cigar, finished his Brandy, and excused himself. Hastings was looking at the last picture from the briefing. Side by side pictures. There were four. The subtitles read, Camp Two - 0615 hours. Camp Two - 0645 hours. Camp One - 0645 hours. And, then there was the photo on the TV of Peshawar, Pakistan - 1530 hours. Now that was impressive. Craters were everywhere. That was some support and at a Million dollars a shot, the Cruise Missiles had done what they were designed to accomplish. Money well spent to take out the cowards who had destroyed so many innocent lives.

Parker left the mansion and drove to where Elder had set up his new life after working with Chuck Taylor. Parker recalled his conversation with Chuck the previous week. His comments and accolades were consistent with his work ethic in the Marines as well as in the U.S. Marshals Office. His background was exemplary. He was in deep thought about Hasting's willingness to pay $100 Million dollars for a piece of cloth. He muttered out loud, "Oh well, it's not my money and he has plenty."

It would take him about an hour to get to Elder's modest home. It was right off U.S. 1 at one of the Melbourne exits and at the exit was a large Ford dealership. Ken turned into Elders' driveway off Magnolia Avenue. It was just beginning to get dark outside. Streetlights were on as were the lights in Elder's house. Ken walked up to the door and knocked.

John Elder had been home for several days. He was very tired and was in no mood to deal with anyone - newsmen or women. John opened the door. Standing there was Ken Parker. Elder asked, "Are you a reporter?"

Parker instantly replied. "No sir. Mr. Elder, I work for Mr. George Hastings III and I'm here to extend an invitation for you to have lunch with him on his private yacht."

Elder looked at Ken Parker like he was crazy. He knew who Hastings was and what he did for a living. Who, in the entire civilized

KIDNAPPING JESUS

world, did not know who one of the ten richest men in the world was, and was practically living next door? "What the hell does George Hastings want with me?"

Parker quickly replied, "It is a private matter to be discussed between Mr. Hastings and yourself." John Elder looked Ken Parker in the face and liked what he saw. This was no errand boy. This man has seen things. There was more to this man than met the eye. Elder was positive he was standing with an equal. Here was a soldier standing in front of him. John took the envelope from Parker's hand and opened it. He looked at Parker and instantly knew he was privy to the contents and to what Hastings wanted to discuss with him. "It says I am to meet with Mr. Hastings on Friday at 0900 hours. It also says you are going to pick me up in a limousine."

Parker replied instantly. "Yes sir. You are one hundred percent correct!"

John looked Ken Parker in the eyes. There was no waiver, no hint of cowardice, not a trace of being someone's servant. "I will be ready for you on Friday. It looks like he went to a lot of trouble for some reason and I am curious as to the reason why. I'll see you then."

"Yes sir. I'll let Mr. Hastings know you have accepted his invitation." Parker turned and walked to his truck, opened the door, and got in. John Elder watched him drive away.

Parker drove back across the causeway admiring the scenery that Brevard County had to offer. The town of Melbourne was conveniently located only two hundred miles from Miami and near famous Cape Canaveral. It was a great place to live without the entire crime wave major cities in Florida and in the United States experience day in and day out.

Parker pulled his truck into the driveway at the Hastings mansion. It had been a routine invitation. He knew he had been sized up by John Elder. What he had read and researched was 100% correct. His instincts assured him this was the case. It was dark and Ken turned the headlights off. Security had checked him at the entrance, yet the security monitors were always active and monitored from the small, yet very efficient, operations center located in the basement of the mansion. It was always operational. Security personnel lived at the mansion with a seven day on/seven day off schedule and the eight-to-twelve-hour shifts depended on where Hastings was located. There was a back-up

THE MEETING

team of six specialists on-call and nearby should the need exist. They all had this type of schedule. One week on (Red Team), one week off (Green Team), and one week of being on-call (Blue Team). It was as if George Hastings III had his own personal SWAT Team. He opened and closed the door of the truck.

He was greeted by James Winfield Jefferson at the massive entry to the mansion. He was then escorted to the den and took a seat in one of the overstuffed leather chairs. George was at the computer. Parker waited for George to speak before he recounted his visit with John Elder.

George looked at Ken and smiled. That was his cue to recap the visit. "Sir, I delivered the message to Elder. Elder was curious as to the invitation and accepted your offer to meet with him on your yacht. He knew who you were but wants to know more. There is one more thing. My instincts confirm the reports I have provided. He is a soldier's soldier. There are no gray areas with him. It is black and white, and he seems to be a man that follows a simple approach, but obtains results. After your meeting with him on the yacht, I would like to hear your evaluation."

John Elder wanted to know exactly who Hastings was and what he could possibly want with him. John sat down at his computer. His search provided information that made John think. Why would a man with a net worth of over $100 Billion dollars want with me. He was the sole, private owner of BIOTECH150, a Fortune 500 company. He mapped the entire human genetic code. He cloned animals from fossils. His company was the first to clone a sheep; however, they were not credited with being the first as they were years ahead of what was in publication. He lost his father and mother in a plane crash while he was in Harvard Medical School. He sold his father's company for a record profit. Hastings then started BIOTECH and then changed the name to BIOTECH150. He won a Nobel Prize for mapping the human genetic code. The question remained, "What does he want?"

<hr>

John hit the sack. It was late and he was soon fast asleep. His dreams took him back to Beirut and to Vietnam. He was in the same firefight and it seemed so real. He woke up. It was dead silence in his house. No sounds and his alarm system was in active mode. This was

KIDNAPPING JESUS

no ordinary security system he had installed. Cameras were inside and outside the house, and the system had back-up power. He would not be caught unaware. Even the windows were bullet proof. When Charles and Pete installed the roofing and helped with the vaults underneath the floor, they subcontracted the windows to a gentleman named Bill who owned a window and door business. The alarm system was private. John did not want any responders coming or calling. It was likely anyone who broke into his house had to have one major objective, to kill John and find out what he knew. They would find his booby traps located throughout his home. Although he kept a low profile, someone would end up dead if they came into his house without hitting the right buttons. Light switches and certain books were merely trigger mechanisms. Even Ken Parker had been checked out. John had done his research well. Although John was armed when Ken knocked on the door, he had been pretty sure Ken knew he was on camera just from his body language, or lack of body language. Professionals knew professionals.

He awoke at 0600 hours for his morning physical training. It was about a three-mile trip to the gym. He routinely rode his bike, worked on the weights, resistance machines and took some time with the medicine ball. He really liked the rhythm boxing provided. It was reassuring. He would often pick up a racquetball game when he hit the machines, but always ran. The days he did not work out on the machines were running days. He kept up his running with a five to eight mile a day regimen. Sometimes he ran on the beach. One day a week was an off day unless he was down in West Palm or Jupiter doing some SCUBA diving. John maintained his physical stamina by working out.

At this time in his life, he was retired, had completed a clandestine operation into the mountains of Tora Bora, but was still itching to get into something that would offer him both a physical and mental challenge. Yet, on the other hand, it sure was nice to be home where he kept in constant contact with his family and the members of the team with whom he still had access. He continuously checked up on Charles and on Justin Carter and looked in on them when he went to Patrick Air Force Base. In fact, John had unlimited access to the facilities with his Military Identification Card and window decal and often ran on the Base after his visits with Charles and Justin. Running around the

224

THE MEETING

airfield was great. It kept him in contact with the airmen and women of the Air Force. This young generation was part of the future of the United States. Justin was due to be released in a couple of weeks. Charles would be in rehabilitation for some time. His doctors were optimistic. Charles should recover, almost completely, given time.

He went out to the garage. There it was. Every time he looked at it, he was astounded. Some people would think he was a little odd. After all, he was 52 years old, yet he still had a love affair with a car. With a smile on his face, John walked into the garage and opened the door of the 1966 Corvette Coupe. Powered with a 427 cubic inch engine with 425 horsepower and a four-speed manual transmission with side exhaust pipes, it was a Detroit beauty. John put the key in the ignition. A low growl came from the motor. It was very distinctive for this type of car. John put the Vette into reverse, backed out of garage and headed east on Magnolia Street. It was only five minutes to the gym.

John waited for his turn into traffic. He gave the Corvette some gas and before he knew it, he was at eighty miles per hour. He backed the trophy car down to around sixty. He arrived at the gym as two women were getting ready to get into their SUVs. They stopped and watched John get out of his car. John knew they were thinking to themselves, that is one good-looking man and machine. They both checked their watches. One of the women turned to her friend. "Sharon, the next time we will have to look him up. Maybe we can invite him to the next singles get together."

Carrie smiled. "I am sure with a car like that, he's loaded." The two of them got into their cars and drove off never knowing how true the statement was.

John went into the gym. Inside the locker room he found a locker and took his lock out of his gym bag along with his towel. Locking up his wallet and changing clothes, he headed towards the weight room. It was very quiet this time of day. Only a few people were inside the weight room. John went through the regular work out he had been doing for as long as he could remember. If a person were looking at him, they would never know he was fifty-two years old. He looked more like he was in his late thirties or early forties. He completed thirty-five minutes on free weights and was looking forward to the sauna. With his shorts on, John went into the sauna to relax. With sweat dripping from his body, he recalled the events from the last several months in the quiet of the sauna's hissing rocks and the steam emanating as the water slowly dripped.

With the workout completed for the morning, he put on fresh clothes. John felt good. He headed home to take care of the calls he needed to make and to check his accounts. LAPEARLE was heading home, and John wanted to check her status. After business, he intended to go out and get into some of the local nightlife. He kicked the Corvette up to 85 miles per hour. What a great sound. He got off at the Vero Beach exit and pulled into a service station.

John went into the store to pay for his gas. The female behind the counter said, "I like your car. What kind of car is it?"

John replied, "I can see you have good taste. I am John Elder, and you are?"

"My name is Katie. Glad to meet you."

John replied, "It is a Chevrolet Corvette and I have owned her for over 20 years. I am kind of new around here so maybe you could show me around. That is, if you would care to show an old Marine some of the nightlife in the area."

Katie quickly replied. "I get off around 8PM."

John stepped out of the way of another customer, to let him pay for his purchase. Katie rang him up. Katie took out a piece of paper to give John her cell phone number. "Call me at 7:30." John handed her $50.00 dollars and headed home.

After taking care of the many calls, he needed to make and the computer searches regarding the day's events, he checked out the time and realized it was 1915 hours and time to make a call. Katie answered her cell phone. It was simple conversation and Katie explained to John she lived in a small apartment complex near the convenience store where John had purchased gas. She would be ready at 8:30.

John hung up the phone and took a shower. He made a call to Seville. At the Consulate, John spoke to Brad Lyons. John got the basics. In fact, Brad informed John, "John, the personnel at Incirlik Air Force Base were first class. We took a few rounds that came close to ending our mission. There was heavy security, so no issues were discussed regarding the mission. However, you should have seen just how

THE MEETING

close two AK-47 rounds missed our control wires for the tail and flaps." With that being said, the call was over.

He headed over to pick up Katie and then headed south on US-1. Once he found one of the famous seafood restaurants, Captain Hiram's Seafood House, he pulled into the parking lot. John decided he would go in and check out what the locals had to offer. John and Katie went into the bar and ordered a beer from the cute bartender behind the counter.

On the television over the bar, Fox News was televising an interview with George Hastings III. The picture of a live Woolly Mammoth was being shown. BIOTECH150 was the only company in the world to have this technology. George Hastings III had crossed another milestone in extracting life from death. It was life from death, death that had no recent memories. No witnesses. But it was life anew; a new beginning for the world.

John's table was located towards the back of the restaurant. A male waiter took their order of stuffed grouper with crabmeat. It was different from the seafood he normally ordered in it was one of the house specialties. It was Cajun broiled. The order was out from the kitchen in about twenty minutes. The waiter refilled John's ice water several times during the meal. They exchanged some small chit chat and each other had a pretty good idea of their backgrounds. John spoke of his Marine Corps days and touched on life after the Marines with the U.S. Marshals office and then as a Bounty Hunter.

Katie asked John a direct question. "Were you on TV not too long ago with President Bush?"

John looked around him and realized some people were directing their stares at him and probably talking about him. The news was recent and broadcasts of the day's events were still being shown on the major networks. John had even been asked to be on FOX News with Bill O'Reilly. At this point in time, John was trying to keep a low profile. It was working, at least to some extent. John looked at Katie and replied, "Yes, that was me. I was the man on TV, but I would rather not talk about it."

John learned Katie was the daughter of an Air Force Colonel, and was working her way through college, albeit at a slower pace. Her grandparents left their three grandchildren a sizable inheritance and one of the stipulations was to travel the world and then go to college. She was

KIDNAPPING JESUS

twenty- four years old and was working on her Master's Degree in Political Science. By traveling, she would learn more about the world and what her life's work should. encompass. She had made her decision. She wanted to join the State Department and work on the diplomatic side of foreign politics. She had not gone blindly into college life without knowledge of the world. John was thinking what a good woman she was. She was smart and was dressed in a summer dress with a kind of a Spanish flair to it. She had nice shoulder length hair. And she was well informed on current events.

Katie expressed her feelings about the war in Iraq and how she felt America should win at all costs. The waiter brought the bill and John left cash on the table with a generous tip. Katie leaned over and kissed John on his right cheek.

On the way out of the restaurant, a man looked at him and mouthed a silent "thanks!" John recognized the man as one of the crew from the C- 141B. He was with his wife and two children. John just nodded his head and looked back at Katie.

"Katie, have you ever gone for a real ride in a 1966 Corvette?" Katie quickly responded, "No, but I would like to...with you."

She had a big smile on her face. John and Katie left the restaurant and headed to Interstate 95. They drove down to Palm Bay and found a quiet little spot and parked. It was about 2200 hours and the sky was dark and the stars were bright. They were both relaxed. John felt good about this woman. You could never judge a book by its cover. Katie was good looking, educated and was mature for her age.

John asked, "Katie, are you having a good time?"

Katie looked at John and replied, "Yes, why do you ask?"

"I know we just met today, but I feel as if I have known you all my life. It's strange. We are different in almost every way, but I feel a kinship to you. You are a kindred spirit. And, although there is an age difference, I feel we are not so much apart."

Katie replied. "John, I am attracted to men who are mature, someone I can feel safe with. You are that person. It may not last long, but life is never about a sure thing. I want you to hold me in your arms. I want you to kiss my lips. I want to be with you."

They headed north on 1-95 and were back in Melbourne in less than an hour. It was nearly midnight. Pulling into the driveway, he pressed

THE MEETING

the automatic garage door opener. John pulled the Corvette into the two-car garage. He pulled out another clicker from his pocket and hit the button twice. Checking the display, it was green.

Had it been yellow, he would have been on alert. Had it been red, the security system would have been armed. He turned the car off and went inside with Katie following. The garage door closed, and the alarm system was reactivated.

"Katie, would you like a drink?" "I'll have what you are having."

John disappeared into the kitchen and mixed two vodka martinis and checked out a replay from the video feeds fast forward. There was nothing to report. He would check the internal cameras next. There was nothing there as well. Of course, the cameras would remain on no matter what took place.

They made themselves comfortable on the leather couch. The lights were dim and the music was low. He had lit the small fireplace. The gas logs were aglow. John had his arm around Katie as they sat and watched the fire and listened to the music. Katie had already broken the ice when she had kissed John on the cheek at the restaurant and then told him she wanted to be with him. This is why Katie liked older men. They treated a woman with respect rather than just groping like a young bull in heat. Katie leaned over and whispered in John's ear. "John, I want you to take me. It has been six months since I've been with someone, and I want you."

A kiss on John's neck seemed like someone had branded him. Her lips were warm, but her tongue was hot. She climbed onto John's lap and started kissing him. Of course, John returned the favor. She was about five-feet, four-inches tall and about 110 pounds with nice full breasts, about a C-Plus, and had a firm ass men would fight over.

He carried her into his bedroom while she was unbuttoning his shirt. They were taking their time undressing each other while they were kissing. It was passionate. They were both in excellent physical condition and the hard bodies collided with sparks flying. Time just seemed to pass as they made love through the night.

They both fell asleep in the early morning hours on John's bed in a sweating pile of human lust. John drifted off into a deep sleep. He dreamed of Katie. This was short-term, and they both knew it. Katie was nice, but he knew she knew he might not ever ask her out again.

KIDNAPPING JESUS

Of course, John always kept his women on some sort of a leash. They would always be ready to come back into his life should he ask. His charisma was powerful. He was not conceited; it was just fact. He did not know why; it was just that way. However, that was all she was to him in a nutshell. He would never let himself get close to any woman.

Then, he began to think about Pearle West. Now this was a woman. In fact, this was the only real woman to him in his life. Still, there were no lasting commitments; even with his unyielding love for her. He needed to call her to see how things were going. A trip to California was in order.

John and Katie drove the Corvette to the IHOP on Highway 192 and ate a late breakfast. They made small talk as they drove back to where Katie's apartment was located. John let her out with a nice passionate kiss. "Katie, you are a very nice young lady. Any man would kill for you. I want you to know I am a very busy man and I operate at a different level than most men could ever understand. I know you know seeing you again may be a problem for both of us. However, I would like to be with you again, I just don't know when it will be possible. I am always traveling, and I think the next few months will occupy most of my time. It's not you. It's me. It's my life."

Katie looked downward with a small pout on her face. What John had just stated was usually her line. Katie looked upward at John. "John, I understand. Remember, I saw you on TV. I feel there's more to the story the world will never know. At least, the world will not know what really happened for now. I am glad we met. You are the type of man I want to meet, and yet am afraid to meet. Just call me once in a while to let me know how you are doing. I'm always ready to take you on a tour around town."

As John drove away, Katie had a strange feeling she would never see John Elder again. Of course, she thought it was too bad because he was a great lover and she had been fully satiated during the night and into the morning. Katie thought she might be giving herself to men too easily, but John was hot. With a smile on her face, she quickly went into her apartment and put on the proper attire to get back to the store where she worked. It would be another boring day. In fact, she was going to quit and concentrate on her studies. She had the money! Why not use it? She hated the job! However, she would go in and quit in person.

THE MEETING

John had left his mark on her. It was time to get on with life. She was no coward and would not use the phone for this type of conversation. It was time, time to move on to the next level.

CHAPTER XII

THE CRUISE

John Elder went to sleep at 2100 hours. He had watched the O'Reilly Factor. He thought of Katie as he drifted off to sleep. He was looking forward to spending time on *The Miss Adventure*, George Hastings' yacht. He wanted to know what George Elmore Hastings III wanted with him and why he had invited John to join him on his yacht for an extended period. It would be fun, and John was looking forward to a few days of being pampered. The one thing John knew was security would be tight. If Ken Parker was any indication of the team behind the man, then John felt confident this cruise would be safe. That is, as safe as could possibly be expected.

It was not a restless sleep, but John dreamed of past events while serving in Vietnam during the TET Offensive. His Marine buddy's faces were vivid. Then there was his tour in Beirut. It was as if he were once again present for duty in honoring those who were massacred.

Just as the alarm clock went off, John was nearly awake, and he was in deep thought regarding the mission in Afghanistan. It was 0530 hours. John quickly washed up, went into the exercise room, turned on the news, and hit the free weights. It was a quick workout, and the news was pretty much a repeat of the previous day's events. After a hot shower, he was dressed. He had packed his bags the night before and had placed them at the door.

KIDNAPPING JESUS

The knock on the door was at precisely 0700 hours. When John opened the door, Parker stood there dressed in a Chauffeur suit complete with a black cap. John looked at Parker. "Ken, you look like Cato from the Green Hornet". They both laughed.

Ken replied, "Good morning Mr. Elder."

Now it was Elder's turn. "Drop the Mister. Ken, it does not become you.

How did you like the French Foreign Legion?"

Parker quickly replied. "I loved it and would have stayed if Mr. Hastings had not have offered me the job of a lifetime."

"Ken, the Legionnaires are good men to be with in a fight. I worked with them in Vietnam, although it was only briefly. Some of the toughest men I've ever encountered."

Parker did not say a word he just kept driving down U.S. Highway 1 on the way to Sebastian. He was thinking the boss was right; Elder had done background homework on both he and Hastings. Why would he not? John sat back and enjoyed the ride. The information he obtained on Hastings and Parker made him feel comfortable.

Parker pulled the limousine into a private Marina just off the highway. He got out of the car quickly, but Elder was out the door before Parker could open it for him. Parker showed John the way to the 100 plus foot yacht. John walked up the gangway of *The Miss Adventure*. John walked aboard and Ken introduced George Elmore Hasting III. "Mr. Hastings, this is Mr. John Elder."

Mr. Hastings replied. "John, it is a pleasure to meet you. I have been looking forward to meeting a real American hero for a long time. It was very nice of you to accept my invitation and join me on my boat." John laughed at the play on words. As he looked past Hastings and Parker, this was no boat.

"Sir, I appreciate your gracious invitation and look forward to the unveiling of this big mystery of yours. Had the invitation come from anyone else, or delivered from an incompetent member of someone's staff, I would not be here. I am intrigued after learning a few things about your background."

"John, the pleasure is all mine. Ken, please inform the Captain to get underway at his earliest convenience and give him my regards. John, please accompany me to my parlor."

234

THE CRUISE

George Hastings III and John. Elder went to the aft of the yacht, down a flight of small stairs that opened up into a very large parlor. Shortly after they had settled in, a Bloody Mary was provided by the incomparable James Winfield Jefferson. As James left, he opened a door to a hallway leading to the cabins located forward of the parlor. The master suite was located in the aft of the large yacht; the parlors were next and located more or less in the center, and forward were eight beautiful rooms.

George escorted John to his room located directly off the parlor. It was stately, and the room was richly appointed with mirrors, wood accents, a TV, and a small bar. He had a very nice bathroom, and the marble inlays were very artistic. His bags had already been unpacked and his Colt 45 caliber pistol was in his dresser. George looked at John. "I know you are accustomed to having your pistol with you at all times. While on board, you may carry it with you or leave it here. It is your choice. I am comfortable with your decision. However, let me show you some hidden compartments in your room."

One by one, George showed John five separate compartments with various handguns and rifles. There was even a Thompson sub-machine gun in one of the compartments. "John, these compartments are for the protection of the ship. My men have strict orders. They are a small army, much like the one you took to Afghanistan. You never know. There are pirates in the Caribbean, as well as individuals who have a personal vendetta against me. I take no chances. There are both passive and active security measures on board."

The engines were revving up and the Captain came on the intercom system. "All hands, prepare to cast off. Ladies and gentlemen, please move to a seated position or come up on deck. There are heavy currents in the inlet and the ride should be bumpy for about 20 minutes."

George and John headed back to the parlor and their Bloody Mary. Shortly, they were joined by six beautiful women. George looked at John and made the introduction. "Ladies, this is John Elder. He is my guest. Please treat him with every courtesy. John, from your left, it is my pleasure to introduce Kelly, Meagan, Beverly, Janice, April, and Michelle. These lovely ladies are not only beautiful, but they are also intelligent. They are our companions for the next few days. John, we are

KIDNAPPING JESUS

on an adventure. Have fun. This is one trip where we can mix pleasure with business."

During the introduction, John could feel the yacht leave the dock. George suggested they all go up on deck as they went out of the inlet. Although the waters were choppy, the yacht moved into the Atlantic Ocean without much effort. The men and the ladies were at the rail. There were many boats of all sizes coming and going through the inlet. In no time, they were out to sea. John exchanged chit chat with the ladies. They were all dressed immaculately, and their make-up was perfect. They could all have been Miss America. They were pretty much the same height, about 5'6" to 5'9" and about 115 to 125 pounds. They were all so very beautiful. Several of them were blondes, several brunettes, and a red head. The eyes were striking, blue eyes, brown eyes and green eyes. One of the ladies hair was so black, it shimmered blue. Her name was April. She was 5'7" tall and probably weighed about 125 pounds. She definitely was an athlete, and her bust was ample. Her eyes were blue along with olive skin. Another lady John was attracted to was Janice. Her hair was a deep rich red; it turned her blue eyes into sparkling diamonds. She could melt a block of ice at 50 feet. She, too, had a physical figure. In fact, they all were physically fit and very beautiful. The staff was serving caviar, crackers with cheese, and small sandwiches. The smoked salmon and cheese were excellent.

George walked over to John. "John, I would like to take a few moments to speak to you alone." He motioned for John to follow him to his private den. Once they were inside the small, yet lavish den adjoining his stateroom, George asked, "John would you like a Havana cigar? They are fresh from the fields of Cuba. I have them flown in special for me."

Elder replied, "Yes, Mr. Hastings, I believe I would like one."

George Hastings III replied. "Please, John, don't call me Mister and I would appreciate you not calling me sir. I would like for us to be on equal terms, regardless of whether you choose to do business with me or not. I would consider it a favor if you would take the whole box as a small token of my appreciation for joining me on this cruise and hearing my offer."

THE CRUISE

For a minute, John was taken aback, but it was ok with him. He was still trying to figure out the angle as Mr. Hastings lit his cigar and then his own.

George Hastings broke the silence, "I am sure you are wondering why I have invited you to my yacht. Am I correct?"

John quickly replied. "I wonder what a man who becomes a Billionaire at the age of twenty-five and has thousands of patents under BIOTECH150 with a net worth of over $100 Billion dollars wants with an old war horse like me. Yes, you better believe, I would like to know." John Elder was sitting directly across from George and looked him squarely in the eyes while he was waiting for an answer.

It was as if an hour had passed before George got up from his leather chair and pulled down what seemed like a map, but it was a drawing. John recognized it in an instant. George looked at John. "John, this is a picture of the Shroud of Turin, the burial cloth of Jesus Christ. This evidence was left on Earth to prove he was here." He opened a small cabinet with an authentic copy of the leather parchment he kept safeguarded in his mansion. "John, let me translate the Latin...

WHEN MAN BECOMES WORTHY,
I SHALL RETURN TO EARTH.
WE SHALL MEET AGAIN.

CASCA RUFIO LONGINUS

Shortly after the crucifixion of Christ, the Roman Centurion charged in carrying out the public execution by the appointed governor of Judea, Pontius Pilate, disappeared from Golgotha and later seems to have reappeared in Turin, Italy. The parchment you see here was signed by Casca Rufio Longinus. It was an odd piece that showed up in a museum I visited, and I purchased it for just a few dollars. John, at the time, I did not know if it was real or not; however, sometimes the past comes to the present to affect the future. I had it carbon dated, and it comes from the time of Jesus. I think now is the right time to test a theory. John, you also have a place in history. History that is being written as we speak."

KIDNAPPING JESUS

John looked up at Hastings. He still did not know what he wanted. "This is very interesting. But what does this have to do with me?"

"John, I own this leather parchment. However, the Shroud of Turin is owned by the Catholic Church." George looked John in the eyes and said, "I want you to steal the Shroud of Turin for me for my private collection. I will pay you and the team of your choice $100 Million dollars. I'll pay $50 Million dollars up-front and $50 Million dollars on delivery. Regardless, $50 Million dollars is yours for making the attempt. But it is my belief that if anyone can do this job, it is you and your team."

It was as if John had been hit by a train. The vision of Jerry Willis, "Choo Choo" connecting a hard-right fist to his left chin years ago came back to mind. That was one tough man. He was silent. His thoughts ran the gamut... intrigue, difficulty, challenge, danger, and money. He chose his words very carefully. Was George Hastings III nuts? Or was this for real? "George, I am no thief. I've never stolen anything in my life. I am going to have to think this over. If I was to be caught at this time, just after killing Bin- Laden's second in command, I would become the Catholic Church's number one target, not to mention the fact I am already a target for the Al Queda network. Talk about squeeze play. I, my family, my friends, even you with all your security could simply disappear. Besides, I am pretty well off myself, George. But, again, I am intrigued by your offer. Please fill me in on all the details. I work with facts and I like to keep it simple. I know you checked me out and you have access to information routinely denied to the public. I also made inquiries about you. Calls to the Pentagon have provided just enough information regarding you and your past to make your investment in time and money with me regarding this cruise a distinct possibility. You certainly have my attention. But, no matter what, even in this case, its business first, pleasure later, even if this mission is in the cards."

Hastings responded. "John, I like the way you think. Ken Parker assured me you were a man, independent and self-reliant. Just to allay any doubts in your mind. I, also, am the type of man who likes to lay his cards on the table. I knew you wanted to know why I wanted to meet you. I also wanted to express my gratitude to you and your men for a job well done in Afghanistan. I believe you killed more than just an Al Queda number two man and the cover story will stand for many years to come...Hell, you did what our military could not do. And, although

THE CRUISE

I know you had support from the highest levels, including Presidential support for the go-ahead, I know you did the mission for your own reasons, even though you are an adventure seeker who enjoys the pure thrill. So, think about what I ask. I know it is huge, but from this mission I am offering you, you will be able to retire and do whatever you want for the rest of your life…You know what is at stake for yourself, but I want to emphasize what is at stake for humanity. The Shroud is probably the most protected artifact in the world save the Declaration of Independence. The Shroud represents a bridge from the past to the future. The parchment is a signal from the past. To bridge the past with the future is the message, the message in a bottle, so to speak. The message is clear. Casca Rufio Longinus placed the message in a bottle when he wrote down the last words of Jesus Christ…The Roman Catholic Church will never open this, the single most valuable time capsule in the world, unless it benefits them. They know what they have. I am convinced you and your team can release the Shroud and place it in my care and under my guard. I understand your trepidation. However, you have enough information to make an informed decision without any pressure. When you are ready to speak of this again, please let me know. So, until then, please enjoy the company of the ladies and make yourself comfortable. Consider my yacht at your disposal. I am taking the helicopter after lunch and will return tomorrow. The Captain has instructions to sail to the Grand Caymans and anchor off the coast. I know you like to dive, and the ladies are all certified divers. I will join you late tomorrow afternoon. Hopefully, you will join me in a dive. I look forward to snagging some fresh lobster, the old-fashioned way, by hand. Let's get back to the ladies."

George and John made their way back to the top deck where the women were drinking and talking. John sat down among the ladies and George motioned to Michelle and Beverly to join him. The three of them disappeared down the stairs. It was around 1100 hours. John was ready to party. James Winfield Jefferson asked John, "Sir, what would you like to drink?"

"James, please fix a vodka martini for me with just a hint of ice." Once he was served, John looked at the remaining ladies and proposed a toast. "Ladies, here's a toast to smooth sailing and getting to know

KIDNAPPING JESUS

each of you. Bottom's up!" Four ladies had their beautiful eyes on this seasoned man. They sparkled.

Lunch was served in the main dining room at 1200 hours. George was escorted in by the two lovely ladies he had disappeared with an hour ago. He sat at the head of the table and was dressed in dress slacks and a dark blue polo shirt. Fresh Red Snapper was on the menu for lunch, but Filet Mignon was also available. In fact, it was a feast fit for a king. The China and silver were beautiful. There were fresh flowers on the table and the ship's staff were wearing their whites. The chef was George's personal chef and traveled with him wherever he went. Salads were first along with a cup of seafood bisque. There was fresh bread and butter. Everyone had their choice of drink, but water in crystal, with lemon, was already at each seat.

George looked around the table and took a spoon to his glass to get everyone's attention.

"John, ladies, I propose everyone on board my ship have a great time and make new friends. John, enjoy the hospitality the ladies have to offer. They are truly what is best about the South."

John saluted his host. As a former Marine, he had been trained to be polite and courteous. His skills had been refined during the years following his service in the Corps, but he had charisma. It was a gift. Some were born with it, some aspired to it and then never succeeded in obtaining it.

John spoke. "George, let me say again my thanks for your hospitality. It was time to take a break and I can think of nothing finer than to be on *The Miss Adventure* with you and these lovely ladies. I hope your trip is successful and I look forward to a dive tomorrow afternoon with you."

Lunch was officially over. It was delicious. And everyone ate like there was no tomorrow. The pilot was starting up the engine to the sleek flying helicopter. It was a beautiful chopper and was painted blue and white. These were George's favorite colors and also his family crest. On the side of the chopper was *Miss A*. Not anything that would jump out at you unless you knew something about George Hastings III.

George shook John's hand and whispered in his ear. "John, seriously have a good time. Look forward to catching up with you tomorrow. Until then, my yacht is at your disposal."

THE CRUISE

John had made another friend. This man was true to himself. John could tell this was no fraud. He had a silver spoon, but not up his ass like many whose fame and fortune were owed solely to their parents. He had made his money with his brains and diligence. While deep in thought, the helicopter gently lifted and headed to the Grand Cayman Islands, the destination of *The Miss Adventure*. George would be back tomorrow afternoon and rejoin the yacht after his meetings with several banks George owned. His assets were closely guarded and to ensure his financial safety, he chose to own his own banks.

John stepped down from the ship's upper deck and landing pad. Six ladies greeted him. He really felt a bit awkward but looked at Meagan and April. Meagan was blond, buxom, and beautiful. She could mesmerize any man on two legs. In fact, they all could. Her skin was lightly tanned, and she looked like she could turn a man inside out. April, her dark hair shimmered blue, and her blue eyes were like fire. Her skin was a dark olive color and her natural tan was only enhanced in the sun.

John turned to the remaining ladies. "Ladies, please excuse us. It's time to take a tour of the ship."

They all laughed. John was in good form. As the party of three headed down the stairs, John kissed Meagan on her left cheek and April on her right. Once down the stairs, they headed towards the bow. John showed the ladies his room. He asked what they wanted to drink, and it was Champagne.

John picked up the phone in his room and James answered. "Sir, what can I get for you?"

"James, please bring a magnum of Champagne and strawberries. Do you have any whipped cream? Please bring it as well if you do. Just leave everything outside the door."

"Yes sir, I'll have everything down to you in about five minutes."

The ladies had opened up one of the closets built into the wall. They each grabbed an outfit and headed into the bathroom. Meagan looked at John. "Give us a few minutes and come join us. The shower is big enough for three."

All John could think of was how seductive these ladies were. He could not help but be aroused. There was a knock at the door. The refreshments were here. John opened the door and brought the ice bucket and tray inside. The bar was open.

KIDNAPPING JESUS

He stepped into the bathroom. Meagan stepped out of the shower dripping wet. She was beautiful. She had a nice line and was completely manicured.

She helped John off with his shirt and then his pants. John stepped into the shower with Meagan and April. They were washing him. John was thinking he had died and gone to heaven. These were two of the most beautiful women in the world. Their hair was wet, and their bodies shimmered. It was hard for John. He had his hands on both women checking them out. This was erotic! This was going to be a day to remember.

The ladies toweled off and were doing their hair. Thank God for mirrors. John brought their drinks into them, and he had slipped on a light robe with *The Miss Adventure* monogrammed just above his left breast. He relaxed in his large bed and dozed off for a few moments.

In no time, April and Meagan came into the bedroom dressed in lace. Meagan was wearing black, and April was wearing white lace with red accents. It was as if they had nothing on at all, however, as the clothes were merely a tease. The ladies were ready for John.

In a sexy voice, Meagan spoke, "John, you are a real man. We are here to please you, but this is our pleasure to meet a man like yourself. Please let us know what you like. We have no inhibitions."

That's all John could think about. And, then it was all over. It was a reaction, not intentional. Meagan was kissing and caressing John. John needed sleep. He shortly fell into a deep sleep with two of the most beautiful women in the world on his left and right.

They were gone for a couple of hours. During their lustful recuperation, the four other ladies had come downstairs and retired to their rooms. They showered and dressed appropriately. The doors to their rooms were suggestively open. Meagan and April asked John if he needed anything else and also went to their rooms. They gave a light kiss to each other on the lips before they left and then both kissed John. It was a threesome.

John asked them what was next on the agenda and April pointed to the slightly opened doors. She looked at John. "It's up to you; pick a door, any door. Have fun!"

242

THE CRUISE

John looked up at his mirrored ceiling and smiled. He had had several women in a single day, but this was going to be a challenge. He was not a young man anymore but was in terrific shape.

He watched two partially clad ladies go down the short hallway, turned around, and jumped into the shower. A knock came at his door as he was stepping out of the shower. He was drying his hair. "Please, come in, the doors open."

It was Janice, the redhead with deep blue eyes. She was all there. Yep, that was it. "Janice, it is good to see you." Shit, he said to himself. That was stupid.

Janice laughed. "John, let's have some fun. You should be able to last awhile, and I like to play for hours. You'll be hungry when I'm done with you."

It was dinner time. Janice had her way with John. She was fantastic. She was insatiable and knew how to keep a man aroused. She played hard and the whispers she spoke to John just kept it going.

John dressed for dinner and Janice went to her room to get dressed. John was soon on deck and somewhat kicked back in the dining room. The Cayman Islands were on the horizon, and they should be anchoring just off the Northeast Coast.

Five of the women were already on deck. The others' noticed Janice was missing rollcall. Looked like she had snuck into John's room and did him. Kelly, Beverly, and Michelle looked at each other. They all wanted to get laid. After all, it was not just about the money, but it was also about being with a powerful man. They would ensure they had a chance at this hero. It was also about memories. Even though George had already made love to Michelle and Beverly, they wanted John too. With all the beautiful ladies, each wanted to be the best. It was vanity.

James broke the ice. "Sir, what would you like to drink?" John replied, "Bourbon on the rocks." The ladies laughed. John asked what was so fumy and Kelly replied.

"John, it was nothing, really. It's just when you said...on the rocks, we all thought that was funny." John got it. He joined in the laughter and looked at Kelly.

"Kelly, please sit next to me. I would like to get to know you."

Janice joined them looking like a Million dollars. She was in a nearly see-through black dress. She wore nothing underneath.

243

KIDNAPPING JESUS

The diamond earrings were about three inches long and the diamond on her neck was huge. It was real. All the ladies looked great, and all were appropriately dressed for a Billionaire's yacht. John was wearing a light black Jacket. His white shirt was unbuttoned revealing his chest hair. He was handsome. The ladies, well, the ladies were breathtaking. Each could have come off the cover of a fashion magazine, or from a centerfold.

They had it all. Mr. Hefner had the mansion, but, for right now, John had six of the most beautiful women in the world at his fingertips.

They sat down for dinner. Out of respect for the owner, no one sat at the head of the table. John had Kelly on his left and Michelle sat on his right. Beverly sat across from John. John thought to himself, and then there were three. The servings were brought out one by one. There was chit-chat.

They exchanged pleasantries on the day's events in the news. It was nothing requiring deep thought or discussion.

They all laughed and spoke of SCUBA diving and some of their past adventures. Kelly's right hand was on John's leg for most of the meal. Michelle occasionally rubbed her left foot on John's right leg. It was sensual. John enjoyed the meal. The prime rib roast was delicious. John thanked the chef. Desert was a dish simply known as "death by chocolate." It was good and whetted the sexual appetite. An after-dinner brandy was served by James to all. They sipped the aged brandy that must have cost a small fortune. The sun was setting, and the yacht anchored just off the coast of the Cayman Islands. They were close to the island as the ocean quickly dropped off into a deep abyss. It was absolutely beautiful. John excused himself from the table. He looked at Kelly and Michelle. "Would you like to join me for a walk around the deck?"

John asked the Captain. "Can you tell me how to get to the game room?" "Sir, of course, I can. However, the ladies know the best route."

John thanked the Captain, and the threesome left the dining room. The remaining four ladies laughed. No one felt left out. They exchanged their encounters with each other and referred to John as quite a conquest. Beverly was looking forward to being last. She would be his best. At least, John would think so. The best was always the last. When the repeated requests for sex with the same woman, or women, came, the group would know who the man thought was best.

244

THE CRUISE

Morning came. It was a new day. The sun was bright. John recalled the night's events. It was another fantastic evening.

He could hear the shower running. He was alone in bed, but someone was in his cabin. He looked around to ensure everything was in its place and then made his way into his bathroom. He did have his Colt 45 caliber pistol beside him, but never needed to point it at his quarry. She was beautiful. In fact, Beverly was quite beautiful. She had a nice heart tattooed on her left cheek. John ran his eyes up and down her body as she slowed and turned. She knew she was being admired and was not shocked to see John. John laid down his pistol and disrobed and joined Beverly in the shower.

Beverly spoke to John. "John, I trust you have had a nice cruise and have enjoyed yourself?"

John replied, "Yes, it is like being on a roller coaster ride. I have had more fun than I could have ever imagined. You all have been perfect hostesses."

Beverly slowly moved her hands around John's waist and then reached for a bar of soap and a small washcloth. She took her time washing John's muscular body. With light kisses and caresses, John was aroused. His tired muscles were gently massaged, and he felt like a million dollars. John responded with his own touching and moved behind Beverly. She was about 5'9" tall. She was the tallest of all the women. She looked like Bo Derek when she was in the movie "Ten." Incredible! Beverly was clearly aroused. Her hands supported her from slipping. John took his time as he slowly made love to this remarkable lady. She was hot. John and Beverly were like one. It was ecstasy. Pure ecstasy!

John turned to Beverly to face him and spoke the words she wanted to hear. "Sweetheart, you were so good I forgot who I was. My mind was transfixed on you and your magnificent body. When two people have this type of timing, it is unreal. Would you care to spend the rest of your time with me while we are on the yacht? I don't want to make any waves, but between you and Meagan, I would like to spend some time with both of you, again, without totally excluding the other ladies."

"John, I agree with your request. Meagan is always free to join in. We have been friends for years and don't mind sharing. When you make your final decision, just let us know. It's not that either one of us

KIDNAPPING JESUS

doesn't care about our feelings, we are realists and know how seldom it is to find one good man. We are all almost like sisters. No one holds a grudge, but we do know how to pout."

John was relieved as he was getting dressed for a late breakfast. He had already called James. He wanted steak and eggs. As John and Beverly ascended the stairs, George Hastings III was approaching in "Miss A". He would be joining John and the ladies for breakfast. John walked up to the landing pad to meet George. Extending his right hand, John welcomed George back to "The Miss Adventure".

"George, I trust you had a good trip. I can assure you your hospitality has been more than perfect in every way."

George laughed out loud and John joined in. George said, "John, I certainly hope so. If you did not enjoy yourself, I would have to wonder about you and whether the information about you is true. I know you fight hard and party hard. It goes together. Let's eat. I'm ready for a great breakfast and then let's get down to business."

John nodded as they descended the stairs to the dining room. All the ladies were seated and rose to meet George. Each made a small exchange of a kiss on the cheek as George greeted every one of them. He treated them with the utmost respect. James held George's chair for him as he was seated. On his left was Michelle and on his right was Kelly. John sat at the other head of the table. On his left was Meagan and on his right was Beverly. April and Janice sat directly apart from each other. George looked around and knew decisions had been made during his absence. It was clear everyone had had a good time.

After a huge breakfast, the ladies headed down to their staterooms. George and John stayed topside up the front of the flying bridge while James served them a mid-morning peach brandy with cigars. George picked up the conversation. "John, hopefully, you have had a few moments to think about my proposition. I would like you to give me your thoughts. I would like to know what you are thinking."

"George, so far, this has been one hell of a boat ride for me. I have thought about your offer. It is a challenge. I have much to do for a mission such as this. Going into Tora Bora to kill Ayman Al-Zawahiri may have been a cakewalk compared to the challenge you have proposed."

THE CRUISE

George laughed. "John, I know you are not faint of heart and are up to the task, but regardless of your decision, I would like to think we have become friends and future associates."

"George, I have a lot of confidence in you and the support needed to accomplish a mission like this. I have no false illusions. This moment has been well-determined in time. It seems as if all the stars have aligned. I will accept your mission on your terms. Now, to complete the deal, you must accept my terms."

George nodded. "Let me hear them."

"While we are in the Caymans, I would ask you to transfer $50 Million dollars to my personal account." George nodded.

John continued…"Then, place the remaining $50 Million dollars in a Swiss Bank account with both our names on the account. If either of us dies, then the other will solely own the account. If we are both still alive, then the funds in the account are mine. If I die, you get to keep the $50 Million dollars. My team will be paid by my estate. I already have provisions protecting them. I have one other beneficiary. Her name is Pearle West. She will always be in my estate, regardless of what the future brings." George nodded once again.

"George, I want Ken Parker to be our liaison between you and me. I may need him during the mission, but I think he needs to stay close to you. Security must be tight. And there is one more thing. I'll take advice from you and your staff. The technical piece is yours. I know you have made arrangements, but if I think we need something, you must ensure the logistics and support I request take place. I won't have time to do everything and distractions, although unintended, take the focus off the mission. Your undivided attention must be on this mission. However, it must be clear from the outset, the final decisions are mine. Should this request not work for you, then we should part as friends now. There can only be one man in charge. This mission will definitely not work if it requires a committee review and final vote. I need to have all involved look at me and to only me for decisions. There are no back channels. Daily SITREPS are mandatory and we talk daily, regardless of where we are."

George looked at John and then out to the ocean for a few moments deep in thought. "Is that all? Are you sure that's everything?"

KIDNAPPING JESUS

"George, I think so. I like to keep it fairly simple, but you know rules change as the mission develops. The battle is fluid, and the plan is only as good as it was moments ago. Time and events taking place may cause a change to pre-determined plans and patterns. It will be up to the entire team to achieve success."

George laughed again, proposed a toast, and loudly exclaimed for all who might be in earshot. "It is done! John, we're in this together. It looks like we are going to be busy. I'm excited to be in this place at this time. History is being written. This is what I live for, to be a part of it, not merely a bystander watching the river of time pass by accepting the destiny others fashion as they weave the very threads of our existence." They shook hands and reclined as James brought a second peach brandy and fresh cigar from George's extensive collection.

Time had flown. George looked at John. "I think it is time to get a dive in while we are off the Caymans. We are anchored in 45 feet of water. This is where we always anchor. We will not be bothered as this is off-limits while we are here. Do you see that ship anchored about two miles from us? That is a backup from one of my teams. They are part of our surveillance and complement our own security." John nodded.

George went on to say. "I think we owe ourselves a fresh lobster dinner. I like to catch my own food whenever I have time. It is thrilling. The ladies are qualified divers. I think you'll enjoy their company. They too know how to catch lobsters. In fact, they are fun to watch as they use their tickle sticks and snares."

John was ready. "George, I am always ready to dive and catch. In fact, I would not mind spearing a Snapper or a Grouper to go along with the meal."

"John, as you know, we dive the buddy system. I take three of the ladies, and you take the other three. This is the new and improved buddy system. In this way, both groups can get their fair share." Again, John laughed, and George caught the inadvertent innuendo and joined John in the laughter.

They all had suited up and were wearing light-dive skins. The ladies, as well as the three men, were ready to make the dive. From, black, blue, white, and pink dive suits, each of the ladies was an admiral's feast in their own right. Each steel tank had a capacity of 100 cubic feet of pure air at 3,300 pounds of air per square inch (PSI).

248

THE CRUISE

This could be some serious dive time for an experienced diver. Of course, the ladies could usually stay down longer due to the size of their lungs. That thought sure sounded contradictory, even if one made only a casual observation, they surely would see this could not be the case.

Ken Parker was in the water first. He had wireless communication with both George and John. He would be on the dive line.

He had a new spear gun with the ability to fire up to three spears in rapid semi-fire. They were short spears and not intended for the spearing of fish. He had two loadable cartridges in case they were needed. Once in the water, hand signals and audio calls were made. One of the richest men in the world was online and of course on camera. Sonar was on, as well as radar. They were covered, both in the air and in the ocean. Both George and John were spare-air equipped in case there was a low-air or out-of-air emergency situation. They all descended to approximately 15 to 20 feet.

George spoke to John, "John, we'll go to about 50 feet at a heading of 360 degrees. Head out 180 degrees and I'll check with you in a little bit."

John acknowledged. "Roger, have fun."

They descended just off the ocean floor. It was fifty-foot-deep and the coral and tropical fish were beautiful. They headed down to where the coral angled out and down into the depths of the ocean. It was magnificent. They had well over 100 feet of visibility and could see how the ocean just started to drop. Meagan spotted a lobster and she and Beverly went in with April following. These ladies were good.

Meagan poked at the large lobster, getting it out of its hole. April had a loop set to snare the lobster as it slowly backed up. Wham! She had the huge five-pound lobster wriggling for dear life. Beverly had the lobster bag and they forced the lobster into the waiting bag. It was the first catch.

"John radioed George. The ladies have one nice bug in the bag." George radioed back. "My ladies here are working on a double. Looks like it's going to be a good catch."

Back to business, the ladies had found another lobster and were getting it under control. John looked around. A large Sand Tiger shark had cast its shadow on the team. John radioed George once more. "We have at least one shark in the water."

KIDNAPPING JESUS

Parker was listening as George replied. "Sand Tiger sharks are often in this water. Keep them in your sight. They should not bother you."

John knew this to be the case, but then; you always must be on your game under the water. John was admiring his ladies.

They had five nice lobsters in the bag when he spotted a nice grouper under an outcropping of coral. He motioned the ladies to back away behind him. The grouper was about 50 pounds. Just about right. He looked up and to his left. He could see the anchor line at about a 30-degree angle. Parker was hovering and they were about 65 feet. No sharks are to be seen. His air was good. About 2,000 pounds left. He pointed at his pressure gauge and the ladies checked their air. They all returned an OK sign back to John.

The grouper was not really interested in John. That was until the spear gun flashed steel and the barb embedded behind his left eye. The grouper fluttered and went for a loop with the 250-pound test line and John following. Then it was over. John secured the grouper on his metal stringer and motioned the ladies to follow him. They took a leisurely swim back to the anchor line. John checked out his space and noticed George and his team were coming close by. The team had about half of their air supply left. This was as good as it gets.

"John, how did you guys do?"

"George, we have five bugs and this grouper. How did your group fare?"

"We have six nice bugs. It should be a feast tonight. Send all but one of your ladies up with the catch. We can spend some time down here."

Meagan and Michelle remained. "John let's have a little fun." John was all in.

"Now, this is fun, George." There were a lot of bubbles and when they headed up, Ken was there to meet them. Their air was getting low, around 200 pounds, but Ken had multiple octopuses as they all took turns. He had almost 1,500 pounds of air as he had never descended below 20 feet. He was constantly on point, checking the surrounding waters. It was clear as they made their final ascent. John was excited. Diving made him aroused, even if he was not diving with six of the sexiest women in the world.

"What? Did someone say Narcosis? Nitrogen Narcosis?" ...John dazedly questioned Ken.

THE CRUISE

John mumbled to himself, rapture of the deep! What was I trying to do with my second stage (my octopus)? The mermaid I saw needed air. And I...I was thinking about reincarnation. The sun was getting low in the sky, so it seemed. I remembered getting to 60 feet and then stopping for about 3 or 4 minutes. I was breathing rapidly. I guess the fight with the fish, Wow, 50 pounds of fresh grouper. Then, I, or we, passed 30 feet heading to our last safety stop at 15-20 feet below the ocean surface. Air was getting low and almost in the red on the pressure gage. And then, I was in Italy, when was it and where was I? A Shroud? Casey...Casey who? Shells...huge, like "Boxcars"! It sounded like trains rushing by!

"What?" John had opened his eyes and stared and blinked a couple of times shaking out the water in his hair.

John spoke to George, "It was nice to have M&Ms on the dive. Best candy ever!"

The dive was over. Everyone was ok and they had a feast fit for a king. The chef met them on deck.

No one really noticed any different behavior from John. But John was having second and third thoughts as he was on his way to his cabin.

Pictures were taken by the only accessible camera on board of the six sexiest ladies in the world and two handsome men with their catch. They were all wet and looking good.

After retiring to their cabins, they met back on deck. This was going to be the final night of a great cruise. Everyone was dressed for the occasion. It was going to be surf and turf. With the lobsters and grouper, the filet minion was served. It was wrapped in bacon. The baked potatoes were stuffed, and the asparagus was fresh. Of course, there was fresh fruit and other sides to go with this feast. After diving, everyone was hungry. It was not only the rush of the dive, but the fresh air and excitement of any dive that seemed to get into the pumping arteries of life.

Everyone had recounted their stories of the dive. The underwater views from the ship's camera were played. The views were vivid, almost as if there was a cameraman with each of them. It was due to the clarity of the water as well as the quality of the camera. There were a lot of laughs.

Even some of the playfulness for George, John, Meagan, and Michelle was displayed. Of course, it was clean fun and then there

KIDNAPPING JESUS

were a lot of bubbles leading everyone's imagination to wander. The Captain notified them they were weighing anchor and heading back to Melbourne.

———————

The sunlight in the room danced off the mirrors. It had been an uneventful trip back to Melbourne. Dinner, that evening, was another meal fit for a king. The lobster, grouper, and fillet mignon as well as the conversation was excellent. John was refreshed. He allowed Beverly to sleep while he shaved and showered and then gently awakened her.

"Beverly, it's time to wake up. Breakfast will be ready in about 30 minutes, and we are just offshore. We'll be at the dock in an hour. See you topside."

Beverly stretched her beautiful body. It was like a work of art. John could not help but admire her. He hoped to stay in contact with her and Meagan after the trip if time allowed. Beverly simply said to John. "I'll be up in a few minutes. I just need to get my second wind."

Breakfast was served. James made sure that a pitcher of Bloody Mary's was ready for those who wanted a drink. Last evening was fairly tame and almost everyone had disappeared by 2200 hours.

George Hastings III was sitting at the table when John entered the dining room. Several of the ladies were already seated. George was drinking his morning coffee.

Everyone said good morning. John sat at the opposite end of the table and James served him a cup of hot coffee. It was black, just the way he liked it.

John looked at George. "George, this was a fantastic voyage. I look forward to working with you in the future."

George responded. "John, it was a great trip. We'll meet again, soon. Once the ship docks, Ken will escort you home. I will have your gear brought to you later."

John understood. They were low-key. The ladies probably could be trusted, but the old adage that loose lips sink ships was not to be trifled with.

Breakfast had been concluded and the Captain came up on the ship's intercom. "Ladies and Gentlemen, we are about to enter the

THE CRUISE

Sebastian Inlet. Please ensure you have a hand on the rails. It could get a little rough." This yacht, due to its size, never anchored at the Mansion. George Hastings owned a small fleet of boats and planes and even had a private rail car. And, of course, there was his pride and joy, a submersible submarine. It was a work of art and George kept the fact he owned one closely guarded.

The Miss Adventure docked and the Hastings' greeting party was on hand. There were three limousines waiting. In fact, the team waiting was some of the security personnel for George from the mansion.

They all said their goodbyes. George left the dock first, followed by John and the last limousine carried the ladies. James was with George and Ken was with John.

Once the limousine pulled up in John's driveway, Ken jumped out of the car and quietly spoke to John. "I'll be back to see you tonight around 2000 hours. Mr. Hastings and I will be reviewing the most current situation. I look forward to seeing you then." John shook Ken's hand. "See you tonight."

With the farewell, John headed up to the house and pulled out his clicker. Security systems were on. There were no problems. John opened the door and went inside.

He checked his internal security systems, and all was as he expected. John sat down in his leather overstuffed recliner and recounted the trip in his mind. He soon fell asleep and had some interesting visions of the past, the present and perhaps, the future.

CHAPTER XIII

PLAN "S", A GOOD PLACE FOR A NEW BEGINNING

K en Parker rang John's doorbell at precisely 2000 hours. John had showered and had a sandwich to eat. Everything had been straightened up inside the house. John checked the surveillance cameras, and Ken was alone. Ken came into the home. John welcomed him as they shook hands. "Ken, hope you had a wonderful day. Sometimes, you have to rest from a vacation." They both laughed.

"John, Mr. Hastings sends his best wishes to you. We met for several hours this afternoon. I have some information for you."

John motioned to Ken to have a seat in his small Command Center. "What would you like to drink?"

"John, I'll have what you are having."

"Be back in a moment." John returned with two large tumblers of Bourbon Whiskey and Cola.

"Ok, let's begin. Let me know what's next. I have to get my team together and Mr. Hastings mentioned a Base of Operations in Arizona. I need the specifics, so I can tailor the training requirements."

"John, yes, the Base is in Arizona. It was an Air Force Base closed in the 1990's under one of the Base Realignment and Closure (BRAC) Commission recommendations. Just for your background information, there were 26 recommended major Base closures and 19 Base

KIDNAPPING JESUS

realignments in 1991. Mr. Hastings purchased a portion of Williams Air Force Base in September 1993. Part of the Air Force Base became the Phoenix-Mesa Gateway Airport, and another portion is now a college campus sponsored by Arizona State University and Chandler-Gilbert Community College, and some of the property, officially, was retained by the United States Government. When I say officially, I mean it is this portion that was sold privately and confidentially to Mr. Hastings. It is not located adjacent to the airport or the campus, but it is remote. The Base is located 10 miles east of Chandler and now is considered part of Mesa, Arizona."

"Williams AFB officially began pilot training on July 16, 1941, as part of our mobilization for World War II. The Base originally was approximately 4,100 acres. Mr. Hastings owns around 800 acres as the remaining 75% or so was turned over to the local community. However, on these 800 acres is a small 7,000-foot runway complete with administrative buildings and four hangers of many sizes. Mr. Hastings efforts at acquiring this land were an interesting part of his overall plan for BIOTECH. Having a private facility in which to conduct experiments without undue interference was instrumental in revolutionizing BIOTECH150 throughout the last five years. I will go into more detail once you assemble your team and bring them to the Base."

"You'll land at Phoenix-Meza Gateway Airport. Transportation will be provided, and you and your team will proceed to the Government Facilities known as Williams AFB, an Annex of the United States Government Research Center for Pilots. Mr. Hastings has provided airplane tickets for you and your team. You will have Military Identification Cards indicating your rank and status, plus Identification Cards that allow access to the Top- Secret Facilities. The guards and staff at the Annex look like military personnel. They are not. They are employees of BIOTECH150, but they are highly trained in their respective fields. Your cover, should you require it, is that you are training for the next series of Space Shuttle missions as Mission Specialists. There are hyperbaric chambers and a staff that actually conducts altitude training for NASA personnel. Do you have any questions?"

John replied. "Ken, you have been very thorough. I will contact my team and they will be here the day prior to departure. I want them to meet Mr. Hastings. I want them to meet you. Both you and Mr.

PLAN "S", A GOOD PLACE FOR A NEW BEGINNING

Hastings have a significant role in this mission." Ken nodded his head in agreement.

As John and Ken walked to the front door of the house, John asked Ken a key question. "Ken, do you feel a bit strange about Mr. Hastings wanting the Shroud for his personal collection?"

Ken replied, "Not at all. You have only seen the surface of what Mr. Hastings owns. His collections rival those held by major governments of the world and on display at such places as the Smithsonian Museum, the Louvre, the British Museum, and the Vatican Museum along with the Tower of London. These collections do not compare with the collection the Hastings family has collected over the years they have been in this country. To say the least, the treasures he inherited and acquired could well be classified as a national treasure."

John slept all night long. It was a restful sleep. For the first time in a long time, he did not dream of Vietnam or of Beirut. Not even a flash back to Tora Bora. He was thinking ahead while he slept. Of course, the latest half-dozen women crossed his mind. They were wonderful; not only beautiful, but sexy and smart— a combination that seemed completely in touch with a world of wealth. He had phone numbers and could call each of them, any of them, at any time. This was not part of their job, but he had struck a bond with each of them. He could fall in love with any one of them; however, his heart still had a place for Pearle West.

The alarm clock was just about to ring. John reached over to the clock and turned it off at 0625 hours. He took a quick shower, dressed for a workout and headed to the beach. The Melbourne Beach on Florida's Space Coast had a lot to offer. Not only were there beautiful beaches, but there were also great accommodations with many notable oceanfront hotels. He headed out in his Corvette. It was time for reflection. He parked his car near the water. He was not the only one with the idea of getting out to the beach early in the morning.

He joined those who were walking and those who were running. Stretching out, he noticed a couple of real beauties out for a jog. It always made it easier to join someone or follow someone for a run.

Although there was no real conversation, he was in his zone after he hit the first mile. His breathing was regulated. Jodie calls from the past were in the back of his mind.

KIDNAPPING JESUS

The Corps was never very far away from his thoughts. The Marines had shaped this man as it had millions of others throughout the Corps colorful history spanning the further most reaches of the world.

He ran thinking of the offer made by Hastings and his meeting with Parker the night before. Stealing the Shroud!

This would put John on the world map as one of the best thieves of all time if he and his team were successful. He wanted to be unknown. He wanted this theft to be a mystery. In all actuality, he wanted the theft to be unnoticed by the Roman Catholic Church. If it was noticed, he would hope the Church would never publicize the fact it had been stolen. Those believers who had placed so much of their faith and hope in the peace and grace the Shroud brought into their spiritual lives would be devastated should the news of theft ever be released to the world. Could this news be a creator of chaos? If it never happened, then life would go on. The world would never know. It would be another secret closely guarded by the Church. John was nearing the end of his run.

As he slowed down his pace, he thought he caught a glimpse of someone he knew. It was nothing he could pin down, but it did raise his awareness. Usually, his instincts were right. He decided to walk off the run in the direction of one of the nicest hotels in the area. Its sparking white towers blended in with the landscape. He had stayed here when he was working for Chuck Taylor. The hunt for scum sometimes ended up in the best places in the world. Although, he never thought this pristine area would experience major crimes. The criminal he had chased to this local area never committed the heinous crimes locally; he had just run to the Melbourne area to hide with his family. He wanted to blend in with the local life. However, Taylor's Headhunters always got their man, or woman, sooner or later.

He said "hello" to a couple who were walking towards the beach and nodded his head to a couple of others who were getting their morning walk in.

He never figured out where he got his feeling, but he did have it and it nagged him. His three-mile run in the white sands always worked the muscles in his legs much better than running on asphalt. He jumped into the Corvette and headed back to his house. He was still deep in thought when he parked in the garage.

258

PLAN "S", A GOOD PLACE FOR A NEW BEGINNING

He automatically checked his security system, entered the house and took a shower. He made an egg sandwich and switched on his computer. The TV was on FOX News.

John went to the Internet to conduct a search for the Shroud of Turin. Like George Hastings III during the early days when he was fascinated with information regarding the Shroud of Turin, or Turin Shroud, his research uncovered facts and myth surrounding the ancient linen cloth, information known by most of the world. The cloth bears the image of a man who appears to have been crucified.

The location of the Shroud was in the Duomo di San Giovanni but was relocated to the Italian Cathedral di San Giovanni Battista in 1997 following a fire; the Turin Cathedral dedicated to Saint John the Baptist.

Debate among scientists and believers regarding the Shroud's origin focuses on the dating of the Shroud. John knew the story well. Those who believed, believed the cloth was the burial cloth that covered Jesus when he was placed in the tomb and his image imbedded into the fibers during the resurrection. And then there are those who believed the Shroud a clever hoax created in the late 1200s or during the 1300s. But, if a hoax, how were the people of the time able to create a hoax resembling a reverse photographic image of a man crucified with all the gory details that would surround such a horrific death. Again, there was no explanation with the ability to explain away the facts easily. However important the presence of the Shroud was to the world, John had to concentrate on the matter at hand. How to steal the Shroud without discovery?

John placed a call to the University of Central Florida, Orlando. The switchboard operator directed John to the Director of Paleontology, a Doctor Lori Summers.

Doctor Summers answered her phone. "Good afternoon, this is Doctor Summers, Paleontology Department. May I help you?"

"Doctor Summers, this is John Elder. I would like to ask you a couple of questions if you have a moment."

"Yes, Mr. Elder, how many I be of service?"

"Doctor Summers, I am interested in a Holy Relic. I have been doing some research on the Internet and I was looking for first-hand information from someone who knows about the Shroud of Turin, or who could possibly direct me to someone who has an interest. Could you help me out or, do you know someone who might be inclined to do so?"

"Mr. Elder, I have some interest in the Shroud as well. The Shroud was the focal point of one of my research projects as an undergraduate at the University of Berkeley, Southern California. I would be interested in discussing this subject with you, but I am scheduled to conduct a seminar in just a few minutes, and I need to gather my notes. Perhaps there would be a better time for us to meet?"

"Doctor, unfortunately, I am going out of town in just a couple of days, and it is extremely important for me to gather as much information as I can regarding the Shroud before I depart. My focus is on archeology, and my team of experts will relocate to a remote, undisclosed location in the Middle East, to further our research into the death of Jesus Christ. As you know, these are tumultuous times, and contact can be sporadic. I am sorry for the late notification, but perhaps I can meet you for dinner at a restaurant of your choice and pay you your consulting fees. I hate to rush you, but I assure you should you have any doubts, I have a number for you to call to check my background should it be necessary."

"Mr. Elder, you have piqued my curiosity. Are you the same John Elder from the news reports responsible for the assassination of Doctor Ayman Muhammad Al-Zawahiri?"

"Yes, Doctor, I am he."

"Mr. Elder, please give me the contact information. If I am successful in gaining the requisite information, I need to validate your archeological expedition, I will meet with you tonight. It will be at the Chaps Steakhouse in Orlando at 8:00 PM sharp. My fee is $200.00 per hour. And, dinner will be your treat, of course. This is business."

"Doctor, I'll call you back in two hours to see if we have a meeting. I certainly appreciate your time. I assure you; it will not be a waste of your valuable time. I look forward to meeting you."

"Mr. Elder, I appreciate you bearing with me. I can tell that you understand."

"Thank you, Doctor Summers, I'll be in touch."

PLAN "S", A GOOD PLACE FOR A NEW BEGINNING

The call went to George Hastings III. It was a direct line. To say that Doctor Lori Summers did not know who Mr. Hastings was would be a gross understatement.

Mt Hastings assured Doctor Summers he was sponsoring an archeological dig near ruins close to Jerusalem with the noted Egyptian Archeologist, Doctor Zahi Hawassa. It was a fact-finding trip based on discovered ruins that might be the burial chamber of Jesus Christ. John arrived early. He spoke to the headwaiter.

He had already called ahead and asked for the best table in the house. John had eaten here on many occasions, and he had Star status since becoming a focal point for TV news stories. He rarely appeared on the shows, but the celebration with President Bush on their arrival at Patrick Air Force Base was still spinning. This included his one and only appearance with Bill O'Reilly and an interview with Larry King on Larry King Live. The only other appearance he made was as a guest of Jay Leno, on the Tonight Show. He was seated and ordering drinks when a beautiful lady was escorted to his table by the head waiter.

John stood up and greeted Doctor Summers. "Doctor Summers, it is a pleasure to meet you. Thanks for accepting my invitation on such short notice. May I ask what you would like to drink?"

"Mr. Elder, I am a woman who is seldom intrigued. From what I gather, you are a man who also has his expectations, and you set the bar at an extremely high level. I did some background checks on you, but for now, I would like a Vodka Martini. And please call me Lori. May I call you John?"

"Yes, of course. Waiter, please make those two Vodka Martinis, stirred, with an olive." The waiter excused himself.

"John, I spoke to Mr. Hastings. He confirmed your assignment. I would like to know more." The Martinis arrived. The glasses had been chilled.

"Lori, here is to a nice evening. Cheers." "Cheers."

The drink was cold but went down hot. John could not help admiring this lady who was in her late 30s or early 40s and kept in great shape. She was approximately 130 pounds and at 5'7", she was beautifully sculpted with blond hair and blue eyes. John thought she was of Scandinavian descent. Either she was Norwegian, or perhaps she was from Finland or Denmark. Time would tell.

KIDNAPPING JESUS

John ordered dinner after finding out what Lori wanted. She opted for the Filet of Salmon cooked slowly on a plank of cedar wood and covered with selected herbs and spices. John ordered a Filet Mignon. They spoke of past events in getting acquainted. It was striking, like a blow to John's forehead when he found out that Lori Summers was married to a Marine First Lieutenant.

"John, yes, Lieutenant Bruce Summers was killed in the Beirut Barracks bombing. I was pregnant. I gave birth almost two months later to a baby girl. She died during childbirth. John, she was so beautiful. I named her Constance Jill and I buried her next to her father in Arlington National Cemetery. Someday I will be buried with them. John, Bruce was my heart. The baby was our bond of love. She still represents that bond of love, even though so many years have passed. I still dream of a life with my husband and my daughter. I am not dead, but a realist. After the baby, I needed to immerse myself. I graduated from the University of Berkeley in 1989 with a master's and a Doctorate. Bruce, and the military, left me fairly well off. And, without the assistance of my parents, I would not be here speaking with you this evening. I am sorry to bore you with my life's story, but I think it important that you know something about me."

"Lori, as you know, I was also a Marine. But what you probably don't know is that I was in Beirut in 1983. One of the many responsibilities I had was that I was the senior NCO in charge of recovering the remains of those who were murdered. I am sorry to hear of your loss. Our Nation sill mourns the loss of these brave men and women."

It was Lori's turn to take a deep breath. "John, I didn't know. Thanks for helping to bring him home to me. When you told me you were the same John Elder in the news, I wanted to meet you. It brings some satisfaction to me that Al Qaeda's number two man met his fate at your hands. I'll be honest. Without this key element of your background, I may not have accepted your invitation, regardless of Mr. Hastings request."

Dinner was served. They ate while exchanging names of Marines they both knew. One of the Lieutenants they both knew was First Lieutenant (Promotable) David Robinson. He was married and had a one-year-old son by the name of Nicholas Tyler Robinson. He would be about 18 now and the last Lori had heard about him was that Nick was a

PLAN "S", A GOOD PLACE FOR A NEW BEGINNING

football star at his High School, was All-State and at 6'3" and 220 pounds could run 40 yards in 4.2 seconds. John made a note that he would have to look this young man up to check on him to see what Nick was going to do when he went in search of a career after high school or after college. After all, it was a small world. After dinner, there was the third round of drinks. John asked Lori what she thought about the Shroud.

"John, it is my belief the Shroud is real. In fact, I believe you should enter into the burial chamber of Jesus with that single thought uppermost in your mind. While we were eating, I thought back to Beirut and the notification I received that my husband was killed. I had a brief vision. It was a mirage of a Pale Horse, just before I received word of his death. John, I know the story in the Bible and what the Pale Horse represents. I believe our meeting is not a coincidence."

John could not imagine this woman also had the same vision he had had. This was not a coincidence even though the visions were at different times. "Lori, it was a wonderful dinner. I have an envelope for you. I am sure you will find your compensation acceptable. I look forward to another meeting with you sometime in the near future."

John paid the bill and left a generous tip. He helped Lori with her light Jacket and escorted her to the door. He thanked the waiter and then walked Lori to her car.

Lori turned to John. "Thank you for a wonderful evening. I really enjoyed our time together. I don't know when I felt so relaxed with someone. I wish you the best of luck. And, yes, I would look forward to seeing you again."

John held the car door for her. "Good night, Lori. Thanks again for a great evening!" John walked over to his Ford F-150. He thought Lori would appreciate the $1,000 dollars he had placed in the envelope in ten crisp $100 dollar bills. The vision of the Pale Horse from the Book of Revelation predicts the path to Armageddon according to the Word of God as written by Saint John. Perhaps it was a signal.

If two people, at two distinct times, and in two separate locations, had this vision, it could mean others had shared experiences; the foretelling of the end of the World as we once knew it was coming to fruition. John thought back to Beirut and the vision of the Pale Horse. The apparition appeared with a rider named Death in his mind over

KIDNAPPING JESUS

the shimmering sands of time. It was as if an hourglass from the past was on a collision course with the future.

The next public display of the Holy Relic was not scheduled until 2025. However, John wanted to find out if the Shroud would be moved back to the Duomo di San Giovanni where the fire caused structural damage. This was a possibility. Also, the Shroud was now located in the Chapel of the Shroud built in the late 1600s. If there was a move scheduled by the Holy See, then John would need intelligence from inside the Church. How the buildings were constructed would be another key piece of information needed by the team.

Plan "S" was in the early stages of execution. However, before any plan could be initiated, fact finding was important. Independent studies by various teams of experts and scientists left the Shroud's authenticity in question. This did not concern John.

But the security surrounding the Holy relic was his primary concern and keeping the theft a secret from the public was paramount to the theft of the century, if not of all time. It was now time to call his friends and assemble the team.

When they captured Osama Bin-Laden and destroyed two of the Al Queda bases deep in the mountains of Afghanistan, the team's name was team COBALT, Company for Elimination of Osama Bin-Laden, and Al Queda Leadership.

John reflected on the mission of this team: to retrieve the Shroud from Turin without public knowledge or discovery. He was sure the Shroud could be taken, but discovery was likely just a matter of time. Masterpieces from the greats including DaVinci, Rembrandt, Michelangelo and other notables have been taken throughout the centuries. This also stirred up a question in John's mind…how many of the world's great masterpieces on public display are real…how many were clever fakes and the real masterpieces were lost to humanity or were in private collections. Probably more than we care to know. Onward with the mission…no time for speculation; however, what about the Shroud. Some owners chose to keep the thefts from public knowledge because knowledge would keep the public from paying to visit the treasures, especially if they were just authentic forgeries.

Before John made the first call, he wanted a name to identify the mission. Team CASCA? Casca Longinus was the Roman Centurion

264

PLAN "S", A GOOD PLACE FOR A NEW BEGINNING

whose mission was to crucify Jesus. He had written the last words spoken by Jesus on the parchment left in Turin 2,000 years earlier. The words were a message in a bottle that bridged the past to the present. This was the message that led George Hastings III to John Elder. This was the message that would lead Team CASCA to the Shroud and would bring the Shroud to Hastings. At the center of Casca's name was the letter "S". On both sides were the letters "CA." and "2CAs?" Plan "S" plans within Plan "S"? Two crucified next to Jesus?

John wanted a name for the team that was both relevant and reverent. Stealing the Shroud of Christ from the Roman Catholic Church was a formidable undertaking. Although John Elder was not a deeply religious man, he did believe in Jesus and in the Bible.

After Jesus had been crucified, his garments were divided by a cast of lots as foretold in the prophecy of the Psalms. Although the Shroud was not his garment, it was his burial cloth. John was stealing this final proof that Jesus died for mankind. There were two additional possibilities, 2CAs or SAC2?

How about this one; the Team would be known as the Seekers of the Shroud. It could be thought of as an SOS, an international signal for distress. Why this name? John did not know. I am Alpha and Omega, the first and the last. Jesus was crucified among two sinners. Surrounded by an S, the 0 was the both the last and was the first.

For all the intrigue, he knew regardless of his involvement at this time in history, so many events had come together that made this mission one of history before it actually took place. In some religious terms, it was in fact known as predetermination.

He pulled out his cell phone and made a call to his brother Jack in California. Jack was living near where he retired, Camp Pendleton. The phone rang two times before Jack picked it up. "How are you?" John asked.

"I'm doing great but haven't heard from you in weeks. I thought you had taken the money and run off to another planet."

John laughed. "Jack, it would seem so. It has been an interesting week. In fact, so interesting that we have allot to catch up on when we are together. I have a ticket waiting for you at John Wayne International Airport. I want you on the flight out tomorrow morning into Orlando International Airport. In fact, I am getting the team together for a

KIDNAPPING JESUS

mission. Charles is going to be released from the Hospital at Patrick Air Force Base and he is on limited duty but will be part of the team. I know Phil Tucker and Justin Carter are in California visiting and thought you might know where they are staying."

"John, your timing is excellent. I am sitting with Phil and Justin. Brad and Phil have been back here for several days now. I know you kept track of their flight from Spain into the United States with LAPEARLE. John, LAPEARLE is in really excellent shape. Brad was called to the Pentagon for a high-level briefing. Justin, Phil and I have been working out, doing a little SCUBA diving, and having a good time recounting our adventures."

"Jack, I need the three of you to get on that plane tomorrow morning. There will be tickets for each of you. Meet me at my house. I'll explain when you arrive."

Jack was surprised by the sound of John's voice. All he could say. "John, you know all you have to do is ask. We've got it covered."

When Jack hung up the phone, Carter asked Jack if anything was wrong.

"Justin, John said to assemble the team and fly down to Melbourne."

Justin scratched his head. "There must be something wrong or he would not ask us to come clear across the United States to meet with him. It sounds like we have urgent business to attend to regarding our last mission or we are being summoned for something too huge to speak of on open communications channels."

They all nodded their heads. "Phil, Justin, we are leaving LAPEARLE. I'll call Pearle West and ensure Chuck Taylor knows LAPEARLE will be at John Wayne Airport. I need someone to check on the plane periodically and Chuck has a crew that can check on it when they are not flying around the country in Chuck's private jet."

Headhunting was a lucrative business commanding top payment of fees. In fact, the rich and famous of Hollywood also used Chuck's services to check out their spouses or fiancées.

It was good business to know what type of relationship you were in or were about to get into. Jack said to the other two, "Let's get the show on the road. We need to get packed."

266

PLAN "S", A GOOD PLACE FOR A NEW BEGINNING

The team of three landed at Orlando International Airport at 1700 hours. John had a limousine waiting for them. They arrived at John's house at 1830 hours. John met them at the door and gave them each a hardy handshake and a slap on the back. "It's great to see each of you. It seems like only yesterday we were hauling ass out of Afghanistan and Pakistan and bullets were flying all around us."

Charles laughed as they all made their way into the living room. The three brothers were back together along with Justin and Phil. Justin's leg had healed although he still had a slight limp. Charles was sore and the stitching underneath the shirt was an art form. He waved off the backslapping from Jack, Justin, and Phil. The small dining room table was set. John had ordered out and pizza had just been delivered moments prior to their arrival. The bar was set up and everyone helped themselves to food and drink.

After everyone had their fill of pizza John looked at the other four men around the table. "I know you all are dying to know what is going on, so I won't keep you in suspense any longer. Fill up your glasses and join me in the operations center."

It was a tight fit. "Gentlemen, and I use that term loosely. Gentlemen, if you thought the last mission was good, wait until you hear what was just asked of me."

It was eerily silent. Everyone looked around the Command Center and on the wall was a picture of the Shroud of Turin as well as of the Cathedral of Saint John the Baptist. John had made a model of the Cathedral located on the table near his computer. Pictures of George Elmore Hasting III were also on the table. "Men, this is why I wanted all of you here. This picture is of George Elmore Hastings III, one of the richest men in the free world. He lives nearby and could almost be called a neighbor in loose terms. This picture is of the Shroud of Turin, the reported burial cloth of Jesus Christ. The Cathedral of Saint John the Baptist is where the Shroud is kept. George Hastings asked me to steal it for him for his private collection. It is unbelievable. This is the mission of a lifetime. Hold onto your hats. He is offering $100 Million dollars. Gentlemen, this is $50 Million up front and $50 Million on delivery of the Shroud. That's why you are here."

Just like John did when Hastings confronted him with the offer, the men were hit in the head like a ton of lead. Charles spoke first "So, Mr.

KIDNAPPING JESUS

Hastings wants to pay us $100 Million dollars to steal the burial cloth of Jesus? And that's all there is to it?"

John replied, "Yes, that about covers it."

Justin was next. "We just captured Osama Bin Laden and killed his second in command. We are American heroes, and some rich asshole wants us to become thieves! Well, hell, you guys can count me in. With that kind of money, none of us will ever have to work again."

John looked around the room. "Can any of you think of why we should not steal the Shroud?"

Again, dead silence.

Charles spoke again. "I'm in."

Jack and Phil looked at each other. They both looked at the others in the room and then at John. In unison, they both responded they were in.

Jack went on to say, "I always liked Italian women."

Phil had a remark as well. "I wanted to start spending some money and I want to be able to go somewhere where I can have my toes in the sand 24 hours a day, seven days a week. It's time. I am more than ready to get out of the States; breathe clean air and live the good life. John, if you would not have signed on for this, I would have told Hastings this mission was a no-go and he could go and pound sand. But, since you heard the man out, I know you gave this mission a great deal of thought. I am 100% in. I know there are dangers, so just like before, I want my family to have my share if something should happen to me."

Team COBALT smiled for the first time in a long time. John thought back to the Jodie call regarding the C-130 rolling down the strip. Bury me in the lean and rest, etcetera. No way!

"Ok folks, we will be training in Arizona at an Air Force Military Base Hastings purchased when William Jefferson Clinton was President of these here United States and downsizing the military was taking place with the Base Realignment and Closure Commission (BRAC). Your cover is that you are Mission Specialists for the next series of Space Shuttle launches. Our code name for this mission is Team "SOS". The meaning is…the Seekers of the Shroud. That's about it. Never use this term unless you are in an untenable situation and need assistance and always camouflage it within another word. You know the drill. We leave in the morning for Arizona. Tonight, we are going over to George Hastings' house for introductions."

268

PLAN "S", A GOOD PLACE FOR A NEW BEGINNING

Two limousines arrived at John's house at exactly 1930 hours. Charles hopped into the limousine with John. Ken Parker had been introduced to the team as the group came out of John's house. Charles spoke up. "John, I don't think I can do the physical stuff right now."

"Charles, that's no problem. You will do the logistics. I have already talked with Stacey Greer to see if he wants in. He is meeting us at the Hastings Mansion. He's ready, willing, and able and wants to join in. He and I have gotten together at Camp Stacey a couple of times since our return. He is filled in on the mission and I gave him a SITREP from our visit to the mountains."

"John, I think Greer is a smart choice. I like him."

John nodded his head. The two limousines went through the massive gates and pulled up to front of the Hastings Mansion. Just like clockwork, they were screened at the gate before being allowed to enter. Ken Parker escorted Team "SOS" to the massive front doors of the mansion.

James Winfield Jefferson opened the door and invited the team into the huge, richly appointed foyer. Stacey Greer had arrived moments earlier. He too had been picked up by a limousine. They greeted each other with bear hugs and slaps on the back and chest. It was a reunion. They sat down while James Jefferson went back to the kitchen.

The staff had prepared trays of huge prawn shrimp from off the coast of South Carolina, lobster from the Keys and wild smoked salmon from Alaska.

James returned to the group and asked them to remove themselves to the library where the appetizers were served by two elderly black ladies dressed in their servant's garb. The whiskey decanters and wine carafes were filled.

James announced, "Gentlemen, Mr. Hastings would like you to make yourselves comfortable. Please enjoy his hospitality. He will join you in a few moments."

Crystal glasses and wine glasses were filled. China plates were loaded with appetizers. The men looked around the library and the study. They were amazed at the opulence. This was just as George Hastings intended. It was about ten minutes later when Hastings entered the room.

John introduced George Hastings III to his team.

KIDNAPPING JESUS

Looking at everyone, George stated "It is indeed a pleasure to meet each of you. I feel like I almost know you. Please call me George. I want each of you to feel comfortable. After all, we'll be working closely together, and I will be involved. Because of your presence here this evening, it is my understanding you have accepted my offer. Is that correct?"

John replied. "I talked to all of the men. They are in. We will be leaving in the morning for Arizona."

Ken Parker had left the room and brought back a briefcase. He placed it down on the desk in the study. The team gathered around the desk as Ken opened it.

Hastings spoke. "Gentlemen, this is traveling money. Your arrangements with John are between you. I wanted each of you to have

$10,000 dollars to use as you need. Please take your envelope. The serial numbers cannot be traced as there is no history behind them. John, I've deposited $50 Million dollars into the accounts as you have stipulated. Ken will be going with you to Arizona."

Ken dropped the screen to the monitor located in the study. "Gentlemen, please direct your attention to the screen." The slide show included a brief history of Williams Air Force Base and how George Hastings had purchased part of the land in 1993.

"I own 800 acres of the original property and there is a small 7,000-foot runway complete with administrative buildings and four hangers. Inside two of the hangers are mockups of how the Shroud is closely guarded. You'll land at Phoenix-Meza Gateway Airport. Transportation will be provided. Your team will proceed to the Government Facilities known as Williams AFB, an Annex of the United States Government Research Center for Pilots. Ken, please hand out the airplane tickets and the Military Identification Cards and Identification Cards. You have access to the Top- Secret Facilities. The guards and staff at the Annex may look like military personnel; however, they are my employees. Are there any questions?"

There were no questions. Pictures of the Cathedral of Saint John the Baptist were still on the monitor. Inside Hanger Number 1 was a mockup of the Cathedral, the vault where the Shroud was kept from public view, a replica of the Shroud, and the Duomo di San Giovanni where the Shroud had been kept until 1997 when a fire had occurred

PLAN "S", A GOOD PLACE FOR A NEW BEGINNING

causing structural damage to such an extent to warrant removal of the Shroud.

"You may ask why this information is important. Here it is 2002. Repairs to the Duomo di San Giovanni will be completed within a matter of weeks and the Shroud will be moved from the Cathedral back to its original location in the Duomo di San Giovanni. That's the timeline. Your team will decide when and how the Shroud will be removed and replaced with a counterfeit Shroud."

"Hanger 2 is the destination for the Shroud. It will be placed in my private collection. Only two people have access to my vault without being escorted by me personally. Ken Parker and James Jefferson have unlimited access, but I have to provide them with the daily password. It constantly changes. I just wanted you to know in case you have any questions. All my cards are on the table. I do not want discovery the Shroud has been stolen. Your mission is to ensure the safety of the Shroud at all costs. If you are detected, you must never reveal the purpose of your mission and my name. Is that clearly understood?"

They all nodded their understanding. It was like the military when covert operations known as Black Ops were in play for National Security.

"One more thing for your information; I visited Turin during the ten- week public exhibition in 2000 commemorating the Jubilee anniversary of the Birth of Christ. The Shroud is closely guarded. Do not take this mission lightly. Now that you are in, you are in until it is over. If someone is captured and cannot escape, one of you must kill him. Regardless of kinship, that man must, and will, die. Gentlemen, thank you for your commitment. I look forward to working with each of you. Please, enjoy my hospitality and join me in a toast. Here's to the Shroud. May we be successful in our quest for this Holy Grail!"

John looked at the ceiling. It was the Holy Trinity—the Father, Son and the Holy Ghost. Shivers ran down his spine and the hairs on the back of his neck were standing on end.

CHAPTER XIV

MISSION TO TURIN

Bright and early the next morning, the team rolled out of the cots John had set up in his house. There was not much room for a small family let alone a small army. The limousines arrived at 0700 hours. It was a short ride to Orlando International Airport (formerly it was McCoy Air Force Base). They passed through security using their new identification cards. It was as if they had achieved some sort of notoriety due to the fact they were associated with NASA and were Mission Specialists assigned to the Space Shuttle Program. They boarded the 737 and were off to Phoenix, Arizona on a direct flight aboard another great American carrier. They sat near the front of the aircraft. They were on one of the distinct aircraft of a fleet of over 500 aircraft in the airplane inventory named after the State of Arizona. What a beautiful aircraft! There was a light conversation on the flight to Phoenix. They would be met by vehicles from the Annex. It was just a short drive from the airport.

Once they arrived at the annex and were assigned quarters in one of the designated administrative buildings that served as guest quarters for personnel and visitors. It was complete with a cafeteria that operated 24 hours a day, game room, exercise room and operations center. It had been a barracks at one time but had been remodeled after Hastings had purchased the small facility from the United States Government.

KIDNAPPING JESUS

There was actual training that took place for the Air Force as well as for NASA or for any U.S. Government agency having a requirement and would pay for the contracted services. Although privately owned, Hastings wanted to profit from the facilities he owned worldwide. Loss of revenue for any facility drew his scrutiny. It had to be very important, or the mission would be dissolved and reconstituted elsewhere, depending on the relevancy and impact of his number one mission to keep his Fortune 500 Company aimed in the right direction and making money.

From what John could see, the security at the entrance was like nothing he had caught sight of for quite some time. This was just like Black Operations Base. What he could not see, he could only imagine.

Ken knew the routine. It was late in the day, and they had a meeting set up in Hanger 1 at 1700 hours. Ken escorted the team to the Hanger. Everyone had to show their IDs. There were no exceptions. Once inside, Ken led them past the mockups and into a high security briefing room.

Ken spoke first. "John, fellow team members...whenever we speak of the mission at this facility, it should be done in this room and this room only. Surveillance outside the facility is state of the art. Security within the perimeter is even stricter. Should something as tiny as a horsefly enter into a building or facility, operations personnel can tell if it is a male or female. I'm not trying to alarm anyone, but there are spies who would like nothing more than to steal a patent before it is ready for primetime. This is big business. Please, for the security of this mission, allow no specific discussions regarding the Shroud. Those entering this facility have a Class II security rating on a need-to-know basis only. As you know, only three people have a Class I security rating, and this includes Mr. Hastings. Besides the Project Manager for Base Operations, only seven other people have access to this building besides you. That makes a total of 17 people including Mr. Hastings and James Jefferson. That is a lot of people who know, or possibly know, there is an on-going mission possibly involving the Shroud. For the last two months, none of these people have been allowed to leave the Base. They know this is highly classified and will not discuss their part in the operations. Once they have completed their duties, they will be debriefed and allowed to go home, with an added cash bonus for their efforts. John, that's about it. It's all yours."

274

MISSION TO TURIN

John spoke to the team assembled in front of him. There was Jack, Charles, Stacey, Phil, Justin and Ken. It was Team SOS. Seven in all formed to make up the team known as the Seekers of the Shroud. "Well, this will be a mission like no other we have done. This is not for revenge, there is no payback, and this is purely for the money and the adrenaline rush. I hope you all are ready for an ass kicking." Everyone laughed.

"This is business. In fact, this is really serious business. We are simply an exchange service. We steal the Shroud; replace it with a counterfeit Shroud, then exchange the real Shroud for the remaining $50 Million. It is that simple. This is the mission of our lives. We are in this for profit, but we are really in for the challenge. I'm not nervous about the mission. I know we will be successful. But you must be dedicated. During this mission, Ken will be my Executive Officer. Stacey will be the Training Officer. Charles will be in charge of logistics and will be the Supply Officer and will work with cleared personnel to get any materials we need or replace any we destroy." Again, another bit of laughter.

"Jack will be in charge of Intelligence. Although, I'm not sure why. Justin and Phil will ensure the equipment we need is coordinated with Charles and it is always 100 percent mission ready. You all know how successful we were in Tora Bora?"

Everyone looked at Stacey and at Ken. Did they know? If they did, they did not indicate they had access to this information. John was quick to pick up on the men's looks towards Greer and Parker.

"Don't worry. They both know." Now it was time for Ken's straight face to show a wry smile. How did John know he and George Hastings had figured out Team COBALT had captured Osama Bin-Laden? Smiles of relief went around. Stacey really did not want to know this information. It could be a death warrant.

John passed out the agenda with a two-week schedule of training with travel to Italy in two or three weeks. Confirmation of the transfer of the Shroud had not been released. This information was closely guarded by the Pope and his inner court.

John added..."Before we leave tonight, I want you to become familiar with the schedule. We will do a leader brief on the mock-ups in the morning following PT. Wake-up is at 0600 hours. Showers and breakfast follow and then into Hanger 1 at 0930 hours. Don't be late. Where we are now is your classroom. Leave all papers here in your

KIDNAPPING JESUS

briefcase and lock it up in your wall locker. Each of you have an assigned locker. Your names are on your briefcase. Ken pulled together the information and sent it here several days ago. It is highly restricted. There are eight copies, and they are numbered one through eight. Mr. Hastings has the other copy and will be involved by remote TV when we are in the classroom. He has a closed-circuit TV and can monitor all facets of our training. If needed, Mr. Hastings can fill the vacancy as a last resort. He is not a Billionaire that sits behind his desk watching his accounts grow. It is not in his DNA! See you in the morning."

John and Ken left. The remaining team members reviewed the contents of their briefcases. Each of them had an assignment for tomorrow. PT would be led by Justin. Phil was to conduct a short overview on the Shroud to include historical information regarding the Shroud.

Jack was going to brief on the Cathedral of Saint John the Baptist and the Duomo di San Giovanni. The rest of the team would have their assignments the following day. This was rotational. Each would become an expert. Each would know what the other knew inside out. There was a hierarchy, just as there was a chain of command. If one fell, another could pick up their responsibilities and so on. It was 2200 hours when Phil and Jack left Hanger 1. They were greeted by the security team on duty and showed their badges. There were roving guards and around the complex, you could hear vehicles outside the perimeter. This was a well-lighted facility and it almost looked like it was daytime.

Once inside the Barracks, they went to the cafeteria to get a bite to eat. The rest of the team was waiting in the dayroom. They went to John's room and had a nightcap. John looked at each of them. "Team, you know the drill. Enjoy this drink. It will be at least another week before you taste any alcohol. We're at it in the morning. I am looking forward to your briefings and walk-throughs. This schedule will rotate three times. Each of you will get a chance to do a better job until we know everything there is to know about the Shroud. Computers are available in the classroom only. We are back to basics. There is no reward unless the job is completed. And to remind you of an old military motto, "No Job is Complete until the Paperwork is done." Although you are my brothers in arms, we are here for one reason and one reason only. We are assembled here to steal the Shroud."

276

MISSION TO TURIN

John received a thunderous "HOOAH"! This was an audible affirmation of the mission yet to come. Traditionally, this term is used by the U.S. Army, but it was universally accepted among the team members. Esprit de Corps was the center of this mission. Success was never a doubt.

John Elder rolled over in his bed and looked at the clock. It said 0530 hours. He was up early and could not sleep any longer. He knocked out twenty push-ups to get his blood flowing. This was more of a way of life than exercise for Elder. He took a quick shower as soon as he was done. It was cold and kept the reflexes at peak performance when he was training for a mission. A person would never know John was almost 52 years old. He did not have gray hair. He jumped out of the shower and put on a pair of light khaki shorts with a military brown T-shirt. Everyone was up. They were outside and waiting on John although he was not late. And they were ready with their gear. There was an old military motto that if you were on-time, you were 15 minutes late.

They loaded into the military 5-Ton truck. "Men, take a deep breath. Smell the fresh air of freedom. We are here because of our freedoms. We are here because of so many of our brothers in arms that have come before us. You know the names that come back to you in your dreams and waking thoughts. They also knew others that had made the ultimate sacrifice before them. Heroes come from all walks of life. This mission will be one of the legends we all see ourselves in as we read the books of life. How can it be that our destiny brings us once again to a point where we are together again? The air is fresh. We train today to complete a mission for which each of us must and will be totally prepared. We each have met the agent of death. We were the victors. Yet, one day, death will embrace us. It will not be this day. It will not be on this mission. There is more for us than this mission in life."

The truck dropped the team into the outreaches of the Annex. John circled the men into their group of seven. It had been a 15-minute drive to their present location. The truck had covered about seven miles of some of the nastiest terrain in the world. All that was in their imagination was the cactus and snakes. The group looked around at their location. John pulled out a compass. The team knew the drill. They were not running, jogging, or walking home on the road. It was cross country. It was orienteering.

277

KIDNAPPING JESUS

John pulled out the map. "Men, we are here. The Base is here. Grab your pack and your buddy. See you back at the Base."

With that, John threw the map into a patch of cactus and headed out. He was playing the scout. The rest of the group would soon follow. However, John took off on a route that was intentionally wrong. He would be close; you could count on that. But he did not want to be followed by the team.

He wanted them to lead. Within minutes he had disappeared. It was like the desert swallowed him. He watched from a short distance with a small pair of binoculars as the men retrieved and then checked out the map.

Teams naturally formed. Jack and Charles followed the two other groups. John was proud that his youngest brother stayed to assist Charles. They would probably be last. However, Phil and Justin and Stacey, and Ken had to run the course as well. Three teams leave at about the same time to one common destination. The sun was rising and the coolness from the desert was quickly disappearing. Phil grabbed Stacey to come with him.

Ken and Justin formed up. This is what John wanted to see. He wanted to see the core members of COBALT take the newcomers under their belt for Team SOS.

The teams were off on a jog. They had their backpacks on and were heading back to the Annex. John was following a parallel course, just out of sight. They all were watching the ground around them. It was not just the snakes, but each team wanted to follow the natural terrain in order not to get into depressions or atop small hills. If they veered right or left, they would have to adjust their compass headings using the natural terrain to orient themselves. They were all trained, but it was Ken Parker who was probably the most skilled in this technique, even though each of the former Marines had the training that helped them in Beirut and later in the first Gulf War. Stacey had received his training in the Army while in Special Forces. None of them were strangers to no-notice type training.

It wasn't long until the three teams began to set their own pace and began to separate from each other.

MISSION TO TURIN

Jack and Charles were last. Ken and Justin were in the lead and looked comfortable. John ambled up to Jack and Charles. They both saw him coming in from their left flank.

John ran up beside them. "Hey brothers, how's it going? Are you going to make it?"

Jack quickly responded. "It's not about who finishes last; it's all about making it together...as a team."

John, Charles and Jack laughed in unison.

There had been so many times when they had seen the fastest, or the strongest, fail in their mission because they wanted to be in the front. They burned out. And, when they did so, the team always suffered.

It was about two hours later when the teams began arriving at the administrative building that had once been a barracks and was now their living quarters. John had passed each of the teams on the way in and had spoken to each of them. Although they all had their own compass and knew the direction back to the Annex, the three teams used their own skills in getting back to their base of operations.

The desert, with the scrub brush, cactus, and tumbleweeds, plus the dried-up riverbeds that became rivers during flash thunderstorms, provided a great course for the team. Unless they were within 50 feet of another team, they probably would not have seen each other. John had brought out some water bottles for the team. The canteen probably contained warm water if any and cold water would be refreshing.

It was about 0900 hours and already the temperature was climbing into the 90s. It was going to be hot. Ken and Justin arrived just as John was getting organized with the water. Justin had set the pace. He was the slowest. Within 10 minutes, Stacey and Phil arrived. Stacey set the pace. And, finally, Jack and Charles walked into the group. They were 20 minutes behind Stacey and Phil. Charles had been working out and doing some jogging as part of his rehabilitation but was not prepared for this shit. However, John learned what he wanted to know. Charles still had the mental toughness to make the run.

Reaching back into his memories of the Corps and of the military in general was one of the oldest military statements in the world. John said it aloud. "Gentlemen, mind over matter. If you don't mind, it doesn't matter. Welcome back!"

KIDNAPPING JESUS

The team, once again responded with a thunderous "HOOAH"! Although, not as sincere as the last "HOOAH", it continued to be an audible affirmation of the mission yet to come and represented the team was still ready and completely focused on this mission, regardless of the toils and sacrifices made by each one of them. Success was never a doubt. John smiled and inwardly, he radiated with pride, although his facial features never hinted anything but business, not as usual, but strictly business.

The team was loosely assembled and talking about the game, the run they had just participated in when Chad Eastman approached them. He oversaw the Base and had just returned from Johnson Space Center in Houston.

He was working with NASA to determine when the Astronauts and Mission Specialists for the next Shuttle Mission would arrive as part of their pre-flight training. He needed to ensure the cover story would be acceptable for the current "Mission Specialists."

"Glad to have your team here Mr. Elder. I have been briefed on your requirements." John introduced Eastman to his team.

"John, please take a short walk with me to Hanger 1." Eastman walked up to the two guards guarding the entrance to the huge building. They both showed their identification badges. Mr. Eastman insisted everyone be checked. He and John walked inside. The guards looked at each other thinking this team of seven Mission Specialists sure did not look like they were part of NASA. Then again, there have been older Astronauts and Specialists, as well as two Senators and a member from the House of Representatives, throughout the program.

"I hope everything meets with your satisfaction. I know you will be spending most of your time here. May I ask what you are training for?"

"Chad, may I call you Chad?"

"Yes, or course you can. I've been instructed to extend every courtesy. We both work for Mr. Hastings. Just one big happy family."

"Chad, I can tell you this. You and a few others can plainly see what is in this building. The accuracy of the replicas is to be commended. But, regardless of what you see here, it is Mr. Hastings who requests the information surrounding our work with him is on a need-to-know basis only. I am sure Mr. Hastings would entertain the same question you just asked me.

MISSION TO TURIN

But, at this time, I report directly to him, just as you do, so I guess you are doing exactly what you were instructed, for which I am very grateful. I would ask one favor of you. Please enter this building only if asked to do so and only if you and I are in each other's company. I don't want any misunderstandings. Hopefully, we can agree anything that happens within this hanger is in my domain."

Eastman did not like anybody talking down to him. He was used to being in charge. This was his Base. Well, not his Base per se, but when Hastings was away, he was in charge.

"John, that's ok with me."

They walked out together, and the guards checked them out to ensure they had exactly what they had taken inside. To have removed anything would have required a form filled out with the items removed and faxed directly to Mr. Hastings. John had the authority on-site to remove items for training purposes, but he was the only one inside the circle of seven who had the authority. Not even Chad Eastman, Base Commander, could alter that fact.

On their way back to the Barracks, Eastman grabbed John's left arm. He squeezed it hard. John did not rip his arm away from his grasp. He looked down at the grip. Eastman was a soft bureaucrat. He was in charge of a large operation, but his leadership abilities were lacking. John suffered from neither. He was a leader and was mentally and physically tough.

"Mr. Eastman. I want you to get something straight. Don't ever touch me again. You and I are here for one purpose and one purpose only. We work for Mr. Hastings. You support me. I need you to provide information and logistics support. You need me to be successful, or we both will be fired. Again, I don't want you to ask me any questions; unless it is what we need and how fast do I want it. If you follow these rules, we will get along fine and we will both have done our respective jobs for Mr. Hastings. Do you understand?"

John grabbed Eastman's hand in a simple flex hold causing Eastman to squirm a little with some pain in his arm. John had to give him some credit; he did not let out a yell. "Do we understand each other?"

"We are clear. You have my support. You can be assured I know what you and your team require."

John let Eastman's hand loose. Eastman placed both hands behind him and rubbed his right hand to regain circulation. John returned to his group in front of the Barracks. Eastman jumped into his jeep and drove away from the Barracks, feeling that if he were to touch Elder again, he would rip his arm off and stuff it down his throat. Eastman had never encountered someone like him.

John walked up to the group. "I hope you all had a nice break. You did well today. Glad to see each of you made it. Let's get cleaned up and have some breakfast and then get over for training. We have two hands-on briefings today. I hope all of you are ready. Pay attention, you may be next in the hot seat."

Once the team was back in front of the Barracks, John had them do two sets of twenty-five push-ups. "Let's get over to the Hanger."

They checked through security. John looked at Phil. "Let's begin with your presentation."

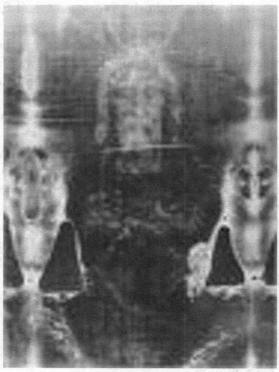

The Shroud of Turin

MISSION TO TURIN

"Gentlemen, the *Shroud of Turin* is surrounded by mystery. Whether the clothes are real or not, these are the facts bearing on our mission. The cloth bears the image of a man. This man appears to have been crucified. It is reported to be the burial cloth that covered Jesus when He was placed in the tomb. His image was imbedded into the fibers of the cloth during the resurrection. The cloth measures fourteen by three and one-half feet. The location of the Shroud is in the Italian Cathedral di San Giovann Battista. The Turin Cathedral dedicated to Saint John the Baptist. It has been in Turin since 1578, except during World War II when it was moved, and hidden, in a Monastery to protect it from Allied bombing. The first time the Shroud was ever photographed was in 1898 during an exhibition of the Shroud. The resulting photograph was a positive image of the negative image embedded in the cloth. It was an amazing picture."

The Shroud of Turin

"Debate among scientists and believers regarding the Shroud's origin focuses on dating the Shroud. There are those who believe the Shroud is a clever hoax created in the late 1200s or during the 1300s. Please look at our replica of the Shroud. It is believed that there are only two forgeries of the Shroud: this one and the one on display at the Cathedral. The real Shroud is constantly monitored by one of four Priests always on duty. Without getting into Jack's presentation, suffice it to say, the Shroud must be authenticated prior to us taking the Shroud. Look at the lower left-hand corner. There is a mark there that is revealed under ultraviolet light. Justin, please dim the lights."

As the lights dimmed, Phil took out a small light from his left pocket of his shirt. It looked like a small pen. However, as he pointed the small light at the counterfeit Shroud, each of the men mumbled to themselves.

"This is very significant. Only the real Shroud and this fake have this mark as far as we have been able to ascertain. It is the mark of the Knights Templar. In 1307, Pope Clement V condemned the Knights, tortured them into false confessions, and then burned them at the stake. However, as a result of a marriage, the Shroud came into the possession of a Knight by the name of Geoffroi de Charny."

"His wife, Jeanne de Vergy, was basically the first traceable owner of the Shroud. Most importantly, the reason the mark of the Knights Templar is on the Shroud is in recognition of Geoffroi de Charny's uncle."

"Geoffrey de Carney was the Preceptor of Normandy of the Knights Templar and was burned at the stake in 1314. Although a member of the Order of the Star, Geoffroi believed in chivalry and wanted to recognize his uncle by placing the mark of the Knights Templar on the Shroud. In fact, many of the surviving members of the Knights Templar were absorbed into other Orders and this could offer a possible explanation why it was this mark that was selected to be embedded on the Shroud. It was added to the Shroud, but no one knows exactly when and how the mark was added. Only a handful of men, including a few scientists, have this knowledge. It is a closely guarded secret by the Church."

"We have placed this mark on our replica of the Shroud as you can see. We obtained information regarding this mark within the last week, and it was embedded on the cloth by one of Mr. Hastings scientists only two days ago. That's all the information I have at this time and that about sums it up. Phil, please get the lights. Are there any questions?"

John looked at the team. No one had any questions. The mark of the Knights Templar was significant information. Yet, John had a question he did not ask, he knew the answer, but the question would not be spoken aloud.

The lack of this mark was the major difference between the fake Shroud and the real Shroud. If there were other marks of authenticity, then the team would be detected.

It would be a matter of time. If not, they could have committed the theft of the century, maybe of all time. It depended on the frequency of the checks. Certainly, the Shroud would be checked when it was moved. John's musings quickly turned back to the next presentation.

Jack was briefing on the Cathedral of Saint John the Baptist and the Duomo di San Giovanni. The rest of the team listened closely. "...

as you can clearly see the Cathedral is a formidable structure built in the late 1400s."

Cathedral of Saint John the Baptist

"The Shroud is currently located in the Duomo di San Giovanni because it was relocated in 1997 following a fire. In fact, the true name of where the Shroud was located is known as the Cappella della Sacra Sindone, the Chapel of the Holy Shroud. For the rest of this presentation, we will refer to this building as the Chapel."

"Ok, moving right along. Getting back to the Chapel. The Shroud is located in a locked vault behind the pulpit. While the architecture is hundreds of years old, the security system is state of the art. There is a copy on display. Someone is always awake and watching the monitor placed within the vault. This is not open to the public. Back-up systems for power are always on stand-by. Should the power go out, the systems kick on within seconds of the electrical outage."

"This may provide us with an opportunity to provide a distraction. Frontal assault would probably prove to be difficult and not part of our

KIDNAPPING JESUS

mission statement. If the authorities are notified, Turin would be virtually cut off from the outside world until the thieves are apprehended. We have to do this right the first time."

"Reportedly, there are sensors and infrared technology protecting the Shroud. These measures are easily countered if we have the right tools for the job. John, we need more information to ensure we can safely assume responsibility for the Shroud. We have to ensure we keep it safe. To destroy, or mutilate this priceless piece of history would be, to say the least, a mark of blasphemy cast upon our names, our families and what little would be left remaining of our reputations for centuries. We literally could be placed into the same categories of Judas Iscariot and Benedict Arnold."

It was late in the day. The team had worked through lunch munching on snacks along with refreshments. After the training was completed, the same briefings were assigned to Charles and Justin for the following day.

John called Greer and Parker into his office at the Barracks. "I need you to take steroids while we are here. They will help you catch up to the other men. Charles began taking steroids only two weeks ago and has really come a long way with his recovery. You guys did well today, and I am not complaining. With the shape you are already in, the steroids will take you over the top. I need you to be in great shape!"

This was nothing new to the two men. Parker took steroids in the French Foreign Legion. It was like Motrin the American military community commonly referred to as M&Ms. Motrin was not steroids, but it did help get through the pain. "We've taken them before. Let's face it. We are not twenty years old anymore."

John walked out with Ken and Stacey into the Barracks. He asked them to bring the rest of the team to his room. They assembled. "Again, today, you did very well. We need to eat dinner and then get ready for the day tomorrow. We will meet for PT at 0600 hours. Ken will lead the group in the morning exercises. Today was a good beginning. Charles and Justin please be prepared to brief me tomorrow. I want more details about the inside of the buildings. The Shroud has been covered in sufficient detail. You know how to identify the original. I know of two fakes. The Church has one and we have one. I am not sure if there is another fake, but I won't take any chances. Remember, assumptions kill!

MISSION TO TURIN

You two team up on the buildings. Work it out. Jack, work with them. Between the three of you, we should expect to be dazzled by your combined intellect." Jack, Charles and Justin looked at John and the others and knew they had their instructions.

John addressed Phil, Stacey, and Ken. "Ok, while the rest of the team is going to the Barracks, I want you three to do some research on the Internet. You have your computers. If you hear something that does not fit during the presentation, or if you think something should be added, I don't want you to say anything until their presentation is over. No spring butts! Got it?"

The team laughed. It was understood they were not to say anything to the others assigned this mission. It was a common technique used by major corporations as well as in the military. Chuck Taylor often checked out his teams doing the same thing when they were chasing down the dregs of society.

John dismissed the team. "What are you waiting for?" They all left. John made a closed-circuit call from a secure phone to George Hastings III. "George, all is going well. I hope you enjoyed the presentation today, but I would like you to tune in tomorrow. This will be a good day for learning about the team's ability to know the material."

"John, there is absolutely no problem with your request. I know you are aware I have remotes to where I can see what is happening virtually everywhere on the Base. I saw your team finish their course this morning. Training was revealing. I enjoyed it. I have not been idle. I have read the papers and my operations staff here continues to feed me any information they are able to find. Copies have been sent to you by special courier. I will keep looking. We need to know when the transfer is scheduled. Please keep me informed."

They ended the call. John reflected. All the men wanted to do the best job they could do for John and themselves not for Hastings.

They could care less about him. He could care less about them. All he wanted was the Shroud.

It was a restless night for John. The clock alarm went off at 0530 hours. It was March 10, 2002. John thought about it. The Shroud had to be moved before Easter. Easter Sunday would be March 31st. Palm Sunday was March 24th and Good Friday on the 29th. John quickly sat up from his comfortable bed!

KIDNAPPING JESUS

He sat on the side for just a few moments before he called George Hastings. "George, this is John. Sorry to wake you, but I think the timetable we were working on may need to be moved up. I am accelerating the training. Please continue to work on finding out the exact date the Shroud will be moved. I need to know soon. But it the meantime, I'm planning on the fact we do not have the luxury of time,"

George responded. "You may be right. I trust your intuition. I'll get on it with my team here."

John went outside. The team was still getting together. Ken began the stretching exercises. They did the daily dozen with 20 repetitions each. Now for the fun part of the day.

John hit them with a curve ball. "Grab your canteen. Leave your gear."

It was 50 degrees outside and crystal clear. The sun was not up, but daylight was on its way. This was known as BMNT. Thirty minutes away from Begin Morning Nautical Twilight.

They began their trot. Justin called cadence. They headed out a mile on the same road they were on yesterday. John stopped the team.

"Men, I am going to let you in on what I believe to be headed our direction: We don't have three weeks, not even two weeks before we deploy. It's a feeling I have. We'll know for sure in a couple of days, I think. I hope. In fact, I'm planning on it. We need to step it up one more level. This is the way it has to be."

The team let out another HOOAH in unison. There was an echo and a coyote howling back to them to let the team know he had heard them and their HOOAH.

"Ok team, you remember where the truck dropped us off yesterday? That's where we are headed. You will follow me at five-minute increments. You will be alone. Each of you has to find your own way. No roads. Cross country. Charles will be first, followed by the remaining. Pick straws or toss a coin, I don't care. Its 0630 hours and I am on my way. Good luck!"

The team would do five to seven miles each day for three days, and then increase it to eight miles. At the end of the week, they would do a ten-mile road-march with a ninety-pound backpack. Then the team would relax the run to just three miles per day for building up speed with endurance and would spend twelve hours a day in the mock-up.

MISSION TO TURIN

That is, if they had the time. He wished Hastings had approached him earlier about this mission.

John's mind raced while he ran. This was his time to organize his thoughts. Each member would have to put to memory what every job entailed in case someone did not make it. All weapons used in this operation would be of the non-lethal kind. Drugs would be used to alter memories. John had run by a small heard of deer at one of the few watering holes in this desolate country. Birds were coming to life and the desert sounded like a neighborhood. He had scared up a fox and even a skunk. They were afraid of human contact and rightly so. Man was their enemy and was to be feared. Man was an indiscriminate killer. He did not only kill for food, but he also killed for fun. It was a passion that would never be contained. The animal kingdom lived, and died, on a different level. It was survival of the fittest. Not who had the technical advantage.

The country was beautiful. Cactus had blossoms in anticipation of the spring about to come. The cactus was a sign of water and life, even in lean times. One only had to have basic knowledge to survive. The moment of truth kept circling his thoughts, the Shroud. His dreams during the night came back to him; the fire fight in Vietnam, his buddies that were killed and those that lived, his Lieutenant who later became a General, and his friends that retired with him from the Corps, and, Casey Long. John wondered where he went after they had been reassigned. It was a puzzle that would not be unraveled in his thoughts.

It had happened to him before. Losing contact with someone he had come to respect. People went in their own direction, sometimes never crossing each other's path again. And, sometimes, you have had a feeling that someone you knew had passed near you only moments before. Life was full of possibilities. John arrived at the RP. It was dead reckoning. He knew where the sun was rising and kept it to his back. The others should be arriving soon. Five minutes was nothing. John sat down on one of the four wheelers while he waited. He had a drink of water. It was not long until the first man arrived. It was not Charles. It was Ken.

He sat next to John. "Nice morning for a jog!"

John laughed out loud. Soon, Phil, Justin, Charles, Stacey and Jack joined the team. Jack arrived within 35 minutes of when John had

KIDNAPPING JESUS

arrived at the RP. He had been the last to start. They came in from a couple of directions, but generally followed the same route.

Nature had created the animals and they in turn established their own highways through the desert. One had to only keep to the same direction.

After the run and a trip back to their quarters on the four wheelers left for them at the RP, the team went over to the cafeteria. The men could order anything they wanted. The food was good. He had to give it to Hastings. He ran a tight ship with only one exception. Eastman would have to be watched. There was something about that man that rubbed John the wrong way. He judged Eastman as he had done so many others. He trusted his instincts so far, and so far, he had been right. When the hair on his neck stood on end, there was always something that would turn up later that proved he was right.

It was not only aimed at the enemy, but even some of his own Marines had caused him grief. John had built up his internal radar through the years. Time after time he was right. Once bitten, twice a fool. And the ever-present thought that assumptions could and did kill. No turning back.

After breakfast, the men had thirty minutes before they went to Hanger

1. Once inside, John handed out a folder labeled Top-Secret that detailed the operational orders everyone would follow.

"To restate your individual participation in this operation. Ken will be my Executive Officer. If something happens to me, you will take your orders from him. Charles oversees logistics and will not be with us directly in the recovery of the Shroud. Charles will be on the ground with Stacey and Jack. The three of them will be providing perimeter security. Justin will be on the roof entry team along with Phil and me. In addition to being Number Two, Ken will act independently between the ground team and the roof team. Should something go wrong, Ken will fill the gap. We will be flying to Rome and then on to Turin. It is a matter of days before we depart. Conduct today's training like it might be our last. Who knows, less pain may mean great gain." They all laughed knowing this could not be more of an untrue statement in the entire world. Work was the answer to success."

290

MISSION TO TURIN

"Transportation will be waiting for us on the ground at Turin International Airport. Again, weapons will be the non-lethal type. Do not kill anyone. The success of this operation is not alerting the vigilance of the Pope. His eyes are everywhere. Sleeping darts will be always used. You will have an aerosol to dispense that is effective within two meters of the subject. Remember to use your filter. We essentially are dealing with cleric, non-violent, men. However, do not rest on that assumption. I imagine some of these caretakers are pretty handy with martial arts. We just want to help ourselves to the Shroud of Turin and replace it with the counterfeit Shroud."

All the men looked at what John had written on the page and was relating to them. They all shook their heads. Silently they liked the plan.

"Let's get the show on the road. Jack, Charles and Justin, you guys are center stage."

The layout of the Cathedral was quite easy to learn. There were four priests always living on the premises and there was one priest on duty.

The Shroud was kept at the end of an altar in a large glass case sealed in a room by itself. This room would be known as the "Vault".

The door was secured at 1800 hours daily. The team discussed how they would steal the Shroud. Several ideas were generated among the group. One course of action was to take out the guard when their shift changed and be prepared to take out the relief shift. This would give the team three hours to pull off the switch until the relief came and found the unconscious priest.

Another course of action Charles brought to the table was to get into the room by going through the roof. The flaw with the first course of action would be a timing issue and taking out the guards. Without enough time, this plan would be doomed to failure. Not to mention the fact the guards would wonder what took place. With coming through the roof, a silk screen of the Shroud could be dropped in front of the camera the priest constantly monitored, or, splicing the cable with a picture of what was only moments before an image of an undisturbed glass case would be another choice.

After the discussion John looked at Charles. "Men, are there any other ideas? If not, let's work towards rappelling through the roof, once the cameras are interrupted with a signal showing the Shroud undisturbed in the glass case. Look at using a power outage. Check to see

KIDNAPPING JESUS

what the history of outages were in the past. If there have not many, then we need to look at another distraction. Again, if it is out of the ordinary, we will be detected. Someone will raise the flag. You can bet your sweet ass! Using that as the premise, we then need to be able to disarm the security devices that are in- place on the glass vault. I imagine we will run into laser beams and motion detectors. Folks, we need to know everything we can know about security and establish the means to avoid detection. This is not a robbery where we can back up a truck to an ATM machine and pull it down the street. Once we have more information from our source, we will make a final decision."

For the next few days, the team was up at dawn every day doing their physical training. They also trained on the mock-up. They had their timing down to an art form in just four days. It was like football teams training for the Super Bowl; however, in this case, they had to be the winning team. They were ready. Although they were not quite the lean mean fighting machine they desired, they were in shape for the mission.

John still believed the Shroud would be moved before March 31st, Palm Sunday was March 24th and Good Friday on the 29th.

It was March 18th. The training was complete, although earlier than predicted. John had been in constant contact with George Hastings. John believed the team should be in Turin by March 22nd.

This would give the team time to recon the actual sites with the crowds drawn to view the resting place of the Shroud. The crowd was the cover the team needed to remain covert. The last road march would be the following morning. A quick walk-through of the mock-up would follow, and then a ride to the airport via the limousines belonging to BIOTECH150.

It was arranged. The team was provided diplomatic passports. This was a nice safety net John liked to have at his disposal. In this case, George Hastings III provided them, not the United States Government. They would be traveling on a commercial airline. Their carrier would provide direct flight transportation to Orlando, Florida. Then they would then fly on another major airline to Rome, Italy the following day. It was going to be busy. They would arrive in Rome on the 21st. Then, one of the small corporate jets belonging to Hastings would take them to a small airport outside of Turin. All the equipment they needed would be on board. They would be staying in a small Villa just

292

MISSION TO TURIN

outside of the town. They could remain relatively unnoticed in that they would be on a vineyard that occupied hundreds of acres. Transportation would be provided. The group would, of course, break up and arrive at the Cathedral at different times. They would not switch. Each group had their responsibilities.

John interrupted his own train of thought. "Charles will be on the ground with Stacey and Jack and will be providing perimeter security and are responsible for our transportation. Two vehicles will be used. The Shroud will be in the first vehicle and the chase vehicle will provide distraction. Just in case, we had a third copy made of Shroud. It is not in the detail of the Shroud we have as the substitute; in fact, nothing is as detailed.

In case we need a temporary distraction, we will sacrifice the vehicle with the fake. That should delay the chase long enough for us to get back to the vineyard. Justin is on the roof entry team with Phil and myself. Ken is our eyes and ears between the two teams. He will act independently. Should something go wrong, Ken fills the gap."

With a big smile on his face, John looked at his team. "Are there any questions?"

The response from the team was a unanimous "HOOAH!" "Let's get the fuck out of here and get to the dining hall. Steaks are on George Hastings III." They all laughed.

"There will be drinks after dinner. No pain, no gain. Tomorrow, we run ten miles of more forgotten terrain. Just don't get snake bit."

They ate, joked, and had a cigar and a couple of drinks. After the regimen they had been through during the last week, the alcohol acted quickly. Lights were out by 2200 hours. They went to sleep early wanting tomorrow to come quickly.

The men were up at 0600 hours ready for the ten-mile road march, if you could call it a road. Like the IGTs (Improved Goat Trails) they used in Afghanistan and Pakistan, these trails were, or probably could be called, Unimproved Snake Trails (USTs). They started at 0700 hours. It was a compass course, and the team had to find a number, go the next route, find a number, and so on. This was a piece of cake for all members of the team. It just took some of them longer. Each had been handed a sheet of paper with their individual course. They all equaled ten miles, but each had a different starting point. There were six points.

KIDNAPPING JESUS

When John said "Go," they each headed in a different direction. John was pacing Charles to the first point. He would cut across to join another member of the team, until he had seen each of them during the course. They all were back at the Barracks by 1000 hours and ready to eat. Greer and Parker were in very good shape from the training and the recent use of steroids. Charles was still behind, but it was remarkable he could almost keep up. Inwardly, John smiled with pride at how his younger brothers could always be counted upon to measure up to any challenge. The rest of the team was once again at peak performance.

After a huge breakfast, everyone took a shower and put on their traveling clothes. John did a walk-through one last time at Hanger 1.

The men had the job down to a split second. They were ready for this last mission, together.

John located Chad Eastman. He had made himself very scarce since their first meeting. John thought Ken Parker might have had something to do with him staying in the background.

Eastman knew that John would be leaving today. It was his business to know what always went on "his" Base.

"Chad, we will be leaving first thing in the morning. I just dropped by to let you know."

Chad replied, "I got the word from the boss last night, but I appreciate you letting me know. I understand you will be back once your mission is complete?"

"That's right. We are making a brief stop then we're on our way back to Florida. In the meantime, take care, and thanks for your support. You run a tight ship. I am sorry if we got off on the wrong foot. My pucker factor had been so tight a doctor could not perform a rectal exam on me even if I was unconscious."

"John, it's not a problem. I watched the way you worked. You take care of the troops, and they see you as their leader. And we both know there is only room for one leader in any outfit. Take care and good hunting."

With that, they parted with a handshake. Chad Eastman watched John Elder walk away. He had a begrudging respect for this former Marine, but would not compromise his own situation for John, or even George Hastings III. What Chad Eastman did not realize was while Chad was watching everything at "his" Base, he too was being watched. It was just a matter of time until his house of cards would collapse.

MISSION TO TURIN

Charles was in charge of all non-lethal weapons. This was the first time John's team would be equipped with rubber bullets, stun guns, and a penetrating gas that would immobilize a charging bull elephant almost immediately. It was non-detectable. The recipient would not even have a headache. He would just have to be placed in a chair and would have no recollection of what had taken place. It was not only a tranquilizer; it was a type of hallucinogenic and caused permanent memory lapses. Often, the loss of memory would be for 30 minutes, but it was usually just for a few minutes. This would allow the team the benefit of an alibi until they were eventually discovered. Hopefully, the team would be in and out before they were ever detected. This was a far cry from what the team had done several months ago.

The team directly and indirectly killed over 200 Al Queda soldiers, cut off the head of the number two terrorist leader, and captured Osama Bin- Laden.

John walked over to Hanger 1. Just outside, he ran into Stacey Greer and asked him if he was ready for the mission. "John, I've never felt better in my life than I do now. The training was right on track. It reminded me of a short course at Camp Stacey. I'm glad you told me to stay in shape. And I do appreciate this once-in-a-lifetime shot. The mock-ups were great training aids. I know the Cathedral like the back of my hand. I know I am ready, and the team is looking forward to the operation."

"Stacey, I agree with you. We are all ready to get this mission over with. I am looking forward to success and a profit. I will not say never again. Training for a mission and then executing the mission is an adrenaline rush."

Greer just smiled when he heard the word profit. He was thinking that he would take his money and go to North Carolina to live. Jack had walked out of the Hanger a few minutes into the conversation.

When John and Stacey finished, Jack looked over at them with a smile on his face shaking his head in agreement. "John, we all are looking for the money. I don't know why this man wants the cloth, but he is paying enough money for it."

By this time, it seemed as if John was holding an informal staff meeting outside of the Hanger where they had spent so much of their time. John told them to get some food and rest. It would be an early

KIDNAPPING JESUS

morning wake-up call and lots of travel. All the men in the team acknowledged this. They headed to their assigned rooms for a shower and then dinner in the cafeteria. The team was up at 0500 hours for a little exercise before chow. They did their road work, took a shower, and had breakfast. They loaded into the two Suburban SUVs and headed for the Airport.

They boarded the plane and settled in while the crew prepared the aircraft for takeoff. They would fly on the airline to Orlando, Florida, and remain overnight. George Hastings III would meet them at the Crown Plaza Orlando Airport Hotel. Suites had been reserved along with a small meeting room. There wasn't much to say during the flight.

With a few exceptions, the team members slept. Those remaining awake watched TV or listened to music. The tunes of "Smooth Operator" played in John's mind. Perfect, just want he wanted to hear. Certainly, all of them were thinking about the upcoming mission.

Hotel transportation was waiting for them just outside the terminal. It was low-key. Once they arrived at the Hotel, they were quickly escorted to their rooms. They had already been checked in. Instructions were given to the team to meet in one of the meeting rooms with a small theater at 1800 hours. All team members rested until around 1700 hours and then prepared to go downstairs and meet with Mr. Hastings III. They were ready to get this mission going.

It was nothing extravagant. It was just a small room. However, Mr. Hastings III wanted to do something special for the team. There was a small, self-service bar and some great appetizers available. No one outside the team would be in the room until later. James Winfield Jefferson would provide the food and drink services. Other than Ken Parker, James was the only member of the Hastings' staff to know the team's mission to steal the Shroud.

Mr. Hastings was already present as the team members joined him. They came in on their own. John was last to arrive. The quiet conversation was in full swing, but the small group just stopped and looked at John. A loud "HOOAH" came from their lips. George was pleasantly surprised at how this leader had gained the respect and admiration of this select group of heroes.

Once John joined the group, James rang a small silver bell. "Gentlemen, on behalf of Mr. Hastings, welcome to this auspicious

296

MISSION TO TURIN

gathering. On the menu tonight is Lobster Bisque followed by Filet Mignon or Salmon cooked on a cedar plank, with a desert of Better than Sex Chocolate Cake. Please enjoy the drinks and the appetizers while I take your orders. Make yourself comfortable."

As James quietly went from man to man, George Hastings proposed a toast to the team. "John, you and the men of the Seekers of the Shroud have made me proud of the way you attacked your mission. I know, with no uncertainty, you will be successful.

While you are in Italy, I have secured one of my small Villas complete with a vineyard for your exclusive use. There will be a chef; doctor, cook and housekeeper to take care of your needs. All of these personnel are in my employ. They will support you in all of your requirements. However, what you are there for is confidential. Please direct your attention to the screen.

This is the Cathedral and Church where the Shroud is kept. This next picture is of the grounds of the Villa. You can continue to conduct any training necessary, except, do not draw attention to yourselves within the local community. I often use this as a retreat."

James looked at Mr. Hastings with that last comment. This was a getaway for Mr. Hastings. And the wine from these vineyards was sought out by connoisseurs worldwide. His private collection dated back over 100 years from this vineyard even though it had only been in the family the last 50 years. His father had purchased it shortly after World War II. The vineyard was near Alba, just far enough from Turin. Milan and Genoa were two of the major cities nearby. George traveled the area and was intimately familiar with the culture, heritage, and a few of the wealthiest and most beautiful women in the world. "With that, I ask only one favor of each of you. Once the mission is complete, I ask each of you to stay in contact with me. I have assets worldwide that can be of assistance should they be needed. Even when you require some downtime, my private yachts must be exercised, so please make my extended homes your homes." With that, the drinking began in earnest.

The team needed to decompress. Their flight to Atlanta was around noon. They would catch a direct flight to Rome around 1700 hours and arrive the next morning. It would be March 21st. A BIOTECH150 Corporate jet would fly them to Turin where they would be met by two

KIDNAPPING JESUS

of the staff from the Vineyard. It was only about a 30-minute ride to the Vineyard from the airport.

It was a nice dinner. One of the best any of them could remember. James ensured the meals from the Hotel were specially prepared. Hastings had provided the beef and the salmon. The salmon was caught in Alaska. The meat was from free-range beef from a small cattle ranch Hastings still owned.

George Hastings was particular about his food and the preparation. He knew that engineering food in this day and age was all part of getting more to the market faster. However, he also knew there were effects of engineering. Affects you can literally see from generation to generation. One just had to get out to the public to see how the growth hormones were affecting the population.

The next few days flew by, literally. John and the team were met by two vans from the vineyards. James had accompanied the team during their flight. He was the eighth man, if needed. And, he was known by the locals. They would think George Hastings III was in town, so to speak. He regularly checked in and out without being noticed. For a Billionaire, anonymity was a must.

John exited the van while the rest of the team unloaded the gear. Parker went to the front door and was greeted by the hostess. She was absolutely beautiful. He could smell pasta cooking in the kitchen. The Villa was like a small chalet. The interior was out of a hunting magazine from the late 1800s. The fire was inviting. It helped to take the chill from the air. The furniture was almost as good as one found in the Hastings Mansion. There were twelve bedrooms, six full bathrooms, a large kitchen and eating area, along with a semi-formal dining room and a large family room able to accommodate up to 30 people. There was a den almost exactly like George Hastings office from his mansion. The animals mounted on the walls or on display were from the local region. Hunting here was not taken for granted. The den would serve as the conference room. A four-car garage was equipped with two vans, a jeep, and a Mercedes Benz. In the den, a large plan had been placed on the wall with a drawing of St. John's Cathedral.

MISSION TO TURIN

The team assembled themselves in the den. John gave them the quick speech telling them to get some rest. They would need it tomorrow.

John and Parker jumped in the jeep with the caretaker and checked the property out.

After dinner, the team turned in early. They had to be adjusted to the radical change in time zones. They slept very well in the comfortable sheets and bed linens. The sheets were stuffed and were like comforters filled with down and were called duvets. Once under the covers, the heat generated was extremely relaxing and comfortable.

On March 22nd, John got all of the men out of their beds. Coffee and pastries were served. Bottled water was provided. They were off for a six- mile run on the property. When they returned, the chef had prepared pancakes and sausages for the men along with orange juice. European three-minute eggs were also ready and egg cups provided with a knife and small spoon to scoop out the insides. This reminded John of his grandfather and grandmother and the breakfasts they prepared when he visited them with his mother in rural North Dakota. This was an art form of preparation, so it would seem. The eggs just gave the impression to be much better when they were prepared in Europe.

The house was equipped with a full weight room. When George Hastings was at the vineyard, he liked to stay in shape. In fact, Ken was no stranger to the vineyard. It was in 1981, shortly after the attack on George Hastings III. Once George Hastings II found out about the attack on his son's life, he flew to Italy. He met Ken Parker and offered him a job for life. He even bought out his reenlistment in the French Foreign Legion. He had to pay to be out of the elite service. Mr. Hastings wanted his son to have a protector. Ken was the man. Although Ken was now almost 50 years old, he was still hard as a rock. The senior Hastings had done well. Ken Parker had more than once thwarted attempts on George Hastings III life. He had been a good friend and mentor.

Shortly after the team had completed their early run and breakfast, they reassembled to take a leisurely trip into Turin via the Autostrada from Alba. The team used two vans and a Mercedes to get to Turin. Charles, Stacey, and Ken left in the first van. They were providing perimeter security and were responsible for transportation away from the Church. Jack, although he was part of the first team (nicknamed

KIDNAPPING JESUS

Team Greyhound), drove the second van with Justin, Phil, and John. The second team was nicknamed Team Reveal. James drove the Mercedes into town.

While the team was in the Church, James would also canvass the area independently.

He would then go to the market on the streets to buy fresh produce and meat for the evening meal. Two vehicles would be used in the theft of the century. The Shroud would be in the first vehicle and the chase vehicle would provide distraction. It would contain a third copy of Shroud. In case a temporary distraction was needed, the chase vehicle would be sacrificed with the fake Shroud. The day prior to the actual mission, the vehicles would be substituted. James would take care of the substitution. It would be necessary to avoid traceability back to George Hastings or the vineyard. In fact, three vehicles would be procured. If all else failed, the third vehicle would act as a blocker. Hopefully, none of the precautions will be needed. Ken was the eyes and ears. Most of the men were equipped with cameras like any tourist. They arrived at St. John's Cathedral at 1145 hours. Both vans were parked in separate lots.

The Cathedral was exactly like the mock-up they used to train located in Hanger 1 back at the Arizona Annex. The one exception was that this Cathedral was so impressive with the décor and trappings a reproduction could just not adequately reproduce. The team members were in awe when they looked at the fake Shroud itself. They had studied it on their own but being here at this place at this moment grabbed them. They were in groups of three. Team Reveal, led by John, noticed the priests were not overly concerned about the security around the fake Shroud. The real Shroud was in a sealed lead glass case that was bullet-proof, fire-proof, and watertight so they really had no worries. And, it was behind a solid rock wall behind the altar they could visually see in the main part of the Cathedral. Even the priest watching the Shroud was out of sight.

From architectural drawings provided by Chad Eastman, John, and the team knew where and when they would have to strike. Keypads were located. John wanted to come back by himself later, prior to closing, to double-check security. He would make it a point to come back at 1700 hours to see how many priests were on duty. The team stayed for about three hours total and photographed the complete

MISSION TO TURIN

Cathedral. They drove around Turin to check the roads prior to going back to the Villa. Everyone left except Ken and John. They continued the surveillance by walking around the area. They checked out the best way to enter the roof from the outside.

It looked like it would be better to cut through the surveillance system, gain entry to the inside, and then drop in from an adjoining room. At least, this is what they were considering as they both had a beer at a small café near the Cathedral.

When they returned to the Villa, they checked and rechecked the plans. The team was assembled around 2000 hours. Film had been loaded into the computer and each team began briefing their findings. They would review once more in the morning following their physical fitness program.

The team was up at 0630 hours. Once PT was completed, the men took their showers and enjoyed another fantastic breakfast. John reassembled the team in the conference room. It was March 23rd. John believed the Shroud would be moved before March 31st.

George and John spoke after the team had been dismissed the previous evening. Chad Eastman had provided what appeared to be the timetable to move the real Shroud.

He had befriended a Cardinal within the Catholic Church years ago and had requested a small favor. Chad had information that would ruin this Cardinal who was in line to ascend to the Papacy itself. Scandal would not only ruin his chance to become the Pope of the Roman Catholic Church but also of the Holy See and could result in a painful descent of power to pauper. Palm Sunday was March 24th and Good Friday on the 29th. The Shroud was going to be moved on the 27th.

"We are taking the Shroud on the 26th. It will be prepared for movement and security will, or at least should be, less stringent. Most of the redundant security systems will have been disconnected. The move will take place at pre-dawn hours. We will enter the Cathedral at 2200 hours sharp. Their shift change is at 0015 hours, just after midnight. Jack and Charles will take care of the pictures. Remember, we have to have a picture of what the new Vault appears to look like. The remainder of the priests will be making the move of the Shroud. We need to be out prior to midnight."

301

KIDNAPPING JESUS

"It's getting to be game time. We not only took pictures, but pictures were taken of us. At this time, we all do not need to go back to the Cathedral. Justin, Phil and I will enter using a side entrance on the north wall. It is on camera. Our robes will provide some anonymity, however, it will be up to Jack and Charles to have already made the initial entry, get the cameras up and running, so we can get up the stairs and in position. Their entry is at 2200 hours. We will enter the room through the adjoining wall where the Shroud is kept. I will repel down to the floor first and Phil will follow. Before I get to the floor, I need to ensure the alarms are off for the change in increased pressure from our body weights. The switch is on the opposite wall from where the glass case is kept. Once I have this disabled, we enter the case through the bottom. This is the weakest point on the case."

"Then, it's simple; we switch the Shroud with the fake. We will secure the real one in the aluminum cylinder. Phil will make the climb out first and join Justin on the winch. I'll follow. I am a little bit heavier than him. We'll pass Jack and Charles. The tape will be removed, the priest should wake up with a slight headache, and the counter will resume time, real time within minutes of the priest waking up. The last image of the tape will be frozen and will last only two minutes.

He should not be alarmed as he should feel like he just fell asleep. Jack and Charles will follow us. We will be rehearsing our Italian for evening greetings and small chit chat. We have cover names, badges, and passwords. With all the activity surrounding the movement of the Shroud, we should just blend in with the rest of the traffic. It is our best cover. And the date of the move is Top Secret.

Once the Shroud makes the journey to the new security system, it would be next to impossible to steal it. This is our best chance. We need to be aware of the weather system that is beginning to gather strength in North Africa. It could affect us in Europe. It is reported to be one of the largest storms in recorded history."

"There is one last thing to be considered. Look at the map. The teams will enter their vehicles at RP (Rally Point) 1 and 2 just outside the Church on the Via Porta Palatina and the Via della Bascilica. We will be joined at the Corso Regina Margherita by James. This is RP 3. This is where the Piazza San Giovanni turns into the Seconda Aiuola

MISSION TO TURIN

Pia. From there, we take the Autostrada back to the Villa. Ken will ensure our routes out to the vehicles are covered.

Once we pass RP4, and it appears we have not been detected, the pilots will be instructed to get clearance for takeoff in the morning around 1100 hours. We will fly to Rome and spend a couple of days of down time. By not appearing to be in a hurry to leave the country, we provide our own alibi. In the meantime, the Shroud will be left on the jet sealed in a container below the floor of the aircraft. This is a change to our original plan. I hope no one minds. James is preparing our itinerary once we reach Rome. We will be going to the Vatican as well as the Coliseum, and we will be staying on as guests of George Hastings. He has another small apartment near the premises of the U.S. Ambassador to the Holy See."

With that final statement, the team's mission was now a reality. The mission was a go. The reason for the change was somewhat of a mystery to the team. John wanted to listen to the chatter regarding the move. And he wanted the team to stay in country until after Easter Sunday on March 31st. There was to be a special viewing of the Shroud on Good Friday. This was totally unannounced and would be limited to a close group directly from Rome. Only the inner circle of the Pope knew of this, and it was limited to 30 of his closest advisors. However, security would be tight.

The morning of March 26th came quickly. Tension within the team was high. Their senses were heightened. They had risen early for their six-mile run. The day looked like it would be clear; however, the weather report was reporting winds and rain early into the evening.

John had an idea and spoke to Ken and James. "Let me ask you a question. What is the chance for this storm to cover our tracks? If, and I do mean if, there is lightning along with this storm, is it possible to fry the power source going into the Cathedral? I don't want to alert the men yet but look into it and get back to me by noon."

The team ate a great breakfast and then showered. Ken and James had gone into the small town of Alba. They picked up a couple of cars modified for protection and speed. Plates were fake but were good enough to stand up to more than just casual scrutiny. There was some small discussion concerning what each of the team members thought about their individual future. The men were in a very good mood. The

KIDNAPPING JESUS

team would disband forever, only coming together inconspicuously. Even the brothers had agreed to keep their profiles off the radar screens.

John kicked the mission off at 1900 hours. That would get everyone ready. They had a light meal at 1800 hours. The team was assembled in the ready room. Jack went over the plan one last time. Team SOS was ready for this, their final mission. Teams Greyhound and Reveal loaded up with Charles and Jack at the wheel. They had driven the route to and from the Church many times. And, they had driven their escape route over the last few days, during different times of the day. They wanted to ensure they could recognize their route no matter the time.

The vehicles were loaded with their weapons and hardware. John was the last team member to get in the new van. Jack was driving. Justin and Phil were also in the vehicle. The other vehicle had Charles, Ken and Stacey. Stacey and Ken would both ensure the way to the awaiting vehicles was clear. Everyone had their responsibilities.

Enroute to their objective, the rain started to come down. At first it was light, and then began to get heavier with gusts of winds beginning to blow. Visibility was reduced. John spoke to George. There were no changes to the schedule for moving the Shroud. It might be delayed for a couple of hours, but that would work to the team's advantage.

John had spoken to James and to Ken. Ken was an expert at demolitions. Literally, throwing a monkey wrench into a terminal down the street from the Cathedral would disrupt the power. There was back-up, but not immediate. It had to be started by one of the priests and it took time. This would only be used if, and only if, they were detected and needed to go to full night vision devices. Their code word, and this could be called by anyone, was Blue. The rain intensified. The lightning was fierce. Of course, they had considered an act of God could cause a power outage. It has happened at least 11 times during the last 50 years. It was never a cause for alarm, just standard procedures would be followed to ensure the Shroud was intact, alarms reset, and/or power generators were on.

The first team arrived at the back door and coded in with their password and badges. Jack and Charles made their way up the stairs. The priests did not look or speak. Their hoods covered their faces.

There was some movement in the building they could detect. They were at the station where the priest monitored the Shroud. Jack and

304

MISSION TO TURIN

Charles could see the Shroud on cameras. Just as expected. They rapped on the glass and showed their badges and asked for directions in Italian. Charles appeared to not understand. The priest behind the glass opened the door to hand Charles a map. The spray put him out on his feet. Jack spliced in the video camera and had the image fixed on the screen with the time still counting.

John, Justin and Phil were making their way by the station. John returned the nod and headed up the stairs. True to plan, the stones in the wall were part of a means to use a winch to move the encased Shroud. The entry was hidden by a tapestry moved by the team. The stones were removed by swinging a bar, then, they seemed like a feather that was counterweighted, and the false wall moved without a sound.

Outside, the rain was coming down in buckets. The wind was whipping up a fierce storm with high winds. And, inside the massive Church, the thunder echoed. John had his goggles on. He was checking out the laser beams of light. They were angled at the front of the case from the entrance. However, John needed to get to the pressure plate switch near the front entrance without setting off the laser alarm. Phil brought out a small cross bow. The bolt was loaded, and a small line attached.

He aimed at a recessed part of a huge timber located about 20 feet above the top of the entrance into the chamber. The bolt hit its mark. Phil tightened the line and then the follow-on cable reached its mark and was locked into place on both sides.

John looked at Phil and slid off his cloak. He was solid black. The belt around his waist was multipurposed. With the help of Justin, he locked into the cable and was off hand-over-hand to the opposite side of the huge chamber. When he reached the other side, he reconnected to another line and started his descent, reversing his posture by rotating his body. Gently, using the wall, he lifted the cover of the plate pressing the weight sensing monitor to the off position. It was a simple code, 747474, that added to 33 years, the probable age of Jesus when he was crucified. John hoisted himself back to the top, reattached his line and moved to a position directly above the case. He descended just behind and to the right of the case.

Justin moved quickly. He was ready and moved out to where John descended. The line was about thirty feet off the floor.

305

KIDNAPPING JESUS

Once Justin joined John, he assisted him by removing the special bolts. They turned differently and only a specific tool could access the slots. This too was a closely guarded secret. All contact points had to be engaged or the head of the bolt would rupture and break off. The contact points of the bolts were in the shape of an Omega, but the bolts were huge. The glass was two inches thick and would have to be lifted. The entry point was located once the bolts were loosened. John grabbed the aluminum cylinder, removed the fake Shroud Hastings had provided and switched the two Shrouds. It was quick. John was wearing gloves, as were they all, that looked like real skin, had fingerprints of priests embedded, so if they were detected, it would take time to work out the mystery. When John was switching the Shroud, a feeling came over him he had not ever felt before. He paused for what seemed liked days. How was this preordained? He felt like saying it out loud.

Justin elbowed him. John snapped out of his stupor. He needed to keep his mind in the game. Quickly, he helped Justin secure the fake Shroud in the case, reset the air to the on position to bring the levels of temperature- controlled humidity and reduced oxygen to perfect conditions for maintaining the integrity of the Shroud.

Justin grabbed the cylinder and headed up the line. John followed when Justin linked up with Phil. He did a pivot and reset the floor panels to register any added weight and then made his way to the bolt He placed a small panel resembling the timber covering everything. It was the perfect camouflage.

Once on the other side, Phil twisted the line 15 times. It detached and dropped and then was recovered back to the opening. It looked good. It was still dark as the door slid to closure. Both John and Justin donned their robes. The cylinder was under Justin's robe, the bow under Phil's and the cable with John. The goggles were off. They passed Jack and Charles. The count from one to twenty started. Team Reveal was out of the building. With the priest in place and the antidote administered, cables were detached; the view was on screen for another 20 seconds. The "priests" made their way out. The shift change was about to take place at 0015 hours. It was just after midnight. The job took just over two hours to complete.

Everything had operated like clockwork. Contingency plans did not have to be executed. John could not believe the weather. They were

MISSION TO TURIN

the only idiots out in this mess. The traffic in and outside the Church had virtually stopped with the storm. Lightning was flashing as they hit the RPs. They were on their way. James pulled out and flashed his lights. There were no problems encountered, but before they hit the Autostrada, the intensity of the storm heading into Turin was growing. Lightening was coming in fast. John was somber. No one was talking. He was reflecting on the mission. Something was out of whack. Why the hell was Hastings paying so much? It took almost an hour to get back to the Villa. The route was not direct. But, with the weather, it was slow going for safety.

Back at the Church, the shift changed. The new priest brought a fresh cup of coffee to his fellow man of the cloth. "Father, are you ok?"

"Yes, Father, I seem to be unsettled. It seems like time passed by quickly this evening." They both checked the screens. Everything appeared to be perfect.

The first priest provided the following advice. "Father, the weather is in a tempest outside. We all have worked very hard in preparation for moving the Shroud. Get some rest. I believe we will be delayed with the move in the morning. We will wake you. Most everyone has been asleep for hours."

With that, the first priest exited the surveillance area and was on his way to bed. He could not and would not remember what took place almost three hours ago.

CHAPTER XV

REALITY, OR IS IT?

Rome was beautiful. The Pope had gone to Turin to see the Shroud on Good Friday and John and the team experienced Easter Sunday and the blessings of the Pope in front of Saint Peters Basilica in Vatican City. John Paul II was extremely frail, and this was a great occasion for him. He had seen the Shroud one more time and was inspired. The Shroud was a gift sent from the past and a cause for renewed faith for the future. The crowd responded to his speech and to his special wave to those hundreds of thousands who had gathered and those who were watching from around the world. It was a good day for him and for his inner circle.

KIDNAPPING JESUS

Pope John Paul II

John was thinking back to their flight from Turin to Rome a few days back. They left the cylinder with the Shroud in it on the BIOTECH150 corporate jet. Before securing the Shroud into the safe onboard the jet just after takeoff from Turin, Ken Parker had been holding the cylinder. He had asked John how it felt to hold the Shroud in his hands.

John replied to him, although not immediately. He looked Ken in the eyes when he said the following, "Ken, I'm not sure what I felt. It was like nothing I felt before. There was a power in me, something was very right, and something was very wrong. With the weather, it was the strangest feeling I've ever experienced. I've never been so unsure of myself, and yet, I am sure we have set off a chain of events mankind may never believe, and one we are totally unprepared for in this lifetime."

While Parker held the cylinder, it began to have a glow. They were already in flight. He too was unnerved. The two strongest people of

REALITY, OR IS IT?

Team SOS were having butterflies. He felt there was something special about this cloth. As he began to place it into the safe, the entire plane shook as there was a direct lightening hit. The jet bounced and literally threw those inside the jet about like light paper dolls.

Everyone felt like the storm was turning from Turin towards Rome. Was it following them? Then, they all saw an amazing sight. The cylinder was glowing like a rainbow. Colors were dancing. John looked around. "What is going on?"

Charles was the only one who came up with an explanation. "John, this is a result of the electrical charge and the type of material the cylinder is made of, nothing more or less."

It was not a comforting thought, especially when Jack whispered to John as the others were taking their seats and Ken was securing the Shroud in the safe. "John, we feel like we just Kidnapped Jesus!"

With those words, John believed he had just opened a Pandora's Box for the present.

The cloth was the key...the key from the past to the present and to the future. They had gone down the path, and they would all be relieved when the mission was over.

John just turned and looked them each in the eyes. "Team, regardless of what we just accomplished, just suffice it to say I will be very happy when we finally land in Arizona and pass our charge, and our responsibility to Mr. Hastings. What happens after that point is his responsibility. Don't let down your guard."

***

Waiting in the hangar was George Hastings along with a team of what appeared to be scientists. The minute the aircraft was on the ground and John and his men exited the plane; Hastings' men were aboard unloading the Shroud. They were dressed in white smocks. It had been a long trip back from Rome. The team slept and had a few drinks, but mostly relaxed as the flight attendants catered to their every need. They were beautiful ladies. John had the small suite on the corporate jet. It was tiny, but lavishly appointed, nonetheless. The seats throughout the small jet were also very comfortable, allowing maximum relaxation.

KIDNAPPING JESUS

And the meals prepared were like heaven. James Jefferson was with the team when they left Turin and headed to Rome.

Although he did not accompany the team while they were sight-seeing in Rome, he remained on guard with the jet and the Shroud. He was part of the inner circle of George Hastings III. He would give his life to protect the Shroud. And he was a fantastic cook. In addition to the seven flight attendants, there were three pilots. One was always taking a break while the other two ensured the plane was en-route to their destination. There would be two stops for fuel. They would land at Heathrow, and then in New York, before they headed to Arizona. It had been an uneventful trip. In fact, it was eerie. No problems weather or otherwise were encountered.

John did not know what to make of all the fuss. However, he thought back to his mission, the uncovered secrets, and the night Team SOS stole the Shroud for one of the richest men on Earth.

The white uniforms snapped him back to reality. George Hastings spoke to John and his team. "Welcome back to Arizona. John, I understand from Parker your mission went very smoothly. I hope you had a pleasant trip back to the States."

John turned to Charles. "Go ahead and take the men to the Barracks. It has been a long couple of days."

Charles replied. "All right, John, we will see you when we see you... big brother!"

John appreciated the knowing reply from his brother. "I will be conducting our business with Mr. Hastings and will be along in a few minutes."

Charles had the men load into the van and drove to the Barracks. He recalled their training just a few weeks earlier. The hanger housing the Cathedral mock-up was completely gone. A small park complete with grass and tables was in its place. Both Jack and Charles thought to themselves these men do not mess around when they do not want any evidence left behind. They simply made it disappear. That thought, in itself, did not make them more comfortable; it just made them even more vigilant. Jack pulled the van up to the Barracks. The men went inside, grabbed the closest rack, and went to sleep. It would be a well-deserved rest.

REALITY, OR IS IT?

Hastings' men took the Shroud and headed to another hanger, one which John and his team had never been allowed to enter. Hastings, Parker and John watched the team of professionals take the Shroud into a cargo elevator. Hastings turned to Elder. "This is why I purchased this Base. It has a compound two-hundred feet underground. You'll understand when you see it."

"George, I'm not at all surprised. My imagination is already running wild."

As the elevator descended into the depths of the Arizona desert, three men went inside a spacious office within the confines of the hanger. It was a well apportioned office Hastings used when he was at the Base. He wanted to restrict his movements while on Base.

There were spies and often when his plane landed, he would be in disguise. James Jefferson prepared drinks for the three men. Cigars were offered to both Parker and Elder. They lit the mild Cubans.

There was a small tray with caviar and toast completely garnished with sprigs of parsley.

And, there were the huge prawns with cocktail sauce and horse-radish. Hastings puffed a huge release of smoke into the air. It was like a circle with a small hole in it. "John, Parker did very well in keeping open the communications between your team and me. I don't think the job could have gone any smoother than what took place. I've prepared us for the consequences just in case the Roman Catholic Church learns of our involvement. The Church has long arms. I don't think they will make this into a public spectacle due to the relevance of the cloth; however, a private war can be just as devastating as one under the scrutiny of the public. Can you think of any weak links within your organization?"

"George, without a doubt my team can be trusted 100%. I know you believe your team also to be 100% trustworthy. If there is a weak link, I believe you have to look inwardly. My men will die for me. Heck, they will die for you. Not because of your wealth or power, but because they accepted this mission knowing full well the consequences of their actions. They love adventure. They love money. They love security. Most of all, they have a love for each other. If one of them talked, they know they could impact the lives of all the others, including their families. No, George, they would not breathe a word of this to anyone. The team went to Europe, had a great time in Turin and in Rome, and then came

KIDNAPPING JESUS

home. That's all there is to it. And, by the way, my brothers and I are Catholic. A couple of the others are Catholics as well. I know you got this information when you asked me to steal the Shroud, but I want to remind you we did this for the adventure and the money. I trust you will honor and take care of the Shroud. The replica we placed in the Cathedral was moved back to its original location in the Duomo di San Giovanni and is an excellent likeness of the true Shroud. Hopefully, if the disappearance of the Shroud is discovered, they will trace back the major events of its movement since the fire. I can tell you one thing for certain; we did not leave any of our fingerprints. However, we were there, so, it could be happenstance that leads the Pope to our doorstep."

"John, I'm convinced. I will check and recheck my personnel involved in the mission. If something comes up, I'll let you know. Now let's get down to business." Hastings opened his computer and showed John the money transferred into his offshore accounts in the Cayman Islands. These were the accounts John provided to Hastings. "Sir, you are a wealthy man. Now that this job is over, I would like to take a moment to savor this victory."

"It may be a poor choice of words, but I can tell you from the time I was a young man, I was intrigued by the parchment Casca Longinus left in Turin. I know it is a risky business, but I have not made this fortune by not taking risks. I truly believe we are a part of history that was preordained. I realize the consequences as I know you do. But for now, I want to savor this moment. A toast! Here's to Team SOS!"

Ken and John nodded at each other. It was a drink soon followed by several others as they joked and smoked. John thought back to his days in the Marines. It was an old adage, but one an old Marine or an old Soldier would remember. Smoke them if you got them. Once you had smoked your cigarette, the remainder was field stripped and the butts went into a pocket to be thrown away later…or, if you tossed one on the ground, you would be loading up cigarettes all over the base or post wherever you were stationed.

"George, I just want you to know that Parker was very valuable to me and to the success of the mission. He became part of us while we worked to establish our relationship with one other. Without him along, I can't imagine the success we enjoyed. In fact, I would like to plant something in your mind for future reference. Should you entertain

314

REALITY, OR IS IT?

another mission in the future, hopefully not as elaborate as this one was, I would request Parker to be a part of the team we form as well. There is something to be said about having already been through the introductions and the first dance. And, I hope you take care of him."

George laughed at the last two remarks from John. "Yes, I can't imagine Parker in a dance, unless he is fighting with some thugs, but I know what you mean. And, as to taking care of him, already done. Guess I forgot to tell him. Consider this an early retirement contribution. I've placed $5 Million dollars into your account we established when you came to work for my father. You have amassed quite a small fortune over the years. I'm sure this beats the French Foreign Legion retirement program by just a small amount! You have done well. Ken, as you already know, you have my deepest appreciation for your years of trusted service."

Parker looked at the two men with a big smile on his face. "Well, that about wraps this up. John, I am sure you and Ken are very tired and would like to get some sleep before you head back home tomorrow."

"Yes, I am tired and not just physically. Mentally, this was a tough job for the team. I'm sure I told you this story, but I really have to say, that when the container began to glow on the way out of Turin, I thought we were going to be struck by lightning. It was an uncanny feeling that gripped the team. In fact, the feeling was summed up best by Jack when he said, "It is as if we just kidnapped Jesus!"

"I really do need some rest. If I do not see you before I leave, call me if you need me again. And I look forward to another invitation, soon, to join you and the ladies on "The Miss Adventure". Speaking of the ladies, I have one special one I will be contacting when I return to Melbourne. First, I have to fly to California and pick up my airplane. I had it refitted with new engines. The Allison Turboprop T56 adds speed and range to my DC-6C. I'll be flying back to Melbourne once it is completely checked out and all the paperwork is complete with the Federal Aviation Administration. I'll be seeing the inspiration for naming her when I get there. It should be quite a reunion with Pearle West and Chuck Taylor. And, you know where and how to reach me. I will always have the small house in Melbourne, although, it may be difficult to find me. I intend on doing a lot of diving around the islands.

KIDNAPPING JESUS

LAPEARLE and I will be doing some flying. And, I assure you, my brothers will be close by."

"John, it was my pleasure doing business with a professional. Good luck to you and all of your men." John and Ken left the building and headed to the Barracks where the men were sleeping.

Once inside John looked at Ken. "I just want you to know the hairs on the back of my neck have not stopped telling me we have opened the door for some heavy-duty shit. I just don't know when, but I do know something is going to happen. It could be something spectacular. It could be something rather ordinary. And, while I know what George tells us he is doing, I just don't know what I don't know. In fact, I really don't want to know. But, if someone is going to climb up my ass, I want to be warned if at all possible. Ken, I am counting on you to be that trip wire. If you feel something is amiss, anything at all, I am counting on you. Tell me you won't let me down."

"John, you got it. I owe everything to George Hastings. However, if I get wind of something going down, I'll be sure to let you know. By protecting you, I am protecting him. It's like a domino effect. If one goes down, others are sure to follow. And, as one warrior to another, I would be proud to work with you anytime. I know you had my back just as you know I had yours. I'll see you in the morning. Sleep well."

It was 0630 hours. The team was up. They were headed to the Phoenix- Mesa Gateway Airport to fly into John Wayne International Airport. Not all of them were headed to California! The team was splitting up. Only the brothers were on their way to California. The others were heading in their own direction. Stacey was going back to Florida.

Breakfast was, as always, great. It should be a quiet flight. Pearle West and Chuck Taylor were going to meet the brothers when they arrived. It was always good to see old friends. And, of course, they would get LAPEARLE into ship shape. About that time, George Hastings and Ken Parker arrived to wish the men good luck. It was a short good-bye, and if the whole truth be known, it was just a formality for George, but meant a lot to Ken. After all, these had been his comrades-in-arms for more than a month. He knew them as they knew him. This was akin to sharing a foxhole with another soldier. Bonds are forged to last for all time.

REALITY, OR IS IT?

Everyone was looking forward to getting home. It was just a matter of a few days and they would all get back on track with their lives. The three brothers planned to fly from California, stop enroute in New Orleans and visit John's old buddy, David Reed. John was looking forward to slapping him on the back while eating some of the best Cajun food in the entire world.

The flight to California was relatively short, compared to their flights over the big pond a couple of times in the last month. John had already transferred money into the established Cayman accounts for his team members.

Although there was a money trail, they should be safe due to the security surrounding personal accounts. The good-byes were said at the airport. Flights were staggered. And, John and the team agreed to meet in one month in the islands. George Hastings was going to provide the Miss Adventure one more time for a blow-out party. LAPEARLE would be the mode of travel for the brothers while other team members would meet up at the Great Grand Tortugas Hotel. The beaches would be absolutely beautiful! This was going to be a trip to get their minds back into the old reality, before so much came out of nowhere and put all of them in the new somewhere...with allot of money to do anything they wanted to do without drawing too much attention.

This could be the first annual party for the team. It could be like the reunions John, Jack, Charles, David and others attended at Camp Pendleton. Now, those were some parties. The sad thing was the moment when the honor roll was solemnly read of those whom had passed away since the last meeting and those who were ill or dying. The lone trumpet would play Taps for their fallen comrades. And, of course, the men and women would always recall some of their stories keeping the memories of those who died very much alive. A reverent toast to their fallen comrades with a resounding "Semper-Fi" that reverberated through the quiet sent goosebumps down the backs and arms of those present.

This might be their last mission together. It was a somber thought for all of the men. For Stacey Greer, this was the only mission with the team. He thanked everyone for the fun. Phil Tucker was on his way to Atlanta to catch a plane to Costa Rica. He was looking for property to establish his own cattle ranch. And, he really wanted to expand his favorite hobby, hunting. Not just any hunting, but he wanted to hunt

317

KIDNAPPING JESUS

the exotic game of the world, not just the North American variety of big game. With the money he now had, he could just about write his own ticket anywhere in the world. In this case, it was not just about the money, but the adventure of the hunt.

Justin Carter wanted to hang out with John for whatever time he could. However, he was flying to Atlanta and then on to Melbourne to try to find a house and establish a small business. He considered opening up a motorcycle shop specializing in custom made bikes; but he needed to look around. He also thought about going to work for the one of the oil companies in south Florida. He believed OPEC had been making the world dependent on their oil at low prices, taking their countries from barren deserts to a rich oasis, enriching their populace, while, in due time calculating the demand for energy of emerging nations like China, India, and Pakistan that would inevitably drive the prices for a barrel of oil through the roof.

It would not be long until the United States would need the rich oil reserves located off the coast, within the United States, and especially those located in Alaska. After all, he was a Master "SCUBA" Diver and demolitions expert. If Florida didn't do it for him, he could always go back to Mobile, Alabama. His partner in his business would understand; however, at this time, Justin wanted to be a silent partner. He just had to come to grips with what he really wanted to do in life. It would take him some time to gather his thoughts.

The good life was now in every team member's reach. All of them were looking forward to their future. As John, followed by Jack and Charles, exited their plane, John saw Pearle and Chuck. Oh, what a vision! Pearle was still an exceptionally pretty woman. John knew even if there was a man in Pearle's life, he would be on the shelf for a few days. Pearle would have been honest with him. There were no gray areas in her life. It was always black and white with them. It would not mean the man in her life was less important to her than was John. It was just the way it was.

The days went by quickly. And the nights were full of good food, good wine and good friends. Pearle and John were still an item.

Jack and Charles had a lot of fun hanging with Chuck when John and Pearle left every evening. Chuck could entertain with great stories

REALITY, OR IS IT?

about John's days in both the U.S. Marshals office and with him in Taylor's Headhunters.

The flight to New Orleans, and then onto Melbourne, was bittersweet. John enjoyed his time with his old friends. It was time to go. In New Orleans, David Reed and his family, wife and four children, prepared some of the best meals any of them had ever had. It was party city as Reed's guest at Planet Reed, a night club on par with some of the most famous ones located on Bourbon Street. Twelve hours from bottle to throttle. They took off from New Orleans and headed to Melbourne. It was like going home, if any of them had really had a home since they were kids. The days were long and the nights longer. Thoughts of John's childhood, Vietnam and Beirut flashed through his memories. John thought of the Shroud. What was George Hastings III doing with the Shroud?

CHAPTER XVI

THE REBIRTH

It was June 11, 2002. Doctor Samuel Wentworth, the top cloning specialist in the world extracted the DNA he needed from the Shroud. The human genetic code is found in structures contained within the nucleus of each cell known as chromosomes. The DNA in the Shroud lay dormant for almost two thousand years. Technology for cloning began in 1970. In fact, there was even speculation that President John F. Kennedy had been cloned following the tragedy in Dallas where he had been assassinated.

Regardless, the fact of the matter was that Doctor Wentworth had the DNA. What followed was a miracle. The host for the DNA from the Shroud was an orphan Hastings had reared from a small child rescued from the streets of Peru. She was now a grown lady and owed her allegiance to Hastings. He had rescued her from the gutters, sent her to the best private schools and she was highly educated for a high school graduate. Her IQ was recorded at the genius level. Maria Ortiz was an eighteen-year-old virgin. She was kept from the touch of man and reared for this purpose should it ever come to pass. She was informed she would be caring for a child from Hastings and accepted this responsibility with great pleasure. Hastings had no children of his own and in this way; she could help the man that had helped her.

KIDNAPPING JESUS

The laboratory was two-hundred feet underground and it was on Hastings's private property. He was watching the event from overhead in the laboratory located in the observation room with Parker at his side. In essence, this was going to be an immaculate conception. However, it would not be Hasting's prodigy, but that of Jesus.

The process had taken just over thirty years to be perfected. Several attempts at the human cloning process were undertaken before Dr. Wentworth was ready for the actual procedure.

The other attempts would have matured into human abominations during the early days as well as into noteworthy people who were from the past during the later days of research if allowed to mature outside of the womb.

Maria was taken into the surgery room by the Doctor's surgical team. She was lying on an operating table with her legs in stirrups and naked underneath the sheets. Doctor Wentworth's team was waiting for her. At the table, several eggs were taken from Maria and placed in a sterile dish. Under the microscope, a very thin needle pierced the outer membrane of Maria's egg. Dr. Wentworth placed the DNA from the Shroud into the egg. He then placed the fertilized egg into Maria's womb. She was taken to her hospital bed for rest and relaxation and would remain there for several weeks under the Doctor's care and scrutiny.

It was June 29, 2002, when Hastings received a call from a very excited Dr. Wentworth. "I have great news for you, Mr. Hastings. Maria is almost three weeks pregnant with a healthy baby boy."

"You did it Morgan! You finally did it! How is she doing?" "She's doing very well and wanting to please you, George." "I will be down in several weeks. Please give me a daily report." George hung up the phone and walked over to the plaque on the wall and read to himself.

WHEN MAN BECOMES WORTHY,
I SHALL RETURN TO EARTH.
WE SHALL MEET AGAIN.

CASCA RUFIO LONGINUS

THE REBIRTH

Again, he wondered if Casca Rufus Longinus knew of what he wrote almost two-thousand years ago. Yes, I know what you wanted the whole time. Jesus, I know what you meant. It has taken me many years and Millions of dollars, but I know now what it is you wanted. I will bring you back to answer all of humanity's questions. Hastings turned to see Parker standing in the doorway.

"Ken, Maria is pregnant. She will carry the baby to full term. We will be going to Arizona in a few weeks. I want you with me."

"Finally," Parker replied, "He finally got it done. That's real nice. Boss, you know I'm with you whenever you need me." Hastings smiled and walked up to the study closing the door behind him. Parker walked out to the front of the house thinking he hoped his boss knew what he was doing.

Lots of things were happening in the meantime. George provided "The Miss Adventure" to John and his team while they were decompressing from the mission in the Cayman Islands. Yes, the ladies were there also. They had a great time. Absent was George Hastings. Ken was in and out in a day. George was reported as having meetings with his board of directors in New York City. BIOTECH150 was making record profits. George had his responsibilities to ensure his Billions were funding the right projects. He had also had meetings on Capitol Hill as a proponent for Stem Cell research. But his mental focus was in Arizona.

***

Hastings went to Arizona many times in the nine months Maria was with child. He made sure she had around the clock nurses. He also kept track at his mansion in Florida of her movements via live video. He had every room in the underground compound wired so he could monitor everything. All Hastings had to do was open his laptop and tap into the system. He could check on Maria's progress and see what the team was doing without their knowledge. It was a very high-tech system.

It was April 11, 2003, when Hastings received a call from Dr. Wentworth while he was aboard his private jet headed back to New York. Dr. Wentworth asked, "Are you on the way here?"

KIDNAPPING JESUS

"I am on a flight to New York, but I can be in Arizona in a few days. Why do you ask?"

"Maria is in labor. She is two-weeks early. There is no cause for concern. The contractions are about an hour apart. I would say she will give birth in several hours."

"Doctor, I will have the jet change course. Do what you can. I want to be there for the birth."

Hastings called up to his pilot. Soon, the plane altered its course and changed flight levels. He was on the phone changing plans in New York. The Director of BIOTECH150 Operations would be in charge. He made sure the Company was always on-track. He functioned as both the Chief Executive Officer and the Chief Operations Officer. He should be good at what he does. He had $250 Million dollars in stock options and a package deal that paid him $20 Million dollars a year. And, then there were the perks. Once the Doctor got off the phone, he verified Maria was doing ok. The contractions were steady and both heart rates were perfect.

His team was on track. He whispered to the anesthesiologist to try to slow the contractions down a bit, but to continually monitor the heart. He did not want either patient to be stressed during the delivery. Anesthesia was administered through the IV. The heart rate was steady and Maria was more relaxed. The Doctor let her know Hastings was already on his way and would soon be present at her side. Maria had a big smile. As sick as it might seem, Maria felt love and affection for Hastings as both a father role model and as a father to their child. Yet, there was definitely no physical relationship.

It was 2100 hours when Hastings landed at his private runway on the Annex, he had purchased almost 10 years previously. Hastings and Parker were met at the jet by Chad Eastman. In a small John Deere ATV, they were taken to the hanger. Eastman was not allowed inside the hanger or in the underground compound. This was a very Top-Secret program. It was on a need-to-know basis and Eastman did not know need to know anything about Maria or the rebirth of Jesus. He wanted his job with Hastings to be more, but Hastings kept him at a distance to run the daily operations of the Base. Eastman would bide his time but he would find out what was going on so he could get the upper hand. He was the person that always wanted the upper hand.

THE REBIRTH

He pulled the ATV into the parking place. Eastman had wanted to say something to Hastings before they went inside the hanger but had been dismissed. Whatever was going on must be huge.

Hastings and Parker went into the building and took the elevator down the two-hundred feet of elevator shaft to the massive underground compound. The complex was a reminder of the Cold War. Massive Retaliation was one of the terms coined by politicians and strategists. Mutual Assured Destruction (MAD), military doctrine and part of our National Security Strategy, was another such term used by the Administrations.

Had Russia gone to war with the United States back in those years, regardless of the terminology, survival would be guaranteed for a few to carry on a war of recovery or annihilation of the opposing side with the accumulation of the remaining stockpile of nuclear weapons. They each had the capability to deliver those weapons precisely to each other's backyard. The location of the highly secret buildings was classified. There was redundancy should some of the secrets be compromised; so, someone, whoever was in charge, could carry on the wishes of the President, if he was incapacitated or no longer alive.

This complex was indeed an alternate Command Post for the President of the United States of America. Or, to the next ranking elected political official, should the President be unable to perform his duties from another such Command Post. There were several in the United States. As elected officials, each had a designated shelter they should reach depending on their current location. The chaos resulting from the detonation of nuclear devices required as much of the command-and-control structure to remain intact as possible. Days following such an event would be filled with panic and chaos. The men and women elected were trained and prepared to handle these events. Or so the theory goes. Regardless, the Command Post Hastings now used was state of the art in every conceivable way imaginable.

Dr. Wentworth was waiting for them. "Mr. Hastings, I hope you had a good trip. We slowed down the contractions and now we can change the Pitocin drip to help induce labor by helping with the contractions. Maria is doing great. The contractions are only ten-minutes apart. She is in the birthing room. Parker was escorted to the observation tower

KIDNAPPING JESUS

so he could observe the birth. Hasting would join him after he briefly visited with Maria.

Maria was on the table taking short breaths while her nurse coached her and kept perspiration mopped off of her forehead. She was covered with a blanket and several machines were monitoring her vital signs. She looked up and saw George. She was relieved he was present for the birth and right away she felt better about what was happening to her. She wanted to give him an heir to his fortune for all he had done for her. That was the least she could do for him. After all, if it had not been for Hastings, she would have most likely led a life of prostitution or even worse. Yes, when he came to her wanting her to have his child, she did not have any hesitation. And now he was here to watch the birth of their child.

George leaned over and gave her a kiss on her cheek. He whispered in her ear for her to hear alone. "Maria, I love you. Please give us a healthy child we can raise together." This made Maria beam with radiance. She had such an angelic face. What a beauty she was. George squeezed her hand and then made his way to the observation room to join Ken.

A contraction came and pain shot through her back like one she never felt before. She had a spinal block, but somehow it was not working. The Pitocin caused the contractions to be more intense.

Maria let out a yell and she heard a voice. "Push!" Doctor Wentworth was somewhat hidden from her. She could see her belly, a sheet, and the wires and tubes attached to her diminutive frame. "Push!" She pushed. She looked around and could see Hastings. The nurse wiped the sweat from her brow and comforted her. The anesthetist checked her vital signs. Everything was normal. She could feel the baby move. Another shooting pain racked her small body. "Push!" The pain! "Maria, you're almost there. I can see the head of the baby." The pain! "Push!" The tears were from both the pain and the joy of giving birth. The sweat was flowing.

Hastings was grimacing. He hated to watch the pain on her face. Even the hardened Parker had backed away from the glass but was still watching from the corner of his eyes. And then, it seemed all of a sudden, the baby was born. "We have a baby boy!"

THE REBIRTH

The Doctor spanked the boy on his butt three times. With the third slap, there was an audible cry and then, an incredibly bright, multi-colored light, entered the room. The operating lights dimmed while the lights danced over the birth table and were centered just above the baby. Although the light was bright, it seemed somehow warm, non- threatening. The light was very much like the same light Parker saw aboard the jet when they left Turin. It was one of the worst storms of the century for Asia and Africa. The light danced and radiated over the baby just as it had danced over the metal casing housing the Shroud.

Hastings was in awe of the whole event. He could not believe his eyes. What was he was seeing? Time was standing still. It was as if they were puppets and put to sleep. They stood motionless and speechless for what seemed like hours. They had no control of their bodies.

The surgical team was in the light. And all around them it appeared as if there were manifestations with wings and golden hair with angelic faces. They hovered over Maria and the baby.

Doctor Wentworth moved in slow motion with the child in his hands towards Maria while he wrapped him up in a white cotton baby blanket. He placed the baby in his mother's arms so she could see the child and hold it. The Doctor slowly backed away and disappeared outside the light.

Once Maria embraced the child and the child was safe the lights moved around them looking inwards, then they swirled around the room and rose above the bed.

In an instant they appeared to move through the ceiling and diminished as the colors just disappeared through the twelve-foot reinforced concrete bunker that was two-hundred feet below the surface of the Earth.

Hastings hoped his recorders were working so he could exam it later. The baby had been born at precisely 2211 hours on April 11, 2003. He knew deep down what he had seen. These were Angels. They entered the room two-hundred feet below ground to protect the baby. The team of medical personnel would have to be well compensated for the job and some extra compensation to keep their mouths shut. Hastings knew that events from this point forward would change the face of humanity. Casca Rufio Longinus had written down the words spoken to him by Jesus almost two-thousand years ago. Hastings could see

KIDNAPPING JESUS

the parchment on the wall in his mind's eye. Jesus Christ had just been reborn on earth and only a few people knew it at this time.

WHEN MAN BECOMES WORTHY,
I SHALL RETURN TO EARTH.
WE SHALL MEET AGAIN.

CASCA RUFIO LONGINUS

Doctor Wentworth wheeled Maria and her new son into her private room so they could bond. Once she was resting comfortably, Wentworth had a private meeting with Hastings and Parker where they would watch the film of the event all of them had observed.

Wentworth entered the room where Parker and Hastings were already seated at the table looking at a fifty-inch plasma television mounted on the wall. Hastings pulled up the DVD from the birth room. All three men were taken aback by what was not shown on the plasma screen. It was as if what they saw in the birthing room had never occurred. Yet, it did. Mass hallucination…probably not, just the technology of man could not connect with what they had been allowed to witness.

Hastings turned the TV off. Parker was the first to speak. "It was the same on the plane on the way here to deliver the Shroud."

Doctor Wentworth was next to speak yet was much more subdued with his statement. "We must make sure we are the only ones who know of this event."

Hastings looked at Doctor Wentworth and Ken Parker. "Ensure we are the only ones that know of this." Parker knew that meant everyone except Maria, the Doctor, and the baby would be taken care of. Parker moved out of the room to ensure the three staff members in the room during the birth understood their positions. It was life or death. They each would receive a bonus in their pay of $100,000 dollars. If they spoke of this to anyone, they would never be seen or heard of again. They probably would find Jimmy Hoffa before they ever found these people. They would still be needed for the care of the child.

The next day, Parker met up with Hastings informing him everything was under control. Hasting looked over at Parker and smiled. Hastings entered the building with Parker bringing up the rear. They

THE REBIRTH

entered the elevator and pushed the button to the ground floor taking them two-hundred feet below ground. Hastings and Parker entered Wentworth's office.

They sat down in the seat waiting for Dr. Wentworth to return from his observation of Maria and the child.

Walking into his office, Wentworth seemed a little shaken. He had a seat at his desk and spoke to Hastings. "I would like to move Maria and the child in two months to another location. It would be best to stay in a home environment like your mansion in Melbourne. This would be best for both the mother and the child. Also, regarding this Immaculate Conception, I don't believe you should infer you are Maria's surrogate husband. That she was with a child is truly amazing, but in today's state of affairs, not unusual. We'll need a cover story. Think of someone who could be the father. And I also suggest you call the baby something else besides Emanuel or Jesus. It should be a Spanish-American name, but not one that links the birth to you, or to something more sinister."

"I agree. Thanks for your advice. I will go and see Maria and ensure she understands. I know she thinks this is my baby. Nothing will change her thoughts, agreed. However, I want her to believe it is safer for the baby if others don't connect him directly to me. I need to know if there is someone we can use as a surrogate father, at least for the time being. I have a name in mind for him. We will name him Joshua. Joshua Ortiz. Joshua Jorge Ortiz. We should be ready in two months. We will have everything we need in place. In this way, the child will have the company of other people around him. I will make all the arrangements."

Hastings rose out of the chair looking at Wentworth. "Relax! The hard part is over. We get to watch him grow and see if the powers and the knowledge he had two-thousand years ago manifested within him. Hopefully, there is a divine spark. If not, we will find out what was embedded in his memory. This is our mission. We are some very lucky people. Think about what he may be able to tell us."

"FOR AS LIGHTNING THAT COMES FROM THE EAST IS VISIBLE EVEN IN THE WEST, SO WILL THE COMING OF THE SON OF MAN. WHEREVER THERE IS A CARCASS, THERE THE VULTURES WILL GATHER."

KIDNAPPING JESUS

MATTHEW 24:27

"What? Did someone say Narcosis? Nitrogen Narcosis?" …John dazedly questioned Ken.

John mumbled to himself, rapture of the deep! What was I trying to do with my second stage (my octopus)? The mermaid I saw needed air. And I…I was thinking about reincarnation. The sun was getting low in the sky, so it seemed. I remembered getting to 60 feet and then stopping for about 3 or 4 minutes. I was breathing rapidly. I guess the fight with the fish, Wow, 50 pounds of fresh grouper. Then, I, or we, passed 30 feet heading to our last safety stop at 15-20 feet below the ocean surface. Air was getting low and almost in the red on the pressure gage. And then, I was in Italy, when was it and where was I? A Shroud? Casey…Casey who? Shells…huge, like "Boxcars"! It sounded like trains rushing by!

"What?" John had opened his eyes and stared and blinked a couple of times shaking out the water in his hair.

John spoke to George, "It was nice to have M&Ms on the dive. Best candy ever!"

330

BOOK II, ECHOES FROM THE PAST, of the
KIDNAPPING JESUS

Trilogy, will be available in the very near future. Our website, kidnappingjesus.net, will be updated with information regarding the publication and release of this action-packed Christian thriller. Additionally, story bytes will also be provided and clues from BOOK I revealed.

"FOR AS LIGHTNING THAT COMES FROM THE EAST IS VISIBLE EVEN IN THE WEST, SO WILL THE COMING OF THE SON OF MAN. WHEREVER THERE IS A CARCASS, THERE THE VULTURES WILL GATHER."

MATTHEW 24:27

ACKNOWLEDGEMENTS

The Authors wish to thank their friends and family for their patience during the writing of this book. Without their help and input the book would not have taken on the breadth and depth as intended. It is a fictitious writing and any resemblance to those living or dead may appear to be coincidental. The point of writing the book gained ground when members of the families of the two authors became involved due to their participation in the military. Some of their stories have been recounted exactly as they had occurred and others were embellished. Battle scenes from World War II, Vietnam, and Desert Storm may or may have not occurred.

You know who you are even if your names were changed during the course of writing the book or if you are not listed, to safeguard your involvement.

>Lieutenant Colonel (Retired) Payne O. Lyons, (United States Army)
>Lieutenant Colonel (Retired) Bradley J. Lyons, (United States Army)
>Lieutenant Colonel (Retired) Mike Harbin, (United States Marine Corps)
>Sergeant Jack Franks
>(United States Marine Corps) (Marine Corps Raiders)

KIDNAPPING JESUS

Professor R. Williams,
RB, SJ, JB, TH, DL, DK, CK, PO, CO, MR
J. McCoy
(The Real McCoy and a fantastic friend)
V. Garcia
(Artist and family friend)
…and many, many others.

Thanks also go out to all the Military Branches of Service. The information available to the public helped with keeping many historic details in perspective. Wikipedia, the Free Encyclopedia available on the Internet, was also used as a reference. We hope you enjoyed this book.

Ohers in this series:

ECHOES FROM THE PAST BOOK II

BREACH OF FAITH BOOK III

There will be a time for RETRIBUTION

STAY TUNED FOR:
CHRONICLES OF CASA
A JOURNAL OF EPIC BATTLES SINCE THE CRUCIFIXION OF CHRIST

KIDNAPPING JESUS

Kidnapping Jesus was discussed and written over a ten-year period and re-released with updates almost 15 years later. Bringing to life an action-adventure story of this magnitude was a challenge, but well worth the emotional roller coaster for the authors and those who helped with their ideas. Those who listened provided much- needed encouragement and direction along the way.

There are many characters in the book, but the major characters are based on the real-life adventures of six former Marines that wanted to make a difference. While this is a fictional story, it is based on fact and the possibility that man could bring Jesus back to life when man becomes worthy and the technology to do so is available. There is the question then if man is smarter, is man wiser? Has man learned? Has man earned the privilege of being able to talk to Jesus in the modern world?

These Marines, and others, will take the reader on an emotional tour around the world, allowing the reader to experience their adventures and discoveries along the way.

This book may question your belief in God and your belief in man. You may ask yourself, "Why has it taken thousands of years for us to come face to face with Jesus?"

If Jesus could speak to man, would he tell mankind why we exist on Earth? Would Jesus tell mankind how we came to exist? Would Jesus be able to answer the questions we have had for thousands of years? What have we done? Jesus, what have we done?

> WHEN MAN BECOMES WORTHY,
> I SHALL RETURN TO EARTH.
> WE SHALL MEET AGAIN.
>
> CASCA RUFIO LONGINUS

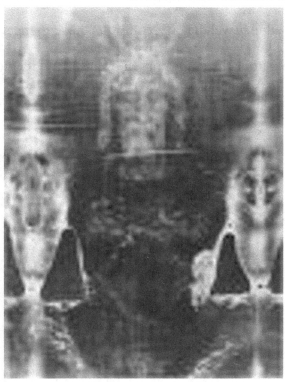

"We all may well be on a collision course to meet our
respective Maker
no matter the name chosen by any given religion.
A pale horse with a rider named Death
appeared in Elder's mind, or was it just a mirage over the
shimmering sands of time?"

Samuel L. (Lyons) Brodie

ABOUT THE AUTHORS

Author **David Barnard** resides in Newberry, South Carolina. He served with honor in two branches of military service - the United States Marine Corps and the United States Army. His training included Tank operations training at Fort Knox, Kentucky, and Ranger Training with the 2nd Ranger Battalion and Parachute Jump School at Fort Bragg, North Carolina. He is SCUBA certified and currently holds an Open Water Certification.

He attended and graduated from the Non-Commissioned Officer's Training course at Camp Pendleton, California. After Barnard medically retired from active duty, he attended and graduated from the San Diego Police Academy, the U.S. Marshals Academy, and the East Baton Rouge Sheriff's Department. His experience includes tours of duty as a Deputy Marshal for three years and as a Police Officer for five years. His background includes police investigation, interrogation of suspects, and crime scene investigation.

Samuel L. (Lyons) Brodie, Co-Author of Kidnapping Jesus, is a retired U.S. Army Lieutenant Colonel. His assignments included tours of duty with the 2nd Armored Division, the 101st Airborne Division (Air Assault) and the 1st Armored Division. His overseas assignments led him to Germany, The Republic of Turkey and to Egypt.

KIDNAPPING JESUS

His military training included the Officer's Basic and Advanced Courses, and the Intermediate and Senior Service Colleges. He has a B.S. Degree in Aerospace Administration and a Master's Degree in Public Administration. Brodie served in the Army for 26 years. Brodie is a Master Instructor in SCUBA Diving. He learned to dive and became a Dive Instructor while assigned in Turkey.

Kidnapping Jesus is an action-adventure novel and is based on fact and imagination. The groundwork for writing *Kidnapping Jesus* began in 1997. It has taken a very long time for the possibilities to unfold. Hold on to your imagination, for it will be challenged!

MORE FROM THE AUTHORS OF KIDNAPPING JESUS

Brodie and Dave are friends and worked on this book together. This is Dave's story and Brodie was fascinated with the adventure and wanted to help his friend bring the story to readers worldwide. It was a lot of fun pulling the story together and Dave and Brodie rediscovered many things that happened not only during their lifetimes but from the chronicles of many lifetimes. *Kidnapping Jesus* is fictional in nature, but many of the events described did in fact take place. Similarities to those living, or who have died, may or may not be coincidental. The fabric of imagination often lies in stark reality.

Printed in the USA
CPSIA information can be obtained
at www.ICGtesting.com
CBHW011554110724
11462CB00008B/61